RIKER'S APOCALYPSE: THE PRECIPICE

(Book 3)

SHAWN CHESSER

D1563645

2023

Return *Sherry Middleton*

CONTENTS

ACKNOWLEDGEMENTS

For Steve P. You are missed, friend. Maureen, Raven, and Caden ... I couldn't have done this without your support. Thanks to our military, LE and first responders for all you do. To the people in the U.K. and elsewhere around the world who have been in touch, thanks for reading! Lieutenant Colonel Michael Offe, thanks for your service as well as your friendship. Larry Eckels, thank you for helping me with some of the military technical stuff. Any missing facts or errors are solely my fault. Beta readers, you rock, and you know who you are. Special shout out to the master of continuity: Giles Batchelor. You helped make this novel a better read. Thanks, George Romero, for introducing me to zombies. To my friends and fellows at S@N and Monday Steps On Steele, thanks as well. Lastly, thanks to Bill W. and Dr. Bob ... you helped make this possible. I am going to sign up for another 24.

Special thanks to John O'Brien, Mark Tufo, Joe McKinney, Craig DiLouie, Nicholas Sansbury Smith, Heath Stallcup, Saul Tanpepper, Eric A. Shelman, and David P. Forsyth. I truly appreciate your continued friendship and always invaluable advice. Thanks to Jason Swarr and Straight 8 Custom Photography for another awesome cover. I'm grateful to Marine veteran Buck Doyle of Follow Through Consulting for portraying Lee Riker on the cover. For technical help, in no particular order, thanks to: Norman Meredith, W.J. Lundy, Ted Nulty, and Stephen Knight. Once again, extra special thanks to Monique Happy for her work editing "The Precipice." Mo, as always, you kicked butt and took names in getting this MS polished up! Working with you over the years has been nothing but a pleasure. I truly appreciate having a confidante I can trust. If I have accidentally left anyone out ... I am truly sorry.

***

Edited by Monique Happy Editorial Services
www.moniquehappyeditorial.com

Chapter 1

New Mexico

Under Steven "Steve-O" Piontek's watchful eye, former Army truck driver Leland Riker tapped repeatedly on the Shelby Raptor's dash-mounted touchscreen. Coinciding with each press of the **+** button, the green line representing the miles-long run of U.S. Route 84, a laser-straight stretch of the four-lane currently visible beyond the idling pickup's flat hood, slowly grew in size on the display.

Pressing a different icon switched the SYNC screen's navigation pane from *Map* to *Satellite*. When the onscreen image refreshed, the pixelated green line superimposed over a light tan background gave way to an overhead photo of their immediate location.

On the touchscreen where the green pixels had been, twin gray strips of oil-stained blacktop split the desert landscape down the middle. Left and right of 84, the desert was represented exactly as it appeared outside the truck. Riker noticed at once that what they were all seeing through the pickup's bug-spattered windshield was *not* depicted on the stock satellite image. Instead of the clear sailing promised by the green line on the previous screen, and despite the current image which showed their route to be unimpeded, the highway dead ahead, for what seemed like a mile or more, was choked with static vehicles.

In the middle distance, maybe a quarter mile ahead, was a pair of dump trucks. They were safety-orange and easily the largest wheeled vehicles Riker had ever seen. Likely liberated from some kind of mining or excavating concern, the trucks were parked grille to grille. The dirt medians and all four lanes of travel were blocked completely. Nobody was going north or south without moving the trucks. A difficult endeavor, by any stretch.

Partially obscured by the towering trucks was the first echelon of vehicles to encounter the roadblock after having fled downtown Santa Fe, ten or so miles to the south.

The dump trucks had been strategically positioned on a spot in the highway where the desert terrain on both sides was choked by scrub and dotted by rocks and therefore not conducive to overland travel. To render the thirty-foot-tall behemoths unmovable, every one of their massive tires had been flattened.

Perfect placement, Riker thought. He'd seen the same tactic used to block feeder ramps from Florida to Texas. Finding their passage blocked completely, the first wave to arrive had tried to get turned around. The result was complete gridlock: a veritable sea of glass and metal in which the first thirty or forty vehicles were inextricably trapped, some touching, some all alone in pockets yet still unable to go anywhere. To the naked eye it presented as an imperfect mosaic featuring all the colors of the rainbow.

Having gotten stuck trying to navigate his old F-150 through Turner Field's congested lot after an Atlanta Brave's home game, Riker had a good idea of the hairball the roadblock had quickly become.

Faced with hundreds of frightened citizens, many of them likely already carrying the Romero virus, some probably harboring infected loved ones in their vehicles, the human element of the roadblock no doubt folded faster than a Texas Hold 'em player dealt a seven-deuce off-suit.

Whether originally manned by state troopers, New Mexico National Guardsmen, or just concerned civilians trying to halt Romero's spread, the roadblock was but a Band-Aid on the sucking chest wound Riker guessed Santa Fe had quickly become.

Upper body balanced precariously between the front seatbacks, Steve-O strained to reach the touchscreen. Finger shaking wildly, he clumsily traced the length of highway centered on the screen.

Speech a little slurred due to the genetic disorder that had left him with a tongue a bit too thick for his mouth, Steve-O said, "Those monster dump trucks are *not* showing up on this picture."

While most people born with Down syndrome, also known as trisomy 21, possessed an IQ of around 50, in that department Steve-O had won the extra-chromosome lottery. While shortchanged a bit in the height and dexterity column, where IQ was concerned, the forty-five-year-old authority on all things country-and-western had scored high up on the chart among those with Down syndrome.

"That's because we're looking at old imagery," Riker responded. "I bet every satellite up there is now tasked with things way more important than updating traffic conditions in real time."

In the passenger seat, leaning as far away from the window as his shoulder belt would allow, thirty-nine-year-old Benjamin Sistek said, "Doesn't anyone care that a *hisser* is tonguing my window over here?"

Voice betraying zero concern, Riker said, "As long as it's not a Bolt and slam dancing into Dolly, I say let her tongue away."

"Looks like the Sicko loves you," stated Steve-O. "Are you gonna marry her, Benny?"

Doing the *gimme hands* in Benny's general direction, Riker asked for the binoculars.

Benny dipped into the center console and came out with the laser range-finding Steiners. "I can smell her through the glass." Suppressing a dry heave, he passed the binocs to his left.

Riker powered on the Steiners. Glassing the roadblock told him it had initially been an around-the-clock endeavor. Parked beside a mobile electronic reader board left facing the northbound lanes was a pair of mobile light standards. Basically large wheeled generators, with their extendable poles retracted and lying flat, the equipment was easy to miss if you didn't know what you were looking for.

The brief flashes of movement in and around the inert vehicles were impossible to miss. As more dead things took notice of the metallic-blue pickup, Steve-O said, "They see us, Lee Riker."

"Nothing gets by those rotten bastards," lamented Benny. He sighed and zoomed the navigation screen out a couple of stops. Tapping the satellite image, he went on: "We're going to have to turn around. If we take the exit we passed back there, we'll circumnavigate downtown to the west and avoid all this."

Half joking, Riker said, "Circum—what?"

Benny said, "Go around. Backtrack to the Santa Fe Bypass. There was a sign a ways back."

"I know what circumnavigate means," Riker said. "We're driving, Benny, *not* sailing the Florida Keys."

Benny said nothing. He was engaged in a staring contest with the undead woman to his right.

"She's almost as tall as you, Lee," noted Steve-O. "And she's *not* wearing high heels."

Looking over his shoulder, Riker said, "I go thirty-eight years on planet Earth without finding *the one*. Now, in the span of a couple of weeks, I come across three women I can *literally* see eye to eye with."

"And the first two were *lookers*," reminded Benny. "Drop-dead hotties. I'd put this one at about a seven or eight."

Eyes narrowing, Riker growled, "Rub it in, *Sistek*."

Hefting his fully automatic battery-operated Nerf gun, Steve-O said, "They *were* lookers when they were still alive, Benny. *None* of the Sickos … whether they are Slogs or Bolts, are pretty once they become zombies."

Already steering the Shelby into a three-point-turn, Riker said, "Agreed, Steve-O. I'll eventually find *the one*. I just need to be patient."

Benny turned away from the window and glared at Riker. "Did you really invoke my last name?" After a beat, his stony countenance cracking, he said, "Hot damn, Lee. I think I finally struck one of your deeply buried nerves."

"*Struck?*" shot Riker. "Hell, Benny, you grabbed ahold and went all Indiana Jones with it. Remember, I've been on a desert island with no female companionship for a few months now."

Steve-O said, "No pretty ladies on your Fantasy Island, Lee Riker?"

Though the question was innocent, it was still funny as hell.

Unable to contain his laughter, Riker halted the Shelby mid-turn.

Wiping away tears, Benny said, "Shocked me to hear it, that's all. Mom and Dad only invoked the Sistek name when I was in deep-shit trouble."

"My bad," Riker said. "In the Riker household, hearing a first, middle, and last name cross Mom or Dad's lips was the death knell. The trifecta usually preceded a big-time ass whoopin'. At the very least, one or both of them would make the offending party—me or Tara—volunteer for a day at the soup kitchen. Dad figured it would humble us a bit."

"My middle name is Clarence," divulged Steve-O.

Shaking his head, Benny said, "Oh no. You shouldn't have let that leak, Steve."

"It's Steve-O, Benny. We're friends now. Which is why I stopped calling you Benjamin."

"That was four days ago. What changed?"

Matter-of-factly, Steve-O said, "You gave me some of your bacon."

Smiling at that, Riker let up on the brake and tapped Dolly's gas pedal.

There was a screech of nails on metal as the female zombie lost purchase on the pickup's right front fender. One second it was there, eyes locked on the meat in the truck. The next it was out of sight and crashing hard to the road.

As Riker cranked the wheel counterclockwise and threw the automatic transmission into Drive, in his right-side vision he detected flashes of color and sudden bursts of movement from within the tangle of cars and trucks.

Pulsing his window down, Steve-O said, "I see Bolts. Want me to distract them?"

Before Riker could respond, the Shelby shuddered and there was a loud *pop* as the pickup's right front tire crushed the fallen zombie's skull.

"Can't unhear that," quipped Benny, his voice all nasally on account he had covered his mouth and nose with his tee shirt.

Answering Steve-O, Riker said, "Save the ammo for later." Crinkling his nose, he added, "And close your damn window; smells like turned hamburger in here." Flicking his eyes to the rearview, he saw that the Bolts had negotiated the roadblock and were now shoulder to shoulder and sprinting damn near straight down the centerline. Already half the distance from the roadblock to the Shelby's tailgate, staring dead ahead and mouths agape, the creatures clawed the air ahead of them as they ran.

At first glance, it seemed to Riker as if the twenty-something males were still alive. If he didn't know any better, he'd have assumed the Bolts were just a couple of guys hopped up on some real bad drugs and looking for trouble.

But he did know better. In fact, he knew that if he didn't get his ass in gear, the runners would slam into his pickup, the twin impacts adding to the myriad of scratches and blood and road grime already marring her once pristine exterior.

In the distance, dozens of Slogs—slow moving zombies—had threaded their way through the matrix of cars and were emerging single-file from behind the dump trucks.

Hearing the fleshy slaps of road-rashed feet drawing nearer, Riker took it upon himself to toggle Steve-O's window shut with the master switch.

"Go, go, go," blurted Benny, who was now leaning forward, straining hard against his shoulder belt, head craned to the right and watching the zombies in his side mirror. Voice rising an octave, he said, "Objects in this mirror are *way* too close for my damn comfort. Tromp the pedal, Lee."

Smiling, Riker said, "As you wish, *Sistek*," and matted the pedal.

Everyone aboard was pushed into their seatbacks as the Whipple supercharger kicked in, feeding the 6.2-liter V8 motor an instant rush of cool, compressed air.

The pickup ate up a hundred feet of blacktop in the blink of an eye.

Easing up on the accelerator, Riker regarded the mirror in time to see the zombies get tangled up and carom away from one another.

After cartwheeling in two different directions, the Bolts ended up in individual heaps, arms and legs bent in unnatural angles.

A little disconcerted from driving north in southbound lanes, Riker kept one eye on the road ahead and turned to Benny. "Think some of those cars back there still have gas in the tank?"

Head wagging hard side to side, Benny said, "Not a drop."

Riker said, "C'mon, man ... you know folks don't leave their rigs idling in a traffic jam. They shut them down."

Benny said, "If it's cold out they don't."

Gesturing at the digital readout on Dolly's dash, Riker said, "It's sixty-two outside right now. I'm not buying it."

"That's about what we were seeing last week," Benny said. "But it dipped into the forties at night."

Riker shook his head. "They didn't wait here for long. With what was happening in Santa Fe the other day, the fires and helicopters crisscrossing the sky, no way these folks stayed the night in their rides with the motor running. They probably up and ran for the hills, leaving plenty of gas behind for us."

Buckling in, Steve-O said, "Every time we came to a roadblock, Tara made you shut off Dolly's engine."

Though the man helped to prove his point, Riker said nothing. He was eyeing the approaching exit and about to create his own shortcut. One that would see the tuned and lifted Baja model tackling terrain it was designed for.

Hand instinctively shooting for the A-pillar grab handle, Benny said, "Point taken, Steve-O. But there's one problem." He went quiet while the pickup juddered and shimmied across the arcing strip of dirt sandwiched between the highway and single-lane feeder. Then, as Dolly transitioned from dirt to smooth pavement, the tires giving an audible *chirp* upon contact, he finished by saying: "The problem is that we don't have the pumps we would need to siphon enough gas to make a difference before those things chomp our asses to bits."

Riker said, "Where there's a will, there's a way, Benny," and steered the Shelby along the ramp, toward a sign that read: VETERANS MEMORIAL HIGHWAY/ SANTA FE BYPASS.

Flanked by grass and juniper shrub, the divided four-lane curled north by west through sparsely inhabited range. After the short jaunt that had them backtrack slightly, the bypass took a hard left and plunged due south. The straightaway quickly transitioned into a left-to-right arc as Veterans Memorial Highway continued its descent through a wide arroyo, toward its eventual terminus on the outskirts of Santa Fe, almost twelve miles south by east.

While Riker watched out for rotters and steered wide of the occasional vehicle left parked on the right shoulder, he went over his plan to fill the empty gas cans in the truck's bed. For it to succeed, they needed to get their hands on a hand-cranked siphon. While his idea of how they would distract the dead while they went about the time-consuming task of drawing enough fuel to top off Dolly's tank and then fill the spare cans seemed plausible, as his words hung in the cabin's carrion-tinged air, Benny scoffed, deeming it "way too dangerous."

Steve-O unbelted and planted his elbows on the seatbacks. "Walking can be dangerous," he said soberly. "Especially in cowboy boots." He adjusted his Stetson. "But I like your idea, Lee Riker. I'm on board."

"First things first," Benny said. "We need to get where we were going and follow through with our promise to Rose." He paused. "Last thing I want to do is piss her off and end up on the same no-nookie-gettin' island as Lee."

Shooting Benny a dose of stink eye, Riker tossed the Steiners onto his friend's lap, achieving a direct hit to the family jewels. "Now you won't have a choice," he quipped. "Employ those bad boys. Keep a sharp eye out for deaders or breathers. But first, since we'll be out of range soon"—he fished the two-way radio from a pocket—"better call Trinity and tell Tara and Rose that we're taking the long way into town."

Keeping to himself the anger management barb he was about to hurl at Lee, Benny took the radio from his friend and placed a quick check-in call.

Chapter 2

Tara swung the machete on a flat plane, right-to-left, dipping and twisting her hips at the exact moment the gleaming blade struck the wrist-thick sapling. A second swing was necessary to cleave through it completely. As she tossed the fledgling tree aside, her gaze fell on the three-inch nub protruding from the ground.

Being quite the Type-A personality, it had bugged her when Lee had insisted that a few inches of stubble left behind wasn't going to be an issue in the grand scheme of things. When she had pressed him on it, he had parted the hardy underbrush and scraped the ground with the machete, revealing to her a small portion of the field of oversized pavers underneath the thick accumulation of decaying leaves and intertwined twigs.

It's a landing pad, Lee had said. *If you pull the trees out roots and all, it'll disturb the pavers and leave us with a surface less even than the one we have now.*

Tara admitted he had a point. Though she was a thirty-two-year-old grown ass woman, she still hated it when big brother was right. Lately, as hard as it was for her to admit, he had been right more often than not.

The circular plot of land she was clearing was roughly a quarter of a mile uphill from Trinity House. A worn path climbed from the door in the back wall to a break in the mature trees ringing the plot.

Long ago, likely in the eighties or early nineties, the plot had been clear ground. Taking into account how uneven the trees on the periphery had grown since, it was likely they had once seen constant pruning on the sides facing the clearing. In the years since, Mother Nature had come a long way toward reclaiming what had once been hers.

Tara and Rose had spent several hours over two days under hot sun clearing underbrush. Today, Tara was working solo. With Dozer lounging nearby, watching with canine indifference, she had chopped her way across a third of the clearing, leaving standing in her wake a half-dozen juvenile trees that would require an axe to fell.

On the far edge of the clearing, partly shrouded by early morning fog, were a number of trees Lee had marked with big white Xs. To bring those down, they would definitely need a chainsaw—a tool they didn't have.

Running down a chainsaw was one of the many reasons Lee, Benny, and Steve-O had gone on their road trip south. Finding out if Rose's friend, Crystal, was still alive was the prime objective. In Tara's opinion—which she hadn't had the heart to share with Rose—going out of their way to find Crystal was all risk and no reward. Tara hadn't known Crystal before the woman brought danger to their doorstep; therefore she couldn't empathize with her situation. She'd made her own bed, may as well sleep in it.

Tara paused to take a sip of water. As she ran the back of her hand over her sweaty forehead, she felt a subliminal tingling caress the nape of her neck. Last time she had experienced the sensation was at Shorty's boat ramp. At the time she had been standing guard over the truck and had caught some teens watching her. That they had come with bad intentions was a certainty. Tara's gut had been the judge of that. Showing them the business end of a stubby shotgun was all it took to set them on their way armed with the message that she was not to be fucked with.

As Tara looked about the clearing, eyes probing the depths of the shadowy tangle of flora surrounding her, Dozer raised his massive head and did the same. Nose twitching, he rose and took a few tentative steps toward the yet to be cleared portion of the plot.

The hackles along Dozer's spine sprang to attention. Ears cocked forward, pink nose probing the air, he went statue still, all of his attention directed north, where something or someone was prowling the edge of the property still to be explored.

She capped the bottle and stuffed it in a side pocket of her cargo pants. She sheathed the machete and drew her compact Glock. With an extended magazine holding seventeen nine-millimeter rounds stuffed in the magwell, the playing field was now tilted in her favor.

"Dozer ... leave it." Last thing she needed was for the pitbull to go crashing off into the woods. As far as she knew, animals were immune to Romero. Still, she didn't want to test the theory. Meeting Dozer's gaze, she pointed at the ground by her boots. It was one of the handful of silent commands she had taught the dog over the course of a week and a half.

Still growling, Dozer sauntered over to the patch of ground beside Tara, sitting when she flashed him her clenched fist.

Tara rewarded the dog with a kibble, then took a pair of two-way radios from a pocket.

"Red or Green?" she asked herself. *Teal for Trinity* suddenly came to her. Teal was a shade of green. Teal begins with T. It was a word association technique she'd applied to help remind her which of the radios was on the same channel as Rose's two-way.

Pressing the Talk button, Tara made herself a mental note to mark the radios with indelible ink once she returned to the house.

"Rose. You there?"

Nothing.

While Tara waited for a response, the other radio came alive. It was Benny relaying the change in plans.

Hearing the familiar voice, Dozer regarded the radio, then rose and spun a tight half-circle. Facing the trail leading back to Trinity House, the dog pressed his body flat to the ground and let out another low growl.

"Thanks for the heads up," Tara said. "Tell my bro to be careful." She paused. Rose's radio silence on her mind, she went on, "You guys bring Steve-O back in one piece, you hear?"

After a short pause, Benny said, "Steve-O wants me to tell you he will make sure no sickos hurt me or Lee."

Smiling at that, Tara said, "I bet you will, Steve-O. See you guys later." She rolled the volume down and pocketed the red radio.

Pressing the teal radio to her lips, she hailed Rose. *Still nothing.* She tried three more times, the urgency in her voice rising exponentially with each new attempt.

Finally, after thirty long seconds, during which the only sound in the clearing was Dozer's incessant growling, the radio came to life with a burst of squelch.

"I'm here," Rose blurted. "Sorry, Tara. You sounded worried. I'm *really* sorry to have kept you hanging on like that."

Thumbing the Talk button, Tara said, "Why in the hell weren't you answering?"

"I didn't have the radio on me," Rose admitted. "I got to cleaning the fireplace in the great room. When I heard your call, I had to go and retrace my steps to find where I had left it." She paused, drew a deep breath, then went on, saying: "I found something in the communal room that you're going to want to see. Something I can't do justice by just describing it over the radio."

Tara shook her head. The ease at which Rose could bounce from something so serious to the mundane was astounding. *Everyone* was supposed to keep a radio *on* their person at all times. Just because someone was indoors and passing the time cleaning a room that had already been thoroughly scrubbed didn't mean they were exempt from Lee's most important house rule.

If Trinity House were to come under attack and everyone forced to flee, the radios would be their only lifeline. Their only way to eventually link back up. And though Tara wanted to lay into Rose over the transgression—the third over the last two days—she let it slide. The *something* Rose had alluded to could also wait. At the moment nothing down at the house was more important than finding out what had Dozer so on edge.

Adding the task of making a lanyard for Rose's radio to her lengthening mental to-do list, Tara said, "Dozer is going nuts. You see anything on the monitors?"

In addition to solar power, geothermal heating, and its own artesian-fed water supply, Trinity House had come equipped with a web of cameras that covered the sprawling estate's entry, parking pad, interior courtyards, and its entire perimeter.

"I got nothing," Rose answered. "No movement. No stinkers. Do you smell anything? Can you hear them breaking brush?"

Early on, the vast majority of the living dead Tara and the others encountered hadn't given off much of an odor. Now, nearly three weeks after Romero had burned its way across the country, springing from mass casualty events in the big cities and spreading across the countryside like ripples on a pond, the appearance of bloated walking corpses was usually preceded by the sickly-sweet pong of their decaying flesh.

While the stench of carrion *was* a welcome early warning system, knowing the dead things were out there without actually being able to see them was, in a way, more disconcerting than the alternative.

Tara cocked an ear toward where Dozer was directing his attention. After a few seconds of hard listening and drawing in deep breaths through her nose, she said, "I didn't hear a thing. Don't smell 'em, either."

There was a long pause. When Rose finally came back on, she said, "What is it that your brother is always telling us to do?"

With no delay, Tara said, "Trust your gut."

"What's your gut telling you?"

"It's saying blast the woods in the direction Dozer's looking. But that would be stupid. You're down there and my bro says rounds fired can travel a long way. They also drop a bit while they're on the fly."

"Why don't you come in and have an early lunch? Call it brunch. You deserve a break. You've been going nonstop since me and Benny got here."

"I can wait," Tara said. *We're getting low on food*, was what she was really thinking.

Though she couldn't beat Steve-O up for it because he had meant well, the impromptu shopping trip to the overrun Smiths in Santa Fe had netted them more junk food than the kind high in nutritional value. Another thing high on her mental to-do list was to conduct a foraging mission to one of the homes down the valley. She figured if she could find one occupied—and they didn't shoot prior to hearing her out—she might work a gold for food swap. She also held out hope that some of the homes were uninhabited. Several times over the past week she and Lee had walked the road to a nearby break in the trees and scanned the valley through binoculars. Not once had they detected signs of life at any of the half-dozen or so homes visible to them. No movement behind darkened windows. No telltale wisps of smoke coming from chimneys. No sounds other than the occasional muffled gunshot or engine noise lifting up from Santa Fe's distant suburbs.

The first time they had walked beyond their vantage point, to the first fork in the road, Lee had arranged a line of dirt clods across the juncture in places where they would likely be crushed under the tires of passing vehicles.

Over the ensuing three days, during which there had been zero precipitation, Tara and Lee had returned twice daily to the fork in the road. When the third day came and went with Lee's dirt clods having gone untouched, they concluded that the majority of the homes on the hillside below Trinity House were likely uninhabited.

While Tara had proffered that they were most likely vacation homes or investment properties being used as Airbnb rentals, Lee insisted that some of them had to be inhabited.

Only way to find out, Lee had said, was to go down and knock on some doors.

Before leaving on the current foray south, he had made her promise to not go it alone.

Voice a bit strained, Rose asked, "You still there, Tara?"

"Sorry," Tara replied, "I was zoning. Lost in thought, that's all."

"You coming back soon?"

"No," Tara answered. "I'm going to keep at it for a while longer. If I smell anything, I'll wrap it up and come in for an early lunch. Or brunch."

Sounding dejected, Rose said, "Whatever. It's *your* gut. I'll watch the monitors real close. Keep the volume up on your radio so you'll hear me if I call."

"Best if you keep the radio in your pocket," Tara said primly. "I'll check in with you in a bit."

Before stowing the radio in the pocket with the other, Tara rolled the volume down to a level she hoped would let her hear the soft warble without giving her position away to the whole world. Without the constant noise pollution emitted by planes, trains, and automobiles, sound up here tended to travel great distances. Which was why Tara had added a pair of Motorola ear buds to the many other must-haves she'd snuck onto her bro's shopping list. She wished she could see his expression when he unfolded the page and saw all of her additions to *his* list.

Smiling at the adverse reaction her scribbles were likely to bring, she grabbed hold of another sapling and swung the machete. Tossing the cutting aside, she recognized how much work still lay in front of her. It was at least a day's worth. Two if Lee came back with an axe instead of a chainsaw.

How Lee had determined how much extra clearance Clark would need to land his helicopter on the pad was still a mystery. Hell, Lee had yet to tell her how he came to see this overgrown hole in the woods as anything but an ideal spot for nude sunbathing or to throw a late night stargazing party—the latter of which she had done, albeit solo, a couple of times now.

If the world ever got back to normal, first thing on her list was to have a contractor come out and give her a bid on putting in an infinity-edge pool. Lord knows there was room for one. Maybe even a sauna and hot tub.

She crossed her arms and scanned the perimeter one last time. Yeah, she thought, this would be the perfect place for a little oasis. Far enough removed from the house to ensure privacy, yet close enough to have a pool boy on standby to run down and fetch her a cold Corona.

Then, like a sneaker wave on a docile beach, reality came crashing back on her. Mood taking a sudden turn for the worse, she spit a few choice curse words and attacked the next sapling with newfound vigor.

Chapter 3

Front and center on the Shelby's navigation pane was the thirteen-mile-long stretch of Veterans Memorial Highway they were currently barreling down. After curling around Santa Fe's west side, the desolate four-lane eventually cut back on itself and crossed underneath I-25, which in turn fed southwest to Albuquerque, and north by east to Santa Fe.

For the first couple of miles or so, the opposing lanes were tied up completely by a series of horrendous wrecks. As they neared the beginning of a long stretch of divided four-lane, Riker was forced to slow the high-performance pickup to a crawl and bull through a sizeable herd of undead clustered around an especially nasty multi-car pileup.

Five miles from the first roadblock, Veteran's Memorial bypassed the Santa Fe suburb of Agua Fria. Once home to nearly three thousand souls, the city looked like a ghost town, every stoplight dark and no vehicles cutting the streets.

The closer they got to their ultimate destination, the smoother travel became. Which seemed strange to Riker, because they were nearing the junction with US 84, maybe six or seven miles ahead.

The longer Riker had to dwell on what he was seeing, the more he came to believe that the people responsible for the first roadblock had likely set ones similar outside the cities fed by I-25. Adding fuel to his budding roadblock theory was that the only vehicles they saw moving the entire time they'd been driving Veteran's Memorial came as they were closing on the I-25 overpass.

They heard the convoy of two dozen shiny Harley Davidson motorcycles well before they saw them. Scooting away from the cloverleaf feeding onto I-25, at nearly double the posted limit, the noisy train of chrome and painted metal, ridden by figures dressed in leathers and wearing helmets, blipped by in the blink of an eye.

Returning his eyes to the road ahead, Riker said, "What do you think, fellas? Weekend warriors or outlaw bikers?"

"Wall Street Angels," Benny replied. "Their gear and bikes were way too put together for them to be one-percenters."

"I'm with Benny," Steve-O said. "Hell's Angels have tiny helmets and beards and tattoos."

"They also have those winged-skull patches on back of their jackets," Benny added.

"I didn't see any of that," replied Riker as he craned to get a look at an upcoming overpass. On the navigation screen the span was labeled Interstate 25. It ran east to west over Veteran's Memorial, with Santa Fe presenting as a wide-open sprawl way off in the bottom left corner of the display, and Albuquerque somewhere off screen to the right.

As the Shelby gobbled up the distance to the elevated highway, Riker saw zombies beginning to congregate at the low rail. Flashes of color among the multitude of vehicles stalled out up there suggested more were still to come out of the metaphorical woodwork. By the time the pickup had drawn to within a hundred feet or so of the shadow of the overpass, it was clear to Riker the twenty or more zombies drawn to the edge of the precipice by the thundering Harleys were now fixated solely on his shiny blue pickup.

Before the viewing angle was cut short by the front edge of the pickup's roofline, everyone aboard was privy to the surreal sight of the first row of zombies pitching over the rail.

Realizing the deadly predicament unfolding before his eyes, Riker said, "Shit, shit, shit," and stomped the pedal. Shouting to be heard over the supercharger whine, he implored his friends to brace for impact.

This is going to be close, Riker thought as he instinctively jerked the steering wheel left.

Eyes gone wide and one hand crushing the Stetson to his head, Steve-O made a sound like air rushing from a popped tire.

Close was an understatement. In response to Riker's input, the pickup jinked left. As the first of the tumbling bodies entered his side vision, he saw snatches of pale skin, a sneering face, then, finally, a flailing arm that smacked the flat of the hood on Benny's side. With the impact resonating through the cab like a struck gong, the arm whipped from view, bones obviously broken and reshaped into all kinds of unfamiliar angles.

As the Shelby slalomed through the danger zone, the heavy thuds of bodies hitting the road and subsequent cracks of bones breaking rose over the engine noise.

When the still-accelerating Shelby shot out from under the overpass, leaving fifty-some-odd-feet of shadowy two-lane and a growing mound of squirming bodies in its wake, the drawn-out gasp was still escaping Steve-O's yawning mouth.

Clutching the grab handle by his head in a white-knuckled death-grip, Benny said, "If that thing would have hit a foot left of where it did, I'd be wearing the windshield and drenched in its guts."

"You'd probably be dead," Steve-O noted.

"You're probably right about that," agreed Benny. "Then I'd come back as one of them." He curled his fingers into claws and reached back for Steve-O.

Flicking his eyes to the rearview mirror, Riker saw more bodies cutting the rectangle of daylight bordered by vertical support columns, the underside of the span, and patch of freeway the Shelby had just vacated. Curiously, as the dead tumbled head over heels, rocketing toward a most certain and sudden deceleration, there was no show of self-preservation on their part. No hands shooting to cradle the head in a futile attempt to ward off the coming impact. No arms and legs kicking furiously against the deadly onrush of bone-crushing, unforgiving pavement.

Nothing.

No cares at all.

They just kept on coming, the prospect of a meal of warm flesh the sole thing driving their actions.

Head craned around, owl-like, Steve-O said, "It's still raining Sickos."

"I see," Riker said. "We just dodged a bullet."

Watching the last of the falling bodies land atop the growing mound, Benny said, "We dodged a whole damn barrage. Looked like a meat waterfall coming off the overpass." He paused to regard Riker. "And you know what?"

Riker shot him a questioning look.

Throwing a visible shiver, Benny said, "If we come back this way, it's going to be on us to drag them off the road."

"You're right," Riker acknowledged. "Still, it'd be smart for us to return this way. Known quantity and all. Besides, there's no way I'm going to try negotiating all the stalls and snarls along the outbound lanes. Easy for a pack of motorcycles. Damn near impossible in this rig."

Steve-O had been staring out the back window the entire time. He said, "A lot of the Sickos survived the fall."

Benny said, "Most of them, from the looks of it."

"Yeppers," Steve-O said, "You're right, Benny. Some of them are already back on their feet."

As if reciting an undeniable fact proven through years of research and backed by empirical evidence, Benny said, "They are going to follow us." He drew in a deep breath and exhaled. "And that means we are going to have to deal with them when we come back through."

Locking his gaze on the road ahead, Riker said, "We'll cross that bridge when we come to it." He paused for a beat as he tapped the brakes. "Right now," he went on, "we have this shit show to deal with."

Chapter 4

The *shit show* Riker had alluded to was a massive vehicular pileup. It was maybe a quarter mile out and coming up blindingly fast.

The southbound lanes dead ahead of the speeding Shelby were clogged with a myriad of vehicles. The first two-thirds of the run of cars were soot covered and sitting on melted tires. A few vehicles at the rear of the column had plowed into the burning cars but somehow had been left untouched by the flames. In the northbound lanes, separated from the conflagration by a short median that quickly transitioned to a long run of Jersey barriers, was a cluster of first responders' vehicles. Beyond a boxy ambulance and what looked to be a Santa Fe County fire engine sat a medium-sized helicopter. It was painted black and green, the writing emblazoned in white on its flank an illegible jumble.

The entire stretch of four-lane highway was hemmed in on both sides by thirty-foot-tall dirt embankments that seemed to go on forever. They were steeply graded, dotted with vegetation, and completely blocked Riker's view of everything east and west.

The fires that had engulfed the vehicles in Riker's lane had long since gone out. There was no smoke. No heat shimmers. No lights strobed on the emergency vehicles. Nothing moved in or around the static vehicles. It was as if a set for a disaster movie had been assembled on the road and then all the actors and crew had gone to lunch.

Mere seconds removed from the encounter with the falling dead, the Shelby was still clipping along at close to eighty miles per hour. When Riker first became aware of the scene filling up the windshield and had made his *shit show* proclamation, his right foot was already going for the brake pedal.

When the big Brembo brakes caught, Dolly fishtailed and her front end dipped substantially. As the brake's antilock feature kicked in, the rear end snapped back around and the speedometer needle crashed precipitously toward zero.

Seatbelt still unbuckled, Steve-O was thrown into the back of Benny's seat.

One hand going for the grab handle, the other clamped white-knuckle tight around his shoulder belt, Benny let out a surprised yelp.

And just like that, Riker's seemingly never-ending headache was back with a vengeance.

Flaring from the back to back stresses of the zombie shower and having run up unexpectedly on the multi-vehicle accident, the twin daggers of pain stabbing his retinas, as per usual, had come at a most inopportune time.

As a result of the IED explosion that stole Riker's lower left leg and left his body permanently scarred by shrapnel and third-degree burns, he suffered from CTE—chronic traumatic encephalopathy. It was a brain injury that, in addition to the headaches, sometimes affected his mood.

Fighting a rising wave of nausea, Riker wrestled the pickup onto the right-side shoulder and stopped them close enough to the tangle to see what they were up against, while still leaving room to beat a quick retreat should the need arise.

Relaxing his grip on the grab handle, Benny said, "What the hell happened here?"

For fear the act of speaking would hasten the flow of bile from his stomach to the great outdoors, Riker dragged out his pill bottle and dry-swallowed a couple of ibuprofen.

"That bad?"

"Yes ... and then some," Riker gasped.

"Looks like someone was texting and driving," Steve-O theorized.

"If they were, they paid the ultimate price," Benny said.

Just off the Shelby's left-front fender, blocking both southbound lanes, were the blackened husks of the vehicles they had spotted from a distance. Viewed up close, the human toll was literally staring them all in the face. Lips drawn back in perpetual grins, charred corpses sat gripping the steering wheels in most of the cars. Bringing up the rear was a pair of vehicles that were just as mangled as the rest but had somehow escaped the flames. Thankfully they were both unoccupied. To their immediate left was a low median that quickly gave way to the long row of Jersey barriers stretching off to the south.

A hundred feet beyond the front of the pileup sat the modern-looking helicopter. It was in the southbound fast lane, cockpit facing the first of the burned-out autos, and angled forty-five degrees in relation to the Jersey barriers. Save for having skids instead of wheels, the aircraft was quite similar to the one Riker had chartered to ferry him, Tara, and Steve-O from the winery in Pennsylvania to the golf course in New Jersey. The words *Rapid Life Flight – St. Vincent Hospital* dominated the side of the fuselage facing Riker.

Parked the wrong way on the northbound passing lane, its right-side wheels aligned with the low median, was a Santa Fe County ambulance. Its rear doors had been left wide open. If there was anyone strapped to the wheeled stretcher in back, either living or dead, the gloom was concealing it from prying eyes.

Backed up close to the ambulance was a triple-axel turntable ladder-truck. It bore the Santa Fe Fire Department insignia and had been left parked diagonally across the northbound fast lane. Hoses unspooled from the rear of the firetruck rose up and over the cement barriers and curled around behind the rear of the pileup, where the brass nozzle had been abandoned mere feet away from the vehicles untouched by fire.

A third emergency vehicle, a red Chevy Tahoe, was part of the pileup. It had come to rest at the culmination of a fifty-yard-long run of dark skid marks that stretched diagonally across both southbound lanes.

Benny said, "Looks like he braked a *little* too late."

Eyes tracing their own faint skid marks in his rearview mirror, Riker said, "Could have just as easily been us."

On the SUV's roof was a trio of needle antennas and a low-profile light bar. Barely visible on its rippled passenger-side door was a gold-leaf shield. Written across the shield: *Santa Fe Fire Department*. Below that, also hand-lettered in black, were the words: *Chief Ronald Hickok*.

A compact car was jammed up underneath the Tahoe's rear end. No way to tell what make or model, nor if the driver had survived. Riker thought it highly unlikely, seeing as how the rear portion of the tiny white sedan's roof had been cut open and peeled back.

It was a wonder the sedan hadn't ruptured the Tahoe's gas tank.

Steve-O said, "Looks like a crushed sardine tin."

Drawing a deep breath, Benny said, "Chief Hickok's ride would have benefited from some brakes like Dolly's."

"I don't think Chief was a responding unit," replied Riker. "Looks to me like he got caught up in the wreck as it happened. No time to do anything but stand on the brakes."

Benny said, "You think he survived?"

Riker shook his head. "Doubtful. If he survived the wreck and extraction, that helicopter wouldn't be here."

He transitioned his foot from brake to the accelerator and slow-rolled the pickup forward a few feet. From the new angle, he saw that the Tahoe's once-rounded nose was buried deep into the rear of a Volvo station wagon. With the bumper and grille pushed in a couple of feet, he guessed Chief Hickok's lower extremities had made the acquaintance of the Chevy's big V8.

The impact had been so severe that the Volvo's many windows were now a sea of glass scattered across the blackened asphalt, the pea-sized pebbles glittering like so many diamonds. Next to the Volvo, reduced to a blackened windowless hulk, was a minivan. Several human forms were frozen in place, burned to death where they sat.

On the ground near the Tahoe's elevated rear tire was an empty backboard. Near one end, sporting a white cross, its top hinged open, was a tool-box-sized medical kit. It was filled with supplies. Some of them—bandages, rubber gloves, rolls of gauze—had spilled out onto the ground.

Impossible to miss, even from a dozen yards away, was the massive pool of blood. It was several feet across and had dried to a shiny black. The backboard was also soiled with like-colored splotches of dried blood. Gauze bandages and paper wrappers were fused to the pool and flapping in the wind like little flags of surrender.

No doubt some kind of life and death battle had occurred here. And the longer Riker stared at the pileup, the clearer it became to him that the Grim Reaper had come out the winner.

Riker brought the pickup to a stop alongside the minivan.

Suddenly sitting forward on the edge of his seat, belt pulled tight across his shoulder, Benny said, "Why are we stopping, Lee?"

Riker didn't address the question. He was craning around, looking up and down the highway, a concerned look on his face. "See anything moving, Steve-O?"

Steve-O pulsed his window down. Pointing to a four-door sedan up near the front, he said, "So far just the Sicko in the car up there." He looked over his shoulder, out the back window. "Then there's the ones back there ... the *jumpers*."

The truck's cab was filling up with the sooty chemical smell of burned rubber and plastic coming off the vehicles. A single gust brought with it the stench of carrion coming off the zombies upwind from them.

"We've got a little time before they get here," Riker said. "I'd guess the overpass is a quarter mile back. Should give us five minutes or so."

Steve-O said, "Not if one of them is a Bolt."

Fingers still locked around the grab handle, Benny asked, "What are you planning, Lee?"

Riker looked at Benny, then swung his gaze to the rearview mirror. Finally, he said, "I didn't stock up on much in the way of medical supplies."

"You mean to tell me that after your huge online end-of-the-world shopping spree, you failed to include basic prepper stuff? Hell, I watched that Discovery show—"

Interrupting, Steve-O said, "Doomsday Preppers?"

"Yeah, that one," Benny said. "Even those wingnuts thought to stockpile bandages to go with their beans and bullets."

Riker nodded. "There was *some* stuff in the bugout bags I bought. Not enough, though. What with Rose changing that dressing of yours twice a day, we're almost out."

Running his window up, Steve-O said, "Tara thinks Lee was too busy buying toys. Says he is no good at thinking about the"—he made air quotes—"*big picture stuff*."

Eyeing Steve-O in the mirror, Riker said, "The very same *toys* you seem to find plenty of time to play with. And as far as Tara's assessment of me: She's dead wrong. I just put a bit more emphasis on the things I figured everyone else would be making a Black Friday run on. Besides," he went on, "nobody could have known Crystal was going to bring that asshole Raul to Trinity House."

"Murdering asshole," Steve-O reminded.

Smiling smugly, Riker said, "And that, Steve-O my man, is another buck for the swear jar."

Steve-O harrumphed. Then he said, "Newsflash, Lee Riker. Money is no good. The Sickos saw to that. *Sooo* ... I'm done playing that game."

While the odd couple was exchanging barbs, Benny had taken his semiautomatic Glock from the holster on his hip. He'd already press checked to ensure a round was chambered and was aiming the muzzle at the floor, trigger finger pressed to the slide, just as Riker had insisted he do.

"Daylight and gas," Benny reminded. "We're burning both."

Chapter 5

Riker regarded the scene on the road just outside his window. Resting on the Tahoe's rippled hood was a piece of life-saving equipment. It had beefy handles on one end and alligator-like jaws on the other. Next to the tool was a pair of leather gloves. It looked as if the operator using the tool to breach the Tahoe's passenger door had hastily tossed it aside once the mission was accomplished.

"Jaws of Life," Riker said to no one in particular. In his head he was back in Iraq, stuck in a smoking Land Cruiser on Route Irish, and reliving the day in 2005 the particular device had been used to extricate him from behind the wheel.

His extraction had been a noisy affair: Rescuers shouting instructions. Soldiers forming a security perimeter and screaming warnings in Arabic at the locals to keep them at bay. He could still hear the passengers all around him moaning and screaming, each one of them in the process of dying.

Thanks to the hard work on the part of his comrades, Riker's life had been saved that day. Despite their best efforts, his foot and several inches of his lower leg had not. In its place now was the titanium and carbon-fiber prosthesis known affectionately as his *bionic*.

Chasing the nightmare away with a shake of his head, Riker said, "You want to grab the med kit?" He regarded Benny. "Or do I have to?"

"Can't we get it on the way back? We can take our time and go through the helicopter and the ambulance. Then there's all the compartments on the fire engine. Bound to be lots of stuff we can use stashed in there."

From the backseat, Steve-O called, "I see Sicko number two."

Benny said, "Where's Sicko number one?"

Steve-O pointed to the half-burned corpse wedged between the partially opened door on a big American sedan a couple of cars from the front. "Same place she was when we pulled up … stuck in her seatbelt."

"Helluva way to go," Riker said. "She must have already been infected with Romero."

Benny said, "She probably attacked the driver and caused this whole thing."

"We'll never know," Riker said soberly. "Where's the second one, Steve-O?"

"I saw him walk by the front of the fire engine. Looked like he used to be one of them."

"Them?" Riker asked.

"A fireman," Steve-O answered.

Noticing the hose spooled out behind the ladder truck, Riker said, "My guess is the engine crew dropped what they were doing and sped over here to help Chief Hickok. And when they saw what they were up against, they called in the Life Flight chopper." Which was exactly how Riker had been spirited away from Route Irish all those years ago. Only his *life flight* had been a CASEVAC HH-60 Black Hawk.

Benny said, "And they walked right into a situation they weren't equipped for. Fire drew Slogs and Bolts from all around. They come rolling up on that sirens all blaring and with no police backup … might as well have been wearing a sign that said *eat me.*"

Riker shook his head. "I think the helicopter was the draw. They wouldn't have landed if the place was already crawling with the dead."

"Who am I to argue?"

Riker said, "Question is: Who's grabbing the kit? Rock, paper, scissors for it?"

Benny was saying, "I got it," when the left-side passenger door flew open. Before he could think of the words to reel Steve-O back in, the man was out on the road and striding toward the abandoned medical kit.

Shrugging, Riker looked to Benny. As he pulsed his window down with his left, and dragged the Sig Sauer Legion from its holster with his right, he uttered the five words made famous by Tara the day they both met the diminutive wanna-be gunslinger: "He's a grown ass man."

Clicking out of his belt, Benny said, "He's still gonna need back up." On the end of the statement, he winced and his hand shot to the shoulder where he'd recently been shot.

"Better take it easy," Riker said. "I got this."

"I just forgot about it for a second, that's all. Easy to do when one of those dead things comes on the scene."

Watching Steve-O in the side mirror, Riker said, "Better get going, then."

Having already failed at getting the med kit's bi-fold top closed and latched, Steve-O had crouched down next to it and, with a closed fist, was tamping down the contents.

Sicko number two appearing from behind the ladder truck drew Riker's attention. He tapped the glass to alert Benny. Making eye contact, he pointed toward the zombie.

Nodding, Benny gripped his Glock two-handed. Holding the pistol at a low-ready, he edged around the front of the Shelby. Finding Steve-O's back turned toward him, he went down on one knee and said, "There's a Sicko coming your way. Better hurry it up."

In the Shelby, Riker was watching Sicko number two. He saw it stagger along the firetruck's rear bumper. He also saw it get tripped up by the still-deployed hose. Before it was lost from sight, he had also seen enough to know it was a fit middle-aged male before returning for its encore performance. He also noted it was still wearing a helmet and heavy turnout gear. And that the gear hadn't been sufficient to prevent the serious damage done to its cheek and neck. The former was a lip-to-ear gash, the flap of pale tattered skin fronting a gaping chasm of clacking teeth. The latter was the wound that had done the man in. That was clear to Riker. The laceration was nearly a foot in length. It began just under the left ear, where the firefighter had received one hell of a vicious bite. From the raised ridges ringing the bite, the deep fissure arced underneath the thing's jaw line.

The bleed had been extreme, soiling from the neck on down the front of the Nomex shell and shirt beneath it.

One moment Riker had been subconsciously cataloging all the details, the next he was back to staring at empty space where the zombie had been.

In his mind's eye, he saw the undead firefighter struggling to rise from the road. But in the mirror, way off to the right near the breakdown lane, maybe thirty feet from the Tahoe, another zombie suddenly appeared. It was male, too. And roughly the same age as the other. Only this one was tall and well-muscled. That it was wearing a navy-blue polo-style shirt over black polyester slacks instead of the bulky turnout gear meant its movement was not hampered by anything save for its undead state.

Puffs of dust rose up from the embankment behind the runner. Sometime during its travels, one of its black dress shoes and the sock on that foot had come off.

A subtle clue to One Shoe's former profession was the empty shoulder holster snugged tight against its ribcage and the shiny badge on a lanyard banging its barrel chest.

Seeing Steve-O, the zombie found another gear. The *slap, klunk, slap, klunk, slap, klunk* reverberating across the road as it closed the distance to Steve-O was mostly drowned out by the Shelby's idling motor and tuned exhaust.

As Riker was screaming "Bolt!" at the top of his voice, two things happened simultaneously: arms windmilling, Benny screamed an expletive and pitched over sideways. Then, rising over the combined commotion, there came a resonant *bang* as One Shoe, with a full head of steam, slammed hard into the Tahoe's left front fender.

Chapter 6

After tangling with the spooled-out firehose, the
Fireman Zombie didn't pop back up behind the Chief's rig. Nor
did it come scrabbling on hands and knees around the rear of the
high-centered SUV. Instead, while Riker's attention was being
hijacked by One Shoe's noisy arrival, Fireman Zombie had
crawled over the low median and wormed its way underneath the
Tahoe.

At the same instant One Shoe put its head down and set
out across the highway, making it clear to Riker they were about
to come face-to-face with a Bolt, Benny was feeling the cold
crush of a hand clamping around his ankle and being drawn off
balance. It was at this moment Benny had screamed his expletive
and the Bolt was putting a sizeable dent in the Tahoe's fender.

As all of that was going down, Riker was bringing his Sig
to bear on One Shoe. However, whereas the Fireman Zombie
had gone low, One Shoe went high, hitting the Tahoe at full
speed, upper body ahead of its feet, in the middle of what was to
be a very long stride.

Instead of being repulsed by two-and-a-half tons of
Detroit steel and glass, One Shoe pitched forward, arms
extended, back bowed, and began what would be an inelegant
face-first slide across the hood.

Bearing a stark resemblance to former Cincinnati Red
Pete Rose, only stiff and unsmiling, the zombie continued its
journey, on its stomach, slowing only when its face bashed into
the life-saving tool left laid out on the hood.

Lips turned to pulp, lower mandible split in two, One
Shoe followed the tool and a multitude of his own broken teeth
off the hood. As the zombie face-planted on the road, body
folding over like a wet paper bag, Riker threw open his door.

Kneeling on the road beside the Tahoe, Steve-O was just getting the top of the medical kit closed when the dry rasp of something dragging against asphalt drew his attention. At about the same moment he was turning to locate the source of the out-of-place noise, he received the tap on the shoulder from Benny and heard his friend exclaim, "What the fuck!"

Starting from the sudden outburst, Steve-O hinged up and turned his head to see what Benny was going on about. But instead of seeing Benny standing over him, he saw his friend spinning around, face turned up to the sky, and the rest of his body speeding toward the road like a felled tree. As that was registering, he spotted the reason for Benny's rare use of the eff word and sudden loss of balance.

Wrapped around one of Benny's ankles was a pair of hands. They were obviously a man's, the knuckles white and craggy, like barnacles on a rock at the beach. There was nothing slender about them. Following the wrists and forearms with his eyes, Steve-O caught a glimpse of a face emerging from the rectangle of gloom beneath the Tahoe. Wild-eyed and open-mouthed, the Sicko coming into the light was focused entirely on Benny. Both gnarled hands released and clamped down again, only higher up on Benny's leg. The pale fingers were curled claw-like and pressing deep divots into the denim. The force of the opposing struggle was quickly relieving Benny of his jeans, exposing the north forty of his butt for all to see.

Just as the Sicko began drawing Benny's boot-clad foot toward its gaping maw, Steve-O swung his right arm on a flat plane. Tracking right to left, all his might behind the action, the medical kit came along for the ride.

Riker was planting his bionic on the road and craning around when One Shoe rose up off the pavement. With no other choice than to engage the zombie before it could get to his friends, even though it meant his rounds would be hitting dangerously close to them, he bracketed One Shoe with the Sig's Romeo red-dot sight and pressed the trigger.

One Shoe was lunging forward when the first round punched a neat little hole in its chest an inch or so above the sternum. Save for a slight tremor shaking its torso, there was no discernable effect. No bloom of blood. No wheezing gasp. No crashing to the ground as Raul had done when he'd been on the deadly end of Riker's Sig Legion.

As the recoil pulled Riker's aim up, he pressed the trigger a second time.

Round number two punched a quarter-sized entry wound in the V of soft flesh just below One Shoe's Adam's apple but did nothing to stop the advance.

Gun hand still tracking a vertical arc, a third press of the trigger sent another round screaming through space on an upward trajectory whose terminus was an inch below One Shoe's pronounced brow.

Unbeknownst to Riker, just a few yards to his fore, a life and death struggle was ensuing on the ground beside the Tahoe.

One of the latches to the lid on the medical box Steve-O had swung at the zombie wasn't secured. Mid-swing, the box popped open, spilling its contents over Benny's face and chest. Now but a shell of its former self—both literally and figuratively—the empty box had no heft when it connected with the zombie's head.

Instead of inflicting any real damage, the empty box came apart, the individual pieces skittering away in opposing directions.

Left holding a plastic handle, Steve-O could only watch as Benny struggled to bring his Glock to bear.

Ears just beginning to buzz as a result of the three booming reports, another barrage of gunshots rang to Riker's fore. They had been fired rapidly, out of sight to him, somewhere behind the Shelby. From first to last maybe a second had elapsed. *Spray and pray* was what he'd heard it called in the Sandbox.

Clearly no kind of time had been taken to aim.

To Riker's ears, it had been an engagement birthed by pure panic.

As he stepped away from the Shelby, fully expecting to see one or both of his friends mortally wounded, instead he saw Benny pushing his way out from underneath the zombie dressed in firefighting gear. In his hand was the Glock, its barrel still smoking. Splattered across the side of Chief Hickok's rig were the contents of the zombie's cranium.

The rest was confusing to say the least: Steve-O was no longer kneeling and fiddling with the medical kit. He was now on his butt, legs crossed Indian style. On his face was a shocked expression. A miasma of brain and congealed blood painted his jacket and pants. Clutched in his hand was a thin plastic item Riker couldn't immediately identify.

Further muddying the waters, the medical kit was broken in two, the box's entire contents scattered about the ground all around the two men.

A wind gust sent some of the bandages tumbling and skittering away from the surreal scene.

Riker said, "Benny, please tell me it didn't get you."

Now on his hands and knees and pushing up off the road, Benny shook his head. "I'm good, but it was damn close."

Exhaling sharply, Riker posed the same question to Steve-O.

Steve-O said nothing. He remained statue still. As far as Riker knew, this was the first time the man had seen the inside of a person's skull. He was damn sure it was the first time he had taken a face full of it. It was pretty clear shock was setting in.

After confirming the Bolt was truly dead—an absurd worry to address, seeing as how he had witnessed the bullet fired from his Legion collapse the monster's face—Riker stepped over the leaking corpse and offered Benny a hand up.

Grimacing, Riker looked all around. Only when he had confirmed they were all alone did he make his way over to Steve-O. Placing a hand on his friend's shoulder, he said, "Are you OK, buddy? Did the Sicko bite you?"

Steve-O blinked but said nothing. He was staring off into space, seemingly focused on something down the road, somewhere well beyond the helicopter.

Riker followed the man's gaze. Saw only the burned-vehicles which quickly gave way to a long run of gray asphalt leading to the distant horizon. The oil-stained stretch of road was framed on two sides by the dirt embankments and skeletal power poles. Crushing down on it all and moving in fast from the south was a bank of steel-gray clouds.

Riker had seen the expression worn by Steve-O on the faces of fellow soldiers: men and women who had seen things their minds couldn't quite process. Awful things. Incomprehensible things. The aftermath of evil acts perpetrated by extremists who believed they were acting on orders from their God.

It had been a regular occurrence in the Sandbox. Recently, in places like Middletown, Manhattan, and, most recently, the Miami Panhandle, Riker had seen the same expression on the faces of fellow Americans just waking up to the harsh realities foisted on them thanks to the Romero virus.

The look frozen on Steve-O's face was called a thousand-yard stare. In all the pictures that had been taken of Riker at the hospital in the days after he had lost his leg and suffered the burns that scarred him for life, he had been the one wearing the faraway look.

Benny brushed by Riker, crouched down next to Steve-O, and looked the man in the face. "That was some quick thinking, big guy. Probably saved my life." He paused and took a deep breath. Exhaling, he went on, "Check that. You *did* save my life. Now let's get you up off the road." Looking a question at Riker, Benny took a hold of one of Steve-O's arms.

Doing the same, Riker said, "The gunfire is going to draw more of them to us."

"On one," Benny said, beginning the count at *three*.

Working together, as the count hit *one*, they hauled Steve-O to his feet.

Riker removed Steve-O's Stetson. Tiny dots of blood stood out on the stark white brim. A quick swipe across Riker's sleeve took care of that. The man's glasses were another story. They had picked up a thin film of something that was going to need a thorough cleaning to remove.

The Stetson went back on Steve-O's head. The glasses Riker removed and passed over to Benny to clean.

Unzipping Steve-O's soiled Carhartt jacket, Riker said, "Let's get you out of this." He removed a few odds and ends from the pockets and tossed them onto the Shelby's tonneau. Peeling the jacket off, he turned it inside out, then used the clean liner to brush the detritus—flecked bone, brain goop, and drops of blood—from the man's stiff denim pants.

After discarding the jacket, Riker gripped Steve-O's elbow and gently steered the man alongside the Shelby. Steve-O remained silent and offered zero resistance as Riker helped him into the pickup and got him belted in.

Finished cleaning Steve-O's glasses, Benny handed them to Riker, who placed them atop Steve-O's lap with the rest of his stuff, then closed the door.

After a thorough visual recon of their surroundings, Riker faced Benny.

"What happened that caused you to *burn* through half a magazine?"

"You weren't watching?" said Benny sarcastically.

Hanging his head, Riker said, "I missed it."

Planting his hands on his hips, Benny said, "I thought you had my back."

"I did up until those things showed their faces. They both appeared at the same time, Benny. Mine was a *Bolt.* Damn thing got to running straight away. Hit the Chief's rig before I knew what was happening. I drew my gun, got out of my seat, and barely had one foot on the road when lo-and-behold, there it was, back up and about to pounce on you two." He paused long enough to brush a hairy chunk of skull off the front of Benny's jacket—a conciliatory gesture meant to mend the rift he sensed opening between he and his longtime friend. Continuing, he said, "I'm real sorry I fired my weapon in your direction." He shook his head. "It couldn't be helped."

Benny shrugged out of his coat. Removing the spare magazines for the Glock from a pocket, he tossed the soiled coat on the ground. Eyes roaming the road, he said, "Before we stop again, we're going to have to figure out some kind of protocol. Got to make sure this doesn't happen again."

"I'm still learning the rules," Riker conceded. "I'm sorry, man. It won't."

Benny said nothing. His gaze was locked on the ambulance where a steady knocking had just started. It was coming from inside the rear compartment's gloomy environs.

"Look," Riker said, "let's hash this out in the safety of the truck."

Benny nodded but remained tightlipped. Eyes never leaving the ambulance, he drew his Glock, dumped the partial magazine, then inserted a fully loaded replacement.

Striding toward the partially open driver-side door, Riker said, "I'm worried about our friend. I think it's going to take the two of us to bring him back to the land of the living."

Finally Benny spoke. "Agreed," he said. "I think what he just saw messed him up pretty good." As he slipped around back of the still-idling pickup, he got a dig of his own in, saying, "We're still *burning* gas."

Once they were inside the pickup, Riker said, "Buckle up and grab onto something. We're about to see what this hundred-thousand-dollar Shelby Baja is capable of." He turned the traction selector to Crawl and steered across the far shoulder. When the front wheels came into contact with the steep embankment there was no slipping. Just a steady forward pull.

In the backseat, Steve-O was still in a near catatonic state.

Once all four off-road tires were digging into the loose soil, Riker inched the steering wheel to the left, slowly, hand-over-hand, until the scenery out the windshield switched from blue sky to a sea of brown.

With the long train of burnt vehicles gliding by on the left, and the horizon over the hood tilted at an extreme angle, Riker let the idling motor pull the Shelby forward. Once they reached the clear patch of two-lane adjacent to the Life Flight helicopter, Riker inched the steering wheel to the left.

The dirt visible outside Riker's window was quickly replaced by the six-foot-wide asphalt shoulder. Once all four wheels were off the embankment, he hauled the wheel hard left and brought the pickup to a full stop.

Plucking a pack of Reese's Peanut Butter cups from the center console, Riker dropped it in Benny's lap. Hooking a thumb over his shoulder, he said, "See if that'll coax Steve-O out of his shell."

Thrusting the Reese's into the airspace between seats, Benny said, "Want it, Steve-O? It's your favorite."

Strangely, there was no reaction from the backseat. No hand broke the imaginary demarcation line in order to snatch the candy bar from Benny's hand. No elbows banged down on the seatbacks, a common occurrence whenever Steve-O reclaimed his usual perch between the headrests. And highly out of character, the self-sufficient Steve-O did not insist he be engaged directly instead of being talked around while in their presence.

"All right," Benny said. "You had your chance." He ripped open the orange wrapper and removed the pair of peanut butter cups. Handing one to Riker, he discarded the wrappers and wolfed his down in one bite.

While Benny had been conducting his little experiment, Riker had been staring at the short run of two-lane between the front of the pileup and where the helicopter had landed.

On the blacktop were the remains of more than one person. A mangled arm had come to rest against the base of one of the Jersey barriers, fingers curled tight, like a bug in repose. A leg missing the foot was nearby. A limbless torso was wedged underneath the car at the head of the pileup. It was totally naked and partially burned, the skin blistered and weeping a viscous yellow and red liquid.

Whether the person had been a living breathing specimen when he or she suffered the horrific fate was a mystery to Riker. They were dead for good now. No disputing that.

Chapter 7

Their final destination, the place where Benny hoped to fulfill the promise he'd made to Rose, was a couple of miles southwest of the pileup. Backstopped by mostly open range, it sat on a huge tract of flat desert terrain at the end of a short run of two-lane that began at New Mexico State Route 14 and ended at a closed gate abutting an unmanned guardhouse.

Identical runs of twelve-foot-tall fence topped with coiled razor wire encircled the entire facility. The no-man's-land between fences was maybe a yard wide.

Inside the perimeter was a pair of lined parking lots that looked as if they could accommodate at least a hundred vehicles. At the moment, a scant few dotted the larger of the two lots. The smaller lot fronting the building, likely used for short-term visitors, held less than ten automobiles.

"Nobody home," Riker said.

"There goes Plan A," replied Benny. "I had a feeling that just rolling up and having someone answer my question was probably not going to happen."

"You know who Murphy is?"

"Murphy Brown?"

Riker chuckled. "No," he said, shaking his head, "not the lady on that show. In the Army, Mr. Murphy was the fictitious guy who everyone blamed when things went sideways. I just chalk how my cards fall up to fate. But some people ... my buddy, Cade, for instance, thought Murphy was out to get him. A malevolent force always conspiring to muck things up."

"Is Cade one of the reasons why you do the pushups every morning?"

Riker nodded. "He didn't come home."

"Want to talk about it?"

Silence fell heavy in the cab. A gust rolling over the flat plain pushed a cloud of dust over the pickup. As Dolly was rocked on her suspension, Riker shook his head.

Purposefully steering conversation back to the previous topic, Benny said, "You know who you remind me of when you dismiss Murphy like that?"

Riker looked a question at Benny.

"I'll give you two a clue." Benny took a pull off a bottled water. Turning in his seat, he regarded Steve-O. *No participation.* The man was staring out his window. The reflection told Benny the thousand-yard stare hadn't left the man's face.

"Well?" Riker said. "Who do I remind you of when I dismiss Murphy? Whatever that's supposed to mean."

Meeting Riker's expectant gaze, Benny said, "Hokey religions and ancient weapons are no match for a good blaster at your side, kid."

Nothing.

Crickets.

Riker yawned. "Doesn't ring a bell."

Benny looked to Steve-O. The man hadn't moved.

"*Han Solo.* You know, the arrogant scoundrel from Star Wars."

"I don't get it," Riker said. "When I did watch sci-fi, which was pretty rare, I was more of a Star Trek kind of guy. Or Alien. Those were some badass monsters."

Palming his face, Benny said, "Never mind."

Riker said, "I prefer to be grounded in reality. Trust my gut and my eyes." He opened the center console and came out with the Steiners. Powering on the binoculars, he glassed the facility, panning slowly left to right.

In the distance, abutting the larger of the two lots, encircled by yet more razor-wire-topped fence, was a cluster of two-story buildings. The main structure consisted of four separate buildings arranged in a diamond shape. Each building was square, the outer walls mostly windowless and roughly the length of a football field. Square guard towers, each rising a few yards above the main buildings anchored each corner. Each building was connected by a slightly shorter elevation Riker figured was for allowing passage between cell blocks. Narrow barred windows were inset high on the throughway.

Coiled razor wire was strung horizontally along the entire flat roofline. Where roof and wall merged, razor wire was strung vertically. Boxy car-sized heating and ventilation equipment rose up from the four main buildings. Smaller units were perched mid-run atop the passages and encircled by razor-wire-topped chain-link. Branching off of both sides of the smaller heating and cooling units, twin runs of identical fencing ran diagonally along the entire length of roof, to an eventual merger with the larger main buildings.

A long, squat building ran away from the right side of the main parking lot. It was connected to one of the cubes and had more windows than the rest of the facility combined. The glass was mirrored and reflected the angry pewter-gray bank of clouds pressing in on them from the south. On a trio of poles rising up in front of the building was a trio of flags. Old Glory, the yellow and red New Mexico banner, and a dull white flag he guessed was a county item. All stood at half-staff.

Benny said, "What's your gut telling you?"

Riker said, "Nothing."

"Your eyes?"

"There's no way to see inside. Therefore I have no firm opinion on occupancy, other than the lack of vehicles in the lot. There may be a separate lot for correctional personnel that we can't see from here. That could change things." He paused for a beat, the binoculars still trained on the front of the windowed building. Finally, he went on. "Flags are all at half-staff. Tells me that, at the very least, the warden was aware of the attack on Manhattan. Means they probably knew about Romero and went on lockdown."

Gesturing at the brick guardhouse straddling the road thirty feet in front of them, Benny said, "What do you make of *that?*"

The sign affixed waist-high on the guardhouse read *Santa Fe County Adult Detention Center*. Another sign was planted in the dirt beside the road, just opposite the guardhouse. Spelled out in large attention-getting red letters was the dire message: WARNING! DO NOT BACK UP OVER SPIKES OR SEVERE TIRE DAMAGE WILL OCCUR.

The "that" Benny was alluding to was taped to the inside of the window facing the pickup. It was a sheet of copier paper bearing a message handwritten with a fine-tipped black pen.

Riker squinted and focused hard on the cramped scrawl. The result was a bunch of black squiggles cutting horizontally across a field of white. So he brought the Steiners into the equation. Expecting to have to pan slowly and read the message in small chunks, thanks to overmagnification, he instead saw nothing but a bunch of *blurry* black squiggles cutting horizontally across a field of white.

Regarding Steve-O, Riker said, "You're wearing glasses. Can you read that from here?"

Nothing from the backseat. The man was hunched over, hat pulled down low, and unmoving. He'd been like that for the duration of the short drive here. Five minutes spent statue still. No observations on the outside world had been levied by the man. No country and western song lyrics had been sung, either.

Not a peep had crossed the talkative man's lips since he'd been splashed in the face with zombie brains.

Hearing no response, Riker posed the question to Benny.

Benny shook his head. "I can't read it from here."

Riker took his foot off the brake and let the idling engine pull the Shelby forward half a truck-length to a spot in the road equidistant from their previous position, but still about a yard shy of the horizontal gash in the asphalt where curved metal spikes clawed upward.

Stepping on the brake pedal, Riker scanned the road all around the truck. Finished, he said, "I still can't make it out. Can you? If not, one of us is going to have to dismount."

Leaning forward, Benny focused on the paper. "It says: 'Back in ten minutes. Turn motor off and have identification and all pertinent paperwork ready for inspection.'"

"Pretty straightforward," Riker said as he slipped the transmission to Park and killed the motor. Along with the silence came the realization the headache had subsided. Same with the tinnitus.

With the hot engine block ticking as it cooled underneath the hood, Riker spent the first couple minutes of the promised ten-minute wait scrutinizing the lots and adjoining buildings through the Steiners. After two slow sweeps, left and right and back again, he said, "Still nothing moving—living or dead."

"Let me get this straight," Benny said. "Plan A was to have us just roll up and ask if Crystal Wagstaff is here?"

"If any place was still up and running, I figured it'd be this place," conceded Riker. "It's where I would stay until the military gets a handle on things."

"You said all the military vehicles you saw on your cross-country jaunt were either heading south or east."

Riker nodded. "No doubt there's still a sizable presence in the Midwest. Around the Great Lakes, too. I'd even bet they're amassing a blocking force along the Ohio River Valley."

"Illinois was highly active with military. We saw a few Humvees and some tank-looking things in Missouri. We didn't see anything once we got into Kansas. What makes you think they're operating here? In the desert states?" Benny shook his head. "Case you didn't notice … we're in the middle of effing nowhere."

"Better than being near a major metropolis full of those things. You just saw how one Bolt can ruin the day."

"That reminds me," Benny said. "When are we going to talk tactics?" He looked back at Steve-O. "Any thoughts on the matter?"

No response.

Riker said, "Clearly this place is operating with a skeleton crew. Might take them awhile to come out to check on us." Silently, he hoped the inmates weren't running the asylum. If that were the case, the risk wouldn't be worth continuing on with the mission.

Benny said, "This is where we need to do something to see if there are dead things here. Draw them out into the open. How about you lay on the horn for a second or two?"

"Agreed," Riker said. "From now on that'll be our protocol. But no need to do it now."

"Why not?"

Opening his door, the Sig Legion already clear of its holster, Riker said, "Because once Plan B is up and running, we might as well be ringing the dinner bell."

"Let's get set up." Elbowing his door open, Benny drew the Glock and stepped to the road. Peering back inside, he said to Steve-O, "Sure you don't want to get out? We could use your expertise."

That didn't move the needle. Steve-O was completely withdrawn.

Wondering what it was going to take to draw the man out of his shell, Benny closed his door and stalked down the flank of the Shelby, head on a swivel, his attention focused solely on the immediate surroundings.

Chapter 8

Plan B was tucked away inside a specially built case stowed out of sight in the pickup's bed. Riker had the tailgate down and the upper half of his body underneath the rigid tonneau cover when Benny emerged from around the passenger side.

"Coast is clear for the moment," he said.

Emerging with the case, which resembled a large backpack, complete with shoulder straps and a zippered outside pouch, Riker said, "Let's hope it stays that way. Keep watch while I set this bad boy up. This is Steve-O's department, so it might take me a minute."

Without making eye contact, Benny said, "Lots of open ground between us and the main road. Then there's the fence. Unless they can climb, I think we'll be safe out here."

Riker flipped the pack over, then worked the zipper all the way around. Flipping the top half onto the tailgate, he said, "If nobody comes back to the guardhouse, I figure we have less than fifteen minutes to finish the job before it starts pissin' rain."

Voice a bit strained, an obvious sign that being so exposed was not to his liking, Benny said, "Then quit with the play-by-play and get on with it."

Five minutes after taking all of the components from the pack, Riker had the quadcopter fully assembled, he'd checked and confirmed the battery held a full charge, and to get reacquainted with the remote controller, he'd given the manual a cursory glance.

About the size of a manhole cover, and maybe a foot or so from landing gear to the top of the props, the exotic-looking gloss-white drone was much bigger than Riker had expected it to be when he purchased it online weeks ago.

On each corner of the drone was a sleek vertical nacelle. Atop each fixed nacelle was a white two-bladed prop. From tip to tip, each prop was roughly five inches across. Positioned between the landing gear and nestled in a belly-mounted three-axis gimbal was a camera capable of transmitting moving images in stunningly high resolution.

Riker had acquired the drone during one of his late-night spending sprees at Villa Jasmine. Back in the good old days. Back when the Internet was still up and working and having seven million dollars in the bank was still brand new to him.

All of that didn't matter now. Save for the gold and guns and supplies he'd bought in Florida in the days prior to them all heading north, he was back to square one. Back to being who he was before he boarded the bus to Middletown: broke as a joke and unemployed.

Not that he desired work. Staying alive, he'd quickly learned, was a fulltime job.

The drone's handheld remote controller was roughly eight inches across and six inches top to bottom. A six-inch color touchscreen positioned horizontally on a swivel protruded from the controller's top edge. Milled from some kind of alloy, the centrally located pair of joysticks seemed incredibly small once Riker wrapped his mitt-sized hands around the controller.

After swiveling the monitor so that the watery sun wasn't glaring off the glass, Riker searched the multitude of buttons and thumbed the one labeled Start.

The four electric motors came to life. In no time they were emitting a high-pitched whine that reminded Riker of the sound made by an overworked weed whacker. With the noisy craft getting light on its dual landing skids, Riker started the timer running on his Casio G-Shock.

Benny asked, "You sure you can fly the thing?"

Setting the drone on auto-hover, Riker said, "It's idiot-proof. It's got a panic button. I hit that and it recovers from whatever trouble I get it in. This button here"—he pointed to one labeled Return Home—"brings it right back to us."

Benny scanned the distant road. He let his eyes linger there for a beat, then walked his gaze along the feeder road. "All clear. Let's see what you got."

Gripping each dainty joystick between a thumb and forefinger, Riker broke the drone from the hover. Applying throttle—a little too much, as he soon found out—the drone shot into the sky, the high-speed climb reined in only when Riker pressed the Return Home button.

Sure enough, after halting its climb and adopting a hover that lasted a couple of seconds, the drone began a slow and steady descent that had it tracking straight for the Shelby.

Nodding toward the parking lot, Benny said, "Why don't you go check out the cars before committing to the prison."

"Jail," said Riker.

"Is this where they fitted you with the ankle monitor?" asked Benny. "The one you promptly cut off."

"Nope," Riker said. "That happened at the precinct where they questioned me." He shrugged. "No need for it now. I don't think the courts will be convening any time soon."

Riker watched the quad getting near the end of its return flight path. At seemingly the last second, the drone throttled down, flared hard, and settled softly on the tonneau, just inches from where it was when he ham-fisted the initial launch.

"Just like you know what you're doing," quipped Benny.

"The learning curve isn't as steep as one would think," Riker admitted. "I've flown it a few times at Trinity. It's damn useful when you don't want to go out and check the perimeter on foot." Biting his lip, he stepped back from the pickup and worked the controls, relaxing only when the quad was in the air again and well on its way toward the parking lot.

"Ever thought of using it to ferret out the Bolts from the ... what does Steve-O call the slow ones?"

Eyes narrowed and tracking the quad, Riker said, "I've heard him call the slow ones Slogs. Never crossed my mind to use the drone to draw out the fast ones. Sounds like it would work. But I sure wouldn't do it out in the open. Those things cover ground so quickly. And the way they snarl and growl ... I'd hate to get caught with this remote in my hands in place of a gun."

Benny said nothing. He was watching the drone cross the open ground to the parking lot. A couple of times along the way the wind picked up, causing the craft to yaw and careen groundward while still under full throttle. Both times Riker hit the panic button, which sent a radio frequency command across the distance, instantly saving the craft and likely sparing them all from having to get any closer to the prison than they were now.

After the second brush with disaster, Riker set the quad on automatic hover and took a moment to let his heartrate return to normal.

"How long do you have on this charge?"

"Twenty to thirty minutes," Riker answered. "And that's dictated by flight distance and how much you hotrod the thing. Steve-O usually milks the full twenty-five out of a fresh battery."

"So what you're seeing on the screen is what's being recorded onto the onboard memory card?"

Riker nodded. "It's a sixty-four giga … mega … something byte. I'm not tech-savvy at all. It seems to capture everything you point the lens at, though."

Working the joysticks, he got the quad moving again. As he popped the craft up and over the distant fence, the timer on his watch indicated he'd already burned two minutes of flight time.

Giving the half-dozen thirty-foot-tall light poles a wide berth, Riker piloted the drone across the parking lot to the cluster of vehicles parked near the far edge, then brought it to a hover fifteen feet off the lined blacktop.

No sooner had the noisy quad entered the airspace directly over a white minivan than Riker saw on the display before him signs of movement.

First, the driver door on a Japanese compact hinged open. While Riker couldn't see the culprit, he guessed it wasn't a person whose midday siesta he'd just interrupted. While that was happening, a man in a suit and tie stumbled from behind a midsize SUV, took a few stilted steps toward the drone, and thrust his arms over his head. Even viewed from a good distance, and at a steep downward angle, there was no disputing the middle-aged man had tied his last Windsor knot.

While the cause of first death wasn't in plain sight, the torn jacket sleeves and deep, red fissures on the knuckles of both hands suggested he'd put up one helluva fight trying to remain among the living.

Finding the drone's gimbal control with his thumb, Riker panned and zoomed until the distant compact car filled up the screen. Witnessing a second zombie poke its head over the car's curved roofline, Riker said, "Look at how she's bloated. My guess is she died a few days ago in her car."

Benny said, "I'll buy that. But how'd she open the door? They can't do that, can they? 'Cause if they can. If they're evolving or something, we … are … hosed."

The thought had already crossed Riker's mind.

Out loud, he said, "The daytime highs were pushing seventy in the days right after we got to Trinity. Maybe she was in her car with the door open. Burning up with infection. I'd want a breeze on my face."

"Why didn't she leave?"

"Maybe she couldn't. Maybe the gate guard was already gone on his"—Riker let go of the gimbal control and made air quotes with one hand—"*ten-minute break*. Maybe when he failed to return, she went ahead and called emergency services from her car. Settled in for a long wait."

They went quiet and watched the female zombie shamble around the little green compact.

Losing her momentarily on the display, Riker nudged the camera controls until he reacquired her, then slowly pulled back on the zoom as she trudged the open ground, face upturned, dead eyes locked on the drone.

The zombie kept up the same steady pace, jaw pistoning up and down until she made it to the businessman zombie's side. Riker imagined the smell coming off of her as she took a futile, slow-motion swipe at the drone. The move hiked her tank up, revealing a bloody compress taped to her abdomen.

Nudging the throttle, Riker put more altitude between the quad and the bloated kielbasa-like fingers straining to get ahold of it.

The undead woman's once-dark eyes now had a dull sheen to them. With her high cheekbones and coal-black, braided hair, Riker figured she must have had some kind of American Indian ancestry. She looked to have been nudging the south side of forty before contracting the Romero virus.

Another time and under a different set of circumstances, Riker would have asked her out for a coffee.

Looking over Riker's shoulder, Benny said, "She couldn't leave."

Nodding, Riker said, "The fence here is designed to keep people in. Then there're the spikes. With no guard to retract them, they would have torn up her tires. She knew that."

Having seen enough, he nudged the drone to a higher altitude, then rotated the craft until the mirrored building filled up the display.

After checking their surroundings, and finding it still clear of threats, Benny said, "How'd she get the bite?"

Riker shrugged. "Maybe she was a nurse inside. Or a head shrinker."

"Or a guard," Benny proffered.

Riker said nothing.

"Maybe she got bit outside," Benny added. "Then she came here to see a husband or boyfriend."

It was as if they were mapping out the last days and hours of her life without her input. Riker suddenly felt uneasy speculating about what had befallen the woman. As if the wrong conclusion might somehow tarnish her former reputation. To halt the conversation, he said, "She's dead, Benny. Get over it."

Benny said, "No shit, Sherlock. You don't have to be a dick about it."

Riker's neck was getting stiff from peering down at the screen. Another of the headaches that had plagued him since he received the head injury in Iraq was manifesting as a calypso beat behind his eyes. Thankfully, the ringing in his ears remained at a manageable volume.

Fingers working the controls, he set the drone rocketing off toward the trio of flags standing sentinel before the mirrored building.

A hundred feet short of the parking lot fronting the mirrored building, Riker slowed the drone's forward momentum. Coming to the white cement sidewalk encircling the lot, he threaded the drone between a pair of vans parked there and brought it to a hover a yard or two from the pair of glass doors set equidistant in the building's stark facade.

For obvious reasons, the doors were not mirrored. Instead they were tinted just enough to block the sun's UV rays and still allow people coming and going to see through them.

On the display, Riker saw furniture crowding a cramped lobby. In the middle distance, parked on a square of burnt-orange carpet, was a low table piled high with magazines.

In the far distance, thick glass rose up from a waist-high counter. Riker's best guess was that the partition was bulletproof and put there to keep the waiting public from wandering into the jail's sensitive areas. Which seemed a waste because the door next to the partition was hanging wide open.

The recon was just seconds old when they saw the first flicker of movement behind the glass. At first, it was just a man-sized shadow, slithering the periphery of the lobby, jinking between chairs, all pertinent detail obscured by the gloom.

The shadow grew larger and larger until finally it neared the tiled section of floor and completely filled up the display.

"That thing's one of them," Riker spat. As he pulled back on the zoom, behind him, Benny said, "Maybe it's the gate guard. See all the keys on his belt?"

Both statements were confirmed when the form entered the dim rectangle of light just inside the double doors. Centered on the display was a middle-aged man with a high-and-tight haircut and a gym rat's physique. A thick neck and bulging biceps stretched tight the white short-sleeved shirt. On the breast of the shirt was an embroidered shield. Words Riker couldn't read were stitched in black below the shield. The uniform pants were navy-blue and bore the obligatory light-blue stripe down the side of each leg.

Holding up the pants was a wide black belt. It was glossy and reflected the meager light spilling through the tinted windows. The ring of keys Benny had spied was there, too, bouncing and jerking wildly with each forward step.

Strangely, the holster on the belt was empty. Same for the ring meant to retain a baton.

The fireplug of a man didn't slow or even seem to notice the doors when he slammed into them.

On the right-side door, like a forked lightning bolt, a series of thin cracks shot diagonally from the single pane's upper left corner.

Voice showing no kind of satisfaction at being correct in his original assumption, Riker said, "Looks like your guard is dead, Benny."

For a long three-count, the undead guard continued the relentless forward march, only to be repulsed again and again by the door glass.

So close, yet so far, thought Riker as more runners sprouted from the initial crack.

Though the action taking place on the display was out of earshot, with each new impact Riker heard in his head the *clack* and *screech* of the keys on the guard's hip striking the glass. Each *bang* of the guard's lug-soled boots striking the doors resonated as if Riker was standing beside the hovering drone.

Benny said, "Put a gap in that thing's front teeth, you got a dead ringer for young Ahhhnold Schwarzenegger."

Focused intently on keeping the image centered on the touchscreen, Riker grunted but made no comment.

"You keep that thing hovering so close, he's going to break out," added Benny.

Riker said, "I'm trying to see if there's anybody alive in there. Maybe someone's holed up in a back room and can hear the drone." He paused and pulled the drone back from the doors. "If there is, maybe the distraction of the drone will buy them the time they need to find a way out."

As if to punctuate the statement, a second zombie rammed the doors.

A beat later a third outline skated across the dim lobby and careened into the others from behind.

The combined weight of the three finished what the stocky zombie had started. Bowing outward, the slightly misshapen pane tumbled to the ground at the base of the door. Instead of disintegrating into a thousand tiny shards upon impact, the window skittered across the cement walk, to the curb, where it finally came to rest, intact and clouded with a multitude of scratches.

Following the same path to the ground as the glass, Arnold stutter-stepped over the bottom door frame, then fell through the void, feet tangled and arms outstretched. Practically climbing up Arnold's back, totally oblivious to their coming fate, the other two zombies pitched forward and followed him to the ground.

Now out in the open, without the tinted glass and shadows obscuring their features and clothing, Riker saw the pair crushing down on the undead guard for what they were: inmates. The young men both wore blaze-orange county-issue uniforms. *Property of D.O.C - Santa Fe County* was stenciled in white across the back of each smock-like top. To add insult to injury, both men wore plastic jailhouse shoes over faded pink socks.

"None of them is Crystal," Riker said.

"Master of the obvious," Benny shot.

Just as the fallen zombies were getting to their knees, another wave of orange-clad monsters filed out of the building. It was a diverse mix. Most races were present, with the men outnumbering the women two to one.

Squinting hard to see the tiny figures on the screen, Riker muttered, "Still no Crystal."

Having just made another visual sweep of the feeder road and the prison grounds surrounding their position, Benny said, "That little amount of footage won't be enough to satisfy Rose. She'll want proof of life ... or death. Let's humor her. Can you still fly that thing when it's out of your direct line of sight?"

"Never tried. I'm not opposed to giving it a shot." He glanced at the G-Shock. *Six minutes.* "I'll just pop it over the building, find the yard, and see if anyone made it out alive."

While Riker had sounded confident in his delivery, deep down he harbored doubts in his ability to maneuver the thing once it was out of sight.

Benny asked, "How much juice does the thing have?"

"Twenty minutes flight time ... give or take."

Riker was already flying the drone away from the squat building's mirrored façade. Once it was in the center of the smaller lot, he gave it power and started it on a return path nearly identical to its approach.

As the noisy craft rounded the corner and shot south, hugging tight to the outside wall and moving quite fast, Benny said, "Make it quick. We've got five slow movers coming our way. Right now they're at the junction with the highway. Figure they'll be on us in five minutes or so."

Putting his trust in Benny, Riker bumped the throttle to the stops and flew the drone balls-out to the facility's distant southwest corner, watching it with the naked eye until it was but a white speck. When he was just about to lose it from sight, he throttled down, initiated an auto-hover, and glued his eyes to the screen.

While Riker had been getting the hang of flying the two-thousand-dollar *toy*, once he was beholden to orienting it to its immediate surroundings using just the image on the tiny screen, he was quickly humbled.

He was saying, "Keep me updated on the zombies' whereabouts," when the camera—still facing dead ahead—transmitted a picture worthy of mounting and framing. Desert in the foreground. What looked like an arroyo, running left to right, in the middle distance. And backstopping it all the way off to the west: low, scrub-dotted hills that rambled away to an eventual merger with a sliver of blue sky.

What made the image so spectacular were the bars of honey-colored light lancing groundward through the billowing cloudbank. Like a swipe from God's paintbrush, the shafts accentuated everything they touched across the miles-wide swathe of desert.

With dark, angry clouds edging ever closer from the south, and the rest of the land but a drab sea of earth tones, what Riker was seeing on the screen was an oasis for the eye.

After getting his bearings, he disengaged the auto-hover, skimmed the flat roof, and dropped the quad over the edge of the distant cube. Reaching a point on the interior wall where he guessed the windows would be, he again engaged the auto-hover.

With the southernmost cellblock and connected passage standing in the way of the wind building ahead of the storm, the craft provided a rock-solid viewing platform. Manipulating the camera controls, which started the sphere spinning clockwise in its gimbal, Riker located the upper floor windows. They were set high up on the wall. One for each cell, he guessed. Each window was a two-foot square fronted by industrial-looking wire-mesh panels.

There were two rows. One for each floor.

Way too many to count. Especially on the tiny screen.

Zooming in on a couple of nearby windows didn't give Riker a clue as to what may be happening inside. Panning the camera groundward, however, painted a much clearer picture.

As the screen suddenly filled with an orange mosaic in constant motion, he intuitively knew what he was about to learn, even before the camera responded fully to operator input.

A beat later, with the lens fully pulled back, his hunch was confirmed: the inmates, most still clad in their Santa Fe County smocks, owned the yard. They milled about in small packs; no rhyme or reason as to why they had glommed onto their pack mates. Men and women, blacks and whites and Hispanics—all hanging together. There were even a few white shirts intermingling with the orange. The common denominator: They were all zombies.

Slowly but surely, the dead things became aware of the buzzing interloper.

Bodies still in motion turned to locate the sound. Sallow faces aimed expectantly skyward, the undead inmates surged toward the trampled soccer-pitch-sized parcel of grass thirty feet below the drone.

Riker's best guess as he panned the camera over the yard was that he was looking at more than a hundred former human beings.

Over his shoulder, he said, "Where are the Slogs?"

"They've covered about a hundred feet of road. Still about three football fields to go."

Having played some football in his day, Benny's way of breaking it down made it easy for Riker to picture the road in his mind's eye.

"Tell me when they're a hundred yards out."

Benny grunted an affirmative. Back to peering at the screen, he said, "How are we supposed to pick out Crystal from the crowd?"

"I'll fly a grid pattern over top of them. Low and slow. Your eyesight is better. Keep a lookout for a bleached blonde. She should stand out pretty good against all that orange."

Benny crowded Riker on the right. Focused intently on the screen, he said, "You know this isn't going to fly with Rose. She will want proof of life." He paused. "Or death."

"This is going to have to be good enough," Riker said. "Short of going inside and checking every one of them, this is as good as it's going to get."

***

After a full minute spent crisscrossing the yard, the drone buzzing just feet above the upthrust arms of the undead, neither Riker nor Benny had spotted a zombie with a single platinum hair on its head, let alone a whole shock of it.

"We gave it our best shot," Riker said. "When we get back, Rose can pop the memory card in the laptop and watch the footage for herself. Hell, she can watch it in slow motion if she wants. That's a thing, right?"

"I think so," answered Benny. "I just hope it appeases her."

Finishing the final pass, Riker found the Auto-Hover button by feel. Only when the craft had leveled off and come to a complete halt did he shift his attention from the scene on the display to the remote control's many buttons.

"You see the *return to home* button?" he asked.

"No," Benny replied. "But I do see something on the display that may warrant a closer look."

Chapter 9

The *something* on the display Benny had alluded to was a cluster of human forms far off in the distance. Setting them apart from the rest of the crowd was their clothing, location, and the way they moved.

The former Riker and Benny had seen before. It was the same white shirt and navy-blue pant combo worn by the stocky guard. Additionally, a few of the dead things patrolling the yard had on the same shirt and pant combo.

How the people got to their present location—a ten-by-thirty-foot rectangle of rooftop bordered by ventilation equipment, all of it head-high to them and encircled by razor-wire-topped chain-link fence—was not immediately evident.

As the quadcopter closed the distance to the far northeast corner of the yard, Benny asked the obvious: "How'd they get themselves up that tree?"

Indicating a portion of the yard showing on the bottom of the remote-control screen, where a fully extended aluminum ladder lay on the ground along the interior wall, Riker said, "That ladder is how they got up there."

Benny said, "They should have pulled it up after them. Used it to get over the rooftop fencing and then down on the other side."

Slowing the drone and enacting a hover that put the camera lens level with the roof, maybe ten feet from where the four people stood waving and gesturing, Riker saw the reason they hadn't done exactly as Benny had suggested. On the ground by the ladder was a pair of corpses. The brittle, brown grass surrounding the corpses was black with dried blood. Scraps of fabric clinging to the dead bodies suggested the pair had been wearing guard uniforms. They had also been clad in black body armor. Some of the individual components had been torn away and sat in the grass nearby. Both corpses had on white helmets, chinstraps stretched tight, and clear face shields deployed over gruesome death grimaces.

While the smaller of the two still wore elbow and knee protection, it had suffered the same fate as the other. Both arms, from the fingerless hands on up to where the shoulder ball-joints connected, had been reduced to blood-slicked bones held together by stretched-out lengths of tendon.

Though the unfortunate duo still wore their contoured breastplates, the hungry zombies had torn through their shirts and mined all the soft morsels from their abdominal cavities. Bristling with twisted ribs and knobby vertebrae, the carnage left behind made Riker think of that scene in Alien in which the screeching little imp burst unexpectedly from the *Nostromo* crewman's chest.

The damage inflicted on the guards by tooth and nail of the dead—while far from precise—had *literally* erased any chance of identifying them by gender.

More evidence of the feeding frenzy that had taken place: human detritus and bits of uniform littered the trampled ground all around the ladder and bodies.

There were also signs that the pair, before being overrun, had attempted to fight off their attackers. At one end of the ladder, headshot corpses in county-orange littered one particular patch of flattened grass. That to a person they ended up in twisted heaps, heads pointing *away* from the wall suggested to Riker that they had fought off some kind of surge with the ladder still propped against the wall.

Having taken it all in, Riker started the camera panning from the ground to the roof. Once the camera was horizontal in the gimbal, with the guards on the roof again framed fully on the remote-control screen, he said, "When the attack happened, one of the deceased was probably bracing the ladder for the others. No doubt the second dead guard was unloading his or her rifle while the lucky ones were climbing their asses off."

"Begs the question," Benny said, "why weren't these guys who made it up the ladder wearing body armor?"

The *guys* were in fact three men and one woman. Like the diversity Riker had spotted in the yard, the roof-bound guards checked most of the boxes.

By some stroke of luck, they were assembled left to right, shortest to tallest.

The first guard was Caucasian, maybe mid-thirties, with a build similar to his undead counterpart who had ridden the pane of glass out onto the sidewalk. The similarities ended there. While the undead guard's exposed skin had been white as driven snow, this man on the rooftop was a walking sunburn. Face, neck, forearms. Only skin on him not beet red were the palms of the hands he was waving at the drone.

Guard number two was African American and nearly as big around at the waist as he was tall. Clearly, the man had never ignored the dinner bell. Riker guessed he had probably been passed up by the local police and took the corrections job only because they would have him.

The third man in line, the one who'd seen the drone first and started flapping his arms, looked to be of Hispanic origin. He was thin and shoeless and never stopped moving, constantly shifting his weight from one foot to the other, eyes wild and darting in their sockets. It was clear he was beyond ready to be down from the roof.

The lone woman of the group also looked to be Hispanic. She stood half a head taller than the rest. Maybe a year or two north of fifty, her rat's nest of graying hair was stuffed under a black ball cap with the words *Santa Fe County Corrections* embroidered across the front in gold. She was stocky and well-muscled. Looked healthy for her age. Squished between a blunt stub of a nose and a wide, flat forehead, her piercing brown eyes never left the drone.

Squint lines and the hard set to her jaw suggested to Riker that the face staring back had never cracked an easy smile.

Looking over one shoulder, Riker saw that the zombies had covered half the distance from the road. A football field and a half in just a couple of minutes. Thankfully, none of the approaching figures were of the fast variety. A quick check of his watch indicated the quadcopter had fifteen to eighteen minutes of flight time left. Finishing the quick recon with a half-second glance at the encroaching clouds, he concluded the fast-moving squall would be here well before the drone's onboard battery was anywhere close to dying on them.

Dropping his gaze back to the screen, Riker said, "She's the warden."

"What makes you say that?"

Dismissing his initial assumption of the lady being Hispanic, Riker said, "Says so on her shirt. Right here." He pointed it out on the screen. "Benny Sistek, meet Warden Littlewolf."

"She's Native American," Benny stated.

"We *are* in the desert southwest," Riker said.

"What are we going to do now?" Benny asked. "What *can* we do?" He pointed at the nearby fence. "We're out here, they're in there. Lots of fence and ground standing between us."

Without warning, pangs of guilt from what Riker did to the couple and their nephew at the ferry landing in Florida welled up within him. Last thing he had wanted was to see anyone get hurt, to leave them exposed to attack from the dead things swarming Shorty's operation; however, at that moment, with all the roadblocks being thrown up in front of them, ensuring the safety of Tara and Steve-O had superseded everything. With all of that in mind, he said, "We can't just leave them up there, Benny. We've got to do something."

Back to staring at the screen, Benny said, "How can you be so sure these aren't *inmates*? Maybe they killed the guards and stole their uniforms."

Referring to the space blankets set up as a rainwater catch, pair of riot shotguns propped against the fence, and small cache of chips and candy bars piled by the rifles, Riker said, "They escaped by the skin of their teeth. Nobody had any time to kill anyone and change into their clothes. Besides, the black guy looks like he kills pizzas and doughnuts, not fellow humans."

Benny shot Riker a skeptical look.

"You see the Hispanic guy's arms?"

Benny nodded. "He's got a shit-ton of tattoos. Doesn't that prove my hostile takeover theory?"

Even on the tiny screen it was obvious the line work was top-notch. Furthermore, the colors were vibrant and laid on real thick. On the man's deeply tanned left forearm was a pair of theatrical masks—one smiling, the other frowning. A snake done in black and gray, the shading exquisite, wrapped the man's other forearm.

Riker said, "Take a closer look. *Those* are hundred-and-fifty-dollar an hour tattoos ... *not* prison work."

Benny shrugged. Looking at Riker, he said, "Can you talk to them?"

Riker shook his head. "Even if this model had the capability, probably couldn't hear them answer over the engine noise."

Benny looked down the drive. The zombies were now three, maybe four hundred feet distant. Confirming Steve-O was still inside the pickup, the doors all closed, he said, "So what's your plan, Lee?"

"Let's get the drone coming back and I'll lay it all out for you."

Deciding to let the drone follow its own GPS trail back to its launch point atop the Shelby's tonneau cover, Riker engaged the Return Home feature.

Responding at once, the out-of-sight drone broke the hover, lifted a few feet over the building, then slowly moved away south by east.

As soon as the drone began the initial ascent, Riker saw looks of desperation settle on the guards' faces. More so on the men, though.

The chubby man was shaking his head and beckoning for the drone to come back.

The Caucasian guard sat down hard, a look of utter dejection washing his face.

The tattooed guard threw his hands in the air and tracked the drone as it passed overhead.

Still standing, hands on hips, Littlewolf's eyes narrowed and she grimaced.

As the drone spun on its axis, the last thing Riker saw was that grimace morphing into a tight smile. A smile that suggested to him that she was at peace with the drone moving on.

Watching the yard and multitudes of orange-clad zombies scrolling across the screen, Riker laid out his plan to Benny. A plan, should it come to fruition, that would soon satisfy many unanswered questions and, at the same time, reveal Crystal's fate.

Chapter 10

The drone rose up and over the heating and ventilation equipment, crossed over the razor-wire coils atop the chain-link fence, then immediately began to shed altitude. As it left the near side of the prison wing and passed over the perimeter fence, the down-facing camera picked up movement on the ground between the jail walls and guardhouse. Curious, Riker stepped around the Shelby and walked his gaze down the short drive and gave the pair of parking lots beyond the abandoned guardhouse a quick once-over.

Expecting to see only the handful of zombies that had followed the undead guard through the destroyed front doors, instead, what Riker saw gave him pause. It was way worse than he feared. *Ten-fold* worse. A damn *disaster* considering how he had hoped to get the warden and her men off the roof.

The parking lot, once home to only a pair of zombies, was now teeming with more of them than Riker could count. Most of them were barefoot and dressed in county-orange. On a positive note, they *were* contained by the fence running around the parking lots. On the flip side, in order to access the no-man's-land sandwiched between the jail's east wing and its twelve-foot-tall razor-wire-topped perimeter fence, all those acres of asphalt the dead now owned would need to be crossed.

"Great," Benny said. "Not only do we have biters coming up the road behind us, now we'll have to deal with these."

Standing clear of the truck bed as the drone came in for a landing, Riker said nothing. He was deep in thought, searching for a solution to their newest problem.

Though he didn't need to, Benny ducked as the quadcopter drifted down from the heavens. Craning to watch the thing touch down on the exact spot it had launched from ten minutes prior, he said, "You know, if Steve-O was out here, no doubt he'd be singing that song about clowns to the left of me, jokers to the right—"

Interrupting, Riker sang the chorus. "*Here I am. Stuck in the middle with you.*"

"Yeah," Benny said, smiling, "that's the one."

"He would also know the artist. I, unfortunately, do not," admitted Riker.

After quickly stowing the drone under the tonneau and slamming the tailgate home, he prompted Benny to board the truck.

The zombies from the highway had closed to within thirty feet of the tailgate. Though Riker had no way of measuring their speed, it seemed as if they had somehow found another gear.

Hand on his door handle, Benny drew his Glock. "What about them?" he asked.

"Just get in. I have a feeling we'll need the ammo where we're going."

Leading by example, Riker tromped around the driver's side. As he was climbing in, a strong gust following the storm's leading edge closed the door on his leg. The metallic *clink* of the door's lower edge hitting his bionic was instantaneously drowned out by a huge clap of thunder that seemed to have originated directly overhead.

The stink of death riding the wind was beaten down as the first sheet of rain pummeled the truck. The rain infiltrated the cab, drenching Riker's left side before he could haul the door shut.

Firing the engine, he slammed the transmission into Reverse and started the first leg of the three-point-turn necessary to get the Shelby facing back the way they'd come. No sooner had the pickup started backing away from the tire spikes than the zombies careened into the tailgate.

With the hollow bangs of dead flesh striking sheet metal rising over the staccato pings of rain pelting the roof and windows, Riker hauled the wheel hard left and slammed the brakes. Only when he saw that the zombies were just outside his window did he spin the steering wheel back around and get Dolly moving forward again.

"You hanging in there, Steve-O?"

No response. Only the fleshy thumps of splayed-out hands coming down hard on the window next to Riker's face.

As Benny was thrown back in his seat by the sudden acceleration, he hooked a thumb toward the prison. "The ones set free from the main building are almost to the gate."

With the shriek of nails raking the paint loud enough in the cab to set everyone's hair on end, Riker stomped the brakes. Ignoring Benny's warning, he performed the same maneuver. Reverse across the road, more spinning of the steering wheel, then another sharp stab of the brakes.

"C'mon," Benny urged. "Stop here for a few seconds. Let's do these ones." He started his window running down. "Eventually we're going to have to deal with them."

"Until we find more ammunition," Riker stressed, "we need to be mindful of how we use what we have." That being said, he used his master control to run Benny's window back up.

The action earning him a prolonged dose of stink eye, Riker spun the wheel right, all the way to the stops. Then, with the power steering pump emitting squeals of protest, dead hands beating steadily on the window glass, and a sudden fork of lightning cutting the sky overhead, he fed the motor gas.

Without a shot fired, Riker had gotten them around the dead things and headed for the road that would eventually spill them back onto Highway 14.

Trinity House

Tara stood in the center of the clearing, hands on hips, admiring her handiwork. Though the field of pavers exposed by hours of back-breaking work was shot through with splintered nubs of wood, the surface was solid and level underfoot. *Perfect place to land a helicopter.*

In the hour since Dozer had first detected something prowling around in the woods, the fog had lifted completely, leaving the clearing awash in the flat light of midmorning.

Done for the time being, Tara sheathed her machete. She gathered up the waist-high pile of saplings, lugged them across the landing pad, and dumped them unceremoniously between a pair of marked trees awaiting their date with the chainsaw.

You get to deal with those, bro.

Pausing where the pavers ended and the forest started, Tara sniffed the air. Detecting the faint odor of decaying flesh, she looked to Dozer. "Where's the stinky?"

Dozer rose from his spot on the pavers, sauntered over to the piled saplings, and cocked his head to one side. He sniffed the air in the general direction of Trinity House, then answered with a single yip.

"That's what I thought," she said, peering into the trees to her front. With the watery sun at a higher azimuth, she could now see dozens of feet into the tangle. Nothing moved in the gloom. There were no dead eyes staring back at her. And unlike the earlier non-event, she kept her imagination in check and the Glock holstered.

Satisfied that whatever had Dozer on edge earlier—be it a wild animal or newly turned zombie—was not an immediate threat, Tara set off for the overgrown trailhead. Faced with the daunting task of getting the pad ready for Wade Clark's pending arrival, she had put off widening the trail until the pad was ready to go. Though she couldn't see it as the forest closed in around her, Trinity House was down there somewhere. Unfortunately, she reminded herself, so was the source of the stench.

Chapter 11

Pushing the Shelby hard, Riker had shaved a minute's travel time off the short ride from the county jail to the pileup near the I-25 overpass. And just as he had feared, the earlier gunfire had drawn the dead from whatever lay beyond the freeway embankments. As he slid the pickup in next to the Life Flight helicopter, in addition to the small herds of dead already vectoring in from the north and east, he detected a flash of movement in his side vision.

Looking off to his two o'clock, Riker spotted a pair of zombies cresting the embankment beyond the northbound lanes. They were still a couple of hundred yards away and, save for one of them turning out to be a fast-mover, no immediate threat.

"I see them, too," Benny said. "They're on my side. I'll take care of them. While I'm at it, you go ahead and draw the rest over to the left-side embankment. I'll meet you there when I'm done over here."

"Good idea." Riker slammed the transmission into Park and killed the motor. "We grab the high ground, the headshots should come a little easier."

While the television shows and movies featuring zombies tended to make the double-tap look easy, actually hitting a Slog on the move with one bullet on the first try was, at best, still a 50/50 proposition for Riker. If not for the limited range time he had put in before fleeing Florida in the early days of the apocalypse, he probably would have never survived the cross-country sprint that followed.

"I've got three magazines," Benny stated. "If that don't do it, I deserve to get bit."

Riker didn't like that kind of talk. After shooting Benny a concerned look, he said, "Squash that negative crap. It's contagious. Glass *half full*. Always!"

As Benny pushed his door open, letting in air rife with the stench of death from the advancing corpses and the faint odor of ozone from the lightning storm dogging them, Riker glanced back at Steve-O. Seeing that nothing had changed since the man had slipped into the state he was currently in, Riker said, "Locking you in, big guy. I promise you won't be left alone for long."

Receiving what he took to be a subtle nod from Steve-O, just a micro-movement of the Stetson's brim, Riker elbowed his door open and stepped out.

No sooner had Riker's Salomon hit the road than he heard the low growl of a hard-at-work diesel motor. Though he couldn't be sure, he pegged it for a big displacement item. Eight cylinders, at least. It was coming from the north, beyond the overpass where a lone zombie, deprived the use of its legs, was just dragging itself out of the shadows.

Just as the crawler was transitioning from dry pavement to wet, the source of the engine noise revealed itself. It was maybe a half-mile out, coming down the highway toward them, moving fast in the same lane as the zombies that hadn't survived the plunge from the overpass.

Leaning back into the Shelby, Riker dug the Steiners from the center console. He pressed the binoculars to his face and glassed the road ahead, picking up first the charred roofs of the cars and SUVs in the immediate foreground, then, after dragging the Steiners up a degree or two, he had the oncoming vehicle fully framed.

At first blush—judging by the gunmetal-gray rig's wide stance, high-rising cabover, and multiple amber marker-lights ablaze on the latter—Riker thought he was looking at a big rig, an eighteen-wheeler to be precise.

As the truck got to within a few yards of the pile of corpses, the driver jinked the wheel, causing the rig to follow the same path Riker had steered the Shelby to avoid the falling zombies.

Afforded a better view of the rig thanks to the slalom maneuver, Riker saw it for what it really was: a supersized pickup fitted with an equally large camper shell.

Instantly Riker's brain was warning him that the rig might belong to the folks he'd stranded on shore so he could have Shorty's ferry all to himself. Feeling the first pang of worry stabbing his gut, he dredged the image of Tobias Harlan's rig from memory.

Both pickups were the same color, but this one barreling down on them was much newer, the blue oval on the grille marking it as a *Ford*, and the badging on the driver-side fender identifying it as an F-550 model. While Tobias's pickup had been an older model of American pedigree, it shared none of the design cues like the one currently filling up the rectangle of light below the overpass. Furthermore, Tobias's pickup was fitted with a vintage Caveman shell. While it had also been framed by amber lights, it was a lower profile item, all sharp edges and right angles.

The shell mated to the F-550 was aerodynamic, rounded and slippery looking. Additionally, the dearth of daylight showing between the top of the shell and underside of the overpass suggested it was much taller than the Caveman shell.

The piece that finally convinced Riker this wasn't the Harlans' rig was the single word spelled out in foot-high white letters: *EarthRoamer.*

"Who is it?" Benny asked.

"Not sure," Riker answered, "but it's just the distraction we need."

In the middle distance, their interest piqued by the drone of off-road tires and rattle-clatter of the EarthRoamer's diesel powerplant, the zombies that had once been locked onto the Shelby were all conducting an abrupt about-face.

When the last of the slack, pale countenances of the dead were facing north, Riker lowered the Steiners and turned his gaze to the zombies coming down the embankment to their right.

Having been unfazed by the appearance of the new vehicle, the zombies picked up their pace. One was male, the other female.

Regarding Benny over the hood, Riker said, "I'm calling an audible. Get back in the truck."

Retaking his seat, Riker trained the Steiners on the I-25 overpass.

Benny was clambering aboard at the very moment the EarthRoamer emerged from the second of I-25's dual east/west running spans.

With the gray sky reflected in the F-550's curved windshield, determining who was behind the wheel was impossible.

As the truck began to slow, two things happened, one right after the other.

First, a horn sounded. Not a single, short *I see you, blue pickup* kind of thing. Instead, it was a long, drawn-out affair produced by an extremely loud air horn.

Like an air raid siren announcing an impending tornado, it droned on as the rig's speed bled off.

Clearly, the driver was trying to keep the approaching zombies on the hook.

Then, coming to a complete stop, maybe two hundred feet short of Chief Hickok's Tahoe and the stretched-out throng of zombies filing past it, the EarthRoamer's horn went silent and its brilliant HID (High Intensity Discharge) headlights began to flash.

"What the fu—"

Shushing Benny, Riker said, "They're communicating."

Benny looked a question at Riker.

Watching the lights as they switched on and off, Riker said, "Three short. *Pause*. Four short. *Pause*. Three long. *Pause*." He went on like that, calling out the length of each individual strobe until the driver extinguished the lights for good.

Benny said, "What was all that about?"

"Morse code."

"You can read it?"

Riker nodded. "I was required to learn it to earn my *Signs, Signals, and Codes* merit badge in Boy Scouts."

"What'd it say?"

After a soft chuckle, Riker said, "One word: *Shorty*."

Hearing that stirred something within Steve-O. He sat bolt upright and clicked out of his seatbelt. In the next beat, he slid to the center of the backseat, planted his forearms on the shared seatback, and locked his gaze on the EarthRoamer.

After a long three-count, his voice adopting the tone of someone who'd just won a game of *Clue*, Steve-O said, "As I *suspected*. Shorty *does* have a small penis."

Unsure of whether he should laugh or be truly concerned by the subject matter of the first thing said by Steve-O since the man had received the brain facial, Benny looked to Riker for a cue.

Clearing his throat, Riker said, "It has to do with the direct correlation between the size—or lack thereof—of a man's penis and that of his vehicle. The larger the latter, the smaller the former. Steve-O, here, has his suspicions. And apparently, the fact that Shorty has traded up from the Tahoe he *was* driving, to the big ass EarthRoamer he is now, is all the confirmation Steve-O needed." Looking over his shoulder, he went on, "Am I right?"

Steve-O nodded.

Riker said, "My truck is much smaller than Shorty's. What does that mean?"

One hand covering his mouth, Benny worked hard not to laugh.

Not really expecting an answer to his loaded question, Riker said, "Good to have you back among the living, Steve-O. How was your time away?"

Steve-O sighed. Adjusting his Stetson, he said, "I'm a changed man, Lee Riker." Jabbing a finger at the pair of zombies coming up against the Jersey barriers near the static ambulance, he went on, saying: " Those things out there are no longer *Sickos*. From now on I am back to calling them *Monsters*."

Benny dropped his hand to his lap. Again with the questioning look, he asked, "Another suspicion confirmed?"

"Nah," Riker said, "he's just coming back around to my way of thinking. Wearing someone else's brains does have a way of enacting change within a man."

Again the EarthRoamer's air horn sounded. A short *blap* that started the nearest pair of monsters trudging north, away from the Shelby.

As the leading edge of the storm passed and the rain started falling in sheets, the EarthRoamer's driver-side door hinged outward.

Not needing binoculars to know what was coming next, Riker said, "Step right up, Monsters."

The zombies did just that, crowding the open door like kids swarming the Good Humor man.

Instead of handing out Bomb Pops or Fudgesicles, Shorty dealt the dead a fusillade of gunfire.

To Riker's ear, the soft pops drifting down the road were identical to the reports made by Benny's Glock.

"Shorty's got the high ground," Benny noted. "If it was me sitting up in that truck, I wouldn't have opened the door."

"If it was you sitting up in that truck," Riker said, "you would be able to reach over the window channel. The man is called *Shorty* for a reason."

"We see eye to eye," Steve-O said. "But he is still a grown ass man. Don't you forget that, Benny."

More gunfire from up the road. Swinging his gaze forward, Riker saw that the zombies were falling en masse. Maybe ten of the original twenty still stood. The ones dropping to the road were becoming an effective barrier, which forced the ones still on their feet into a single file line in order to get to Shorty.

"We better help him," Benny said.

The back to back to back *booms* of a shotgun discharging seemed to contradict Benny's statement.

"Let's go," Riker said, setting the Steiners aside. "Unlike me earlier, he's firing *away* from us."

Holstering his Glock, Benny asked, "Am I still getting the two by the ambulance?"

Riker shook his head. Not only did he see the two zombies staggering away as contained by the freeway divider, but he also saw them as a perfect learning opportunity. An opportunity for Steve-O to graduate from shooting bottles and cans to becoming someone who could be relied upon should the need arrive. While he didn't ever see the man carrying his own weapon, it would be nice to know if he was capable of pulling the trigger if it came down to it.

Doing so in a controlled environment, well away from Trinity, seemed the best approach.

Riker opened the glovebox. Inside was a plastic case. He removed the case and popped the lid. Inside the case was a small black pistol and box of shells.

He removed the magazine. *Empty.*

He pinched the slide between thumb and forefinger and did a quick press check. *Clear.*

Taking a single .22 round from the box, he thumbed it into the magazine, inserted the magazine into the pistol's magwell, and dumped the Sig Sauer Mosquito into his pocket.

Having been watching intently, Benny said, "You sure about this?"

Dragging his Legion from its holster, Riker said, "After that last episode, I *need* to know."

Benny made no further comment.

Meeting Steve-O's gaze, Riker said, "You ready to bag your first *Monster*?"

With zero hesitation, Steve-O nodded, saying, "I shall do my best, Lee Riker."

Chapter 12

Riker, Benny, and Steve-O remained inside the Shelby and watched Shorty finish blasting his way through the herd. Judging by the booming reports rolling down the highway, it was clear he had stuck with the shotgun to put down the last ten zombies, pausing only long enough, Riker guessed, to load more shells into the weapon.

Once the shooting had ceased and Shorty had again retreated back into the EarthRoamer, Riker said, "While I'd like to wait for the storm to blow by, our friends at the prison are in the thick of it."

Taking that as his cue to get out and do his part, Benny grabbed his parka from the backseat and shrugged it on. Yanking the hood over his head, he stepped from the Shelby.

When Shorty had fired his final shot into the face of the last zombie standing beside the EarthRoamer, the pair of zombies that were to be used for Riker's experiment had only managed to cover half the distance to the far end of the pileup.

Dipping his head as he passed underneath the drooping rotor blades, Benny skirted around the helicopter's rounded nose. A quick peek through the rain-mottled cockpit glass told him that no one was home. He opened the right-side door and liberated the small fire extinguisher strapped to the bulkhead.

At the cement freeway divider, Benny leaned his upper body into the open and began shouting and waving the red fire extinguisher at the retreating zombies.

"Hey pusbags!" he called. "Come and get it."

If the zombies were the bulls, and Benny the toreador, then the extinguisher was the red cape.

At once, in response to the new stimuli, the rain-soaked creatures halted in their tracks.

The male was first to whip its head around and fix its dead-eyed stare on Benny. As the female zombie took notice, the male was already turned around and on the move, arms and legs working considerably well for having no blood pumping through them.

By the time the female zombie had performed the series of movements necessary for its lower extremities to get pointed the same direction as its cocked head, the male had halved the distance to the tangle of cars at the front of the pileup.

Farther down the two-lane, the EarthRoamer was reversing from the drift of face-shot corpses.

Inside the Shelby, Riker was giving Steve-O one last chance to change his mind.

Using a tone he figured Tara would employ—equal measures of empathy and concern—Riker said, "You sure about this, Steve-O? Because I'm good with whatever you decide."

"I'll pretend it's a NERF gun."

Riker shook his head, vigorously. Tone all business, he said, "You can't pretend it's anything but a deadly weapon. This is the real deal. A real gun shoots *real* bullets made of copper and lead, not *foam*."

At that, Steve-O rattled off the four tenets of gun safety, beginning with "Always treat a gun as if it's loaded" and ending by saying "And always be sure of your target and what is behind it. My target, Lee Riker, will be a Monster and the dirt hill over there will be behind it."

"Good memory," Riker said, clapping Steve-O on the shoulder. "You nailed all the rules. Now put on a coat. I think you'll find one of Tara's extra waterproof shells on the floor back there."

Seeing Benny approaching the Jersey barrier with only a red fire extinguisher in hand, Riker unbuckled and elbowed open his door. Fairly confident his friend wasn't going to lose it again and put a hole through anything but a zombie skull, he turned up his collar and exited the Shelby.

Benny was just out of the male zombie's reach when it arrived at the point in the road where he'd been waiting. As soon as the snarling creature lunged for him, it received a short blast to the face from the fire extinguisher, its unblinking eyes and open mouth accepting the lion's share of the powdery, white chemical.

The cold drizzle immediately began to scour the thing's forehead and cheeks free of the residue.

Meeting up with Steve-O by the freeway divider, Riker plucked the Sig Mosquito from his jacket pocket.

"Benny," he said, "give it another shot, then make room for Steve-O to work. He's told me he wants to put this one down."

Without a word, Benny sprayed a liberal dose of fire retardant at the zombie's face. Thoroughly blinded, it lunged across the divider, missing everything but the air where Benny had been standing.

Staking a position behind Steve-O, Riker pressed the Sig into the man's palm. "Just like you did it at Trinity. Aim, throw the safety, finger on the trigger, then press it—*slowly.*"

Extending his arm, gun aimed at the growling zombie, Steve-O nodded.

Rain cascading off the Stetson wet the gun and sent a constellation's worth of droplets onto Steve-O's waterproofed sleeve.

Taking a step closer, the gun hand beginning to waver, Steve-O said, "I can't see its eyes. Isn't that where you're supposed to shoot them?"

"With this gun, yes," said Riker, as he positioned the shorter man just out of reach of the zombie's grabby hands. "Just shoot at where you think one of its eyes *should* be."

While all of this was taking place, Benny was watching Shorty maneuver the EarthRoamer to the spot on the highway where Riker had driven the Shelby up the embankment. Certain there was no way the man was going to try and drive the top-heavy beast on the incline, but instead was getting it turned around, Benny turned his attention back to the female zombie. Still a dozen yards away, it posed no immediate threat.

Ignoring the revving diesel engine, Riker drew his Legion, then took a couple of steps back to give Steve-O some room.

Rolling his shoulders, Steve-O leaned forward, gripped the pistol with both hands, and drew in a deep breath. As the seconds ticked away, with the zombie blindly clawing the air directly over the barrier, the Mosquito's muzzle again began to waver. At first, it was just a subtle little tremor. The tremor soon became a full-blown case of the shakes, the barrel carving a huge counterclockwise circle in the air.

Riker was about to throw in the towel and shoot the zombie himself when the single report sounded. And as Steve-O had done every time a gun he was shooting discharged, whether the target be an empty glass bottle, soda can, or milk jug, he closed his eyes and a shudder wracked his body.

Amazingly, given his inability to keep his hands steady and his eyes open, the lone round struck the zombie an inch below its right eye socket.

Unlike the many items Steve-O had used for target practice, maxillofacial bone was *not* forgiving. Instead of fracturing and collapsing inward, the angled cheekbone altered the round's trajectory, sending it plowing underneath the flesh and into the zombie's roving, powder-coated eye—*exactly* where Steve-O had been trying to put it in the first place.

Like a marionette with its strings cut, the zombie crashed vertically to the road.

There one second, gone the next.

Most importantly, there was no blowback whatsoever. No spritz of blood and brain matter went airborne. No flecks of bone or scalp splashed Steve-O. Even the caked-on fire retardant stayed put.

It was a clean kill, the bullet remaining inside the skull along with the brains it had just scrambled.

"I did it," Steve-O gushed as he lowered the pistol.

"Sure did," Riker said. "Good job. One down, one to go."

Engaging the Sig's safety, Steve-O turned to Riker. "Here." He handed the pistol back, butt first. "The lady Monster is all yours, Lee."

Given Steve-O's reaction after being splashed with brains and bone, slipping into a near-catatonic state for the better part of thirty minutes, Riker hadn't expected the man to follow through with the morbid task. That Steve-O wasn't aware that the Mosquito's .22 caliber round would not inflict the same damage to a skull as the much larger 9mm round, and still followed through with the task, told Riker the man had put the brain facial in the rearview mirror.

If push came to shove, Riker decided as he pocketed the Mosquito, Steve-O could be trusted with something *other* than a NERF rifle.

Deciding to put his own squeamishness to the test, Riker holstered the Legion. With the female zombie just arriving across the divider from him, he dragged the Randall Model 18 from the scabbard on his hip and warned Steve-O of what he was about to do.

The handcrafted survival knife was a single-tang item measuring eleven-and-a-half inches from its spear-point tip to its weighty brass pommel. Sporting a razor-sharp six-inch blade complete with sawtooth top edge, the knife looked like something Rambo might wield.

Flush with new money, Riker hadn't balked at the eight-hundred-dollar price tag when Jon, the owner of the gun store in Florida, had placed it on the counter alongside the assortment of firearms Riker was already purchasing.

The petite blonde had been in her mid-twenties when she had died and come back as a zombie. It looked to Riker as if she had fought hard to survive the attack that did her in. Both arms were riddled with bite marks and crisscrossed by deep scratches. As if ripped by brute force, a jagged half-moon tear—beginning on the left side of her mouth and running away toward her ear—had left her with a perpetual lop-sided grin.

The young woman's dirty LSU tee shirt was torn down the front, exposing a flesh-colored bra and a pair of bloodless, dime-sized gunshot wounds. Black gunpowder burns around the entry points suggested the weapon had been pressed against her ribcage when she'd been shot. That there was very little blood in the vicinity made Riker think the damage had been done postmortem.

Judging by the bloat and intense stench, Riker figured this one had contracted Romero in the early days of the outbreak. A couple of weeks spent hunting the living while exposed to the elements had left her hair matted to her head and given insects time to make her body their new home.

Jaw hanging open and breathing through his mouth, Riker lashed out and snatched up one of the grabbing hands.

Crushing down on the wrist, he found the pale flesh ice cold to the touch, the sensation triggering an eruption of gooseflesh all up and down his ribcage. As he yanked the undead thing off balance, his eyes were drawn to the thin silver bracelet encircling its wrist. Shiny beads spelling out *Petra* jangled out a tinny rhythm as he changed his footing to keep the majority of his weight on his good leg. As he did, he couldn't help but note how the nails on the hand he was holding were uneven and cracked in places. And how flesh and dermis had collected under the nails and blood had dried around the cuticles—evidence, Riker decided, that Petra had killed in the not too distant past. Maybe the one who had shot her. A person who had not been versed in the *rules* and had aimed for center mass instead of the head, thus signing their own death warrant.

Just like the cause of the pileup spread out before him, the whereabouts of the Life Flight pilots and crew, and the true reasoning behind the dump trucks parked across the highway south to Santa Fe, Riker would never know Petra's true backstory.

Last kill, lady, was what went through Riker's mind as he stabbed at her left temple with his new blade.

Unlike the way this particular killing stroke was portrayed in movies and on television—the blade slipping in quietly with little to no resistance—Riker felt a lot of initial pushback.

Immediately following the strike, there came a grating sound and the blade tried to twist from his grip. As he added more muscle, the tip speared through the bone offering resistance, dug in a few inches, then struck something solid and came to a *grinding* halt.

Similar to the male zombie's second death, as if a switch had been thrown, Petra's body went limp. However, instead of disappearing behind the barrier, the unmoving corpse remained upright, the entire hundred or so pounds suspended on Riker's blade, its sawtooth serrations acting like the barbs on a fishhook.

While Riker had expected some kind of a physical response after killing one of them in such a deliberate manner, maybe a cold shiver or wave of nausea coursing his body, he felt only empathy. For the first time since this had all started in Middletown, he saw the act of killing the dead as not an affront to who they used to be, but a favor to them and anyone they may have left behind. For if the shoe were on the other foot, he would want someone to afford him the same courtesy.

Standing there, staring his ultimate destiny in the face, he said a silent prayer. A prayer asking that when it *was* his time to go, the person performing the act be anyone but Tara.

Last thing Riker wanted was for his only known living kin to see him as one of these lifeless automatons, let alone have her shoulder that kind of responsibility.

Seeing that he had been mistaken in assuming Shorty was going to find an alternate route around the pileup, Benny mouthed, "What the hell?" Tapping Riker on the shoulder, he said, "Snap out of it, Lee. She's gone." He paused and pointed at the EarthRoamer. "I think you're going to want to take a look at what Shorty's about to attempt."

After stealing a final glimpse into Petra's dead eyes, in which not a flicker of life had been detected before, during, or after the clumsy killing stroke, Riker gave the knife a quick twist.

Sliding free of the blade, Petra's head and upper body pitched forward. A hollow *thunk* sounded as her forehead butted the top edge of the barrier. Following that was a wet slap as one arm hooked the barrier. Then, as if in slow motion, the diminutive corpse slithered from the top of the barrier and rode its angled cement face to the shoulder, where it finally came to rest, arms and legs bent in crazy angles, yet another life cut short by a heinous act against humanity Riker was still struggling mightily to comprehend.

Chapter 13

From Riker's first contact with Petra, to her lifeless shell riding gravity to its final resting place, ten seconds had elapsed.

During that ten-second span, a lot had happened.

Off of Riker's right shoulder, acting on the simple instructions Benny had given him, Steve-O was beginning to strip the helicopter of its medical supplies. A pair of white boxes sporting the ubiquitous red cross already sat on the road beside the helo's open left-side door.

Beyond the pileup, Shorty had driven the EarthRoamer as far south on the shoulder as he could. It was now awfully close to running over the backboard left behind by the ambulance crew.

Remembering how the road had seemed so close to his window when he drove the Shelby on the embankment, Riker said, "I don't think Shorty knows that thing's limitations."

On the heels of Riker's assessment, the squall line passed them by and the sun got back to shining its flat light of winter over the scene. As wisps of steam lifted off the road all around the EarthRoamer, the sound of a second motor kicking in emanated from the vehicle's undercarriage. It was much quieter than the rig's V8 and definitely not running on unleaded or diesel.

Recognizing the rapid-fire piston noise for what it represented, Riker said, "I spoke too soon."

Benny said, "What do you mean?"

Showing up at Riker's elbow, Steve-O said, "I put the boxes in Dolly. What next?"

Scanning their surroundings, Riker said, "Keep an eye out for Monsters. A real keen eye."

Steve-O threw a salute and trotted off toward a spot in the road nearby where his view north and south was unimpeded.

Indicating the EarthRoamer, Riker said to Benny, "Watch what that thing does next."

Barely perceptible at first, the EarthRoamer's left side began to lift up. After running for a few seconds, the second motor went silent. A beat later, with the rig already adopting a little bit of a sideways lean in the embankment's direction, there was a soft hiss of air and the EarthRoamer's right-side suspension began a slow, controlled collapse.

"You did speak prematurely," Benny said. "Dude knows what he's doing."

Feeling a bit foolish for having doubted the crafty survivor in the first place, Riker flashed a pained grin in Benny's direction. "I should have known he had something up his sleeve. What he's doing is no different than altering ballast on a seagoing vessel."

Benny said, "Like his ferry ... what'd he call her?

Riker said. "Miss Abigail." He paused. "Shorty named her after his late wife."

"She had the big C," Steve-O called.

"We still good, Eagle Eyes?" Riker asked.

"Coast is clear the way we just came. There is one monster walking and one crawling towards us from the overpass," answered Steve-O. "But they're still a long ways away."

Riker craned to see past the pileup. Confirming Steve-O's report, he directed his attention back to the EarthRoamer just in time to see it slow-roll onto the embankment.

Crossing his arms, Benny said, "He's fuckin' going for it."

Keeping the driver-side tires tracking on the soft dirt just outside the frost-heaved shoulder, and with the passenger-side tires carving a deep furrow into the embankment, Shorty maneuvered the EarthRoamer around the pileup.

It was slow going, the rig bobbing to and fro as it crept along at a walking speed. And though Shorty's close-up view of the road was likely similar to Riker's when he had skirted the pileup in the Shelby, thanks to the EarthRoamer's adjustable suspension, the towering vehicle was clearly in no danger of turning turtle on Shorty.

"That man," said Benny, "has King-Kong-sized balls."

"Shorty still has a small penis," Steve-O said.

Riker removed his Braves cap. After beating it against his leg to shake the rain from it, he said, "I don't think we need to go back down that road, Steve-O. Especially not in front of Shorty."

Steve-O harrumphed. Planting his hands on his hips, he said, "Shorty made it. He's on our side now."

Once they reached the end of the clogged stretch of road there was a hissing noise and the EarthRoamer's driver-side suspension began to compact. As the vehicle transitioned from the embankment to the southbound lane, maybe fifty feet from Riker and the others, the compressor motor started up again.

Slowly but surely, as the air Shorty had bled off before the maneuver was being pumped back into the passenger-side suspension, the vehicle crossed the shoulder and steered into the far lane.

By the time the EarthRoamer had come to a complete stop on the rain-slicked freeway, the compressor was silent, the ride height had returned to normal, and the vehicle was again sitting level with the road.

After seeing up close all the craftsmanship that had gone into the EarthRoamer, Riker was convinced he had seen it, or one just like it, on the cover of one of those extreme overlanding magazines he liked to thumb through at the QVC.

The big diesel ceased rumbling and the driver-door swung open.

The second Shorty poked his head out, in complete disregard of Riker's warning, Steve-O blurted, "Looks like I was right about your penis, Shorty."

If Shorty heard Steve-O, he didn't let on.

Shooting Steve-O a look that all but screamed: *Did you have to go there again?* Riker greeted Shorty, saying: "Hell of an entrance."

When Shorty took hold of the grab handle and climbed down to the road, he did so gingerly, favoring his left hand, which was wrapped with a blood-stained bandage.

Hand hovering near his Glock, Benny cast a suspicious, side-eye glance at Riker. Whispering, he asked, "How do we know he's not infected with Romero?"

Shorty said, "Because I'm not infected with anything, *Slim.*" He reached up into the EarthRoamer's footwell and came out with a stubby shotgun. "Long story on how I got this"—he showed off the bandaged hand—"but I assure you, it was *not* the work of a *biter*." As if just the idea of being infected had put a bad taste in his mouth, Shorty spit a long stream of tobacco juice onto the road.

Still not sold on the middle-aged midget with the face only a mother could love, Benny regarded Riker. Still whispering, he asked, "You *sure* about this guy, Lee?"

Placing a hand on Benny's shoulder, Riker said, "Stand down. He's good people. Saved our lives more than once."

Nodding emphatically, Steve-O said, "Lee's right, Benny. Shorty let me drive Miss Abigail, too."

Riker said, "Miss Abigail's a boat. You *pilot* a boat, Steve-O."

Ignoring the correction, Steve-O said, "Nice boots, Shorty! Where'd you get them?" He paused. Then, smile growing wider, he said, "Did you go to Dollywood?"

Resting the shotgun on his shoulder, Shorty said, "Nope."

"Graceland?"

"Guess again."

"Nashville?"

Shaking his head, Shorty said, "I got 'em at a tack and feed store just outside of Thompson's Station, Tennessee. They're Stetson Outlaws. Hand-tooled. I figured they'd be right up your alley, so I picked you up a pair."

Smile growing even wider, Steve-O pumped a fist.

Closing the door behind him, Shorty started across the lane toward Riker. His bib-style ski pants made a swishing sound as he walked. They were bright yellow and held up by the attached suspenders. Apparently a little bit on the long side, the pant legs were rolled up, leaving the fire-engine-red cowboy boots impossible to miss.

Perched on Shorty's head, complete with a mesh back and perfectly shaped brim, was a black trucker's-style hat. *Booty Hunter* was screened in red up front. Below the words, the image ubiquitous to anyone who had spent time on the road behind long haul rigs, was the silhouette of a buxom, seated woman. And in keeping with the hat's theme, the crude caricature was encircled by red crosshairs.

Partially obscured by the bunched-up fabric of a wool button-up shirt was a shoulder holster containing a boxy black pistol. Clutched in Shorty's right hand, its stunted barrel aimed groundward, was the Mossberg 590 Shockwave Riker had given him when they had all parted ways in Mississippi roughly two weeks ago.

Boot heels clicking on the road and a wide smile appearing on his face, Shorty quickly covered the distance to the Shelby.

Knowing that Shorty had likely spoken to Tara once he'd gotten within radio range of Trinity House, Riker spared the inquisition for later. While he wanted to hear how the rest of the country was holding up, he spread his arms wide, saying: "You finally made it to our neck of the woods."

Shorty spread his arms wide, too, and wrapped them around Riker's midsection.

The men slapped each other on the back then quickly disengaged.

"I was almost to your place and then I came up on a roadblock."

"Couple of mega dump trucks?"

Shorty nodded. "Hailed Tara from there. She told me you'd gone south. I had no choice but to turn around and backtrack anyway. So here I stand."

Riker said, "You think about going through Santa Fe's suburbs?"

"Lots of biters," Shorty said, grimacing. "No way I was chancing getting my ass trapped on some side street and becoming walker chow. So I went south to 25 and—"

"And here we all are," Riker finished.

"And here we all are," repeated Shorty. Looking to Steve-O, he said, "About your penis wisecrack. It ain't the size of the boat, my friend." He pumped his hips. " It's the motion of the ocean."

Steve-O's cheeks flushed red.

Regarding Benny, Shorty asked, "Where's Scooby Doo, *Shaggy*? The biters come between you two?"

Glad to see that Shorty knew how to take it *and* dish it out, Riker smiled and shook his head.

Responding to Shorty's barb, Benny said, "Never heard that one before, *Napoleon*. And now that we've got the insults out of the way ... tell me how you heard what I said to Lee? The thing about you and Romero? I didn't exactly say it through a bullhorn."

Shorty said, "Jamie Sommers I am not."

Benny furrowed his brow.

Catching the reference, Riker cupped a hand behind his ear and made a *che-che-che* sound with his mouth.

Reacting to the blank look on Benny's face, Shorty said, "Does *Bionic Woman* ring a bell?"

Throwing Benny another bone, Riker said, "She's that hot blonde with the bionic ear." He paused. "Hearing so good she could hear a mouse pissing on a cotton ball from across the room."

If Benny knew who Jamie Sommers was, he didn't let on.

Finally, Shorty said, "I read lips, Slim. Spent a lot of time out on the water. Deep-sea fishing. Crabbing on the Bering sea. Captaining boats inside a nice warm glass-enclosed wheelhouse. It's just a little something I picked up along the way."

Only response out of Benny was, "Whatever, Napoleon. By the way, my name's not *Slim* … or *Shaggy,* or whatever other slight you got loaded up."

To break the Grand-Canyon-sized rift growing between the men, Riker interrupted and proceeded with long-overdue introductions. Finished, he said, "Now kiss and make up, fellas. It's time to get to doing what we came here to do."

As the men buried the hatchet, Riker instructed Steve-O to keep watch.

Finished shaking Shorty's hand, Benny looked a question at Riker.

Handing Benny his Gerber multi-tool, Riker said, "Get the radios out of the Chief's rig and the ambulance. Save as much of the wiring as possible."

Taking the multi-tool, Benny drew his Glock and started off down the road, toward the Tahoe, all the while giving the grabby zombie in the crumpled sedan a wide berth.

Going up on his tiptoes, Riker called out to a retreating Benny, "Be careful, bro. I think there's a biter in back of the ambulance, too."

Benny acknowledged Riker with a wave of the hand holding the multi-tool.

Shorty asked, "What do you need me to do?"

"There's a length of hose and a bunch of empty gas cans in back of Dolly. Why don't you start siphoning fuel? I figure the Chief's rig has a pretty deep tank. The ambulance, too. When you're finished with that, we need to use that winch of yours to move a couple of these Jersey barriers."

"No need for the hose," Shorty said. "I've got a cool little *toy* in back of Marge. You can keep your cans. I've got plenty of those, too."

Cocking his head, Riker said, "Who's Marge?"

As Shorty strode off toward the EarthRoamer, he called, "It's short for *Large Marge*. She's the bad guy in Pee-Wee's Big Adventure."

Standing ten feet away, Steve-O heard what Benny had said and launched right into a pretty damn fine rendition of The Champs' smash hit, *Tequila*.

Riker said, "Never saw that one. Is it a movie?"

Still within earshot, Shorty called, "What fuckin' rock were you living under during the eighties?"

"I was in the third grade and busy watching Pee-Wee's *Playhouse*," Riker shot. "Never even knew there was a Pee-Wee *movie*." Shifting his gaze to Steve-O, he said gruffly, "Keep your eyes on the road, shit-stirrer."

Flashing a pretty fair salute, Steve-O uttered one final, albeit muted, *"Tequila!"* then went quiet, head back to panning the road and embankments and long tangle of burned-out cars sandwiched between it all.

Shorty returned carrying a trio of plastic five-gallon cans and the "cool little tool" he had alluded to. It was a hand-cranked pump trailing two lengths of rubber tubing, one about a yard long, the other nearly twice that and dragging on the road behind him.

"Wish I would have had one of those when we came up from Florida."

Grinning, Shorty said, "You swallowed some gas, didn't you."

Riker nodded, the memory of the rancid taste kicking his salivary glands into overdrive. "The second I did I thought for sure I was going to start breathing fire."

"Don't worry, nobody's swallowing anything," Shorty promised. He nodded toward the pileup. "Let's do this."

Riker put his hand on the shorter man's shoulder, stopping him mid-turn. Looking him in the eyes, Riker said, "I didn't want to say this over the phone. Thought it best to wait until you got here so I could say it face-to-face." He paused for a beat, then, in a funereal voice, added, "I'm sorry you didn't find your kids. Even though they're both grown, I imagine it's hitting you pretty damn hard."

Hanging his head, Shorty said, "Getting turned back before I even got a glimpse of Lake Michigan was a punch in the gut." He swallowed hard. "But I'm a realist, Lee. Chicago and all points beyond are lost to the biters. Leads me to believe so are New York and Jersey. Unlike what I did after I lost Abby to cancer, completely going off the deep end … I'm going to move on from this. Nothing in a bottle is going to bring my kids back to me, let alone ease the pain of losing them."

Always the optimist, Riker said, "There's still a chance—"

Pulling away from Riker, Shorty stalked off toward the Tahoe, hose skittering along the ground behind him.

Riker had nothing to say to that. Sticking to the far left of the narrow shoulder, he followed Shorty through the shadow of the EarthRoamer, down the length of the pileup, and to the rear of the Tahoe, where the man set the empty cans and siphon pump on the ground.

On the other side of the red SUV, Benny was just rising up from the footwell. Meeting Riker's gaze, he showed off the newly acquired radio, then displayed the knuckles he'd bloodied in the process of prying it out.

Caught in gravity's pull, rivulets of red encircled the man's wrist and flowed down the jacket cuff.

The sight of blood acting as a reminder, Riker said to Shorty, "How'd you do that to your hand?"

As Shorty worked at prying off the Tahoe's gas cap with a Tanto-style blade, he said, "It's a long story. Happened when I *acquired* Marge." He looked up from his task. "It wasn't pretty what I was forced to do. I'll tell you all about it when we get to your place."

Taking the man for his word, Riker nodded. "I'm all ears when you're ready to talk about it."

Seeing that Benny was still rooted on the other side of the Tahoe, a questioning look on his face, Riker waved him away, mouthing, "It's OK."

After plucking the empty backboard off the road, Riker stepped over the face-shot fireman and picked up the cumbersome Jaws of Life.

With Benny on the other side of the barrier and already approaching the ambulance, Riker set off for the fire engine.

Chapter 14

Riker stopped at the rear of the Santa Fe Fire Department engine to stow the Jaws of Life and backboard. Finished, he noticed the spooled-out hose by his feet. With the task of reeling it back in untenable—both in respect to the time it would take him and the expertise needed to do so—Riker drew his blade and sawed through the hose, leaving maybe a yard or so of it hanging over the back deck and a steady stream of residual water leaking onto the road.

Sheathing the blade, he looped around to the driver's door, where he stopped and uttered a prayer only he could hear.

After stepping up on the running board, peering inside, and finding the cab free of dead things, Riker opened the door and climbed behind the wheel.

Glancing at the dash, he learned that the first part of his prayer had been answered. The key was still in the ignition. Icing on the cake was the fact that the driver's last act had spared Riker the grim task of searching for them in the zombie fireman's pockets.

Turning the key in the ignition told Riker that his second and third requests to the Big Guy in the sky had also been heard.

All at once, the instrument cluster lights lit up and the fuel needle rocketed from Empty to a hair below Full.

Key in the ignition, battery juiced, and diesel in the tank.

Three batters up, three fastballs smacked over the right-field wall.

The one ask Riker hadn't thought to posit during his silent appeal was that the motor would actually turn over and remain running. Biting his lip, Riker turned the key the rest of the way in the ignition and fed the motor some fuel.

Immediately the motor roared to life. It rumbled and vibrated the cab as Riker stabbed the accelerator pedal a couple of times.

From the driver's seat, Riker had a commanding view. At his one o'clock, roughly fifty feet ahead and adjacent to the pair of dead zombies, Steve-O was smiling and flashing two thumbs-up. Behind the man, the entire run of road—all four lanes of it—showed no signs of movement.

Knowing his tank of good luck was probably trending contrary to the fire engine's fuel gauge, Riker consulted the massive side mirrors. Though the reflection was a bit blurred due to vibration caused by the thrumming engine, Riker was still able to see the entire passenger side of the ambulance where, inexplicably, Benny appeared out of nowhere. He was falling backward and being pursued by a wheeled stretcher with a thrashing zombie strapped to it.

While the stretcher was fully collapsed, its wheels were not locked.

After hitting the road on its wheels, the stretcher wobbled and bounced and nearly toppled over. Somehow remaining on all four wheels, it continued on, spinning a lazy clockwise circle, the end where the zombie's head lay on a collision course with Benny's prone body.

Fearing Benny was about to get bit, Riker kicked his door open, seized the grab handle by his head, and threw himself from the cab.

After an off-balance landing that saw Riker planting a hand on the ground to keep from pitching over, he rose up and sprinted the length of the engine, along the way drawing the Sig Legion from its holster. Going left at the engine's back deck, high-stepping to keep from getting tripped-up on the remaining length of hose, he slipped past the ambulance's wide chrome grille.

As Riker squirted from between the vehicles, Benny's calls for help suddenly rose over the rough-idling diesel motor.

Still moving at a near sprint, his bionic squealing in protest, Riker made a hard right. Going a bit too fast for the maneuver, he bounced off the ambulance, then hip-checked the cement divider.

With about twenty feet to go, having just caromed off the freeway barrier and about to get slapped in the face by the ambulance's right-side wing mirror, Riker saw that things had gone from bad to worse as the occupied stretcher pushed up hard against Benny's left side.

Seeing as how the undead man completely filled up the stretcher, ample belly riding over the hip straps, Riker had a sinking feeling that once one set of the stretcher's wheels had left the back of the ambulance, there was no way a person of Benny's stature had a chance in hell of stopping it.

Weighing in at maybe one-sixty fully clothed, and having come to rest on his back with the freeway barrier pushing in on him from the right, Benny was a perfect example of someone caught between a rock and a hard place. To put it in Steve-O speak: Benny was in a pickle.

Though the *hard place* was still atop the collapsed stretcher and constrained by the strap across its knees and hips, it still strained mightily against the bonds to get to the fresh meat. With each wild swipe the zombie took at Benny's upturned face, its lower body inched up on the compressed mattress.

In the middle distance, still turning the handle on his siphon pump, Shorty was just becoming aware of Benny's predicament.

On the ground to Riker's front, Benny was struggling to free his Glock from its holster.

On the stretcher, the zombie had gotten both arms free of the blanket. From all the struggling to get to Benny, the zombie had succeeded in getting its upper body rotated damn near one hundred and eighty degrees contrary to the angle of its trapped hips. And like one of those possessed creatures in the independent horror flicks Tara was always talking up, this one's torso kept on turning until a resonant crackle of bones snapping sounded over the throb of the motor and, just like that, its torso was hanging over the stretcher's side rail.

To Riker, still a few feet removed from the melee, it looked as if his friend had given up on going for the Glock but instead was focused on creating some separation between him and his attacker.

Arm outstretched, the difficulty of the shot making the Sig in his hand seem much heavier than its measly two pounds, Riker bellowed, "Lay flat, Benny!" and threw off the safety.

No time to inspect the mag or press check the slide to ensure a round was chambered. Riker superimposed the Romeo's red pip over the zombie's nose and pressed the trigger.

On the road, his shirt wet and sticking to his back, Benny found himself in a fight for his life. Head dangerously close to the zombie's snapping teeth, out of the corner of his left eye, he read the script stitched in gold on the left breast of the zombie's polo shirt: *Chief Hickok - Santa Fe Fire Department.* He also noted the blood-stained sheets stuck fast to the undead man's thrashing lower extremities.

Though it hadn't been evident in the ambulance's gloomy interior, it was clear now that the Chief had suffered severe damage to his legs, leaving them both twisted grotesquely inward from the knees down. Also not visible until coming under the light of day were the multitude of ragged, purple-ringed bite wounds running from wrist to elbow up the Chief's left forearm.

Laying there on the wet ground, the fire engine's rumbling exhaust beating a cadence, Benny was gripped by the fear-filled realization that his only backup this side of the barrier was the person responsible for starting the motor.

From his compromised position, all Benny could see was the gray sky up above, the passenger side and rear end of the ambulance rising up over his outstretched legs, the Jersey barrier in his right side vision, and the zombie and stretcher crushing in on him from the left.

A hollow moan emanated from deep within the zombie's chest. Along with the hair-raising sound came a concentrated stench of death the likes of which Benny had never smelled.

As Benny was making the split-second visual recon, the fingers on both of his hands snapped open and they came under attack by what felt like a million pins and needles. When he went for the Glock, the numb fingers failed to cooperate. Every time he thought he had ahold on the grip, his hand came away empty.

Feeling a cold hand fall across his face, he gave up on the Glock, planted both feet on the stretcher, and drew in a deep breath.

Core muscles coiled, fast-twitch fibers in his quads and calves just receiving the electrical impulses instructing them how to act, a whole slew of things happened all at once.

91

While the creaking of the ankle joint of Riker's prosthesis didn't register to Benny, the barked admonition and single *boom* of the pistol discharging certainly did.

On the stretcher above Benny, Chief Hickok's head snapped violently up and away. As a shudder raced through the stretcher underneath the corpse, the head was already on the rebound.

Having just been hit full-on in the face with a spritz of some kind of awful-smelling bodily fluids, Benny was then showered with clumps of brain tissue when the Chief's mangled face reentered the picture. *Welcome to the club.*

Cursing and spitting out sticky clumps of ice-cold who-knows-what, Benny thrust both legs out straight, the action sending the stretcher on a slow roll away from him and freeing his trapped upper body.

Heels kicking the road and with both hands propelling him backward, Benny scrabbled away from the growing puddle of ooze, shredding the seat of his pants and balls of both palms in the process.

"What the hell were you thinking?" Riker barked. "You were supposed to get the radio." Voice softening, he went on, saying: "I warned you that thing was in there. Did it bite you?"

Extending his hand, Benny said, "I don't think so. Help me up."

Just as Benny was getting his feet underneath him, Shorty and Steve-O arrived from opposite directions.

Indicating the brains and fluids splashed across the front of Benny's shirt and parka, Steve-O said, "Isn't that the second jacket you ruined today, Benny?"

Winded from running, Shorty slung the Shockwave. Fishing a red handkerchief from a pocket, he handed it across the barrier. Back heaving, hands going to his knees, he said, "What the hell happened here?"

Benny said nothing as he went to work cleaning himself up.

Having already spoken his mind to Benny regarding the foolhardy deviation from the plan, Riker said, "Someone forgot to lock the stretcher when they put it into the ambulance. Benny was grabbing hold of it to get inside to check for supplies." He shook his head. "Thing rolled out on top of him. Could have happened to any of us."

Obviously skeptical of the story, Shorty shot a side-eye look at Riker.

Keeping with the *everything is alright, nothing to see here* attitude, Riker asked Shorty how the siphoning was coming along.

"I got about ten gallons out of the Chief's rig and was about to move the operation over here when you went all Wyatt Earp on this biter here." Regarding the corpse on the stretcher, he added, "Damn fine shooting, Lee."

Grimacing, Riker said, "Steve-O, can you help Shorty *and* keep an eye on the road?"

"I'll be OK," Shorty said. "I've grown eyes in the back of my head."

That response drew a curious stare from Steve-O.

Benny said, "It's a figure of speech, Steve-O."

"No duh," was Steve-O's response to that. Regarding Shorty, he said, "Just like on Miss Abigail, the First Mate helps with the gas."

Clapping Steve-O on the shoulder, Shorty said, "I missed you, man."

"Ditto," said Steve-O. "You need to tell me what it's like out there."

As the pair walked off toward the Tahoe, Riker said to Benny, "Let's get that hand patched up."

Chapter 15

"Yes, I can drive," Benny assured Riker. "I don't care if it's cut to the knuckle, I can still flex my fingers." He held his right hand up and wiggled them to prove his point.

"Can you still shoot?"

Benny flexed his trigger finger. "I'll be fine," he said, the tone none too convincing.

Nodding, Riker climbed into the idling fire truck. Looking down on his friend, he said, "Two hands on the wheel. And be careful … Steve-O's singing and constant stream-of-thought conversation has a way of distracting a fella."

Benny flashed a thumbs-up with the bandaged hand, then strode off for the Shelby where Steve-O was sitting shotgun with the Tahoe's radio on his lap.

Less than thirty minutes had elapsed since their arrival at the pileup. In just fifteen minutes, thanks to the hand-cranked pump, Shorty's siphoning operation had netted them a combined forty gallons from the Tahoe, ambulance, and two compact cars that had survived the conflagration.

They had burned the rest of the time collecting a second backboard from the helicopter, looting the ambulance of its supplies and removing its radio.

As Riker took a few seconds to get acquainted with the fire engine's controls, he caught a whiff of something dead. It was coming from the crew compartment and reeked like rotten fish.

If there was one thing that gave the stink of the dead things a run for their money in the gut-churning department, it was rotten seafood.

Holding his nose, Riker craned and searched for the source.

Turnout jackets, gloves, and helmets were scattered about the crew cab. On the floor was a thick novel: *The Stand* by Stephen King. Next to the novel was a battered metal lunchbox and matching thermos. Reaching over the seatback, Riker snatched them up.

The items went on the seat next to the radio he'd pried from the ambulance. The radio was a long-range unit. Mounted underneath the dash, it had come out of the ambulance easily, leaving his knuckles unscathed and all of the attached wiring intact.

In the lunchbox along with a baggie bulging with Cheez-Its and blueberry Pop-Tarts still sealed in their foil packaging was a tuna sandwich long past its prime.

Rolling his window down to dispose of the sandwich, Riker scanned the mirrors. Just coming up on the Tahoe was the lone zombie Steve-O had pointed out some time ago. The thing was a slow mover, yet still it had come a long way since leaving its crawling companion alone on the road north of the pileup.

In the left mirror, he saw the long stretch of highway spooled out behind the engine. Here and there cars and trucks and SUVs were stalled out. Most had been abandoned on the side of the road, some piled high with belongings, all of them coated with a couple of weeks' worth of dirt.

Straight ahead, maybe a quarter of a mile beyond the spot on the opposing lanes where the Life Flight helicopter had made its final landing, both northbound lanes were also choked with static cars.

About five yards past the helicopter was the beginning of the breach in the freeway dividers Shorty had created. Utilizing the EarthRoamer's bumper-mounted Warn winch, he had displaced three of the ten-foot-long, two-ton concrete Jersey barriers from the miles-long uninterrupted run.

Flinging the sandwich out the window, Riker raised the two-way radio to his lips and pressed the Talk button.

Though all of their handheld radios were now tuned to the same channel and sub-channel, Riker singled out Benny by name. "You ready, *Sistek?*"

After a short burst of squelch, Benny's voice came from the tiny speaker: "Ready as I'll ever be, *Riker*."

Shorty came on next, saying: "I'm good to go." After a brief pause, he added, "Age before beauty, Lee. Get that big red beast of yours moving."

That's the pot calling the kettle black, thought Riker. For one, Shorty was older by a decade or so. Secondly, the EarthRoamer was not much smaller than the fire engine. Probably cost more, too.

Just as Riker started his window running up, he heard over the engine noise a woman's shrill screams. They were coming from somewhere off to the left and behind the engine. It was growing louder and drawing nearer. And while it didn't sound like the woman was under attack, she sure as hell was trying hard to make it happen. For nothing, in Riker's experience, excited the dead more than the wailing of the mortally wounded.

Looking up the embankment, Riker saw a woman. She was running flat out, the long knitted scarf around her neck flapping in her slipstream. She had just made the apex and was on her way downhill toward him when, with maybe fifty feet left to go until she made it to flat ground, a single head broke the crest of the hill behind her.

As she halved the remaining distance to the highway, arms and legs pumping furiously, Riker realized the thing coming down the hill behind the woman was a Bolt.

In the split second it took Riker to decide to reach back and open the rear door so the woman could get inside when she arrived, or, on second thought, *if* she arrived, a half-dozen more pursuers appeared behind her. As the things chasing her crested the embankment, their upper bodies silhouetted against the gray sky, it was evident they were having trouble making the transition—stretched out in a long, ragged Congo line, staggering and slipping, their heads lolling around. Riker had a good feeling he was looking at twenty or more slow movers—or so he hoped.

The woman running downhill in Riker's direction was all arms and legs. If she wasn't as tall as him, she was damn close.

As the woman dodged the low-scrub clinging to the incline, she tore the scarf from around her neck, letting it fall to the ground behind her.

Walking his gaze uphill from the woman, Riker saw that the female Bolt was quickly gaining ground on her. The Bolt was lean and muscular, likely mid to upper twenties when she turned.

As it careened downhill, everything in its path was secondary to the fresh meat it was pursuing.

Behind the Bolt, the other dead things were focused solely on the runner, too. Some, their shark-like dead-eyes locked onto the moving target, staggered through the scrub totally oblivious to the ankle-grabbing branches. Obviously excited by the prospect of catching up to the woman, a couple of slow-movers got tripped up by their own feet. Aided by gravity, pale arms and legs batting the air, they tumbled head over heels through the hardy ground cover, dark rooster tails of damp earth erupting in their wake.

As the young woman crossed the breakdown lane, her long strides eating up the distance to the fire engine, the Bolt's feet got tangled in the discarded scarf. As the Bolt pitched forward, it didn't try to arrest the fall by throwing its hands up. No *Oh shit!* expression altered its slack alabaster face. Its eyes stayed locked on the woman even as its mouth was filling up with dirt.

After going down hard face-first, its spine bent unnaturally. Dirty soles of both bare feet clearly visible to Riker, he witnessed the pent-up kinetic energy send the contorted body on a hard-to-watch, out-of-control tumble.

Like a big-mountain skier catching an edge at the beginning of a steep run, the zombie rocketed downhill, completely out of control, going totally airborne, head and feet trading places faster than an Olympic caliber gymnast tumbling her way to Gold.

Grateful for the stroke of luck, Riker twisted around in his seat and, with his long left arm, opened the door for the woman. As he did so, over the radio, Shorty asked, "What's the holdup?"

Ignoring the call, Riker turned his face toward the open window and bellowed, "Get in!"

Running shoes squeaking on the still-wet pavement, the woman covered the last ten feet to the fire engine in two long strides. Hollering, "Drive, damnit!" she dove for the open door.

Launching off of one foot on wet ground didn't deliver the runner the distance she had needed. While she did get her fingers hooked into the mesh cargo pocket on the rear of the driver's seat, and her upper body part of the way onto the rear passenger seat, her legs, from the knees down, came nowhere close to making it inside the cab.

Having already acted on the shouted order, Riker matted the pedal and steered toward the break in the freeway dividers.

Finding herself being dragged outside the accelerating vehicle, and wholly pissed that she had miscalculated her leap, the woman let loose a string of expletives. Hearing this, Riker looked to his side mirror. Seeing the rear door still open and swinging back and forth, with the runner only partway inside and hanging on for dear life, he stabbed the brakes and reached blindly into the backseat area.

As Riker probed the space behind his seat, hoping to catch hold of the woman's hand, he flicked his gaze to the side mirror.

He didn't like what he saw.

While the Bolt getting tripped up on the scarf had initially seemed to be the Godsend the fleeing woman had needed at the time, in reality, the ensuing series of somersaults and awkward cartwheels delivered the creature to flat ground much faster than pure bipedal locomotion could have.

Having reached the asphalt shoulder with one arm clearly broken in multiple places and flopping about like a limp noodle, the lone Bolt rose up and immediately resumed the chase, loping diagonally across the two-lane, the ruined arm in no kind of sync with the other three appendages.

Finding the woman's hand by feel, Riker held on tight and tromped down on the gas pedal.

Slow to respond to the input, the multi-ton rig spent the first second or two lurching and shimmying before finally gathering speed.

Seeing the woman's free hand come up and slap down on the seatback, the slender fingers clawing deep divots into the cloth, Riker let go of the steering wheel. Keeping the rig tracking straight by bracing the wheel with his knees, he reached his left arm out his window and closed the crew cab door.

No sooner had the door thunked shut and the woman released her vice-like grip on Riker's right hand than a loud *bang* drew his eyes to the side mirror where he saw reflected back at him the humorous sight of the female Bolt crashing into the fire engine's rear quarter panel.

Instantly repulsed—the jarring impact causing the limp, broken arm to whip the air—the Bolt took a few stilted steps backward, then sat down hard on the wet pavement.

Retaking the wheel in a two-fisted grip, Riker said, "What's your name?" Feeling a little sheepish at having followed up the woman's close brush with death with such a mundane greeting, he took his eyes off the road just long enough to meet her gaze in the oversized rearview mirror.

Instead of answering the question, the woman crawled over the seatback. Once she was in the passenger seat and buckled in, she took a deep breath and stuck out her hand. "I'm Amelia. Friends call me Lia."

Riker nodded to indicate the upcoming break in the freeway barrier. Keeping his hands at the proper ten and two on the wheel, he said, "Leland Riker. Pleasure is all mine, but for safety's sake, the handshake has to wait."

Chapter 16

Reeling in the offered handshake, Lia said, "You're driving *this* … through *that?*"

Riker said nothing. He was focused solely on threading the forty-foot-long engine through the thirty-foot-wide opening. While the fire engine's width and length wasn't a problem, the angle he had to work with was.

As the fire engine entered the breach, the helicopter's drooping rotor blades banged off its light bar, then raked along the ladder apparatus atop the rig, creating a metal-on-metal keen that had the hair on Riker's arms standing to attention.

Finally clear of the helicopter, its blades all aquiver, Riker eased the rig into the far lane and stole another quick peek at his side mirror.

The first wave of slow movers was just reaching the dry patch of pavement in the fast lane where the engine had been parked. The embankment behind them was teeming with zombies, many more than he could possibly count. And closer in, having just used the gap in the Jersey barriers to cross over into the southbound lanes, the female Bolt with the damaged arm was definitely still in the hunt and gaining ground on the lumbering engine.

Shifting his attention back to the road ahead, Riker spotted the EarthRoamer forming up with the Shelby. Thanks to the unscheduled pause to collect the unexpected guest now occupying the passenger seat, the other two vehicles had opened up a bit of a lead on the engine.

Tightening his grip on the steering wheel, Riker said, "Where did you pick up your undead posse?"

Before Lia could answer, the radio came to life; it was Steve-O: "Benny's driving, so he had me call you. He says that you better make sure the woman you picked up hasn't been bitten."

The radio went quiet again, but the silence was short-lasting because half a beat later another burst of squelch preceded Shorty saying, "And check the chick for weapons first chance you get."

As silence returned to the cab, Riker directed his gaze at the woman calling herself Lia. For the first time since he had set eyes on her, she was *not* a blur of movement. As if one of the infected chasing her had taken up residence in the gloomy footwell, she had drawn her long legs up to her chest and trapped them with her arms.

The quick once-over told Riker that the twentysomething blonde's bobbed hair was damp with sweat and that she was dressed in skintight runner's spandex—top and bottom both black and sporting the Nike swoosh. On her feet were black Nike trail runners.

Considering the woman's attire, if she *was* concealing a bite or had a weapon stashed anywhere on her person, neither would go undetected for long.

Finally getting around to answering Steve-O, Riker said, "Nothing I can do at the moment. I've got my hands full driving this monster."

Lia let go of her legs long enough to make a *gimme* gesture with one hand.

Riker examined the hand. It was deeply tanned, the skin smooth and unblemished—definitely no bites or scratches. Walking his gaze over her long, toned legs, he couldn't help but let his eyes linger on the contours of her firm backside. It wasn't a leer, just an action dictated by some kind of prehistoric instinct buried deep within his brain. Getting to her neck, he noticed the skin there was inflamed. Just a thin raised red line. Like maybe she had a rash. *Nothing to be worried about.*

Finally ending the not-so-surreptitious visual recon by looking her straight in the face and matching her blue-eyed gaze, he said, "Where were you headed?"

Nodding at the radio, she said, "Where are *you* all headed? Only thing down this way is the county jail, the Sheriff's station, and a whole lot of open desert." She paused and looked about the cab. "And why go to all the trouble to steal the fire truck? You planning on breaking someone out, or something?"

Riker shook his head. "Or something. We were at the jail earlier. Doing a kind of welfare check. Ended up coming across some people trapped on the roof."

Lia cocked her head. "People?"

"The warden and some of her guards."

She stretched her legs out, real slow, one at a time, and planted her feet flat on the floorboard. "How do you know they're not inmates wearing stolen uniforms?"

"Because that's not what my gut's telling me."

"My gut's telling me I just got dropped into the middle of a sausage party. Any women in the other vehicles?"

Riker shook his head. "I can stop and let you out right here if you want."

She shook her head. A hard side to side wag. "I want to get as far away from where you picked me up as possible."

Riker said, "You didn't answer my question. How'd all the zombies get on your trail?"

Lia looked at the headliner, then said, "I was foraging and came upon a tent city. It was surrounded by Army vehicles. On the side near the embankment, they'd parked a long line of FEMA trailers. That's where I picked up my *posse*."

"So the authorities are still there and running the place?"

She shook her head. "Nope. Nothing but deaders inside. When I tried to sneak past the front gate one of the things on the outside saw me. Next thing I know they're all moaning and pressing against the fence."

"Then the fence failed."

Crossing her arms, Lia said, "Nope ... that's when the Random spotted me. She was about three blocks east at that point."

Brow furrowing, Riker said, "*Random?*"

"The fast ones. I call them Randoms. She took off chasing me right away." Lia paused. She bit her lip and looked out over the hood. "If it hadn't been for you, I'd probably be fighting that *bitch* to the death right now."

Seeing Benny steer the Shelby onto the detention facility's feeder road, Riker took his foot off the gas pedal. Not familiar with how the fire engine handled, he slowed the behemoth to a walking speed and eased her into the sharp right-hander.

"So why are you out and about during the day?" he asked. He also wanted to know why she was on foot and unarmed but didn't want to bombard her with too many questions all at once.

"I just can't deal." She shook her head. Slowly this time. "It's a long story. You wouldn't understand." She drew one foot up onto the seat and began worrying the shoelace with those slender fingers.

"Try me. Start from the beginning."

Staring at the distant jail, Lia said, "I was at a high-elevation running camp when this thing started. When I finally got back to civilization ... to Santa Fe, the power was out. No streetlights. No heat in my place. No television to show me what had happened. I wanted to move on but decided not to. I guess I was holding onto hope that the government would get stuff straightened out. Hell, we have the best military in the world, right? They handled the Nazis and the communists, right? So what the fuck? How'd they let it come to *this*?"

Riker said, "Governors across the east called up their National Guard units real early. The Four World Trade Center building had been down less than a day when I started to see signs they were losing control of the situation. Battery Park in New York was chaos. Pure madness. Never seen anything like it. Not even in Iraq."

Lia said nothing.

Steering clear of an unmoving corpse splayed out in his lane, Riker asked, "So you only go out during the day? That's pretty risky to do on foot since the dead hunt mostly by sight. And with no backpack or weapon."

"I *only* go out during the day." She didn't address the other questions.

"Why is that?"

"About a week ago I got tired of cold soup. I'd been back barely two days and the only water I had left was in the toilet tank. I had used up the last of my batteries and was down to one candle." She went quiet and stared off into the distance.

"So something happened to you when you were out and about at night." Riker was checking the road behind them, so he didn't see her draw her legs up again and plant her heels on the seat.

103

She took a deep breath and exhaled sharply. It was clear she was reliving something. Finally, she said, "I was creeping around inside a store by my place and came *literally* face to face with one of *them*. I'd seen plenty on my street from a distance. First time, though, that I'd been that close to one. Coming around a corner and bumping into it in the dark." She threw a hard shudder. "Feeling that cold cheek coming up against mine"—she made like she was batting a spider web away from her face—"I just about shit myself right then and there."

"So it was your first kill."

She shook her head. The thousand-yard stare returning, she said, "I screamed like a ... *girl*." The way she had spit the word "girl" led Riker to believe the strong personality traits she had exhibited so far were not put on. Not some kind of false bravado.

She wasn't playing the role of survivor. She *was* a survivor.

"So that changed you?"

"Hell *yes*, it changed me. I had no flashlight. No weapon. I shouldn't have been there in the first place. Damn near got myself killed."

"So you only forage during the day, without a pack, and on foot," Riker said slowly. It was more of a statement than a question. Something about her story seemed way off. Slowing the rig with a tap of the air brakes, he said, "We're here. Staying in or coming with?"

After chewing on it for a second or two, she said, "Let me have a quick word with your friends."

Knock yourself out, Riker thought, handing her the Motorola. *This ought to be fun.*

Suppressing a smile, he said, "Benny's the blue truck in the lead. Steve-O is riding shotgun with him and was the one who came over the radio first. Shorty's the one driving the vehicle making the turn right now."

Lia lifted the radio to her face. After licking her dry, cracked lips, she pressed the Talk button. "This is the *chick* Leland just picked up. I haven't been bit and I am unarmed. That being said, I am *not* stripping down for *anyone*. You all are not the TSA, so, *no*, none of you guys are frisking me and there will be no *patting me down* over the top of my clothes. You will just have to take my word for it that I'm not going to stab you in the back when you're not looking." She paused, radio an inch from her lips, thinking. After a long three-count, she added, "You have my word I won't turn and come back as a *Random*. I'll kill myself first." She closed the channel and handed the radio over.

Impressive, Riker thought as he took the radio back.

Thumbing the Talk button, he said, "Did you all get that?"

There was a ten-second patch of dead air, during which a fusillade of gunfire could be heard from inside the fire engine's cab.

Riker was craning to see beyond the distant EarthRoamer when the radio came alive with Shorty's voice. Sounding a bit winded, he said, "I've been listening. And I get it all right. But when she sees what we're seeing right now, she's going to want to hop out and run her butt back to wherever it is she came from. Hell, it's even got me thinking about turning tail and getting out of Dodge."

Coming up behind the parked EarthRoamer, Riker steered the fire engine off the asphalt feeder road, rolled the right-hand-side wheels up and over the curb, then drove forward a few feet on the white cement sidewalk.

As Riker parked the fire engine parallel to the other two vehicles, its front bumper even with the Shelby, he saw that Shorty and Benny were dismounted and had made quick work of the zombies that had gathered at the gate while they were gone.

Unbuckling his seatbelt, Riker got his first good look at what had rendered Benny speechless and Shorty contemplating retreat. Clear of zombies an hour ago, the larger of the two lots was now home to scores of them. Looking right, he saw that the lot in front of the main, glass-fronted building was also crowded with zombies. And to make matters worse, dead things were still staggering through the building's destroyed front doors.

Eyes wide, forehead just inches from the engine's nearly vertical windshield, Lia said, "You've got to be shitting me, dude. We're not going in *there* ... are we?"

"Not *we*," Riker said as he set the brakes. "Just me. I'm going it alone."

Chapter 17

Lia was on her knees on the passenger side of the bench seat, hinged over the seatback and rooting around the backseat area when Riker elbowed open his door. Pausing before stepping to the ground, he said, "I'm going to need you to get out."

Voice muffled, Lia said, "That's my plan." Coming up clutching a gray sweatshirt a size or two too big for her, she followed Riker's lead, shouldering open her own door and climbing down to the sidewalk.

Working swiftly, Riker collected the Jaws of Life and backboard he'd stashed in back of the fire engine. While there, he also grabbed a specialized tool he guessed was used to breach locked doors, vent the roofs of burning buildings, and pry open uncooperative windows. It was almost a yard in length and milled from some kind of alloy. A super-sized version of the claw-like nail-puller found on most garden-variety hammers protruded from one end. Affixed at a ninety-degree angle on the opposite end of the weighty tool was a sturdy-looking wedge sprouting two sharpened tines.

Riker lugged the items to the Shelby and set them on the ground by the open tailgate.

Under the watchful gaze of the others, Riker retrieved the second backboard he'd stashed under the Shelby's tonneau.

Shorty stepped up to Riker. "Benny told me about the warden and her men. You want to read me in on this rescue operation of yours?"

Riker held up a hand. "In a second. Wait until everyone is here. In the meantime, I need a few shotgun shells. Got any?"

"In my rig. Be right back."

Riker gave the pair of lots a quick look. The zombies were now acutely aware of their presence and migrating en masse

106

toward the gate. They were coming from all directions. Thankfully, there were no Bolts breaking from the pack—*yet*.

Shorty returned with a box of shells which Riker distributed between several of his pockets.

A couple of seconds apart, Benny and Lia arrived from entirely opposite directions.

"What's going on?" Benny asked.

Lia stood back from the group, apparently content being the fly on the wall.

"Steve-O," Riker called, "come on out and give me a hand." Regarding Benny and Shorty, he said, "I need you guys to go ahead and take care of any deaders that make it to the gate. Do it quietly. I figure this place holds several hundred inmates. The ones already out in the open are probably just a small fraction of them. You discharge a firearm right now, the ones still inside won't be for long."

Benny asked, "What are you doing?"

Riker spent a few seconds going over his plan. When he was finished, he looked over the assembled group.

Shorty said, "Sounds like you're trying to be a hero."

To which Riker responded, "I'm no hero. Just putting myself in their shoes. It's what I should have done at your place. Can't turn back time, though."

Benny said, "I don't like it." He ran a hand through his lengthening salt-and-pepper hair and looked skyward. "Tara will kill me if anything happens to you."

Grateful his choice of words didn't have Steve-O launching into a Cher song, Riker said, "She'll kick my ass posthumously, too. I'll be careful."

Fixing Riker with a serious look, Steve-O said, "Do you need a wingman on the inside?"

Trapping a backboard under one well-muscled arm, Riker picked the Jaws of Life off the ground with one hand, entry tool with the other. Gripped by a sense of urgency, he said, "Steve-O, you can help out by grabbing the other backboard and following me."

Benny had parked the Shelby a few yards farther back from the guardhouse than when they were here last. The tire spikes were a full truck length beyond the Shelby's front bumper.

Arriving at the tire spikes, Riker took a knee and deposited the items he'd been carrying. Forgetting about the tools for the moment, he took the backboard from Steve-O.

"Oh," exclaimed Steve-O, "these aren't for hurt people on the inside. They're to cover the spikes so you don't pop your tires coming out."

"Nail on the head, Steve-O. Easier than breaking into the guardhouse and trying to figure out how to get them retracted with no electricity going to them." He paused and fixed the man with a serious stare. "But they won't be needed to cover the spikes until I drive out of there." Riker laid the backboards down near the retractable spikes. "It's going to be your job to place these *over* the spikes *after* I drive the fire engine through the gate." He demonstrated the task, then said, "Just like that, *Wingman.*"

"I got it," Steve-O said. Then, as Riker scooped the tools off the ground, Steve-O asked with all the exuberance of a kid on Christmas morning, "Can I sit in the fire engine when you get back?"

"Sure you can."

"Make the lights flash?"

"And sound the siren, too. Sure Steve-O, you can do all that when I'm done in there."

Steve-O pumped his fist.

Leaving Steve-O at his assigned position, Riker hurried over to the guardhouse and again set the tools on the ground.

The up-close look at the guardhouse confirmed Riker's suspicion: The gate was going to be the path of least resistance. While the door to the tiny guardhouse at the entry to Sunset Island in Miami Beach had been simple to breach—as easy as tearing the sliding door off the tracks and walking right in—this fortified number would be nothing of the sort. With bulletproof windows and steel-reinforced doors, even if he used the Jaws of Life, Riker was afraid that getting inside to disengage the gate would take a lot of effort and burn precious time they didn't have.

The rolling gate consisted of chain-link panels that had been welded and trussed for extra stability. Multiple strands of tightly strung razor wire ran the entire length up top. Electrically operated, the gate moved left-to-right, the wheels guided precisely by the sunken V-track.

Though the gate was designed to take a beating, Riker was afraid that if he used the pneumatic expander the frame would get crushed and the gate would be rendered inoperable.

Part of the plan called for Shorty and Benny to close and secure the gate once Riker was on the inside. Which left Riker no choice but to rely on the firefighter's entry tool and his own brute strength.

Entrusting Shorty and Benny with the task of culling the zombies that were soon to arrive, Riker quickly inspected the gate's mechanisms.

The end of the gate nearest the guardhouse was secured by a pair of electric solenoids. That the power was out and the gate remained secure told Riker there was also a mechanical latch. A failsafe in case of a complete power failure, backup generators and all.

Crossing to the opposite side, some thirty feet from the guardhouse, Riker identified the third locking mechanism. It was incorporated in the track and wheel system and solely mechanical in nature. *Maybe, just maybe*, he thought, *I can defeat all three with the entry tool.*

The recessed receiver was secured to the brick building with masonry screws. The screws were flush-mount items and partially concealed by the gate's locking mechanism when it was in the closed position.

Acting on that glass-half-full attitude, he worked the flat end of the tool through the narrow slot between the gate and guardhouse. Facing the guardhouse, he dropped to one knee— the left, on which his prosthetic was attached—then planted his right Salomon against the low curb of the walkway encircling the guardhouse.

Drawing a deep breath, he tightened his grip on the tool and hauled back on it. Neck muscles corded and with beads of sweat forming on his brow and upper lip, he increased the pressure until the brick started to release its hold on the masonry fasteners.

A full minute of prying on the three edges he could access with the tool brought mixed results. Though five of the eight screws were now lying on the ground before Riker, the ones on the inside edge were being troublesome.

Trying hard to ignore the mental image of the advancing dead, with their reaching hands and gnashing teeth, Riker slid the tool across the ground to Benny. "Work on the wheel latch." He pulled his multi-tool from a pocket, opened it up and selected the flathead screwdriver.

By this time, the lead element of the dead streaming from the main lot was within fifty yards of the gate.

"Be my eyes," Riker said to Shorty and pressed his cheek to the brick wall. Literally trusting life and limb to Shorty, Riker threaded one arm through the widening gap where the recessed latch was coming loose from the guardhouse wall. Working blind, he got the multi-tool wedged under the inside edge of the stubborn latch. After expending a lot of energy prying and moving the tool and then going at the latch again from a different angle, Riker popped out two of the three remaining screws.

"I think I got it," exclaimed Benny. "You almost ready?"

Before Riker could answer, an agitated Shorty was telling anyone listening that time was running short.

Letting his actions do the speaking, Riker collected the Jaws of Life off the ground and relieved Benny of the entry tool. "Be ready," he said, shooting his friend a serious look. "We only have one shot at this."

"Open and shut," Benny said. "We'll make it happen."

Standing near the guardhouse, Lia said, "What can I do?"

In passing, Riker said, "Just stand by and be ready to offer a hand if needed."

Lia crossed her arms. Classic defensive posture. *I don't like being underutilized* was the silent message Riker received.

The Jaws of Life and entry tool went in back of the still-idling fire engine.

Riker quickly took his seat at the wheel and got the truck rolling past the Shelby.

At the gate, Benny and Shorty each had a handful of fence. They were bundles of nervous energy, coiled and ready to spring into action on cue.

One eye on the advancing dead and one on the approaching fire engine, Shorty uttered a foxhole prayer, asking for their portly bell cow in county-orange to trip on a shoelace or something. Not that jailers let inmates have such a thing, but it was the thought that counted.

Seeing that the dead were nearly at the gate, a shuffling wall of orange enveloped by the sickly-sweet stench of death, Benny said, "You think we'll get it closed before they reach the threshold?"

"In case we don't," Shorty mumbled, "you better be Quick Draw McGraw with that Glock of yours."

Though Lia was anticipating the *"Go"* signal, she nearly came out of her skin when the fire engine's horn blared. When the long, drawn-out blast sounded, she was standing with her back pressed to the guardhouse windows. Shorty and Benny were to her left and just beginning to haul the gate back in its track, and, on her right, Steve-O was watching the fire engine roll over the front-facing tire spikes.

With the fire engine a looming wall of red to Lia's fore, and the chain-link gate clattering madly nearby with Benny and Shorty muscling it open ahead of the slow-moving monstrosity, the young woman suddenly felt compelled to do something she clearly hadn't thought through to the end.

Seeing a number of biters being swallowed up beneath the accelerating fire engine, she put her head down and ran after it. Staying in the engine's blind spot, she sprinted through the open gate, acknowledging Benny and Shorty in passing with a wan smile.

Negotiating a minefield of crushed zombies leaking internal organs and bodily fluids, Lia kicked away a pale hand reaching for her then leaped onto the retreating fire engine's cluttered rear deck.

Thinking for a split second that he'd been seeing things, Shorty kept to the plan. As soon as the truck was inside the perimeter and roaring across the lot toward the far fence-line, he immediately switched his hold on the gate and started running it back in its tracks.

Knowing for sure what he had seen, Benny was rooted in place and staring at the surreal scene laid out before him. In the foreground, body parts and flattened torsos, some with snapped bones jutting forth, some still moving, were scattered amongst puddles of rainwater reflecting the front edge of more bad weather moving in fast from the south.

In the middle distance, the fire engine was growing smaller, its every light ablaze and siren wailing.

Finding the noisy vehicle and the stowaway out back irresistible to ignore, the throng of orange shirts altered course and gave chase.

Inside the fire engine, having just been privy to all the stomach-churning sounds associated with a multitude of walking corpses being ground to mush, Riker was donning earmuffs left behind by one of the firefighters. Steering clear of the vehicles left parked on the lot, he aimed the rig at the fence bordering the prison's east wall. Fifty feet from the fence, he steered hard left and commenced a sweeping counterclockwise turn that brought the guardhouse and feeder road back into view out the flat windshield.

Chapter 18

Coming out of the wide turn, the fire engine rapidly bleeding off speed, Riker stomped down hard on the accelerator pedal. As the perimeter fence slipped by off his right shoulder, he couldn't help but think about the jam he'd gotten himself into. The knowledge that he, and only he, stood between the Reaper, Lord knows how many more zombies that were sure to spill from the main building, and the ultimate fate of the four survivors on the prison roof had started behind his eyes a pounding unlike any he'd experienced since coming face-to-face with the Pale Rider himself in the courtyard of Trinity House just a handful of days ago.

Back then it was the lives of loved ones that had hung in the balance. Now it was only strangers. Strangers who represented to Riker a trio whose fates he longed to learn. Had the Harlans been killed that night on Shorty's boat ramp? Or had they succeeded in fighting off the unexpected zombie attack?

He figured the prospect of the older couple and their teenage nephew getting out of that scrape wasn't too far of a stretch. After all, they *had* come cross country during the initial outbreak, managing to get by some of the same hastily thrown together military and state police roadblocks that he and Tara and Steve-O had successfully circumvented. At face value, Tobias and his nephew, Jessie, had seemed more than capable of taking care of themselves. Maria, though, was the wild card. She had remained alone in the truck with the Caveman camper when it all went down. If she had possessed a modicum of the confidence Lia exuded, Riker had a good feeling that Maria had gotten their truck turned around, got her husband and nephew back aboard, and they all had lived to fight another day.

RIKER'S APOCALYPSE (THE PRECIPICE)

It was the last part that troubled Riker. For if they had survived, he knew he was the top dog on their totem pole of retribution, Shorty coming in a close second.

The only thing standing between success and failure was roughly a hundred feet from the fire truck's grille. To say the wide expanse of wet asphalt between the slow-to-accelerate fire engine and distant guardhouse was a target-rich environment would be a monumental understatement.

Speedometer needle creeping past ten miles per hour, Riker lined up the largest group of dead things with the approximate center of the windshield, then firmed his grip on the steering wheel.

While the vibrations from plowing over the zombies near the gate had barely registered inside the cab, Riker knew the scores of rotters in his sights were going to have the truck bucking on its suspension like a wild bronco.

Standing just outside the main gate, mouth agape, Shorty could only watch in horror as Lia monkeyed her way from the fire engine's rear deck to the top-mounted ladder assembly. Though the sinewy young woman did so while exhibiting the agility of a Parkour master, once, when Riker jinked the wheel abruptly, she had been thrown overboard—just the fingers on one hand keeping her life literally hanging in the balance.

Next to Shorty, a two-way radio poised just inches from his mouth, voice an octave or two above normal, Benny was frantically trying to get Riker to pick up his radio.

Thanks to the earmuffs, the cacophony of human flesh thudding against the rig's wide front bumper was lost to Riker. The vibrations that came with each new impact, he felt to the bone.

Like one of the souped-up imports in a *Fast and Furious* movie, the fire truck actually started to drift sideways atop the gore.

One more lap, Riker thought as he regained control of the truck and again nosed it away from the gate. With the guardhouse and vehicles parked beyond it scrolling by in his side vision, he was so caught up in the grim task at hand that Benny's wild gesticulations failed to grab his attention.

The final pass was more of the same: former humans wearing county-orange and slack expressions going down like wheat to a combine.

Slowing the truck to a crawl, Riker drove the length of the prison's east fence, the buildings scrolling by maybe thirty feet to his right. Craning to see through the windshield, he scanned the entire length of the mostly flat roof, on the lookout for something to orientate himself as to where the warden and her men were located.

Choosing a spot in the fence adjacent to where the prison wall bumped out a bit, an architectural element that had stuck in his mind during the aerial recon, he wheeled left and brought the engine to a complete stop.

Watching the fence in his left mirror, he backed to within a few feet of it, put the transmission into Park, then set the brakes.

Unsure of whether the motor needed to keep running to operate the turntable and ladder system, Riker let it idle.

As he removed the earmuffs, the constant vacuum of silence he had enjoyed was replaced at once by the growl of the siren and clattering of the diesel engine. Leaning over, he found the toggle and silenced the siren. Next, he switched off the light bar and headlights.

Having rendered the fire engine less of a draw for the dead, he clicked out of his belt and promptly popped a few more ibuprofen.

Before committing to the great outdoors, where anything could be lurking—a zombie wrapped around the axle, or maybe one that had been caught up under the truck and dragged around only to be freed once the ride ended—he scanned all points of the compass.

Left mirror: *clear.*

Right mirror: *also clear.*

There was nothing worth worrying about between the truck and gate, where, for some reason, everyone save for Lia was crowding the fence and waving at him.

Remembering that he'd rolled the volume down low on the two-way and stowed it in a pocket, he patted himself down, feeling for the telltale lump.

As soon as Riker felt his fingers brush the smooth plastic item deep in his jacket pocket, a series of knocks sounded directly above his head. He thought for sure there was a certain cadence to them. Something familiar to it. Then it dawned on him that what he had heard was the old *shave and a haircut, two bits* number.

As he took the radio from his pocket, thumbing the volume up as he did so, his gaze was drawn to the pavement in front of the fire engine, where, the outline hazy due to high clouds and a watery sun, he saw the shadow of the thing knocking. It was long and lithe and crouched down low against the blocky outline of the roof-mounted light bar.

Riker's gut clenched at the thought of a zombie climbing onto the moving fire truck and somehow finding its way past the ladder apparatus and onto the roof directly above him. The fact that the thing was showing signs of intelligence—indicated by the intricate sequence of the knocks—not to mention the dexterity to perform a feat the likes of which he'd never witnessed one of the dead attempt was one hell of a game-changer.

If all of it is true, he thought as he drew the Sig Legion and aimed it toward the exact spot on the roof where the monster's shadow indicated it should be, *then God help us all*.

In the next beat, as Riker was flicking off the Sig's safety and finding the trigger with the pad of his finger, Shorty's voice sprang from the tiny speaker. He was speaking rapid-fire. The message: "You picked up a passenger, Lee."

No shit, thought Riker, finger drawing up some of the trigger pull. While he knew his hearing was about to suffer great damage from the discharge in the enclosed space, leaning over and snatching the earmuffs off the seat next to him was out of the question.

"It's the woman," Shorty blurted. "Lia followed you through the gate and had latched herself on back of your rig before I could do anything about it." A short pause. "And answer your *damn* radio from now on."

Riker made no reply. Recognizing the ramifications had Shorty's call come in just a half-second later, he was struck speechless and feeling sick to his stomach. As he holstered the Sig, Shorty said, "She's not moving, Lee. Your driving nearly threw her off. I think maybe she was injured getting back aboard."

Riker threw open his door. Muttering expletives under his breath, he gripped the grab bar and planted his bionic on the fire truck's running board.

Coming in at six-foot-four in shoes meant that Riker didn't need to stand on his toes to get a clear look at the roof. Actually, as he rose to full extension, both feet on the running board, he was looking *down* on the roof.

Immediately Riker saw that it was indeed Lia casting the lithe shadow. However, she was now on her knees, back arched, chest rising and falling. When their gazes met, a sheepish grin broke on her face.

Riker felt a wave of relief wash over him. In the short time since he'd met the woman, he'd actually taken a liking to her. While she was easy on the eyes—beautiful, actually—this liking, for now, was more of a big brother platonic kind than the romantic variety.

The relief was short-lived, though, because the anger that was always simmering just beneath the surface—a side effect of CTE—reared its ugly head.

"That was a damn fool move, Lia. For a hot second, I was convinced a *Bolt* had gotten on the roof and was communicating with me."—Lia's sheepish grin morphed to a look of incredulity—"That somehow it had *evolved*." He held up his free hand, just a sliver of light showing between pointer finger and thumb. "I was this close to putting a few rounds through the roof. It would *not* have ended well for you."

Still breathing hard, the look of incredulity now a full-on frown, Lia said nothing.

"Are you hurt? Did one of them bite you?"

She shook her head. "No, just winded. Holding on to this thing while you whipped it around was more of a workout than I've had in days."

The hard edge to his voice softening, he said, "Why risk your life like that?"

Before she could answer, Shorty was back on the radio issuing a warning that more biters were exiting the main building. "And we have an assload of them coming down the feeder road," he added.

Wondering how many zombies constituted an *assload,* Riker said, "No sense in keeping up the noise discipline. Go ahead and deal with them however you see fit." Before signing out, he asked Shorty to keep a close eye on Steve-O. Finished, Riker regarded Lia. Her eyes said she wanted to talk about what had happened, but her mouth remained clamped shut, lips a thin white line against her deeply tanned face.

After a brief pause, during which Riker grabbed a Nomex turnout coat off the backseat floor, he said, "You can tell me all about it whenever you're ready to. But I need you to stay right here while I set the ground pads."

Seeing her nod, and taking it as a sign that she understood and would comply, he closed the door and jumped to the ground.

A quick glance underneath the truck's chassis told Riker it was free of ankle-grabbing biters.

Having been exposed to all manner of emergency vehicles while in the Army, it didn't take Riker long to find the controls and extend the ground pads—twin opposing outriggers essential in keeping the truck from tipping once the ladder was put to full extension.

At the rear deck, Riker collected the Jaws of Life, balancing it on his shoulder, over top of the draped turnout jacket.

Making his way to the side-mounted ladder, Riker lugged the tool and jacket up to the telescoping ladder deck, placed the items on the floor of what looked to him to be a three-man basket, then beckoned Lia over.

Chapter 19

With Dozer off-leash and leading the way, Tara traversed the path between the clearing and Trinity House without incident. Once she reached the trailhead across from the rear door, the smell of carrion hanging in the air was enough to make her grab a fistful of shirt and cover her mouth and nose.

"Holy shit," she said under her breath. "Methinks somebody forgot their Axe Body Wash."

Before stepping into the open, she paused off to the side of the trail and hailed Rose on the teal radio.

A burst of white noise, then, "This is Rose."

Tara asked, "Where's the rotter? I can smell it."

"Rotters. Plural," Rose replied. "We have three of them roaming the turnaround. Another one is standing dead still right in front of the driveway gate. And there *was* a kid zombie. I don't see him at the moment."

"Are any of them fast movers?"

"I think they're all Slogs."

"*Think* and *know* are two very different things," Tara shot back. "One of those can get you killed."

Exasperation showing in her tone, Rose said, "What do you want me to do? Go bang on the gate? Throw one of Dozer's balls across the cul-de-sac and see if any of them take off running after it?"

"Forget it," Tara said. "I'm coming in. Just make sure you let me know if you see any change in their behavior."

"My eyes won't leave the screen," Rose promised.

Taking the *discretion is the better part of valor* road, Tara drew the Glock. After press checking the weapon to ensure a round was in the chamber, she did a quick turkey-peek in each direction. The stretch of open ground between the trailhead and where the east wall made a shallow left-to-right bend, maybe fifty feet total, was clear. To her right was a run of nearly a hundred feet. It, too, was clear.

She said, "OK," to get Dozer moving, then stepped from cover. As if somehow the thing had been alerted to their presence—which was absurd as hell to even think, let alone say out loud—a child-sized zombie emerged from behind the near corner. It was head-down and staring at the ground, all of its attention drawn to the fallen leaves crackling beneath its road-worn sneakers.

Caught fifteen feet from the wall, Tara had to choose quickly between making a mad dash for the recessed door or standing her ground and confronting the threat.

Reaching the door before being seen by the zombie might be doable. Working the keys in the pair of locks without the junior rotter catching on and giving chase was not going to happen.

Tara hated seeing any kind of zombie. But the ones she hated seeing most were the kids. They should be home playing video games, out riding bikes with their friends—doing the things kids do.

This one's days of doing the things kids do had been over for a couple of weeks. Pustules dotted both arms. An inch or two north of its shirt collar, dead center on its scrawny neck, was a golf-ball-sized hole. The blood that had flowed from the wound and soiled the collar was dried and crusty. The kid had died the first time wearing blue jeans and a DAB CAT tee shirt. On the front of the shirt was a cat performing the pose Tara had most recently seen performed by none other than Usain Bolt. God, she hoped the shirt was false advertising.

That hope was dashed when the undead kid grew tired of the noise made by the leaves, leveled a dead-eyed stare in her direction, and broke into an all-out sprint. Stick-thin arms pumping in near-perfect unison with equally skinny legs, the kid covered the first ten feet without a sound. No guttural grunts. No animalistic growling. And, of course, on account of its lack of a pulse and respiration—no heavy breathing.

Getting the Glock online to fire seemed to happen in slow motion. Tara was sticking her finger in the trigger guard and thrusting her hands out in front of her body at about the same time she heard her brother's voice in her head reminding her the Glock's safety was on the trigger. Which, at the moment, with sixty-some-odd pounds of hungry zombie barreling down on her, was one hell of a convenience.

Jumping the gun, so to speak, Tara pressed the trigger before she had the sights fully aligned. The first round struck the undead boy's clavicle, shattering it in several pieces and sending him off course by a few degrees.

Still, the thing made no sound whatsoever.

At the very moment Tara had been pressing the trigger, Dozer was already halfway across the open ground. Little rooster tails of damp earth erupted as the dog's paws found better purchase and its pace quickened.

Ignoring the furry missile vectoring in on the zombie, Tara sighted on a spot in space where she figured the zombie's bobbing head would soon be and gave the trigger a second press.

With the dog and undead kid a half-beat from one hell of a collision, the second round, tacking on a downward angle, entered the hollow cheek facing her and exploded out the other side, dragging in its wake a spreading cloud of congealed blood and shredded skin and shattered teeth. On account of the muzzle climb, Tara's third shot plunged into the runner's right eye socket, the kinetic energy snapping his head back and literally stopping him in his tracks.

Coming in fast and from the left, every muscle in his eighty-pound low-to-the-ground frame gone rock-solid, Dozer launched at the incoming threat. While the dog's aim was off, the impact with the undead kid was jarring. And though Dozer's weight advantage further altered the zombie's course, his bared teeth missed their mark. A good thing, considering nobody really knew Romero's true effect on animals.

Instead of clamping down on the arm sweeping past his muzzle, Dozer got a mouthful of the Dab Cat shirt. In the next second, as the equal and opposite reaction part of Newton's Law kicked in, Dozer was sent spinning away from the true prize, the large swatch of tee-shirt clutched in his pointy teeth the only thing to show for his effort.

The odd-looking pirouette that followed—the kid's arms and head all jerking in one direction, entire torso torqueing in the other—struck Tara as a move she'd seen at an interpretive dance performance.

As the zombie crashed to the ground, face-down, she bellowed, "Leave it," and motioned for Dozer to back off.

Still clutching the scrap of shirt between his teeth, Dozer backed away from the fallen ghoul. Once he reached the forest edge, he sat on his haunches and cocked his head.

Tara took another tentative step toward the prone figure, aimed the pistol's still-smoking barrel at the back of the zombie's head, and pressed the trigger.

Ears ringing, she plucked her keys from deep in her pocket and advanced to the door.

The radio in her other pocket emitted a soft electronic tone. After a follow-on hiss of white noise, Rose said, "I heard that. And so did they. They're coming your way."

No time to answer. Tara stuffed the key in the lock and drew back the first deadbolt. She was working on getting the other lock open when two things happened back to back. First, Dozer rushed over and put himself between her and the corner the kid zombie had just come around. Then, the zombies Rose had described—all of them waxen-skinned, their bloated bodies draped with torn and tattered clothing—doddered around the corner.

Though the door wasn't to a public restroom of an inner-city gas station, the ring of keys suddenly felt as if they had a cinder block hanging off them. The perceived weight was all in her mind, brought on by the sudden emergence of the trio of flesh-eaters.

Fighting through the rising panic, she jammed the key in the second lock, rotated it counterclockwise, and shoved her way into the courtyard.

Placing her hand in the breach where the growling canine could see it, she said, "Dozer, touch," and got ready to close the door.

Hindquarters appearing first, Dozer backed his way through the narrow opening, the ongoing low growl subsiding only when Tara had the door shut and both locks thrown.

Chapter 20

Lia had crabbed over the top of the fire engine's ladder and crawled into the basket with Riker. After spending a minute or two poring over the ladder controls, Riker got the basket rising clear of the truck. With the ladder canted at a forty-five-degree angle, he started it telescoping out.

Compressor noise similar to that made by the EarthRoamer sounded as he worked the controls. For some reason, his mind went to the people on the roof. He imagined the warden and her men wondering if the siren meant imminent rescue. He was certain they had been crestfallen when it ceased, that they were up there right now, craning and maybe crawling up the fence to the coiled razor wire and straining to see beyond the razor-wire topped parapet rising up at the roof's edge.

To be sure the coast was clear enough for him to take the next steps necessary to proceed down his own personal road to redemption, he scanned all points of the compass.

Seeing Shorty and Benny on the feeder road and just seconds away from their close-range engagement with the small pack of zombies, and knowing their fate and Steve-O's now lay firmly in their own hands, Riker started the ladder telescoping over the first layer of fencing, creeping ever so slowly toward the distant roofline.

The ride was smooth as they crossed over the perimeter fence, the basket eventually rising over the building's east wall without incident. Once there, with gunfire sounding at their backs, it took a little finessing of the controls on Riker's part to get the basket past the parapet and to a spot above the coiled razor wire where the ladder's under-mounted hoses and hydraulic piston were in no danger of becoming snagged.

After locking the bucket in place, Riker let go of the controls, then turned and looked to the east. From the elevated perch, the second he set eyes on the guardhouse it was clear that his new friends were still standing and a whole bunch of zombies were not.

Looking north, Riker saw another hundred or so zombies spread out on the pair of lots. While they were a clear and present danger to him, Lia, and the people they were hoping to bring down off the roof, how to deal with them would have to wait.

Pleased that he had gotten them to within fifty feet of the heating and ventilation equipment where the survivors were hunkered down, Riker surveyed the flat rooftop. It was encircled by a foot-wide parapet. Mounted parallel atop the parapet was a two-foot-high barrier of coiled concertina razor wire. Running away diagonally from the inner parapet to where the outer parapet met a wall that rose up over what Riker guessed was the main building the zombies were spilling from was an unbroken length of twelve-foot-tall fence. Like all of the fence surrounding the prison, this was also topped with coiled razor wire. Which is why Riker brought the Jaws of Life up with him.

From the bucket, he could only see the warden and two of her men. They were crowding the inner parapet and looking groundward, through the curls of razor wire. The third guard was nowhere to be seen and didn't emerge during the scant few seconds Riker and Lia spent observing them.

Considering the wailing siren and mechanical sounds the turntable and ladder had made while Riker moved the basket into position, he was amazed they weren't being greeted by expectant stares.

"What's going on? Lia asked.

"I have no idea," Riker conceded. "We're going to have to dismount this thing to find out." He draped the turnout coat over the razor wire to keep their clothing from getting snagged, then climbed down from the basket, crushing the jacket down under his Salomons.

Once he made it onto the roof, Riker had Lia pass him the Jaws of Life. Setting the tool down, he extended a hand, saying: "Why'd you do it?"

She leaped from the basket, easily clearing the razor wire. Landing cat-like on the roof, she said, "I did it because your little friend was giving me a case of the heebs."

"Shorty's a good man." Riker picked up the tool. "I've spent many hours in close proximity to him. If I thought he was a danger to Tara or Steve-O, I never would have invited him to Trinity House."

She looked a question at him.

Setting off walking toward the run of fence bisecting the roof, Riker described the mansion in the foothills north of Santa Fe. Told her what he knew about the nuclear physicist who had once called it home.

"So Tara and Rose are real?" Lia asked.

"I'll show you pictures of them when we get done here. We've got a house dog, too. Name's Dozer."

This seemed to put her at ease.

When they got to the fence, Lia was the first to call out to the others.

The second the warden rose and faced them, even across the distance, Riker could tell by her expression that something awful had happened. As the warden opened her mouth to speak, he noticed someone had been busy fashioning a rope from tied-together jackets and emergency blankets. One end of the makeshift rope was tied to the mounting bracket of the van-sized air-conditioning unit, the other, he guessed, was dangling somewhere out of sight below the parapet.

Hustling over to the roof's edge, the majority of the mostly zombie-free yard was revealed to Riker in increments. The reason for the warden's obvious concern became clear only when he got a good look at the ground immediately below where the jacket rope snaked over the parapet.

Initially, seeing more brown grass and asphalt than zombies in orange seemed to Riker to be a good thing. Whereas the aerial recon had shown hundreds down below, now there were just under thirty, most of them clustered in the northeast corner where a single door stood wide open.

Upon reaching the parapet, Riker cast his gaze at the ground thirty feet below. Prostrate on a patch of mud, surrounded by tufts of crushed grass and with a long length of the *rope* coiled about his body, was the badly sunburned guard. He was in pain, grunting and writhing and pounding the ground with both closed fists.

Voice betraying the fear he must be feeling for his coworker, the Hispanic guard said, "Norm fucking volunteered to go down there and get the ladder set back up. God damn it, *dude*." He began to cry. "I told him it wasn't his fault."

That ladder's staying where it is, Riker thought. The lower half of Norm's left leg was jutting off at an unnatural angle. Just below the left knee, a long length of jagged bone protruded from a hole in the bloodied uniform pants.

"You're the one with the drone," said the warden in a solemn voice. "I didn't think you were coming back." Her jaw took on a granite set. After a couple of seconds of silence, she added, "There's no helping Norman now. You're going to have to do *it* before they get to him."

Glad that she had been the one to recommend the dreaded "it," Riker drew his Sig, threw off the safety, then gave it a quick press check to confirm a round was chambered.

Making slow but steady progress, still maybe thirty feet from the fallen man, was a group of twenty or so dead things. They were becoming more vocal with each plodding step, grunts and moans and animal-like growls escaping their wide-open maws. A thought flashed through Riker's mind telling him the gang in orange moving on the guard had likely not devolved as much as their appearance would suggest.

Stepping forward, Lia said, "Shouldn't we at least *try* to save him? Shoot the things before they get to him?"

"Scoring headshots on that many moving targets with a pistol isn't going to happen," said the warden soberly. "At least not before one of them gets to him."

"And all it takes is one," Riker stated.

Lia said, "Then throw the gun down to him."

The warden shot her a look. Shaking her head, she said, "Too many variables. Plus, that would leave all of us defenseless."

The lady is all business, thought Riker as he stared down at the fallen man. "Hey there, Norm. My name is Lee. I'm going to need you to close your eyes. Can you do that for me, Norm?"

The man's eyes were wide open and flicking between the people peering down on him and the zombies drawing nearer.

"You have to save me," Norman wailed. "I have two kids. They're with their sitter. Been there for a week now."

This new information sent a shiver up Riker's spine. Trying not to let his own emotions show, he said, "Just close your eyes and try to picture their faces."

Instead, the will to live strong in the wiry man, Norman tried to sit up—pushing off the ground with both hands as he did so. The result: He let loose a guttural scream and his upper body slammed back to the ground.

After the wave of agony contorting Norman's face subsided, he stared skyward and professed his love for his young kids, calling them each by name.

At this point Riker's right arm was extended, the Romeo's red dot superimposed over the bridge of the doomed man's nose. As Riker transitioned his finger from the Sig's frame to the trigger, a tremor rocked his hand.

"Please close your eyes," Lia cried.

The zombies were almost upon the man.

The warden took a step closer to the fence separating her from Riker. "Do it," she implored. "Do it or give me your gun so *I* can."

After drawing a deep breath, Riker let it out real slow and pressed the trigger.

There was a booming report and a tiny dirt geyser erupted a few inches left of Norman's right ear.

Norman opened his eyes. Locked them with Riker's. Norman's mouth was moving now, but no sound was coming out. Riker could have sworn the man was mouthing "Do it" when the Sig discharged a second time.

The man's face imploding had the opposite effect on Riker than had Raul's, who was already mortally wounded and bleeding out on the pavers in front of Trinity House. The parolee was halfway to Hell at that point. Plus, the life-long criminal had already shot Benny and killed several others at Clines Corners.

Raul had definitely had it coming: He had earned every round Riker had pumped into him.

Norman, on the other hand, did not deserve this kind of death. In a way, Riker felt responsible. For if he had just spent a few more dollars and bought the best drone available, he would have been able to communicate his intentions to the warden. Let them know to sit tight and wait for him to return.

Woulda, coulda … didn't. No changing past history.

The rotund African American guard said, "Norm beat himself up for letting go of the ladder. None of us could talk him out of going back down there to get it."

Even hearing that failed to fill the dark hole opening up in Riker's heart. Peering through the fence, he fixed the warden with a tear-filled gaze. "I couldn't tell you I was coming back." He shook his head slowly, side to side. "It's not that kind of drone."

"I know," said the warden, "it's not your fault. I take full responsibility. It's my jail. He was my guard. My fault Norm set the ladder up on the wrong side of the rooftop security fencing. I directed him to do it. Thought we might have a better chance of getting down from here near the front lot where the roof is a few feet closer to the ground. Without the ladder to get us over this"—she gestured to the razor-wire-topped fence surrounding the HVAC components—"we were right back to square one."

The warden turned away and drew her men in close. She draped an arm over each of their shoulders and bowed her head. After saying a few kind words for Norman and his kids, she deferred the prayer to the African American guard.

After bowing her head for the duration of the prayer, Lia reached up and placed a hand on Riker's shoulder. "Come on, Lee," she said, "we need to get this done so we can get back to the others."

Nodding in agreement, Riker had the warden and her men stand behind the air conditioning unit, powered on the Jaws of Life, then went to work breaching the fence.

Chapter 21

Putting the Jaws of Life to work, Riker opened up a two-by-two-foot gap at the bottom of the fence. Working together, he and Lia received the shotgun and gear, put it all aside, then helped the warden and her men through the opening.

Rising up off the roof, the warden offered her hand to Riker. "Josephine Littlewolf," she said, then went on to introduce her guards, beginning with the Hispanic man. "This here is Roberto Flores. His longtime partner-in-crime on C Shift there is Luther Carr." She paused. "Do *not* call him Luke. He hates it."

As if the *deed* he'd been forced to do had left his hands dirty, Riker wiped his palms on his pants legs. "If only we were all meeting under better circumstances," he said, hooking a thumb at Amelia. "This is Lia. Don't know her last name, we just met." He nodded to the guards, then gripped the warden's offered hand. "I'm Leland Riker."

"I know who you are," Littlewolf said. She kept hold of his hand, her grip strong as she sized him up. "You're much larger in person," she added, releasing his hand. "And better looking in person than you are in your mugshot."

Lia took a step back. Fixing Riker with a hard stare, she said, "What the hell have I gotten myself into?"

Ignoring Lia's question, Riker said to Littlewolf, "I called the D.A. like I was mandated. To see if I still needed to appear. I got his voice mail. Then, just for the heck of it, I tried 911. Got a recording." His eyes widened. "It basically said we are on our own."

Nodding, Littlewolf said, "I got the same thing. We've been stuck here since the power went out for good. That was about day six. By then nobody was answering their phone. Makes me think landlines are down all across Santa Fe. Maybe even all of New Mexico. Our cell batteries died shortly thereafter." She cast her gaze at Riker's right leg and quirked an eyebrow.

"I cut it off," Riker admitted. "Santa Fe was on fire. Zombies had started to show up at our place. Figured the law and the courts had their hands full with more pressing matters. Besides," he added, "I shot that man in self-defense. Totally justifiable."

As Flores and Carr started a slow nod, Littlewolf said, "I read your jacket. I also read up on the man you killed. He was a real piece of work. That Bonnie *ride-or-die* of his was no angel herself"—*Bonnie?* thought Riker—"you just happened to be at the wrong place at the wrong time. Crossed paths with the Devil. I would have cut off my ankle monitor, too." Littlewolf unknotted the sleeve of her windbreaker and put it on.

Carr said, "You did us *all* a favor."

Remembering he had friends waiting below, Riker fished his radio from his pocket and hailed Benny. After a short exchange, during which Riker learned that both lots were now crawling with dead things and that they were beginning to surround the fire engine, he signed off. Picking up where he had left off with Littlewolf, he said, "This *Bonnie?* You mean Crystal, right?"

Littlewolf said, "Sorry. Crystal Ellison. Why do you care about her?"

Riker shook his head. "I really don't. Don't even know her that well. It's just that I agreed to this whole side trip to placate my sister and my buddy's girlfriend. Mostly the latter." Tone all business, he asked, "What happened to Crystal?"

"She tried the old Stockholm Syndrome defense," Littlewolf said. "At least through her court-appointed counsel, she did. All bullshit, though. She was a wackadoo. Finally admitted to a cellmate that she was just a thrill seeker who got in way too deep. You want my opinion, she was a *yes man* wrapped in the skin of a pretty little twentysomething white girl."

Riker said, "Was?"

Shrugging his windbreaker on, Flores said, "She claimed she was pregnant. I think she just wanted a way to get out of general population. I was in the infirmary when she was processed in to have the necessary tests. Saw the little *I got over on y'all* smirk on her face. That's where she was when the infection broke out inside and everything went to hell on us."

Nodding, Carr said, "We were severely understaffed at the time. Lots of people calling off. Everything would have worked out if Mary hadn't gone all Florence Nightingale and insisted we open the place up before leaving ourselves."

Riker said, "Open the place up?"

"The nurse on duty insisted we let the prisoners out of their cells. She argued that since we were leaving, it was the humane thing to do." Carr shook his head. "Hell, we were out of food. Delivery had ceased three days prior. The in-processing and administrative areas already belonged to those things. I said no way we were going to contain them before remotely opening all the cell doors. If it was my decision, I would have left them all locked up."

Littlewolf fixed Carr and Flores with a serious look. "Enough," she said. "We may have to go before a judge and answer for this one day. *Clamp it.*"

Though the world they all knew was going to shit around them, it was clear to Riker that the warden still held sway over her men. Both guards immediately began policing up their meager belongings, Carr grabbing the pair of shotguns, Flores donning a pack containing a medical kit and their dead phones and radios.

Riker had heard enough. He could now look both Tara and Rose in the eye and tell them in all honesty that he had done all he could for Crystal. *Mission accomplished.* Turning to Lia, he said, "I'm not a bad guy. Still, if you want to leave ... my offer stands. I'll take you wherever you want to go."

"Honestly, before I met up with you, Lee, I was just trying to get to the airport."

Riker said, "You weren't foraging?"

She shook her head.

"What really happened?"

"Like I said: It's a long story." She crossed her arms.

"When you're ready," Riker said, "I'm all ears."

Interrupting, Flores said, "You don't want to go to the airport anyway. Nothing has taken off or landed there since we've been up here. And I mean *nothing.* Last we heard, a quarantine facility was being set up to house all the incoming passengers."

Littlewolf nodded. Regarding Lia, she said, "Forget about the airport, young lady. I'd take Mr. Riker up on his offer.

You could do much worse. Apparently, his losing-his-temper-problem *has* gotten him in touch with the courts a couple of times." She zipped up her coat. Lifting her gaze to Lia, she went on, "But only enough of a problem to warrant him being ordered to attend a couple of anger management classes. He's got an honorable discharge, which says a lot. His work history is spotty, but whose isn't? Bottom line … he's not the kind of guy we like to keep behind bars."

Carr handed a shotgun to Flores, then fixed Lia with a no-nonsense-stare. "I've seen what an IED can do to a man." He tapped his head. "I've got a touch of post-concussion syndrome myself. Tinnitus, headaches … the whole nine yards." Indicating Riker's left leg, he added, "I didn't leave a piece of myself in Afghanistan, though."

"Iraq," Riker said. "Route Irish." Suddenly he was feeling like a shit for thinking Carr was a reject of the Santa Fe police when in all reality the man had also heeded the call to serve. They really were no different, he and Carr.

Riker dug into his pockets and gave Carr the shotgun shells he'd gotten from Shorty. "That's all I have to offer. Use them sparingly."

Giving half the shells to Flores, Carr went to work loading six of them into his pump gun.

When Riker turned to face Lia, he saw that she had uncrossed her arms. And though the look of disgust was gone, he had a feeling she was suffering from information overload.

"Mull it over," he said. "Let me know when you've made a decision." Hauling the Jaws of Life over to the basket, he looked groundward. What he saw was exponentially worse than what he was expecting: The dead that had been patrolling the prison yard had made their way through the building and, thanks to the newly destroyed doors, were now spread out across both lots. Riker guessed he was looking at two or three hundred of them.

The idling fire engine was attracting the majority of them. Maybe a hundred or so were already three deep and crushing in on it from all sides.

At the gate, a couple of dozen dead things, their alabaster fingers threaded through the chain-link, were pressing into the fence, causing it to flex and bow outward.

The only cars sharing the lot with the fire engine had each attracted a small knot of zombies.

Speaking into the radio, Riker said, "Benny, Shorty ... *do not* kill those things at the gate."

Shorty fired back first: "You sure you don't want to have to drive over a meat speed bump on the way out?"

"Something like that," Riker said, then went on to explain how he was going to get inside the truck and what he needed them to be doing in the meantime.

Lia said, "I don't think all of us are going to fit in the bucket."

"Just three of us," Riker said, "You watched me work the controls. You'll be doing that part."

Voice wavering, Lia said, "I guess."

Maybe, Riker thought, she's beginning to regret her decision to come along. "You got this," he said. Looking to the warden, he asked, "Who's going with you in the bucket? Carr or Flores?"

Littlewolf looked a question at the men. Carr stepped forward at once. "I'll stay back with Lee. Flores can go with you, boss."

Shaking his head, Riker said, "Nobody's staying behind. Two of us will be *climbing* down the boom before Lia gets it moving." This was met by a skeptical look from Carr. Riker went on: "Don't worry ... we'll be well out of their reach." He nodded at the truck below. "Once we're down there, we use the firefighting tool to thin them out." He patted the Randall on his hip. "I also have this to fall back on."

Carr asked, "Why not use the guns?"

"We want as many of them lured away from the rig as possible. Gunfire draws them like moths to a flame. Also, ammunition is a finite commodity. It's best to ration it. No telling when or if we'll come across more of it."

Carr nodded. He said, "You first," and gestured toward the awaiting basket.

Once Riker was across the jacket he'd draped over the crushed-down stretch of razor wire, he took the Jaws of Life from Carr and put it on the floor by the other firefighting tool. Next, he accepted the shotgun—deadly end aimed skyward, Carr's finger nowhere near the trigger—and propped it muzzle-down in one corner of the basket. Lastly, he helped Carr over the wire and into the basket.

It was no easy affair. In fact, after seeing Carr struggle to get over the wire atop the parapet, Riker had reservations about whether the man possessed the balance and agility necessary to navigate the narrow and steeply angled stairs. Doing so in the best of circumstances was a harrowing affair. Attempting it with a hundred hungry gazes tracing your every move and staring the meat from your bones only added to the degree of difficulty.

Though Riker was a little worried Carr might not make it to the bottom without losing his footing, who was he to tell the man what he could or could not do? So instead of having Carr go first, Riker started his descent. At the very least, if Carr did encounter a problem, Riker would be there to help him through it.

Having descended about ten steps, Riker looked up and saw that Carr was just stepping out of the bucket. The man had removed his windbreaker, tied the arms around his hips, and knotted the sleeves in front. The shotgun hung diagonally across his broad back.

Riker cast his gaze at the ground and resumed his slow and steady descent to the turntable. About halfway down, he paused and looked up at Carr. The guard was barely a third of the way down, stalled out and staring off to the side. It was clear he was having trouble breathing, the shotgun on his back rising and falling with each labored breath.

A few feet above Carr, the others were peering down from the bucket, worry etched on all of their faces.

As Riker neared the bottom of the boom, the stink of the dead had started his eyes to water. To make matters worse, it started to rain. At first, it was just a light mist. Then, in the blink of an eye, the sky opened up.

The stinging rain had no effect on the dead. They continued staring up at the boom, unblinking, as if a downpour wasn't pummeling them in the face.

"I can't keep a grip," Carr called. "It's slippery as sh—"

Riker had already finished the sentence in his head and was about to concur and offer words of encouragement when Carr came loose from the stairs. It wasn't like in the movies: feet slipping off of the ladder, followed by a scene in which the victim held on for dear life. Maybe even dangled there for seconds as his or her lives flashed by. This was sudden and jarring. Carr didn't scream or cry out as he detached entirely from the ladder. One second his expletive was cut out mid-word, the next his entire body weight was crashing into Riker from above.

A knee caught Riker on the right shoulder, breaking his hold on the rung in front of him. Even as his arm was being torn backward, away from the ladder, he was reacting to the tragedy unfolding, trying with all his might to get a hand on Carr as he sped on by.

Following the same trajectory as the doomed man, Riker caught a rung on the chin, his head snapping back in response. In the end, it was the extra flex and range-of-motion afforded by the bionic that saved him from the fate swallowing up Carr. When the tip of the Salomon on his good leg slipped off the wet rung, the extra give in the bionic allowed that shoe to stay put just long enough for its opposite to catch the next rung down. Though the stair above Riker's head was slick with rain, he got his hand wrapped around the tread and held on tight.

The screaming began the instant one of the dead plunged its claw-like fingers into Carr's jiggling belly. It rose in pitch, taking on an almost animalistic quality, as the creature yanked out a shiny length of intestine. The death warble ceased seconds later when another of the monsters found the man's exposed neck, clamping down hard with all the pounds of pressure the human jaw was capable of exerting. Instantly, muscle, flesh, and trachea were punctured by sharp canines and incisors. The dog-like back and forth thrashing of the zombie's head rendered loose a pulpy, bloody mess trailing veins and ragged strips of ebony dermis.

Riker cast his gaze up the ladder, past the spot Carr had been seconds ago, to the basket where Flores was just now performing the sign of the cross.

Beside Flores, her upper body hinged over the rail, Lia was crying and mouthing something Riker couldn't decipher.

Next to Lia, one hand clamped over her mouth, the warden was glaring up at the dark clouds overhead.

After stealing one last glance at the dead greedily consuming the contents of Carr's once-ample belly, Riker hung his head into space and emptied the contents of his stomach. Long after the half-digested bits of granola bar had come up in a wave of bitter bile, Riker's back still heaved and spasmed, droplets of spittle the only thing accompanying the air emptying from his lungs.

Going through his mind were the back to back deaths, one by his hand, the other, arguably, chalked up to his negligence. For if he'd insisted Flores accompany him down the latter instead of Carr, in all likelihood this would have never happened.

Shedding tears for both men, Riker resumed his slow and steady descent to the turntable below.

Chapter 22

Trinity House

The first burst of adrenaline was shocking Tara's system as she slumped down, back against the perimeter wall door. It was a solid item. Some kind of hardwood, the vertical boards several inches thick and reinforced by steel plates where the hinges attached.

Like a caged animal trying to escape her chest, her heart hammered hard against her ribs. As if that wasn't disconcerting enough, her back was bearing the brunt of the zombies' ongoing attack on the door. Every hollow thud coursing through the wood rocked her entire body.

Seconds after she had gotten the door closed and locked behind her, the first of three Slogs hunting her had slammed into the door. Soon the others had arrived and the beating on the door had intensified.

Now, with Dozer looking on, she unholstered her Glock, dumped the magazine, and press checked the slide.

One in the chamber, fourteen in the magazine.

Figuring the locks and hinges weren't rated to hold under the constant assault being waged on the door by what she guessed had to be a combined five or six hundred pounds of dead weight, she holstered the Glock, pushed herself up from the ground, and stalked off for the nearby shed.

She came out of the shed lugging a ten-foot aluminum ladder and cursing under her breath.

Back at the wall, Tara erected the ladder to the right of the door, gave it a good shake to ensure it was level and stable, then commenced her ascent.

As Tara reached the top of the wall, poking just the top of her head over the edge, the view that greeted her was exactly what she was expecting. Just feet below her perch, the tops of their heads fully exposed, the dead continued jostling for the limited real estate in front of the door.

Drawing the Glock, she said, "Up here, assholes."

The result she got was also exactly what she was expecting: Instantaneously, all three zombies froze in place and three expectant gazes swung skyward.

The term shooting fish in a barrel came to mind as Tara aimed for foreheads and ended each of their extended time on earth with a single shot. The little bloodless holes punched in the foreheads of the two male zombies didn't faze Tara. It was *bang* and crumple.

Putting down the female zombie was not so clean. One eye dangled from a destroyed eye socket in a head severely misshapen thanks to a thorough beating by something heavy and blunt. As the round struck the zombie squarely on its narrow forehead, the good eye shot from its socket and the undead woman's entire skull opened up like a blooming onion. Expecting to see an entry wound similar to the others, instead Tara was introduced to everything that was once inside the already compromised skull. As the zombie hinged over backward, both eyeballs, still attached to the head by their optic nerves, came together like the clacker toy Tara played with as a young child. In the next beat, what was left of the brain tumbled from the wide fissure.

The entire sodden mess struck the ground with a wet plop.

The sights, smells, and sounds started a revolt that began in Tara's salivary glands and ended only when she had emptied the entire contents of her stomach on the pile of corpses directly below her.

Dragging the back of one hand across her mouth, she mumbled, "I officially hate this shit."

Rose met Tara in the inner courtyard, between the guest house and main residence. On Rose's face was an expression Tara couldn't read. Though the two had just recently met, Tara could read the much younger woman like an open book more often than not. Rose wore her heart on her sleeve and didn't have much of a filter between her thoughts and what came out of her mouth.

This time, though, Rose said nothing. Just turned and motioned for Tara to follow.

With Dozer in tow, they entered the main residence via a side door and padded through the kitchen. When they reached the large open-concept shared living area, Rose stepped aside and said, "I was bored and started dusting the light sconces on the mantle. I was really getting into the cracks and crevices on the left-side one when it moved." She walked over to the mantle and took hold of the sconce in question. "It turned in my hand"—as she talked she was putting on a demonstration—"and then *this* happened."

There was a grating sound, then, slowly, like a scene straight out of an Edgar Allen Poe novel, a three-by-six-foot section of the stone hearth dropped down into the floor and snugged up against the left-side cement wall. Revealed was a run of stairs that disappeared into the gloom.

I found something you're going to want to see turned out to be the understatement of the century. The *something* Rose didn't think she could do justice by describing over the radio wholly exceeded Tara's expectations. And Rose had been right: There was no way Tara would have grasped the scope of what she was now looking at based on description alone.

Tara shot Rose an incredulous look. "Holy crap! Nuclear bomb guy had a *dungeon?*"

Rose shook her head. "It's more like a panic room, I think. It's like one of those rooms the Hollywood stars have in their mansions."

"You've been down there?"

Nodding vigorously, Rose said, "I took a quick look around."

"You have the flashlight?"

Pointing to the thick beam supporting the stairs leading down, Rose said, "Hit the switch."

"Wow! Lights, too?"

"There's more. Just flick it."

Tara threw the switch. There was a faint electrical hum, which was followed instantly by a flicker of soft, white light. After ordering Dozer to stay, Tara descended into the unknown.

Chapter 23

Riker was down on his hands and knees in virtually the same spot on the fire engine's roof where Lia was when she delivered the knocks that had almost gotten her killed. A torrent of blood was running down his neck and soiling his shirt. He was certain he'd lost a sizeable chunk of skin and flesh when his chin had smacked down on the textured stair tread, but when he stuck a finger through his beard and probed the wound, he found only a shallow inch-long gash. Nothing serious, which was shocking to him considering the amount of blood saturating his beard.

Safely out of reach of the dead encircling the fire truck, and in no danger of being crushed by the ladder or getting caught up in the turntable's moving parts, Riker met Lia's gaze and flashed her a thumbs-up.

With no lag whatsoever the basket and turntable began moving clockwise, the former sweeping away from the prison roof and cutting the air above the narrow strip of no-man's-land between the prison and inner run of fence, the latter emitting mechanical noises as it transported the basket and ladder to where Lia's input was directing it.

The rain had gone as quickly as it had come, the afternoon sun now glaring off the many puddles dotting the parking lot.

In the basket, a bit ham-handed on the controls, Lia was working on extending the ladder fully and getting the boom horizontal with the ground. The ride was far from smooth, each sudden directional change causing the basket to bounce more than the previous.

Underneath Riker, the fire engine was moving too. The subtle swaying ceased only when the boom was perpendicular to the fire engine's left side, the ladder at full extension, and the bottom of the basket hovering ten feet above the steaming asphalt.

Sticking to the plan, the three survivors in the bucket started hollering at the zombies. The calls varied from Lia's "Here zombie, zombie. Come and get it!" to Flores waving a shiny emergency blanket and bellowing, "Go back to Hell where you belong!" and Littlewolf chanting loudly in her native tongue.

As expected, the zombies surrounding the fire truck instantly forgot about Riker.

Like bugs drawn to the zapper, the horde broke apart and plodded off in twos and threes for the noisy meat in the basket.

Seeing his plan bearing fruit, Riker fought the urge to make a break for the cab. Instead, fingers kneading the firefighting tool's textured steel handle, he continued breathing through his mouth and kept a low profile.

From Lia's perspective, though the fire truck was a little less than a hundred feet from the basket, it may as well have been a mile away. Surging across the stretch of asphalt, arms outstretched, teeth clacking an eerie cadence, was a sea of jostling bodies. The fact that some were still emerging from behind the truck only elevated the sense of isolation she was feeling.

Though Riker was at roughly her level atop the truck, all that she could see of him was the crown of his head and the rounded hump of his back.

Flores stopped yelling at the zombies and regarded Lia. "You sure they can't reach us?"

"We'll know soon," Lia responded. Eyes watering, she covered her nose with the oversized sweatshirt. It did little to filter the rank odor rising off the decaying corpses.

Flores stilled the space blanket. Hands trembling mightily, he said, "You know what I feel like up here above all these dead things?"

Lia had resumed pounding her fists on the outside of the bucket. Stopping momentarily, she looked a question at the man.

"I feel like a fucking meat piñata." He gestured toward his friend. "Look what they did to Luther. They fucking gutted him. Ripped the meat from his neck and arms and legs. They're soulless eating machines."

Up to this point, Carr had been totally obscured by the feeding zombies. Now, with the crowd receding from the truck, the nearly naked corpse was exposed for all to see. It lay in a pool of blood and was surrounded by human detritus and scraps of fabric from his thoroughly shredded uniform.

The shotgun had ended up a few feet away in a water puddle near the truck's rear tire.

A lone male zombie had stayed behind, its head and both hands buried inside the gaping bloody chasm that once held Luther's internal organs. Two near symmetrical rows of ribs bracketed the zombie's bobbing head. Bloody tatters of the man's shirt still clung to some of the jutting bones.

As the zombie pushed its face even deeper into the disemboweled torso and shook its head, the rib bones followed the movement in perfect unison. And though it struck Lia as absurd as soon as the notion popped into her head, from the elevated perch it appeared as if the zombie was wearing a crown. A crown fashioned from the bones of its most recent kill. *King of the Zombies.* That was nightmare fuel she definitely didn't need added to the bonfire of horrifically morbid sights that had already damn near rendered her an insomniac.

Wanting to help Flores cope with the gruesome sight, Lia said, "He went real quick. I'm sure he didn't suffer." Even she didn't believe the words as she had uttered them.

"The suffering is eternal," Flores shot. He was staring past Lia as if she wasn't there. "They *all* come back. Luther told me their souls are in some kind of purgatory. Like a waiting room for Hell." He paused and pinched the bridge of his nose. Blinking away tears, he pointed at his friend. "He promised me he was *not* going to come back as one of them. Even if he got bit, he was convinced he was going to stay dead and go on up to Heaven." Lia knew where Flores was going with this but forced herself to maintain eye contact. "Luther was a God-fearing man. An assistant pastor at his church," Flores railed, shaking a fist at the sky. "Please tell me I'm imagining what I'm seeing."

Regarding the scene she hoped to never set eyes on again, Lia detected movement in the man's chewed-on limbs. It was a constant twitching that she figured *could* be attributed to the feeding zombie; however, the cold ball forming in her gut quickly dismissed that explanation.

So she lied. "I can't be sure," she said, looking away.

As if the feeding zombie had received an unspoken command, maybe something transmitted from deep within the reptile part of its brain, it abruptly extricated its head from the dead guard's chest cavity and hinged up from the position of supplication.

The zombie's hair was a bloody matted mess that clung to its head like a shiny black helmet. Face slack and glistening with fresh blood, it rose up off its knees and followed in the footsteps of the others.

Though Carr's body was no longer being desecrated by the hungry dead, his bloody, half-eaten limbs continued to spasm. The movements quickly became more pronounced, the fingers clenching into fists.

Barely a minute had passed between Luther falling from the boom and his corpse showing the first signs of reanimation.

Ignoring the dead gathering a yard or so below her feet, Lia said, "Oh no. No, no, no."

Flores hung his head. Knuckles going white from the death grip he had put on the railing, he launched into the Lord's Prayer.

Standing behind Lia and Flores, the warden had ceased her chanting. A lone tear traced an uneven arc down her cheek as she spotted what had the others so transfixed.

As the trio looked on, Luther's head lolled to the side and his eyes locked onto them. Even from a distance, it was evident the windows to the soul harbored no spark of life.

The eyes remained fixed on the boom as the corpse rolled over onto its front. After a lot of slipping and sliding in its own bodily fluids, the reanimated corpse planted its palms flat on the asphalt, rose up on unsteady legs, and again locked its glassy-eyed stare on the meat in the bucket.

Flores exhaled sharply. "I told him I would go in his place." Looking to the warden, he said, "What are we going to do with him?"

"I'm still responsible for Flores. We're going to have to get out of this scrape first," Littlewolf stated soberly. "Then, and only then, do we confront the Luther problem."

Chapter 24

Rising up from the roof, Riker took a long hard look at his surroundings. To the right, save for a couple of zombies on the lot's periphery, the wet pavement was unoccupied.

As to what was lurking in the fire truck's blind spot, Riker had no way of telling. With the fence so near to the rear bumper and nothing back there for them to eat, he doubted he had anything to worry about. Still, he told himself, once he committed to climbing down, if he was to keep from suffering the same fate as Luther, he'd need to keep his head on a swivel.

Peering off the truck's left side, Riker saw evidence of Luther's demise, but no Luther.

Near the rear tire, the black nylon sling severed, was Luther's shotgun. That each end of the sling was frayed led Riker to believe one of the ravenous dead had chewed through it.

Riker walked his gaze the length of the boom, but still saw no sign of Luther. Establishing eye contact with Lia, he pointed to the ground and shrugged. *Where did he go?*

Two of the three in the basket recognized the universal semaphore for what it was. Lia and Littlewolf both pointed at the boom.

Before Riker could move forward to get eyes on the ground below the boom, Zombie Luther ambled into view, all of his attention focused laser-like on the trio in the basket. He was not even halfway to the basket and already coming up against the growing circle of zombies underneath it.

How did he turn so quickly? was the first thing to cross Riker's mind. It was followed immediately by: *Did he come back a Bolt or a Slog?*

Only one way to find out.

Keeping his voice at a level he hoped would be heard by undead Luther, but not the participants of the scrum developing underneath the basket, Riker said, "Luke."

Apparently, the warden hadn't been joking when she had said, "Do not call him *Luke*. He hates it." Because that one word froze Zombie Luther mid-stride. Fortunately, the creatures nearby remained intent on getting to the basket.

Searching for the source of the sound, Luther walked his gaze down the length of the engine.

To hasten the process, Riker got up on his knees and waved at the zombie with his free hand. Nothing. It was looking everywhere *but* up.

"I'm over here, Luke."

The shell of the man who used to be an assistant pastor and good friend to his fellow jailers lifted its gaze and emitted a guttural growl.

Brandishing the firefighting tool like a baseball bat, left hand closest to the claw end, the other a few inches south of the tool's center of balance, Riker shuffled forward on his knees. Stopping just short of the roof's rounded edge, he took one hand off the tool, leaned out over space, and swept his arm pendulum-like in front of the driver-side window.

Locking its dead-eyed stare on the offered appendage, the newly risen corpse lowered its head and charged the fire truck.

We have a Bolt was what Riker was thinking as undead Luther reached the exact spot on the parking lot where he had died the first time. A sudden wave of remorse crashed over Riker as he withdrew his arm and watched the Bolt slam into the engine under a full head of steam.

Undeterred and uninjured, it rose up off the ground and again ran headlong into Detroit steel. Arms outstretched and its growling and grunting rising in volume, the Bolt battered the fire truck's slab-side with its knees and elbows.

Barely a yard separated Riker from the Bolt. Drawing a breath, he said, "Oldest trick in the book, Luther." He shook his head. "I'm sorry I pulled that on you. I'm sorry this had to happen to you. And I'm really sorry I have to do this to you."

Blocking out everything extraneous: the idling diesel engine, the cacophony of the dead trying to reach the others in the basket, undead Luther's vocalizing and incessant slam dancing into the truck underneath him, Riker lifted the firefighting tool over his head, its entire length parallel with his upper body, and brought it down hard as if the weighty tool was a posthole digger and he was plunging it into desert hardpan.

Undead Luther's face was *not* desert hardpan. In fact, the opposite was true: It was more than forgiving. The bladed end struck the Bolt's upturned face squarely between the eyes, splitting the skull wide open and starting a torrent of gray brain tissue spilling from the gaping fissure.

Riker released the tool and paused long enough to do three things. First, as the twice dead corpse was still settling on the ground below, Riker met Lia's gaze across the distance and gave her their predetermined signal. Seeing Lia nod, he rose up from the roof and scanned the lot all around.

Then Riker checked on the gate crew. Though he didn't have binoculars, he could still see the vehicles and guardhouse. The lack of movement on the opposite side of the gate told him Benny, Steve-O, and Shorty were sticking to the plan.

In the middle distance, the zombies that had been hanging around the gate were now fifty yards from the bucket and closing.

Finally checking his right flank, he saw that the handful of vehicles left behind sat all alone. The zombies that had been hanging around the static imports and minivan were on the move and had halved the distance to the engine.

With all of the possible threats pinpointed on the crude map in his head, Riker clambered down from the roof. On the ground, his Salomons fighting for traction in the pooled blood, he tugged the firefighting tool from twice-dead Luther's skull. Sidestepping a glistening length of intestine, he bent over and snagged one half of the shotgun's severed sling.

Since the outriggers were still deployed, he opened the panel and worked the controls. As soon as the metal legs began motoring back into their vertical housings, the compressor came online, blasting his ears with a high-decibel mechanical clatter.

Above Riker's head, the boom was making a slow counterclockwise sweep toward the rear of the truck.

To verify that the passenger-side outrigger was in sync with its counterpart, Riker ducked around behind the engine's rear end. The moment he came into view of the advancing zombies, the entire group altered course. While the zombies angling for him posed a serious threat, unless both outriggers got retracted, the rig was going nowhere.

Seeing the passenger-side outrigger finish its upward sweep and snug into its housing, Riker hustled forward, past the tandem axles, and went to his knees to take a look at the rig's undercarriage and tires.

Clear. No dead things in the shadows beneath the truck. Though the tires were covered with organic matter, all ten appeared to be fully inflated.

All systems go.

With the zombies still ten yards out, Riker brought the shotgun's barrel to a ready position and retraced his steps.

The first thing Riker saw when he came back around the rear of the engine was that the boom had moved past the halfway point and the ladder was partially retracted. In the next beat, he learned that while he was away, the horde had splintered. The majority of the dead—maybe seventy or eighty of them— were still in lockstep and following the basket's slow sweep. Having approached to within fifty feet of the fire truck, the second knot of zombies—nearly twenty strong—were already stalking him. Only explanation he could think of for their deviation from the horde was the sound made by the compressor and follow-on hiss of the outrigger's hydraulics.

From experience, Riker knew it only took one of them taking notice of you to start a chain reaction that *always* led to a whole bunch of them hunting you.

While Riker had already proven to himself he could handle a Bolt or two, double or triple that if they were *all* Slogs, taking on twenty of the things was an entirely different story—a story whose ending was about to be written.

With thirty feet of rain and blood-slickened ground standing between Riker and the cab, and about the same distance between him and the dead, he was afraid if he was going to survive the final act, a whole lot of things were going to have to go right.

As the severity of the situation set in, so did the metronomic throbbing of a headache he knew would soon be a debilitating migraine. He'd been so preoccupied with surviving, he hadn't even noticed the previous banger subside.

With the first wave of pain moving from the back of his head and flanking both retinas, he leveled the shotgun and backpedaled to create room to work.

Off of Riker's left shoulder, just above his line of sight, the shouting from the bucket had turned from epithets being directed at the dead to keep them interested and on the hook to warnings meant solely for him.

"The biters are flanking you!" Flores said, stabbing a finger at the rear of the engine.

Lia was shaking her head and mouthing, "I can't reach you with the basket."

Don't even try, Riker thought. *That'd just bring the horde back together and drop the whole thing on my doorstep.* Heeding Flores's warning, he changed direction, crabbing sideways the length of the engine while firing the shotgun head-high into the crowd spread out before him.

By the time Riker had cycled all six shells through Carr's pump gun, he had winnowed the dead down by four, two of them having had their skulls imploded by slugs fired from a dozen feet away, the other pair dropped in their tracks and left paralyzed by the fist-sized holes blasted through their necks.

Dropping the shotgun, Riker quickly transitioned to the Legion. No need to power on the Romeo optic: It was motion activated. Trusting that a round was chambered, he threw the safety and engaged the zombies.

Breathe in, exhale, press.

Riker saw the first couple of rounds strike exactly where the superimposed red pip indicated they should. Spirits buoyed, he continued down the side of the truck, bringing the undead entourage with him. Unfortunately, since moving and firing was not his strong suit, by the time he dumped the first spent magazine and jammed a second into the magwell, his shot to kill ratio had fallen off a cliff.

Eleven down. Nine to go.

Migraine now in full swing, vision going hazy around the edges, he thumbed the slide home and resumed pumping rounds into the dead. He crossed Carr's pooled blood and continued to fire cross body until the mag went empty again. Out of ammunition, he holstered the Sig, scooped up the firefighting tool, and made a final push for the cab.

The three remaining zombies, all males wearing county-orange, were within arm's reach of Riker when he made the cab. Gripping the firefighting tool like a baseball bat, he paused in front of the driver-side door and took a stance his favorite Atlanta Braves slugger, Freddie Freeman, would be proud of.

Shuffling closer, having formed up three abreast, the zombies lunged at Riker near simultaneously.

Putting everything he had into the *cut,* Riker beat the dead to the punch, the tool scything the air on a flat plane, right to left, head-high to the zombie on his immediate right.

Swing and a hit.

The blade edge of the tool cleaved the zombie's left ear in two, continued on through the temporal, sphenoid, and zygomatic bones, then came to a grinding halt, the leading edge stuck fast in the inner ethmoid bone.

Taking the path of least resistance, the pulped white of the zombie's left eyeball and a torrent of clumped gray matter shot from the collapsed eye socket. As the vibration from the impact transited the tool and shot like a bolt of lightning through Riker's hands and arms, he actually felt deep within his chest the sickening *crack.*

A Freeman solo homerun.

Mimicking the All-Star slugger's follow-through, Riker put a twist in his hips, let his wrists break, and then began the *push.* Tool still stuck firmly in the zombie's misshapen skull, the monster was lifted off its feet and rocketed headfirst into the zombie to its right. The thunk of the two skulls coming together was every bit as loud and disconcerting to Riker as that of the overpass leapers' skulls striking asphalt.

Using the momentum of the textbook swing to his advantage, Riker thrust the tool away from his body and released his grip on it. As the hundred-and-fifty-some-odd-pounds of twice-dead zombie caromed off the others, knocking them off balance and creating a precious yard of separation, Riker scrambled into the engine.

From the first press of the shotgun's trigger to the trio of zombies sprawling domino-like away from the truck, less than a minute had elapsed.

Only when Riker had gotten the door locked, his hands on the wheel and the rig rolling forward, did the full effect of the migraine hit him. He was suddenly nauseous and gripped by cold chills.

So the gatekeepers knew that he was on the move, Riker laid on the horn for a long three-count. No sooner had the air horn gone silent than brief flashes of orange drew his attention to the side mirror, where, as improbable as it seemed, he spotted a trio of zombies break from the horde and give chase.

"What next?" he asked himself as he gave the horn another blast. "The gate still going to be closed when I get there?"

Fishing a backup plastic baggie of ibuprofen from a pocket, he threw down another handful. If a near-fatal dose of what his Eleven Bravo friends not-so-affectionately called "*grunt candy*" didn't temper the pounding in his head, nothing was going to.

Chapter 25

Shorty was wondering what had precipitated the gunfire, and totally in the dark as to what it meant to the plan, when he heard the predetermined signal.

The moment the engine's air horn cut out, Shorty bellowed, "It's go time! You in position, Steve-O?" Without waiting for an answer, Shorty looked to Benny and flashed the younger man a thumbs-up.

Crouched down behind the Shelby, in the same position he'd been holding for nearly twenty minutes, Benny nodded and stood up straight.

Hearing his name called, Steve-O said, "Yes I am," and moved from behind the guardhouse. As he'd already done five times in his mind over the last twenty minutes, he hustled the short distance to the pair of backboards covering the tire spikes and tightened up the gap between them.

Satisfied the boards were centered, the spikes mostly compressed under their combined weight, he retook his position behind the guardhouse.

Out of sight, out of mind was what Shorty had said when he had shown Steve-O where he wanted him to stay until the signal sounded. And though Steve-O knew Shorty was talking about keeping *out of sight* of the monsters, the saying still reminded him of the way people used to ignore him. It had happened most at school—gym class, the cafeteria, recess—where he never, ever felt included.

In the distance, the horn sounded a second time.

Already alert to the fact that Lee was in the fire engine and heading toward the gate, when Steve-O heard the second blast—a predetermined signal alerting them all that Bolts had just entered the picture—he felt a chill settle in his gut.

With the satisfied feeling of being useful to the group at war with the fear brought on by what the second horn meant, he drew a calming breath, purged all of the negative thoughts from his mind, and locked his gaze on the backboards, ready to spring into action when it was time.

The pair of zombies that had stayed behind at the gate still had their fingers wrapped up in the chain-link when Shorty and Benny emerged from cover. Though the zombies had their heads turned in the direction of the approaching engine and trio of fast-movers chasing it, the stimulation wasn't enough for them to give up on the prey that had drawn them to the gate in the first place.

"Stubborn bastards," Shorty muttered, "why didn't you tag along with the rest of your stinky friends?"

Drawing his knife, Benny said, "I got them," and started toward the zombies.

Shorty put his hand on Benny's forearm. "No, put it away."

Eyes narrowing, Benny said, "We need to clear the path for Lee. With those Bolts on his tail, he'll be going balls out when he comes through here."

"If you do them where they stand," Shorty stated, "not only will they be in Lee's path when they fall, but so will you and I as we try to drag them out of his way."

"Lay it on me," responded Benny. "What's your plan? We have about twenty seconds to get them out of the way and this thing open wide enough for that—." He punctuated the statement by nodding at the engine, which, at the moment, was quickly climbing through the gears and gathering speed.

Thinking the dead would be slow to react to their presence, and even slower to release their grip on the fence, Shorty said, "We run it open, they follow us to the side of the driveway, then we do them there. Two birds, one stone."

Yeah, easy peasy was what Benny was thinking as he hustled to the gate, grabbed ahold of it with both hands, and started to run it open.

Seeing their prey reenter the picture, the zombies hissed and mashed their bloated abdomens hard against the gate.

Shorty and Benny had gotten the gate opened a yard or so when Shorty's plan was shot to hell.

While initially the zombies had followed the gate as it rolled away from the guardhouse, the moment they saw that the meat was not getting any closer to them, they released their grip on the chain-link. Though their feet and legs ceased moving, the pent-up inertia sent them both on a one-way trip to the ground.

"Good thinking," Benny shot as he crossed paths with the sprawled-out corpses. "Not only do we have to move 'em out of the way and keep from getting bit, but we have to do it with the truck bearing down on us."

Shorty said nothing. Head down, he leaped over the gnarled hands reaching up for him and kept on going. When the gate clanged against the stops, he let go, yanked the Glock from his waistband, and stomped over to the supine zombies.

Saying, "Nobody's getting bit," Shorty shot each zombie one time in the head. Holstering the Glock, he barked, "A little fucking help here?"

Working together, the two men got the leaking corpses dragged out of the way with, at most, five seconds to spare. As the truck crossed the threshold, Shorty said, "My fault, Benny. I'm pretty good at complicating an easy task."

Wiping blood on his pants, Benny said, "You're quite the asshole. Apology accepted."

When the engine rolled through the gate, it brought with it all kinds of noise: the roar of the diesel engine. A whooshing of air brakes being deployed. The nails-on-a-chalkboard squeal of overworked brake pads trying to bring thirty tons of steel and rubber and glass to a complete halt on an extremely limited run of asphalt.

In the engine, blood dripping steadily from the gash to his chin, Riker had jumped on the brakes as soon as he felt the front tires bump over the backboards. As if he had been driving the forty-foot-long vehicle all his life, he managed to bring it to a complete halt without skidding or slewing sideways *and* kept the tandem rear axles from rolling across the backboards.

One look in the mirror confirmed what he had already guessed: The rear of the truck was blocking the gate from closing, and the Bolts were not far behind.

The second the fire truck had come to a full stop, Steve-O hopped up and hustled over to it. Taking a knee a few feet left of the right front tire, he aimed the small penlight provided by Shorty at the pair of backboards. Seeing that their movement had been minimal, he stuck his thumb up and thrust his arm out to his side, holding the pose until Lee acknowledged the "Go" signal with yet another toot of the horn.

A little incensed at being called an "asshole" by a total stranger, Shorty snatched the Shockwave off the ground where he'd left it, threw the safety off, and stepped forward to engage the onrushing Bolts.

"Forget that," Benny called. He had ahold of the gate in anticipation of the engine getting rolling again. "I need your help with this."

Shorty's response was more of a guttural growl than a coherent sentence. "Shocky needs to eat," he said and thrust the shotgun out ahead of him, its business end tracking the nearest of the three Bolts—a tanned and toned twentysomething female with a full head of blonde hair.

Near simultaneously, the fire engine rolled the rest of the way through the open gate and the sprinting Bolt encountered the wide swathe of pulped flesh and bone spread out before it. After having been run over twice by the engine's massive tires, the bodily fluids once contained within twenty or so zombie corpses were seeping out and mixing with the standing rainwater.

Oblivious to anything and everything but Shorty, the female Bolt came at him like Flo Jo chasing the Gold. When it reached the slick asphalt, its bare feet traded places with its head. If it hadn't been for the deadly nature of the imminent encounter, the sight of it slipping and sliding, pale arms windmilling as it performed a clumsy somersault, might have seemed humorous to Shorty. Instead, wearing a scowl, he continued to track the creature with the pump gun as it slid face-first for his boots.

The zombie's pent-up momentum bled off completely a handful of feet from Shorty, leaving the flailing monster face down in the gore and its hair and county-orange blouse saturated with blood and unidentifiable liquids.

Unable to rise to its knees, the undead inmate lifted its face off the asphalt and locked its dead-eyed gaze on Shorty.

Taking a couple of quick steps forward, Shorty stopped where the tracks for the gate ran underfoot and promptly shot the zombie in the face.

From near point-blank range, the slug—traveling 1,800 feet per second—punched a quarter-sized hole clean through the thing's skull. In the front and out the back, leaving its pale features stippled with black powder burns and the back of its orange blouse painted with scrambled brain and splintered bone.

Shorty was saying "Next" and racking the Shockwave's slide when the second Bolt entered the debris field. Through some stroke of luck, the undead male remained upright, even as the laggard behind it lost its footing and went down hard, the back of its head bearing the brunt of the fall.

The follow-on shot from Shorty's shotgun was also a slug. Though it missed its mark by half a foot, the damage done to the zombie's throat and spine was enough to drop it in its tracks. Paralyzed from the neck down, it didn't move again.

Shorty was racking another shell into the breach when Benny entered the picture from the right. Skirting the pool, one hand held up to tell Shorty to check his fire, Benny leveled the Glock and fired a pair of rounds into the head of the remaining Bolt.

With all three of the fast movers put down inside of the gate, there was no need to get their hands dirty and move them.

Benny holstered his Glock and regarded Shorty. "The rest are still coming. Let's finish this."

Stabbing the Shockwave's smoking muzzle in the direction of the jail, Shorty said, "A lot of good it'll do against those kinds of numbers."

Grabbing a fistful of fence, Benny let his gaze roam the lot. In the short time since Riker had driven the fire engine away from the distant fence line and left the horde of slow movers all alone, another fifty or sixty deaders had streamed from the main building and were on the march toward the guardhouse. Though there was no imminent danger of the two groups converging before making it to the gate, Shorty was right: Though it was reinforced, the chain-link wouldn't hold for long against their combined weight.

"Agreed," Benny said. "It won't hold for long, but it should buy us the time we need to mount up and get the hell out of here."

Chapter 26

Riker had heard the gunfire coming from the vicinity of the yawning gate, but since he was inside the cab, he was blind to what had gone down. Receiving the thumbs-up from Steve-O, and trusting the man completely, Riker had driven the fire truck the rest of the way through the gate. Once he was certain the eight remaining tires were safely over the backboards covering the spikes, he set the brakes and elbowed open his door.

Lia and Flores were already down from the bucket and met Riker on the road beside the cab. Littlewolf, Riker saw, was just climbing down from the engine. She was tentative, choosing her handholds carefully. Riker thought about offering her a helping hand but quickly decided that thanks to her being an Alpha, she wouldn't be receptive to the gesture.

Lia put a hand on Riker's shoulder. Craning, she studied his face. "Damn, Lee," she whispered, "you look like you just saw a ghost. What's going on?"

Still not used to the woman's penchant for being so forthcoming with her thoughts, Riker paused to collect his. Nodding toward the gate, which was now closed against the oncoming horde, he said, "Where in the hell did those Bolts come from?"

Lia said, "They were part of the pack hounding us."

"Carr bled out and turned quick," Riker noted. "He was a recent kill and relatively young. I expected him to come back as a Bolt. The other three"—he shook his head—"they weren't new kills. They looked to be two, maybe three days old. Goes against everything we've learned about them so far."

Nodding, Flores said, "The last of the inmates died thirty-six to forty-eight hours ago. When they first started coming back every fourth or fifth one of them was just as fast dead as it was alive."

"Were the fast ones all younger? More physically fit?" Riker asked.

Flores shook his head. "Most of the inmates lived pretty hard lives before they got here. A stretch to call any of them healthy. The ones hitting the weight pile on a daily are physically fit. Just 'cause they're yoked, doesn't mean they're healthy."

Lia said, "It's random."

"I don't care what you call them," Riker said, "I just want to know what the rules are."

Flores said, "I think she's trying to say it's *random* selection."

"Exactly," Lia said. Regarding Riker, she asked, "When did you come up with *Boli*? Pretty cute naming them after Hussein, by the way."

"My sister started calling them that on day one. I had no idea who the hell the dude was."

Lia said, "How many have you seen since day one?"

"Counting the ones today, maybe fifteen or twenty total. Of those, all but the last three were recent turns. Most of them that I saw, even the first one I killed, died and reanimated in a matter of minutes. A couple might have been dead for hours or days, but I can't be sure. I didn't see them die and come back."

Incredulous, Lia said, "That's it? You've only seen twenty Randoms between the rising and today?" She paused and looked at her shoes. Reestablishing eye contact with Riker, she said, "You consider that enough evidence to make blanket assumptions? We're talking about something happening that's unprecedented in all of human history?"

Flores said, "What about Haitian voodoo? They make zombies, don't they?"

"Those are living slaves," Lia said. "If memory serves, they were drugged into submission."

Riker removed his Braves cap and massaged his temples. Though his migraine had mostly dissipated, Lia's interrogation was reviving it. "I'm no expert," he shot. "Nor am I pretending to know everything about these things. I'm just an average guy trying to survive this bullshit." He shook his head. "Lady, I'm just calling them like *I* have seen them." He donned his hat and pulled it down hard on his bald head. Regarding Lia, he asked, "So what's *your* experience? How many *Randoms* have you seen since day one? And in your opinion, what's the common denominator?"

Jaw taking a hard set, Lia said, "There is no common denominator. It's all random. Old, young, newly dead or starting to stink ... any of them can be fast movers. You get enough of them in one place and there's sure to be a few sprinters. It's like what Forrest Gump said: Life's like a box of chocolates—"

Having just arrived at the periphery of the ragged semicircle, Steve-O said, "You never know what you're going to get," and started laughing. Reining the laughter in, he added, "Did you know that Jenny dies at the end?"

Lia said, "That's common knowledge," and turned her attention back to Riker. "I've seen at least fifty of what you call *Bolts*. And they come in all shapes and sizes."

At the rear of the engine, Littlewolf had just made it to the road and was working her way forward. Finished stowing the backboards, Benny and Shorty emerged from behind the engine a half beat later.

From thirty feet away, Shorty called out, "Gate's secured, Lee," and fell in behind Littlewolf. "You going to introduce us to your new friends?"

Ignoring Shorty, Riker locked eyes with Lia. "You riding with me or him?"

Lia glanced at Shorty. Throwing a visible shudder, she said, "You ... on one condition."

Riker looked a question her way.

"Can you take me to my place?"

In a different time, any time actually before that fateful Greyhound bus ride from Atlanta to Middletown, Riker would have been giddy inside that a beautiful young woman he'd just met would trust a man of his stature and skin tone enough to pop the question—platonic or not. Now, with all of the uncertainty hanging over the direction the outbreak was heading, the question carried with it all kinds of unanswered questions. After a short pause, with a tilt of the head, he asked, "Where is your place?" Though he worded the question so as not to sound skeptical, his tone and body language gave him away.

"Northeast part of Santa Fe. It's a little one-bedroom adobe on a quiet street."

Riker said, "It might work. But we still have a couple of things on our to-do list. If you're flexible, I'll do my best to get you there. No promises, though. Because if we come across another horde or the surface streets are thick with deaders, I'll turn us around in a heartbeat."

Lia nodded. Taking hold of the engine's grab bar, she said, "Let's go. I'll sit in back."

Having just arrived at the huddle, Littlewolf said, "My Durango is stuck in the on-duty lot. Can you drop me and Flores at the Penitentiary?"

Riker shook his head. "I'd steer clear if I was you."

"Did the inmates take control?"

"If they didn't, judging by the lack of cars in the lot, looks like the folks running the place are vastly undermanned. I'd bet the house they're in the same boat as you guys were."

"Or worse," Benny said. "I glassed the place for a couple of minutes." He shook his head. "Only thing moving inside is already dead."

Flores looked to Littlewolf. "How about we walk to the Sheriff's shop and liberate a cruiser."

Riker said, "The place looks abandoned. Lot is empty. No cruisers. No civilian vehicles. Gate was hanging wide open ... like they left in a hurry."

Littlewolf planted her hands on her broad hips and stared at the sky.

Flores turned his back to the others and whispered something to the warden. Nodding, she looked to Riker. "Can you take us to police headquarters downtown? I'm sure Chief Chavez could use a hand."

Riker didn't have the heart to tell her what he really thought: that the rule of law was as dead as the walking corpses just reaching the gate. Instead, he said, "Take the engine. Tank's nearly full. It's County property, anyway."

Littlewolf said, "I don't know how I can ever repay you and your friends—"

Interrupting the warden, Riker made introductions, beginning with Steve-O and ending with Shorty. "I have a place in the hills outside of town," he said. He gestured to the Bic ballpoint in Littlewolf's breast pocket. "Got something I can write on?"

As Littlewolf produced the pen, Flores pulled a scribbled-on envelope from a pocket. "Last will and testament," he said. "Looks like I won't be needing it for now."

Riker said nothing as he jotted something down on the back of the envelope. Handing it to Littlewolf, he said, "I put down the intersection near our place and the channel and sub-channel one of our two-way radios is always tuned to. You get there and need anything, give us a call."

Regarding Riker, Benny said, "We also have the long-range radios I took from the ambulance and Hickok's rig. They're not hooked up yet. I imagine I can get them working by tonight."

Littlewolf said, "If all else fails, I'll get on the radio. How about Channel 18?"

Riker nodded. "Sounds good."

Finished reloading the Shockwave, Shorty fished six shells from his pocket and gave them to Flores. "Those are all slugs," he said. "That's all I have on my person."

"Thank you, bro," said Flores. As he loaded the county-issue pump gun, the steady *snik, snik, snik* made by the shells entering the tube was drowned out by the discordant rattle of dead bodies slamming against chain-link.

Voice a bit strained, Shorty said, "Biters are getting to the gate, Lee. We better get the hell out of here."

Grasping Riker's hand, Littlewolf said, "I am in your debt. If you need anything. And I mean *anything*. Just call and I'll come running."

"Offer accepted," Riker said, shaking her hand. "Godspeed to you, Josephine." Reaching out and shaking Flores's hand, he said, "Godspeed and good luck, Roberto." Looking groundward, Riker offered his condolences as well as a heartfelt apology for not being able to arrest Carr's fall.

Littlewolf looked all around, then said, "Join me in prayer."

After the warden had said some kind words for the recently departed, she walked to the engine and climbed on up.

Patting Riker on the back, Benny said, "We have to go, Lee." Looking to Steve-O, he asked, "Shotgun or backseat?"

Steve-O hooked a thumb at the vehicles. "Where is the pretty lady riding?"

Riker said, "Lia knows Santa Fe. So she needs to navigate. Makes sense she rides shotgun with me."

Adjusting his Stetson, Steve-O said, "Then I'm riding with Shorty."

Riker asked, "You good with that, Shorty?"

Shorty regarded Steve-O. "You promise to keep the fartin' to a minimum?"

Smiling wide, Steve-O said, "I shall do my best."

Suppressing a smile of his own, Riker said, "It's settled, then. Everybody mount up."

Chapter 27

At the mouth of the Santa Fe Correctional Facility's public entry, Warden Littlewolf steered the fire engine left. As she cut the turn a bit short, the rig's rear wheels jumped the curb and rolled over a twenty-foot run of nicely manicured shrubs, leaving every one of them bent and twisted.

Seeing the shrubs being spit out from the engine's rear tires, Riker slowed the Shelby. With the EarthRoamer close on his tail, he steered left at the T and followed the engine at a respectful distance as it motored along Camino Justicio. In no time, Littlewolf's driving went from erratic to semi-controlled.

Inside the EarthRoamer, Steve-O leveled his gaze at Shorty and, without shame or a glimmer of embarrassment, said, "You have a small penis, don't you, Shorty?"

Grip tightening on the wheel, Shorty said, "That's a hell of a way to treat your Uber driver."

If Steve-O understood the rideshare reference, he didn't let on. Twisting in his seat to face Shorty, he went on, saying: "I think Lee has a small penis, too. My caregiver, Marcy, said guys drive big trucks because they have small penises. Dolly is big. The truck you stole from the new car lot was big. Marge"—he slapped a hand on the dust-covered dash—"is bigger than both of them combined." Finished lobbing accusations, he leveled a questioning look at Shorty.

Eyes on the road, Shorty said, "I'm guessing Lee calls his new race truck Dolly. Am I right?"

Smiling, Steve-O said, "I named her Dolly."

"You have the hots for Dolly Parton, eh?"

"She's a talented lady."

"Plus she has big—" Shorty began.

"—Beautiful eyes," Steve-O finished. "And her breasts are bigger than most."

Shorty said, "You know what, Steve-O? Your mouth is like a magician's hat—you never know what's going to come out of it."

Shifting his attention forward, Steve-O said, "I have never had a rabbit in my mouth."

With a block to go to the next turn, realizing the warden had no intention of stopping at the looming merger with New Mexico State Road 14, Shorty kept Marge glued to the Shelby's rear bumper.

Reaching the junction with SR-14, all three vehicles blew the stop sign. Tires screeched as they made the right turn as if they owned the road. In a way, they did own the road. Nothing had changed since Riker had last been through here. Same static vehicles dotting the shoulders. Same sea of stalled vehicles atop the elevated stretch of Interstate 25, the sun glinting off dirt-streaked automotive glass.

At Lia's urging, when Littlewolf hooked a left at the next major north-south arterial, Riker kept the Shelby tracking due east, parallel to 25, downtown Santa Fe still a few miles north by east.

Beating Riker to the punch, from the backseat, Benny said, "I thought your place is north of downtown Santa Fe. Looks like you're taking us somewhere else."

Lia said, "You drive, I'll navigate."

Riker said, "Sticking to a more direct route would burn less gas."

"Ever thought about trading this monster truck for something that gets better gas mileage?"

Riker knew instantly that Lia was trying to change the subject. He said, "You sound like my sister." He didn't go so far as telling Lia about Tara's little Smart car, but he did mention how his sister was more fiscally conscious than he and not prone to making snap decisions and then failing to divulge said decisions until trapped and left with no other option.

Lia said, "I think I'm going to like your sister."

In the next beat, Benny was in Steve-O's usual spot: elbows hooked over the seatback, head thrust into the front of the cab where the action was. "Why not take the wider roads?

More room to turn around if we come up against a roadblock or another horde of biters."

"Benny has a point," Riker said. "We have to think about Marge, too."

Navigating a bit like Riker's late mother—calling out the directions mere seconds before they had to be acted upon—Lia said, "Turn right."

For this very reason, Riker's father always hated taking driving directions from his mother. What started out as a nice Sunday exploratory drive in the Heartland usually ended in hurt feelings after several unintended stops to ask strangers for directions. Remembering that for the first time in his life he was the owner of a rig with a navigation system, Riker pointed it out to Lia. "Input your address."

"That thing still works?"

Benny said, "We've been trying to figure out why the phones are all down but not the Global Positioning System. Lee says it's because the military relies on it. I think it's just a matter of time before orbits decay and the satellites plunge to earth."

"Here we go again," Riker said. "So, Mister NASA, how long does it take for an orbit to decay? Do you know? Or are you just spouting a line from Armageddon?"

They were already several miles east of the county jail when Lia leaned forward and powered on the Shelby's SYNC system. After getting to the Navigation screen, she inputted a destination address and tapped the *GO* icon. While the computer brain worked up all of the possible routes to get there from here, she pushed the screen around with one finger until she found a point of interest to her. Unable to read the street names, she toggled the Zoom feature until the screen was dominated by a blocks-long run of a certain east-west arterial. The divided four-lane was bright red and cut through the center of a slew of sprawling campuses, each dominated by tall buildings and centrally located parking lots. After keying in on the names of individual buildings within the campuses—*Christus St. Vincent Regional Medical Center, Unity Medical Clinic, Lovelace Health Systems, Bonita Medical Center,* and *Alma Family Medicine*—Riker knew exactly what he was looking at and was wracked by an uncontrollable shiver he hoped went unnoticed by Lia and Benny.

Putting a finger on the screen and tracing it right-to-left along the entire run of red, she said, "*This* is why I took us on the scenic route."

Voice dripping with sarcasm, Benny said, "Great scenery. Abandoned automobiles, dead bodies, looted stores, and burned-to-the-ground homes. What's next on the tour? A horde of hungry zombies?"

"If we had gone anywhere near this cluster of buildings, that's exactly what we would be faced with." Lia was moving the digital map by touch as she spoke. "The dead own Saint Michaels Drive from Old Pecos all the way west to Galisteo Street. And each time I've gone out and about, their territory has grown. Better to be safe than sorry."

Riker remembered the area well. After seeing the shit show unfolding outside the hospital in Miami, running out of gas near so many possible flashpoints of outbreak had been disconcerting. It was only trumped by the lonely trek to the gas station, empty can in one hand and the big Legion tucked out of sight. Since coming back from Iraq, Riker couldn't remember feeling that exposed to imminent danger. Luckily, the brushfire that was the spread of Romero had just reached Santa Fe.

Wisely keeping the "*running out of gas" story* to himself—mainly because he didn't want to give Lia more anti-Shelby ammo—Riker asked her if there really were any auto parts or home and garden concerns nearby.

"We're almost there," was all she said.

Having been focused mostly on looking down the side streets as they blipped through intersections, Benny said, "I hope they're close to here because I'm starting to see more and more deadheads the farther north we go."

Lia's home address was represented on the screen by a tiny icon. It was tucked dead center in a subdivision a few blocks north and east of the outermost campus of the cluster of buildings she had just pointed out.

Eyes back to watching the road ahead, Riker asked, "Are you going to be safe there all alone?" He paused long enough to follow her next blurted direction. "I mean, you do live alone, right?"

Smiling, Lia said, "I see that chivalry is not dead." Looking across the seat at Riker, she went on, "Screw the PC crap. I think it's sweet that you care about my well-being. Are you taking a liking to me, Lee Riker?"

Riker felt a sudden warmth spreading up from his collar. The slow creep brought on by the embarrassment of being found out continued up his neck, then spread to his cheeks and forehead. *Showing your cards prematurely. Good going, Lee.* Thankful for the coverage his hat and blood-matted beard provided, he said, "I'd ask the same thing if you were a man." Of course that was a lie. If Lia were a man, Riker would probably stop and offer a fist bump and a curt "Good luck" while thinking *Hurry up* followed by *Don't let the door hit ya where the good Lord split ya.*

But Lia was *all woman*, and *hell yes* he was *"taking a liking to her."* But he was rusty as hell at this game. So he answered with a Cro-Magnon-like grunt.

Playing the wingman role, Benny interjected himself into the conversation. "Do you live alone?"

She said, "I do now," then proceeded to tell Riker to turn right and park at the curb. A beat later she was pointing to a one-level adobe the color of strained yams. It sat on a sloped lot and was crowded in on both sides by larger homes built in the same architectural style. Both homes looked to be recent additions to a part of town dominated by smaller homes surrounded by ample yards. The gate at the bottom of the stairs and wrought iron bars on the windows and front door to Lia's place spoke volumes to the neighborhood's previous disposition.

The rest of Lia's street was more of the same: half a dozen newer homes, all twice the size of her little casa. The block sloped upward at a shallow angle and ended at a car-choked cul-de-sac. If anyone was alive in any of the surrounding homes, they certainly weren't parting curtains or opening doors to show their faces.

Throwing the transmission into Park, Riker scanned the mirrors. Since the EarthRoamer had yet to enter the picture, he said, "I didn't see any of the places we talked about. Is there a Home Depot close by? Maybe an AutoZone?"

"There's a strip mall not too far from here. A mom and pop hardware store is tucked in there with a few other businesses. If it hasn't already been looted, I'm pretty sure you'll find everything you need there."

Riker was about to ask Lia for directions when sun glinting off glass drew his eye to the side mirror. It was Shorty's rig turning the corner. As Riker watched, the EarthRoamer came to a complete stop. In the passenger seat, Steve-O seemed to be leaning forward and craning to see something on the driver's side of the truck. The *something* appeared a tick later. It was a jacked-up 4x4 pickup, red with white racing stripes down the hood. It rolled up on the larger truck fast, left-to-right on Shorty's side, then skidded to a complete stop.

Since Riker couldn't see enough to know who was in the 4x4 or what danger Shorty and Steve-O may be in, he drew the Legion and elbowed his door open. Before he exited the Shelby, the 4x4's engine revved high into the RPM band and the pickup's oversized knobby tires chirped as it sped off, leaving behind a lingering cloud of blue-gray smoke.

Staring out the back window, Glock drawn and aimed at the floor, Benny said, "That was a short-lived encounter."

After turning a quick three-sixty and determining he wasn't being stalked by anything, living or dead, Riker fished the radio from his pocket. Thumbing the Talk button, he said, "What was that all about?"

Shorty came back right away. "A couple of twentysomething kids brandishing cheap pawn-shop pea shooters. Didn't see them on my six until I slowed for the turn. By that time, it was stop there or drive forward and chance getting you all dragged into whatever they were planning."

Lia was on the edge of her seat, literally, and staring at Riker through the open door.

"What do you think they were after?" Riker asked.

Shorty said, "They wanted Marge. No doubt about it."

Though Riker thought he knew the answer to his next question, he still wanted to hear it from the horse's mouth. "What'd you do to change their minds so quickly?"

Shorty said, "I showed them Shocky's lead-spittin' end." He paused. "Didn't hurt that Steve-O here was mean-mugging them. Should have just ran down my window and let him spring the *penis inquisition* on them."

Riker said, "I've been on the deadly end of that thing. Muzzle's big as a manhole cover when it's in your face. And don't get me started on the penis thing. I too have been on the receiving end of Steve-O's penis inquisition."

Shorty asked, "Is Lia's place the one sandwiched between the new builds?"

"Yeah," Riker said, sounding tired. "Figure I'll escort her across the street and make sure nobody's inside before we leave her here alone."

Arms hooked over the seatbacks, Benny regarded Lia. "You have a gun ... right?"

She nodded. "It's inside. Under my bed."

Lot of good it does there, Benny thought. Speaking to Riker, he said, "I'll wait with the truck."

"Watch the houses. Focus on windows and doors," Riker said. "If you see anything at all ... hit me on the radio."

Benny flashed a thumbs-up and started scanning their surroundings.

Pressing the Talk key, Riker said, "Shorty. You there?"

"Standing by."

"Watch the road," Riker said. "Warn me right away if you see those kids coming back around."

"You got it," Shorty said. "Just don't leave us hanging for too long. If those kids do come back, it'll be with reinforcements and better firepower."

Riker had already taken that into consideration but hadn't thought it necessary to say in front of Lia.

"In and out," Riker said. "Two minutes, tops." On the way out of the Shelby, he reminded Benny to lock the doors.

Chapter 28

Riker pocketed his radio, drew the Legion, and followed Lia across the street. He had her pause on the sidewalk, where they spent a few seconds scrutinizing the adobe's front elevation.

"Is everything just how you left it?"

"We'll know real soon," she said cryptically. "Let's go."

A minute after exiting the Shelby, Riker was following Lia up the double stack of stairs, his prosthesis creaking with every step, and a dull ache starting deep within his stump.

He tried his best to keep his eyes downcast as they scaled the steps. It proved to be a monumental task, what with Lia's contour-hugging running attire. The one time he did sneak a peek, he found himself wondering where in God's name she was keeping her house key.

Only when Lia had reached the second of two landings and was standing oblique to Riker did he lift his gaze.

Hanging from the tiny porch roof was a set of bamboo wind chimes. Someone had had the foresight to silence them with rubber bands.

On the landing by Lia's feet was a week's accumulation of the local newspaper. They were folded up and stuffed into clear plastic bags. Though Riker couldn't read any of the old headlines, he knew in those last days none of the news was good.

Before the front door was a colorful welcome mat. It was emblazoned with the ubiquitous Olympic rings and the word: *BIATHLON*.

On a rickety chair next to the door sat a ceramic planter filled with different species of cacti.

A thin coating of dust covered everything. Imprinted in the dust on the landing was a set of footprints. They had been made by the last person to leave the house. A closer look told

Riker the pattern matched the new tracks left on the stairs by Lia's shoes.

Riker asked, "Is this the only door you use to come and go?"

She nodded. "First thing I did when I got home was to barricade the shit out of the back slider. Used some plywood my father had stored in the garage. Put it up with masonry screws he'd left behind."

Why just the one set of prints leaving the house, then? Riker wondered. She'd talked as if coming and going was a regular occurrence.

Parting a pair of cacti with one hand, Lia extracted a single bronze key from the dirt between them.

Though the lack of foreign footprints on the landing was a good indicator the place was as Lia had left it, that might not be the case next time she ventured out. "How do you know you're the only one who has come and gone?"

She pointed out the footprints on the landing.

Good job, Riker thought.

She went up on her tiptoes and plucked something from high up on the door and jamb. Dangling a strand of her own hair in front of Riker's face, she said, "This is my backup. If it's gone, so am I. In a heartbeat."

As Lia worked the key in the lock, Riker asked, "Where'd you learn that trick?"

She pushed in the door. Craning around the door's edge, she said, "A James Bond movie."

Riker said, "I'm impressed."

"Girls watch action movies, too."

Riker thought, *She's a keeper,* and stepped into the house. No sooner had he set foot on the tiny tiled foyer and closed the door behind him than Benny's voice emanated from the radio in his pocket. Though the volume was low, he could detect stress in the friend's voice.

"All good in there?" Benny asked.

"Be out in a minute or two," Riker replied. Turning to Lia, radio in one hand, gun in the other, he said, "Let me do a quick walkthrough. Then I'll be out of your hair."

Pointing to the boarded-over sliding door, Lia said, "We're alone. Be right back," and struck off down the only hall in the tiny home.

Even in the dim light, Riker could make out the home's entire layout from where he stood. The living room was on his left: low couch of Scandinavian design. Funky paper lanterns hanging from the ceiling. An economically sized flat-screen television atop a white ash stand.

In the far corner was some kind of palm. It was a vibrant green, perfectly symmetrical, and nearly as tall as Riker. Nearly every flat surface in the living room was taken up by a different type of houseplant. Clearly, Lia had a green thumb.

The galley-style kitchen was off to the right. Beyond the small kitchen, set up in front of the plywood-covered sliding door, was a glass-topped dining table and two chairs.

The short, narrow hallway running straight off the living room, to what Riker guessed was Lia's bedroom and the only bathroom in the joint, was covered by framed pictures of people enjoying the outdoors. The abundance of snow in the photos told Riker that Lia was a fan of winter sports.

While Lia was in the other room, Riker got Shorty on the radio.

"The kids in the pickup come back?"

After a warble and short burst of squelch, Shorty said, "Negative. But we do have a few slow movers coming to investigate. I'll handle them if they get too close. You're good for a few more minutes, I'd guess." There was a pause. Then Shorty snickered and asked, "What are you two doing in there, anyways?"

Not surprised in the least by the juvenile question, Riker changed the subject. "You never did say how you scored yourself a six-figure ride."

"You didn't ask," Shorty said. "Thing set the previous owners back a cool quarter mil. Found the invoice in their belongings."

Riker said, "That's a chunk of change. More than some homes."

Shorty came back right away. "You could say it fell in my lap. Started out as your classic damsel in distress thing. Young woman by the side of the road waving a gas can."

"With all that's going on, you stopped for her?"

"Of course I stopped," Shorty said. "She was *hot*. And I had plenty of room in the Tahoe."

Riker said, "She was the distraction, right?"

"Yep. When I stopped and ran my window down, her man showed up from behind the guardrail across the way. There was a creek beyond. And some trees. He was hiding out of sight, down the embankment."

"He was armed?"

"Dumb shit had an old hunting rifle pointed at me. Found out after it all went down that he didn't even have a round chambered."

"Did she draw on you?"

Shorty chuckled. "She had a little .38 snubby revolver. Waving it around like a crazy person as she ordered me to get out. Must have seen *Pulp Fiction* one too many times."

"You shot her, didn't you?"

"While I was running the passenger window down, I hit the windshield wipers. Sprayed a good dose of the soap on the window so the boyfriend couldn't see me. It was all the diversion I needed. Brought Shocky up over the window channel and blasted her. Snubby went flying from her hand. Her scalp went the other direction."

Riker said, "What did boyfriend do?"

"He started moving toward my window," Shorty said soberly. "So I shot him, too. Couple of bandits gone to meet their maker. No sweat off my sack."

"Where'd they have the EarthRoamer stashed?"

"Behind a copse of trees just off the road. She was nearly out of fuel. Except for some ramen and a couple of cans of SpaghettiOs, the cupboards were empty. I got a feeling those two were worse at logistics than they were at highway robbery."

Riker cast a quick glance down the hall. Saw shadows flitting across the interior wall. Figuring Lia was changing to different clothes before seeing him out the door, he thumbed the Talk key and asked, "Where do you think they stole it?"

"Paperwork from the glovebox leads me to believe it belonged to a retired couple from Michigan. All the blood I found in the camper suggests they were killed for it."

Riker said, "Too much of that going on." He signed off. Pocketing the radio, he took a couple of tentative steps toward the hall entrance. New sounds coming from the doorway on the left made him think of someone stuffing clothes into an Army-issue duffel bag.

Chapter 29

When Lia emerged from her room at the rear of her tiny adobe home, Riker learned he wasn't far off in his assessment of her stuffing things into an Army-issue duffel bag. She had changed into worn blue jeans and was shrugging a black overstuffed vest on over a gray Wellesley College sweatshirt. Slung over each shoulder was a large sports bag bearing the Olympic logo and the words *Olympic Training Center, Lake Placid, New York.*

Clutched in her right hand was a long, narrow case. It was black and plastered with colorful stickers suggesting it had traveled all over the world.

Riker said, "Looks like we have a change of plans."

Lia said, "Is that OK?"

"I have to ask you a couple of questions. Might want to sit."

Lia set the bags down. She took a seat on the couch, a questioning look on her face.

"Today is the first day you've been out and about since this thing started, right?"

After a short uneasy silence, Lia nodded. "I finally ran out of food." A slight tilt to her head, she asked, "What gave me away?"

"There's a week or so worth of dirt on your porch and stairs. If you had been going out on a regular basis there would be more than one set of tracks on your porch."

"While the story about me coming face to face with the zombie in the store was the truth, I'm not as adventurous as I led you to believe."

"Were you telling me the truth about the FEMA facility?"

"Half-truth."

"What really happened?"

"These three assholes ran me down with their car. Boxed me in by a bus stand. There was no way I could outrun them on my bike. Before I could dismount and make a break on foot, one of the guys had a gun on me." Tears welled in her eyes. "I didn't know what to do."

"Probably did the right thing," Riker said. "You're still breathing." He was about to ask her what happened next when Shorty came on over the radio.

"You two breaking in a new mattress?"

Riker didn't answer.

Flashing a wan smile, Lia said, "Ask him if he wants to watch."

"We don't want to get Shorty started. He's a good guy, but he's got a few rough edges."

"A few?"

The look Riker gave her could mean only one thing: *We are not done here.* He said, "Then what happened?"

She wiped the tears on a sleeve. "There were three of them. Two guys and a woman. They were all a few years older than me. Based on their clothes ... early thirties, I'd guess. They were out scavenging. Car was full of food and stuff. One of the guys tied me up with a scarf. They left her holding a knife on me while they ranged ahead. They must have only had one gun among them because that's all I saw. Just a little pistol."

"You don't really have a gun under your mattress?"

She shook her head. "No. But I keep my rifle under the bed."

Riker sighed. "So where'd the guys go off to?"

"The FEMA facility was a block away. They were both wearing netting with leaves and twigs stuck everywhere."

"Ghillie suits," Riker stated. "Snipers use them to stay hidden from the enemy. The foliage breaks up their silhouette. So the dead got the dumbasses and then she let you go?"

Lia bit her lip. Speaking slowly, she said, "The guys were pretty stupid about it. They opened the gate and then sprinted across the street to hide. That was their entire plan. Last thing I saw was the two of them slipping into some bushes next to a short wall in front of the Park and Ride. I guess they were thinking the bush suits would fool the roamers. It didn't. I heard one of them scream and then start calling for his mom. The other one emptied his gun into the things."

"He got away?"

"Nope. He dropped it and curled into a ball on the ground. It was all over in seconds."

Riker picked up the bags, then beckoned for Lia to rise. "What happened to *her*?"

"The guys dying freaked her out really bad. But not enough to let me go. She had more friends she wanted me to *meet*." The tears were back, rolling down her cheeks and leaving dark spots on her sweatshirt. "I had already worked loose the end of the scarf she had tied around my wrists. When she looked away, I grabbed the knife." She was shaking her head now. Fists balling up, she went on, saying: "We struggled in the front seat of the car for a bit. I was stronger. Turned the knife around and she got stabbed in the neck."

"She bled out?"

"Thirty seconds and she was gone. Eyes open and just staring."

Riker said nothing. Just stood there in disbelief that the young woman was a killer.

"The dead heard her scream," Lia said. "They were coming. Half a block away. So I went around to her side and pulled her out. By this time she was already coming back. Reanimating is what I guess you could call it. She must have already been infected. Maybe she was hiding it from the guys. She seemed tentative around them anyway. Like maybe she'd been in my shoes at one time and they broke her down."

"As far as I know the only way to get the virus is to be bitten by one of the infected. You didn't see any evidence she'd been bitten?"

Lia shook her head. "Nothing. Then again, I didn't check her for one. So I can't be sure."

"You were on foot when I first saw you." He paused, thinking. "Why not take their car?"

She flashed him a sheepish look.

Incredulous, Riker said, "You don't know how to drive?"

"I do. But not a stick shift. All I've ever driven have been automatics. Up until this situation, I biked everywhere." She shook her head. "I tried. Couldn't get it going."

Riker literally palmed his face. Peering through parted fingers, he said, "Let's go. You can explain the long gun in the case and your Olympic ties once we're underway."

"I can come? Even though I lied to you?"

Riker nodded. "I think you and Tara and Rose are going to get along just fine."

She said, "Shorty?"

Riker said, "Leave Shorty to me."

Lia stopped Riker by the door. "I have something else to tell you."

Brows arched, Riker said, "What is it?"

She took a key off a nearby shelf. It was all by itself on a plain ring. She said, "I was supposed to be checking the mail for the Lins up the street. Turning their porch light on and off each day while they were vacationing in Chicago."

Riker said, "Power's been out for a couple of weeks. I'm sure the mail delivery ceased for good about the same time."

Lia said, "Finding food was high on your list." She sighed. "The Lins have five kids. Two of them were away at college. Of the three who are still at home, two are *teenage* boys. Plus ... don't take this the wrong way, they're Mormons. I'm pretty sure they have a fully stocked pantry. At least they're supposed to, right?"

"I don't know about all that. I didn't know any in Indiana." He parted the curtains and checked the street. *Clear.* Regarding Lia, he went on. "So you think they actually went on their trip and didn't make it home?" This caused Riker to think about what New York looked like just days after the terrorist attack that started the outbreak in Manhattan. If the Lins were in Chicago when it went down, the only way they were getting back to New Mexico was in a rental car. Planes were grounded early on. It was also highly likely passenger trains had been sidelined so the DoD could rail vital pieces of armor and command vehicles to flashpoints of infection.

"I wasn't here the day they were supposed to leave. I was still in the mountains." She took a deep breath. "I honestly have no idea if they went on their trip."

"Are their cars in the driveway?"

She nodded. "That doesn't mean much, though. They usually take an Uber or call a taxi van to take them to the airport."

Riker looked at the ceiling and exhaled. "I see what you're getting at. You think they could still be in there. Hunkered down with all their food and hoping to ride this out."

"Or—" she began.

"One of them became infected and the house is now full of biters," he finished.

She said, "Exactly. But I couldn't summon the courage to go up the street to check on them."

"Then let's do it together."

Lia cocked her head. It was clear there was a battle being waged inside her. After a few seconds, she closed her eyes and bowed her head. "OK. We can knock. We knock and see if anything is in there. See who or what comes to the door."

Nodding, Riker radioed ahead to inform the others of the sudden change in plans.

Chapter 30

Trinity House

From the living room to the bottom of the steep, narrow run of stairs, Tara guessed she had descended at least twenty feet. The stair treads wore a thin layer of dust that had gone undisturbed until Rose had ventured down. The dust and cobwebs suggested to Tara that the room hadn't been visited in a long while.

Whereas the grand living room above Tara's head was circular, the wide-open space before her was rectangular, with the wall the stairs were anchored to being one of the short sides of the rectangle.

The wall to Tara's fore was taken up by eight cathode-ray tube television monitors. A long shelf below the wall-mounted monitors was cluttered with desktop computers and all manner of electronic components whose purpose she didn't immediately recognize.

As Tara waited for Rose to join her at the bottom of the stairs, she let her gaze wander the room. Plastic milk crates filled with books and papers were scattered about the poured cement floor. The wall behind her, a counterpart to the one bristling with monitors, was plastered with maps and newspaper articles. The articles seemed to be assembled in chronological order. One headline from the mid-80s screamed about a major stock market plunge that was purported to be the downfall of the United States as a major world power. Another detailed the lightning invasion of Kuwait by Saddam's forces. Next to it was a full-page spread with a photo showing dozens of American tanks assembled and awaiting the beginning of Operation Desert Storm. Near the midpoint of the wall were clippings of the bombing of the Marine barracks in Beirut, Lebanon. Another spoke of the terrorist attack on the *U.S.S. Cole* and showed a photo of the badly damaged destroyer which had been attacked in 2000 while refueling in the port of Aden in Yemen.

A full third of the wall was dedicated to the 9/11 attacks and our Nation's response to that awful day in American history. Tara was especially moved by a front-page photo showing the towers burning after being hit by the second passenger jet.

Dead center on the same wall was a square sign warning against the dreaded Y2K bug. Someone had drawn a black X across the sign. Funny, thought Tara, because, at the time, both of her late parents had been especially concerned about a societal collapse resulting from the dreaded coding anomaly that had been poised to affect computer operating systems the world over.

Large clocks, each displaying a different time in red digital numerals, were mounted at uniform intervals high up on the wall. The first four were set to the United States' time zones and labeled **Pacific - Los Angeles**, **Mountain - Santa Fe**, **Central - Chicago**, and **Eastern - Washington D.C.** Clock number five was set to Moscow time. The clock taking center stage was labeled **Greenwich, England - Zulu Time**. The other clocks were also labeled and displaying the current times in Berlin, West Germany; Jerusalem, Israel; Riyadh, Saudi Arabia; Seoul, South Korea; Beijing, China; and Canberra, Australia.

On the wall underneath the clock showing Zulu time was a small, square sign bearing the easily identifiable radiation symbol known as a trefoil.

All of the evidence Tara had seen so far led her to believe the place was indeed a panic room, only the particular reason for panic wasn't necessarily of the two-legged variety. This hundred-by-fifty-foot cement tomb was to serve one purpose: save whoever had designed it from the immediate effects of a nearby nuclear detonation.

Reaching the bottom step, Rose said, "Cool space, huh? What do you think? Was this a CIA safe house or something?"

Tara shook her head. "Nope," she said matter-of-factly, "it's a fallout shelter. Judging by the fact that one of the clocks is dedicated to West Germany, it's been here a long time. It may have been here long before the house was built."

Hands on hips, Rose said, "Pretty impressive."

Tara said, "Agreed. It's pretty low on tech, though." Figuring the televisions were top of the line in the year 2000, she crunched some numbers. "I wasn't even voting age when those televisions were new."

Rose said, "Beggars can't be choosers."

"Good point," Tara said. She glanced at the top of the stairs. Dozer was there, peering down at them. Clearly, his short legs and the high-rising stairs were not a good match. Regarding Rose, she said, "I guess in realtor speak this *would* be considered a bonus room." Rose shrugged. "Seeing as how our agent didn't mention it," Tara added, "I'm good calling it a *freebie* room."

Pointing toward the concrete ceiling some ten feet over their heads, Rose said, "When I was down here earlier, I noticed these pipes. What are they for?"

Tara shielded her eyes against the fluorescent lights. "Clean air? Water?" she speculated. "I bet Lee would know."

Rose said, "We should call him."

"When he called earlier, he said he was on the edge of his radio's reach. They're well out of range by now," Tara answered. Eyes following the pipes, she walked the length of the room, then stopped before a large oak desk pushed up against the wall furthest from the stairs. All of the pipes converged above the desk and disappeared into the wall.

"Those have got to be for bringing clean air in. I bet there's one for purging the bad air. Wires are probably routed through another of the pipes."

Rose said nothing. She seemed fixated on a bookshelf brimming with well-worn paperbacks.

Tara regarded the desk before her. Instead of the usual office accoutrements, the desktop was home to books, piles of gun and hunting magazines, and what looked like more maps. She stooped and brushed dust from the map atop the pile. She waved the dancing motes from her face, then let her eyes roam the *map*.

The map was actually a blueprint. A little more scrutiny told Tara she was looking at plans for a subterranean structure. There were eight sheets in total. Each sheet was labeled **LAZARUS** at the top and roughly the size of the desktop— maybe three feet by five. Underneath the stack of plans, she found a pair of topographical maps. A to-scale overhead of Trinity House was located centrally on the first map. The circular patch of ground Tara had been working on getting cleared was also depicted. And once again Lee had been right: The crisply drawn circle sprouting well-defined paths to the southwest and northeast was labeled **HELIPAD**.

She said, "The agent didn't mention *any* of this, either," then moved the top page aside. The second topo-map was of the land behind Trinity House. When both topo-maps were aligned, the path shot northeast from Trinity House, then followed a perfect diagonal tack that took it through the helipad and all the way to a to-scale overhead shot of the bunker on the blueprints.

Holy shit, thought Tara, *I hope these plans are more than someone's pipe dream.* Then her stomach churned at the notion that a former owner of Trinity House may now be calling this Lazarus place home.

Rose had been powering on the monitors. Displayed on the slightly rounded screens were color images piped in from the perimeter cameras. Turning to Tara, she said, "Check this out. These are showing the same camera views as the monitors upstairs. There's a bank of radios, too." In her hand was one of the books taken from the shelf. "Ever heard of Jerry Ahern?"

Tara took the book from Rose. "The Survivalist," she said, turning it over in her hand. "Now we know where Mr. Nuclear Bomb got his inspiration." She tapped a finger on the plans. "I think this little hideout of his is just the tip of the iceberg. If this Lazarus place is real, our man was keeping some mighty big secrets from his next of kin who inherited the place."

Chapter 31

The Lins' home was a two-story McMansion positioned at the end of the cul-de-sac. It was the largest of the four homes crowding the turnaround. The main body of the house was a vibrant shade of orange. The trim and shutters were mustard-yellow. Capping it all off was a multi-pitched red-tile roof. Riker got the notion the person who'd chosen the color scheme was a fan of desert sunsets.

A long run of stairs led to the wide front porch. The porch was cluttered with bagged copies of the Santa Fe New Mexican and, like Lia's tiny porch, bore the same thin layer of dust.

Standing before the oak front door, Lia lifted the lid to the mailbox. "There's nothing to bring in," she declared. "What now?"

Riker and Benny were to the right of the door and searching for a seam in the shades behind the huge picture window.

Benny said, "I got nothing. Curtains are drawn tight."

Riker approached Lia. "You think they keep guns?"

Lia said, "How would I know?"

Riker said, "The Lins are Asian, right?"

She nodded. "What's that got to do with anything?"

Ignoring the question, he said, "And you said they're Mormon."

Lia planted her hands on her hips and glared at him.

Benny said, "What are you getting at, Lee?"

Riker asked, "Are they well off financially?"

Lia shook her head, slowly, side to side. Her high ponytail kept pace, nearly whipping Benny in the face. After giving the last question some thought, she said, "I don't know. Never really gave it any thought. They do own a couple of restaurants as well as a small bubble-tea shop." She made a sweeping gesture with both arms. "Look at the house. The Mercedes SUV. Eve's Jaguar. Plus, the oldest son drives a nearly new Audi." She nodded, exclaiming: "They're rich."

Riker said, "They have guns. Key please," and made a *gimme* motion with one hand. Clutched in his other hand was the Sig Legion. Just in case someone was home and willing to defend their castle, he had the pistol pressed tight to his right leg. If that came to pass, better to talk their way off the porch than the alternative.

Lia took a step back from the door. "Isn't this considered breaking and entering?"

Flashing a pained smile, Riker said, "When's the last time you saw a cop?"

She said, "You have a point."

Benny asked, "Do they have any pets?"

Lia nodded. "As far as I know, just fish. Since I wasn't coming back before they left town, a neighbor kid was supposed to be feeding them."

"If a cop comes," Riker said, "we are conducting a welfare check." He regarded Lia. "You were given a key, right?"

Lia shot him a *You think I'm stupid, don't you?* look. She said, "Don't you think we should at least knock? Make sure nobody is home before we go snooping around inside their house?"

Riker flashed her a thumbs-up. "Great minds. That was my next move." For good measure, given the picture window to his right, he hid the hand holding the pistol behind his back. Putting on a fake smile, he pounded on the door with a closed fist.

Nothing.

Staring at one another, they stood back from the door and listened hard for a long five-count.

"One more time," Lia insisted.

Riker shrugged, then knocked again.

Another five seconds passed.

Still nothing.

After stowing Lia's bags and rifle case in the Shelby, Riker had driven the truck down the block, swung a wide three-sixty in the cul-de-sac, and parked it in the narrowest spot in the road, leaving its grille facing the EarthRoamer, which was still parked on the corner a block distant.

Lifting the radio to his mouth, Riker said, "Shorty, Steve-O … whatcha got?"

"This is Shorty. Just a couple of nosy biters coming at us from the north. Nothing we can't handle."

"Copy," Riker said. "We're conducting a … a *welfare* check on one of Lia's neighbors."

Shorty chuckled at that. He said, "Yeah, that's the ticket. Have you met my wife, Morgan Fairchild?"

Lia said, "Old Saturday Night Live. Jon Levitz, I think."

Oh yeah, Riker thought, *you and Tara are going to get along just fine.* Speaking into the radio, he said, "We're going in. Watch our backs." Before signing off, he told Shorty to roll the radio to the next agreed-upon channel, then did the same with his radio.

Lia said, "Why do that?"

Benny said, "He's paranoid. Thinks someone could be listening."

Shooting Benny an icy look, Riker said, "It's a brave new world, my friend."

Lia said, "Aldous Huxley." When Riker didn't respond, she handed him the key. "How is your sister going to get in touch with you if the radios are on different channels?"

Riker turned the key in the lock. *Success.* Half expecting an alarm to begin wailing somewhere inside the house, he nudged the door open with his toe.

When no noise erupted from within, he said, "We're still out of range. I'll roll it back when we get closer to Trinity." Leaning in close, he whispered, "Your voice is familiar. Best if you do the talking."

The tiled foyer had a sunburst motif. An empty coat tree stood in the corner on the right. A pair of Spiderman galoshes sat on the floor under the coat tree. A stairway on the left went up to a landing, then curled to the right.

Glock in hand, Benny squeezed past Riker and Lia and took up station at the base of the stairs.

One foot in the door, Lia called, "Eve, Jim. It's Amelia. Hellooo … anybody home?" She looked to Riker for a prompt.

"Call for the kids."

Benny sniffed the air in the stairwell. "Anyone else smell that?"

While Lia called out the kids' names, Riker edged closer to Benny.

"Damn it," whispered Riker. "Something died in here."

Benny said, "Think it's the fish?"

Riker shrugged. Starting up the stairs, he said, "Let's find out." Turning back to Lia, he added, "Close the door and lock it. We'll stick together."

Bars of afternoon sun lanced through a square window high up on the wall. It illuminated the stairs all the way to the second story.

The run came to a T at a hall whose walls were adorned with photos of the Lin family. There were vacation pictures, formal school portraits, shots of Jim and Eve's wedding, and what appeared to be their honeymoon in a tropical locale.

Benny pointed to his left. At the end of the hall was a door plastered with pictures of Disney princesses. The stench was coming from that room.

Leveling the Sig at the distant door, Riker said, "I hate it when kids turn zombie."

Benny said, "I hate to be a grammar Nazi, but shouldn't it be … I hate it when kids turn into zombies?"

Lia hissed, "Who gives a shit? I want to get out of here."

Riker said, "Screw it," and walked down the hall, the stink growing stronger with each footstep. Along the way, he bypassed three other doors, all closed, and a hall that branched off toward the other side of the house, where he guessed the master suite was located.

At the end of the long hall, Riker planted his left hand on Cinderella's face and nudged the door open. After a quick turkey-peek around the door's edge, he retreated back down the hall.

Lia called, "It's Mary, isn't it?"

Benny said, "Please tell me it's only the fish."

"Neither," said Riker. "Mary had a couple of guinea pigs. That's what we're smelling."

"Good thing they had someone else feeding them," stated Lia. "I can't stand rodents."

Riker said, "Well, they dropped the ball. Poor things."

They banged on the other doors and listened hard before entering. The first two rooms were filled with boys' stuff: video game systems hooked to big-screen televisions. Both had a desk on which sat an Apple laptop and printer. The oldest boy's wall was home to posters of teen divas. Shelves lined every wall in the youngest boy's room. On the shelves were all kinds of figurines: Star Wars characters, Marvel superheroes, Funko bobbleheads, and a couple of hundred Pokémon miniatures.

The beds in the rooms were made up.

The lack of cold-weather clothes in the closets and drawers led Riker to believe the family had indeed packed for a trip to Chicago. Whether they actually made it to the airport was a separate unanswered question.

Behind door number three was a home office. The only thing in there on Riker's list was a couple of Costco-sized packages of batteries. On the wall, above framed certificates of learning, was a beautiful Katana sword.

Benny had taken the sword and scabbard off the wall and was inspecting them when Lia said, "We're here for food. And guns, I guess. We take only the things the Lins can replace if they ever come back from Chicago."

Benny put the sword and scabbard back where he found them. Finished, he said, "Fine. But I don't think they're ever coming home."

Riker said, "I think he's right. Shorty couldn't get anywhere near downtown when he went looking for his boy, Matt."

"Still," Lia said. "The Lins were real nice people. We take what we need. Leave the rest."

"She's right," Riker said. "If they have guns, we'll find them in the master or in the garage."

The master bedroom was meticulous, the bedding taut across the king bed.

They found a gun safe in the master walk-in closet.

Riker marveled at the square footage set aside for clothes and shoes. The walk-in eclipsed any bedroom he had ever called his own—at least up until he and Tara had moved into Trinity.

The safe wasn't one of the high-dollar items that weighed several hundred pounds and could survive anything you threw at it. It was the kind with an extremely low fire rating, likely secured to the joists with lag bolts. He guessed the safe's main purpose was to keep the guns out of the kids' hands.

Wishing he had also grabbed the firefighting tool when he took the Jaws of Life from the engine, Riker led the others downstairs to find the pantry and to check the garage for a crowbar or another tool suitable for breaching the safe.

They found the aquarium in the kitchen. It was a saltwater item, the heaters and pumps no longer doing their thing. The tropical fish were now a technicolor mess, rotting away at the bottom of the tank amongst a forest of stark white coral.

The pantry was off the kitchen. It held what looked like a year's worth of food. While Benny and Lia transferred everything into two-ply garbage bags, Riker ventured into the garage.

The garage was stuffed with *toys*. There was a Harley Davidson Electra Glide in the far stall—all black, the chrome gleaming even in the garage's gloomy interior. A Mercedes AMG roadster took up the near stall. Its top had been left in the down position, which put the red leather interior on full display. It must have been brand new because the instant Riker had opened the door to the garage the new-car-smell hit him full in the face.

Bikes hung from the ceiling above the Harley. Behind the big touring motorcycle was a workbench and a pair of rolling toolboxes. A quick search produced the tools Riker was looking for.

Entering the kitchen, crowbar, flat-blade screwdriver, and ten-pound sledgehammer in hand, he said, "Put the food in the Shelby and wait for me." He tossed the key fob at the pair, then hustled down the hall toward the stairway. Pausing at the front door, he stole a peek at the cul-de-sac through the peephole.

Nothing had changed. The Shelby was parked at the mouth of the turnaround. Beyond the Shelby, kitty-corner from Lia's house, the EarthRoamer threw a long shadow up the street.

One minute after entering the walk-in closet, parting the curtain of Adidas tracksuits, and slipping the flat edge of the crowbar behind the wall-mounted gun safe, Riker had it off the wall and in the center of the bedroom, where he was going to town on it with all the fervor of a fat kid trying to crack a piñata.

A sheen of sweat was beading on Riker's forehead and all of the muscles in his hands and arms were burning when a seam finally appeared between the safe's door and its main body. He worked the crowbar deeper into the narrow opening and put his right knee on the door a foot below the seam. He strained, throwing all his weight on the crowbar, and something finally gave.

There was a loud groan as the seam opened up another inch. Deciding to give it one more try, he adjusted his grip on the tool and repeated the process, this time bouncing up and down, all of his weight on the very end of the crowbar.

The sound of metal properties being irrevocably altered was followed by a loud *pop* as one of the two internal latches gave way. Now that several inches of the door had separated from the inside channel, he could see some of the contents. There were a couple of rifles in the shadowy interior. Above the rifles was a shelf containing a pair of pistols, a half-dozen different-sized magazines, and several boxes of ammunition whose calibers he couldn't discern.

With the hole opened up wide enough to accept his arm all the way to the elbow, he reached inside and removed everything from the shelf. Finished stuffing the items into an Adidas gym bag he'd found in the closet, he tilted the safe up on one end and shook it until the rifle muzzles appeared in the opening.

Threading the shotgun and AR-15 through the opening was an exercise in patience.

By the time Riker was leaving the home with the weighted-down bag in one hand and the shotgun and AR slung over one shoulder, Benny and Lia were waiting inside the Shelby and less than ten minutes had elapsed.

As Riker was stashing the Adidas bag and weapons in the bed alongside the bulging trash bags, Steve-O delivered an ominous message over the radio.

Chapter 32

The moment Riker heard Steve-O say, *"The kids are back and they brought friends,"* his gut clenched. Not because he was scared, though; it was the block of separation between his position and Shorty's EarthRoamer that troubled him.

As he dragged the liberated AR back out into the light, he was already thumbing the Talk button. "Can you guys close the distance to us?"

Steve-O said, "Shorty says he's on it. He also said this time we are going to have to shoot first and ask questions later. Is that true, Lee Riker?"

"I'm afraid Shorty is right, Steve-O. You keep your head down. You hear?"

Steve-O said, "Yeppers," then added, "sure wish I had the Mosquito."

"Just listen to Shorty. Do what he says." Riker banged on the tonneau, shouted, "Get out and gun up!" and dropped the radio into his pocket. Looking toward the main road, he saw that Shorty had already performed a J-turn. The EarthRoamer's brake lights flared red for a second, then went dim when the white backup lights snapped on.

Doors opened and closed and the others joined Riker at the Shelby's open tailgate. While the slab-sided pickup offered both concealment and cover, if the kids and their friends were armed for bear—as Riker feared they were—it wouldn't provide the three of them nearly enough of the latter.

A play-by-play of what was happening down the street emanated from the radio in Riker's pocket. Steve-O said, "They are shooting at us." There was a break in the transmission. A tick later, when the connection was re-established, engine noise and Shorty cussing at the shooters came out of the speaker. In the next beat, a pair of loud booms overrode everything.

Seeing the Glock in Benny's fist, Riker instructed him to
go back into the cab and fetch for him the F4 Defense Small
Frame AR-10 he'd purchased at the gun store in Florida. The
Leupold scope atop the carbine was already zeroed in. And while
Riker had been doing his best to conserve ammo, he'd practiced
with the rifle enough to know that, if push came to shove, he
could put on target most, if not all thirty of the .308 Win rounds
in the F4's magazine.

Riker looked up long enough to see that Shorty had
stopped the EarthRoamer a few yards from the T with its wide
rear end facing the cul-de-sac. The driver-side door was open.
Shorty had one foot on the running board and a knee planted on
the door's elbow rest. His upper body was in the pinch point
between the door and A-pillar, with the Shockwave horizontal to
the hood and belching fire at something up the street.

Though most of the little man's body was shielded by
his vehicle, the shooting angle was awful. If he hadn't already
accidentally peppered the hood or windshield with buckshot, or
put a slug into the engine compartment, it was only a matter of
time before he did.

Worry crept in as Riker inserted a full magazine into his
custom AR's magwell. As he racked the charging handle back, he
hoped he hadn't jinxed himself earlier with his *When's the last time
you saw a cop?* statement. Last thing he needed now was to have to
justify a bunch of bodies in the street and then explain how all of
the Lins' food and weapons made their way into his truck.

Gesturing at the liberated AR-15—a Colt LE6920—Lia
said, "I'm a pretty good shot."

"I'm sure you are," Riker said. "No doubt about it. But
we're talking people here, not targets." He trained his carbine's
business end down the street and switched the selector to Fire.

Voice wavering, Lia said, "I already killed once today. I
will do it again if I have to." She picked up the Colt. Having
watched Riker with his AR, she seated a magazine, then pulled
the charging handle.

There was a metallic *snik-snik* as a round was chambered.

"It's semiautomatic," Riker said. "Safety's on the left.
You have thirty rounds. You'll know you're out when the bolt
locks open."

Lia set the AR on the ground by the Shelby's right rear
tire, got down on her knees, then went prone behind the rifle,

snugging the buttstock to her shoulder, trigger finger where it should be: horizontal above the trigger guard.

Riker said, "Don't shoot until I give the word." Regarding Benny, he added, "Be ready to jump in the truck when I say. Should one of us get hit, the other is driving."

Benny said nothing. His slack-jawed expression did the talking for him. Even though he'd been shot recently, the life and death seriousness of the zombie apocalypse was just now beginning to dawn on him.

A couple of seconds after the last shotgun report rolled up the road and echoed about the cul-de-sac, a whole bunch of things happened at once.

As the EarthRoamer resumed reversing toward the Shelby, a compact car slow-rolled around the corner, then crashed into a tree, its engine still revving. The compact's windshield was spiderwebbed, the driver unmoving and draped over the steering wheel.

White dust from the airbag deploying still danced about the driver's head and shoulders.

Again Steve-O's voice came out of the radio: "A pickup truck and a black SUV is chasing us. Shorty says he is going to squeeze Marge past Dolly. He says *do not* fire until we are out of the way."

Copy that, thought Riker, his trigger finger getting itchy. Out of the corner of his eye, he saw Lia looking up at him. As he established eye contact with her, she mouthed, "Marge? Dolly?"

Riker shook his head. "Long story."

Down the street, tires squealed and a jacked-up pickup appeared. It was the same one described by Shorty. As the lifted ride took the corner, it wallowed like a small boat in rough seas. On the pickup's tail was a shiny black Cadillac Escalade still wearing dealer plates. All of the windows save for the windshield had been given a limo tint. The baby-faced African American behind the wheel was grinning like a madman.

As soon as the pickup straightened out, the Cadillac accelerated and formed up on its right side.

Riker looked grimly at the approaching vehicles. "Wait," he barked. "Do *not* shoot. Let Shorty get his rig past Dolly's front fender. I'll get the pickup. You two focus on the Cadillac. " He watered down his language on purpose. "Get" and "focus" carried a less-lethal connotation than words like "engage" and "target." The Cadillac's deeply tinted windows informed Riker's decision to assign it to Benny and Lia. Out of sight, out of mind. He only hoped those windows kept the targets hidden until the entire engagement was beyond the point of no return.

"Understood," said Benny.

Lia nodded and flashed a thumbs-up.

As the vehicles halved the distance to the mouth of the cul-de-sac, Riker's hopes were dashed when the Escalade's windows rolled down and people with weapons appeared where the impenetrable black glass had been.

It was a diverse group. A Hispanic teen rode shotgun. As he emerged, pointing some kind of pistol over the side mirror, the slipstream whipped the tails of the red bandanna atop his head into a frenzy.

An Asian kid, also likely not old enough to vote, filled up the window behind Bandanna. Though Riker couldn't be certain, the weapon the kid was bringing to bear appeared to be some kind of pump shotgun.

Behind the driver, an obese white girl wriggled her upper body through the open window. Her shock of brilliant blue hair whipped by the wind, massive breasts barely constrained by a white tank, the young woman roared something unintelligible, raised a boxy black pistol, and opened fire.

A bullet crackled over Benny's head. As he ducked instinctively, a second round snapped the air to his left, grazing his bicep. Wincing in pain, he called to Riker. "You are aware we're trapped here, right?"

Riker said nothing. He was focused on keeping his lower body still and the crosshairs parked squarely on the face of the young man at the wheel of the pickup. The wall of wind pushed by the squared-off EarthRoamer hit him in the face a tick before the big vehicle reached the Shelby's left front fender. Pushing Benny's warning from his mind, Riker said, "Now," and pressed the trigger.

The recoil was minimal as the first round left the muzzle traveling 2,600 feet per second.

The damage inflicted on the pickup's windshield didn't show until Riker was six rounds deep into the thirty-round magazine. When the windshield finally bowed inward, the driver had gone totally limp, his cratered head hinged all the way back and resting on a pillow of his own brains.

With the driver out of commission, Riker walked his fire toward the passenger, whose face was a mask of concern. *Nothing like the movies*, he thought as some of his rounds found their mark.

Sorry, kids.

Rising over the hollow pops coming from Benny's Glock was the reassuring sound of Lia's AR entering the fray. With the pickup out of commission, Riker turned his attention to the speeding Escalade. The result of the Olympian's outgoing fire, directed solely at the remaining vehicle, was catastrophic and near-instantaneous.

Turned out the woman was beyond a good shot. Relying on iron sights alone, she had put two rounds through the Escalade's windshield, striking the driver squarely in the face. Her follow-on shots were just as lethal, hitting Blue Hair center mass. As two distinct crimson splotches blossomed on the young woman's tank, her upper body snapped backward, and the pistol fell from her lifeless hands. In the next beat, all the extra weight up top—whether God-given or surgically implanted—dragged Blue Hair's torso groundward.

A loud bang sounded when the shooter's upper body slapped the Cadillac's passenger door. Then, slowly, like sausage leaving the grinder, Blue Hair slithered limply from the SUV's open window. She hit the road face first and, pushed along by the SUV's forward momentum, performed a ragged somersault that left her skinned up and prostrate in the middle of the street.

In the seconds immediately following Riker's initial attack on the lifted pickup, and Lia's well-aimed barrage directed at the Cadillac, both vehicles swerved in opposing directions, crossed paths with just inches to spare, then continued on their altered courses, picking up speed until the pickup ran over the curb and collided with a low wall and the luxury SUV rode up and over a Mazda Miata parked curbside thirty feet from the mouth of the cul-de-sac.

Ignoring the pickup's death throes—revving engine and spinning tires—Riker swung the AR to the Escalade, settled the crosshairs on the passenger's red bandanna, and pressed the trigger three times in quick succession. Without pause, he shifted aim to the left a few degrees, targeted the stunned Asian kid, and repeated the process.

Seeing the Asian kid go limp and the shotgun slip from his hand and clatter to the road outside of the Escalade, Riker bellowed, "Cease fire!" Keeping his eyes glued to the static vehicles, he dumped the half-spent magazine from the AR and jammed a full one home.

To Riker's right, Lia's weapon had already gone silent. To his left, still caught up in the heat of the short, albeit one-sided battle, Benny snapped off another pair of poorly aimed rounds at the stalled-out pickup, then lowered the smoking Glock to his side.

Seeing blood leaking from the inches-long gash in Benny's jacket sleeve, Riker waved to get his attention. "How bad is it?"

Benny shrugged. "Hurts like a mofo. But nowhere near as bad as the through-and-through."

Appearing seemingly out of nowhere, Shorty filled the gap between Riker and Benny. Wide smile on his face, he said, "So much for the General Custer moment I was envisioning."

Riker was surprised, too. He'd had an idea in his head, a picture he'd built up of what the bad guys ought to look like. These kids were the farthest from that picture. No studded leather. No mohawks. They weren't meth-mouth dirtbags missing all their teeth.

It suddenly dawned on Riker that he had just participated in the wholesale slaughter of the Breakfast Club. And it had him feeling sick to his stomach.

Averting his eyes from the carnage, he said, "Out by the road. Did they really shoot at you first?"

A retching sound rose up from the Shelby's passenger side. Benny craned and made a move to investigate.

Riker extended his arm, barring Benny's passage. "It's Lia," he said. "She just killed two people. Best leave her be for a moment."

Benny clamped down hard on the superficial wound and cast a long stare down the road.

Shorty said, "With God as my witness, they shot first." He plucked some shotgun shells from a pocket and started feeding them into the Shockwave.

On the road beside the parked EarthRoamer, door just starting to swing shut behind him, Steve-O said, "Shorty is right, Lee. The driver pulled a Greedo."

The retching had ceased, but Riker could see that Lia was still prone behind the rifle, her face buried in the crook of one elbow. Regarding Steve-O, he asked, "Who's Greedo?"

Planting his hands on his hips, Steve-O walked Riker through a bit of Star Wars lore, explaining that in the Mos Eisley cantina, when the audience first meets Han Solo, he survives a near-miss blaster shot directed at him by an interstellar bounty hunter by the name of Greedo.

Hearing this, Shorty said, "Oh hell no, buddy. I saw Star Wars in the theater. Han shot first."

"Not in the Star Wars I saw," Steve-O countered.

Finished puking for the moment, Lia rose up from behind the Shelby. Wiping a hand across her mouth, she said, "Who gives a *shit* who shot first! Shouldn't we be getting the hell out of here?"

Shorty said, "I like the way Carlos Hathcock thinks." He regarded Lia. "Where the hell did you learn to shoot like that? Wow! You did about the same damage as Big Guy here." Smiling, he hooked a thumb at Riker. "And you used *half* the ammo Lee did. Great return on investment if I may say so myself."

Riker made a mental note to have Shorty explain the Hathcock statement if they got away from this scene without all going to jail. Looking to Benny and Steve-O, he said, "Batten down the hatches and get ready to roll. I'll be right back."

Incredulous, Lia said, "Where are you going?"

"I'm going to go and make sure nobody is suffering." He paused and stared at her for a second. "Are you going to be OK?"

Lia stared past Riker. A gun smoke haze hung over the cul-de-sac. After a half-beat, she nodded, her eyes never leaving the Escalade.

Riker said, "What I'm about to do is necessary. While we didn't start this, I feel obligated to finish it. Plus, if one or more of them is infected, I can't in good conscience let them reanimate." He scanned the immobile vehicles and the road behind them. Only the drivers, Red Bandanna, and Blue Hair were visible. After all of the intense action, the silence was deafening. Turning back to Lia, he said, "You're welcome to come with me."

The sudden adrenaline dump to Lia's system had her entire body shaking. She planted her hands on her knees and wagged her head side to side. "I've seen and done enough today to last me ten lifetimes. I'm staying right here."

Riker said nothing. Part of him wanted to console her. Stretch out his arms and wrap her up and draw her close to him. But he knew it wasn't his place. Probably never would be. Such was his luck. So he about-faced and strode down the street, AR at the ready position, stomach roiling at the prospect of having to dole out mercy shots.

By the time Riker reached a spot in the road where he could see inside both vehicles, he was feeling the first acidic tang of bile tickling the back of his throat. Seeing that nobody was left alive in either vehicle did nothing to relieve the rising tide of nausea.

Jaw clenched, Riker left the grisly scene and trudged on. When he finally reached Blue Hair and discovered she no longer had a pulse, he whispered, "Why couldn't you all have just left us the hell alone?"

He let his gaze roam the scene. It was only when he was back to staring at the lifeless corpse with the vibrant shock of blue hair that he realized he had just lost another small piece of his humanity and the dam was about to break.

Hot tears streaming down his cheeks, Riker planted his hands on his knees and vomited until his stomach was empty.

Chapter 33

Trinity House

Rose was standing in the kitchen, eyes glued to the monitor, one hand worrying a damp dishrag. In one of the monitor's multiple panes, a newly arrived zombie stood in the center of the cul-de-sac, lips drawn over yellowed teeth, jaw constantly moving. Like a big cat searching for prey, it panned its head left and right and back again.

"Biters can't smell, right?"

Tara seated a fresh magazine in her Glock, chambered a round, and holstered it. Regarding Rose, she said, "Huh?"

"The dead ... can they smell us?"

"Never gave it much thought," Tara replied. "I've always acted on the assumption that they hunt by sight and sound."

Rose pointed to a pane on the monitor. She said, "Looks like this one is sniffing the air."

Tara watched the thing for a beat or two. Then, turning so she faced the rear of the house, she said, "You hear that?"

Startled, Rose followed suit, whipping around and craning her neck. With a slight rearward tilt to her head, listening hard, she said, "I don't hear it." She took a step toward the hallway, where Dozer was lounging on the wood floor.

Tara said, "I was just testing a theory."

Rose returned to the kitchen wearing a quizzical look. "Care to share?"

Pocketing a bottled water, Tara said, "You looked just like that thing on the monitor."

Brows lifting, Rose said, "I don't get it."

"When you were trying to hear what I pretended to hear, your body language mirrored that thing on the monitor."

Rose shifted her attention to the monitor.

The *"thing"* had moved a few steps closer toward the driveway gates.

"Keep watching," Tara advised.

"What are you planning? You're not going out the front door, are you?"

"Just watch." Tara swiped a pitcher off the kitchen counter, filled it to the top with water from the sink faucet, then padded off toward the front door.

Rose did as she was told, but first, she quickly walked her gaze over the other eight panes. Nothing was moving around the rest of the perimeter. The camera focused on the perimeter wall door was broadcasting a macabre scene. The zombies Tara had put down earlier were still there, sprawled out in various death poses. From the looks of it, one of them—a woman in her twenties—was nearly headless. Next to the woman, lying flat on its back, an arm bent to a peculiar angle, was a kid-sized zombie. It, too, had been shot in the head. Clumps of what could only be brain tissue lay in a pile beside its ruptured skull.

The third zombie had fallen close to the wall. Due to the camera angle, all that was visible were its lower extremities. Its feet were bare, the pads worn to the bone. On one ankle, Rose saw a deep wound oozing some kind of fluid.

Zombie number four looked fairly fresh. If there wasn't the bullet wound on its forehead, it would appear as if he were taking a nap alongside a bunch of dead bodies. While Rose had heard the gunfire that caused this scene, she had averted her eyes from the monitor at the time.

Wishing she hadn't broken down and looked now, she focused on the zombie near the front gate.

Calling out from the direction of the foyer, Tara asked, "You watching?"

"Yes," Rose called back. *What are you trying to prove?* she thought, when a single gunshot-like *bang* of a door slamming had her nearly leaping out of her skin. Coinciding with the sudden noise, the zombie turned in the general direction of the front door, repeated the head-tilt thing, bared its teeth, then resumed the back and forth pan of its head.

Still watching the monitor, Rose saw Tara creep the length of the curved path connecting the front door to the circular parking pad. She flicked her eyes between panes and noticed nothing new in the zombie's behavior.

Tara didn't stop at the gate. Instead, she made her way to the pair of rolling bins pushed up against the garage. She gingerly lifted the lid to the bin dedicated for garbage, removed the bloody towels she had used to clean the pavers of Raul and Benny's blood, then threw them on the ground by her feet.

After emptying the pitcher on the towels, Tara scooped them off the wet pavers and lugged them to the wall.

A lightbulb went off in Rose's head. "Oh," she exclaimed. "Pretty damn smart." She watched Tara walk around the house. It was kind of strange how she jumped from pane to pane, blipping from one corner to another, seemingly at random, until she was in the back, by the perimeter wall door, and lifting the ladder off the ground.

As Tara retraced her steps, her image bounced from pane to pane in reverse order, until she was picked up by the camera covering the front entry, where she wasted no time erecting the ladder and arranging the bloody towels on top of the wall.

If Tara had exited Trinity House like a lion, she came back in like a lamb, closing the front door at her back with all the care of a teenager sneaking in after an unapproved nocturnal excursion.

Traversing the hall between the foyer and kitchen, Tara said, "Hey Luuucy. I'm hoooome."

The obscure *I Love Lucy* reference drew a queer look from Rose as Tara entered the kitchen. Placing the empty pitcher on the counter, Tara said, "What's Biter McBiteyface doing?"

"Nothing much. Still just standing there. I bet it's waiting to catch sight of something to eat. Or chase." She shook her head. "I hate biters. I've had enough of them to last ten lifetimes."

"You and me both," Tara said. "Did it do anything different after I put the bloody towels up there?"

Rose shook her head. "Not a thing."

"After I wet the blood dried on those towels I smelled that coppery fresh-blood odor coming off them. You'd think if the zombie hunts by smell, he'd be reacting to it by now, right?"

Nodding, Rose said, "You're going back out to work?" She bit her lip and worried the dishtowel she'd been holding.

"I'm going stir crazy in here. Plus, if Flyboy actually shows up and the pad isn't ready, I don't know where he'll land his helicopter. Especially if it's the same one Lee rented to take us to Niagara Falls."

Brows hitching, Rose said, "Why Niagara Falls?"

Tara sighed. "It's a touchy subject. I'm not quite ready to rehash it right now."

Rose said nothing.

Tara said, "I'm going to spend another hour or so cutting back saplings. After that, all that's left to do is trim back the bigger trees."

"You have *both* radios, right?"

Tara nodded. "Right here in my pocket." She tapped the monitor. "When I'm about ready to go out the back, I'll make an X with my arms. OK?"

Rose said, "OK. Then what?"

"I want you to create a diversion for me. Slam the front door hard, like I did. That should keep Bitey occupied while I slip away."

Face tightening, Rose said, "Should I try to get Lee on the radio? Find out when they'll be back?"

"Why? He's a grown ass man. He'll call when they're back in range."

Again, Rose bit her lip.

"Ohhh," Tara said, eyes widening. "You're worried about Benny." Before Rose could respond, Tara continued, saying: "You shouldn't. Lee has a knack for getting out of scrapes. Oh, the stories I could tell you."

Rose forced a smile. "Tonight, then. When they're all back. Storytime by the fire?"

Plucking the set of keys off the counter, Tara said, "Deal. You're going to be"—with her free hand she pantomimed fireworks erupting over her head—"mind blown."

Dishtowel clutched tightly in both hands, Rose said, "I want you to check in with me every fifteen minutes."

Sensing a reluctance on Rose's part to remain alone in the house—especially after finding the bunker and all the questions raised by its existence—Tara said, "Deal. And I'm leaving Dozer with you."

"Sounds good." Rose patted the radio in her pocket. "I promise I'll have this on me at all times."

"If Lee calls," Tara said, "I want you to pick it up. If he needs to talk to me, have him drop off and call back. I'll hear the second chime and pick it up."

Rose said, "Be careful."

Patting the Glock on her hip, Tara said, "Always."

Chapter 34

Northeast Santa Fe

The mini-mall containing the mom-and-pop hardware store Lia had spoken of was roughly half a mile north by east from her house. It shared a misshapen block with a number of other business concerns, all of them facing a small kidney-shaped parking lot. Bordered to the north by a divided two-lane boulevard, and the west by the main arterial that had brought them here, the parking lot was home to only two vehicles: a Jeep Grand Cherokee with faded red paint and a yellow Jeep Wrangler Rubicon whose tan canvas soft top was in complete tatters. It was pretty evident the Rubicon had been set upon by a pack of biters; the side facing the road was dented here and there and covered with bloody handprints trailing feathery crimson streaks. All that was left of the soft passenger-side door was the metal frame and some of the clear plastic that once passed for a window.

Riker pulled hard to the curb, put the radio to his lips, and thumbed the Talk button. "Keep your eyes open," he urged. "I want to get a sense of what we're getting into before we commit to entering the parking lot." *God, grant me the serenity*, he thought to himself. It was tedious work having to game every single move six ways from Sunday. He missed the days when he could just wake up, knock down his pushups, strap on the bionic, and walk to the nearest coffee shop to grab a steaming cup of joe. Now, seemingly, there was danger lurking under every metaphorical rock and in every metaphorical crevice. He imagined this must be how the Aussies felt about their existence before all this. What with all the deadly critters Down Under, every second spent in the Outback demanded one exercise extreme caution.

This new train of thought made him think of Clay, the Aussie gas attendant at the Shell station in downtown Santa Fe. What had happened to him? Santa Fe was a madhouse then. People driving like maniacs. The Smith's store overrun with panic shoppers. Hell, Santa Fe was a ghost town now. Where did everyone go?

The rumble of a diesel motor snapped Riker back to the present. Shorty had pulled the EarthRoamer to within a truck length of the Shelby's rear bumper. The vehicle cast a shadow over Riker's pickup.

Over the radio, Shorty said, "Screw glassing the place. Steve-O wants to bust out the drone. Do a little aerial recon."

"Not for this one," Riker replied. "Way to be thinking ahead, though. I'm going to glass the place. If it looks good, I'll go in on foot and get a closer look." What he wanted was a moment alone with his thoughts. Every time he closed his eyes, he saw the dead kids. The pickup driver's brains dribbling from his fractured skull. Next to him on the blood-soaked bench seat, the passenger curled into the fetal position. What the fuck were they thinking? Maybe this was their idea of living out their favorite video game. The type in which you played the bad guy, cops were the enemy, and citizens the cannon fodder. Or the kind of game where you squad up virtually with people from all over the world, then proceed to engage in digital combat for hours on end. What did they call those games? It came to him almost immediately: first-person shooters.

Sadly, in this new reality, the dead came back to life, the Thin Blue Line was nonexistent, and incoming fire was real as a heart attack. Benny the bullet magnet could attest to that. Thankfully the only medical attention he had needed this time around was a thorough cleaning and a good bandage job. All of which Riker had provided while Shorty went about siphoning gas from the Escalade and diesel from the lifted pickup.

Now, in the passenger seat next to Riker, Lia was already busy glassing the mall with the Steiners.

Benny was in the seat behind Lia, both biceps bandaged, and staring out his window at the mini-mall. Leaning forward, he perched his elbows on the front seats and turned to face Riker. "Assuming we get inside and find everything on your *big ass* shopping list ... how are we going to lug it all across the lot to the trucks? Shopping carts? I don't want to be going back and forth pushing a noisy shopping cart. There could be biters lurking about. What if those dicks we killed have more friends? Surely they'll come looking for them sooner or later. Think about it … If you found a scene like we left back there, and those were your bullet-riddled pals, wouldn't you go on the warpath? Rustle up a posse and start looking for the ones responsible? I sure as hell would." He bowed his head. His body was shaking. Clearly, he was agitated. "If that is the case," he went on, "then I don't want to take the chance of being the one who gets caught out in the open. I've a feeling my luck is spent. I've been shot twice already, Lee. Came away with flesh wounds both times. Third time I might not be so lucky."

"First of all," Riker said, a trace of annoyance in his tone, "why don't you put a little more lemonade in your glass. Positive thinking breeds positive outcomes. Secondly, my *big ass* list was about a third the size it is now before my *sister* got her hands on it." He paused and drew a deep breath. "We'll collect as many of the items on the list that we can find and pile it all near the door. Then we drive onto the lot and load it all at once."

"Minimizes our exposure," Lia said. "But who's keeping watch while we're inside?"

Riker removed his hat and rubbed his temples. Tossing the Braves cap on the dash, he said, "Maybe it wouldn't hurt to have an eye in the sky. So many moving parts, though." He drew another deep breath, then hailed Shorty on the radio.

After a burst of static, Shorty said, "What's up, boss?"

Riker said, "Steve-O may be on to something. If he can run the drone from inside your rig, I think it would be a valuable asset. I'm going to swap out the batteries and bring everything back to you."

"Take your radio," Benny said. "If we see anything, we'll let you know."

Riker said, "Sounds good. Be right back." He checked the mirrors, elbowed open his door, and stepped to the empty boulevard.

"B … R … B," Lia said, then lowered the binoculars.

As soon as the door thunked shut, Benny said, "What?"

"Be right back," she answered. "I've heard that one before." She raised the binoculars, trained them on the mall.

Benny asked, "You lost someone?"

Lia said, "M …Y … O … B."

Benny said, "Point taken. Minding my own business." He craned and looked out the back window. The tonneau cover was now hinged up and blocking everything save for his friend's head and wide shoulders. Every now and again Lee would bend over and disappear from sight. This went on for a minute or two. Finally, Lee closed the tailgate and dropped the tonneau cover back into place.

Benny turned around and checked the mirrors again. Seeing nothing moving, he turned back and watched Lee pass the remote through Shorty's open window. The two men shared some words, then Lee placed the insect-like drone on the EarthRoamer's hood.

Benny regarded Lia. "Still looking good?"

"I don't know," she answered. "Vern's is boarded over. That's going to be a problem."

"Why?"

"Because if I know Vern, like I think I know Vern, the old coot is holed up inside there."

"You know—"

The driver door opened, and the shrill whine of the drone drowned out Benny's question.

Riker climbed in, slid behind the wheel, and closed his door. Looking to Lia, he asked for the Steiners.

She said, "Looks clear to me," then dropped the binoculars into his waiting palm.

Lifting the field glasses to his face, Riker said, "Just to be certain, Steve-O is going to circle the block a couple of times with the drone and tell us what he sees."

Benny said, "Lia knows the owner. She thinks—"

Cutting him off, she said, "I can speak for myself, dude." Fixing Riker with a hard stare, she added, "I buy all my potting supplies from Vern. In fact, we're on a first-name basis."

Riker said, "You think he's in there?"

She said, "I think that's his Jeep out front."

Near simultaneously, Benny and Riker said, "Which one?"

"The red one."

"Good," Benny said. "I don't think the owner of the little Rubicon survived that attack."

Riker said, "Whatever did that to the Rubicon I'd bet is long gone." He donned his hat, collected the AR-10 from behind his seat, and went through the paces of making sure the magazine was full and a round was chambered.

Benny asked, "You still going it alone?"

Riker handed him the key fob. "If I like what I see when I get there, and Steve-O comes back with good news, you can bring her around. Probably ought to back her in next to the red Cherokee. That'll make it easier to load everything."

Lia squared up to Riker and shot him an icy glare.

Eyes going wide, Riker said, "What's this all about?"

She crossed her arms. "While I didn't expect you to ask a complete stranger, one who happens to be a *girl*, to drive your prized pickup, I *was* hoping you'd ask my opinion about Vern's."

Riker thought about it for a few seconds, then shook his head. "Has nothing to do with you being a girl. I just want to go alone. Fewer people for me to let down."

Lia's glare softened. She said, "Suit yourself, *Eli*."

Already halfway out his door, Riker turned back. "Eli?"

Benny said, "As in The Book *of ...* Eli. You know the movie, right? The one where Denzel plays the brooding loner."

Riker said, "You got it half right," then set off for the hardware store, alone with his own thoughts and saddled with guilt that he couldn't quite comprehend.

Trinity House

Tara sidestepped the fallen zombies, then turned and locked the perimeter wall door behind her. As she stood there in the open, with the map vivid in her mind's eye, she cast her gaze north, to the wall of foliage. Somewhere behind the tangle was a road. Or so the squiggle on the map suggested.

Fighting the urge to investigate, she headed off east, along the short path to the clearing. She had a job to do.

Depositing her water and bag lunch Rose had fixed for her on the clearing's edge, she felt a twinge in her lower back.

"You're thirty-two, Tara," she said to herself. "Too young to be breaking down."

Taking advice her mom had often proffered, advice Tara rarely heeded, she placed her palms on a nearby tree trunk, planted her feet a yard back from the gnarled roots, then went about stretching her hamstrings and calves. Just as she felt her back pop and some relief was achieved, she heard a much louder *pop* from somewhere off to her left. Though she wasn't aware of what was happening to her, a millisecond after hearing the out of place noise she was hit in the left side, just below the armpit, by twin steel-barbed darts. In the next beat, thousands of volts coursed into her body via a thin insulated copper wire. As the modulated current wracked her body, causing temporary neuromuscular incapacitation, she tasted metal on her tongue and was falling face-first against the tree.

Her eyes involuntarily rolled into the back of her head. With the ongoing internal explosion of electrical current clenching her fingers and limbs, she crashed to the ground, the pile of cut branches providing a semi-soft bed for her twisting body to land on.

As a cloth was pressed over her nose and mouth, she caught a fleeting glimpse of a pair of black boots entering her field of view. It was the last thing she saw as her vision blurred and she was plunged into an all-encompassing shroud of darkness.

Chapter 35

Northeast Santa Fe

Vern's Hardware and Garden was bookended by two business concerns that seemed totally out of place. To Riker, putting a day spa offering Brazilian wax jobs and manscaping and a wellness center specializing in acupuncture and reiki anywhere near a hardware store was almost as dim as locating a new age shop selling crystals and aromatherapy crap next door to a Marine Corps recruiting center.

To the left of *High Desert Spa* was a chain pet store. Like the spa, it had been completely ransacked, the plate-glass windows reduced to a million little pieces scattered inside and out. A vinyl sign fluttered in the window frame: SELF-SERVICE DOG WASH $10. As Riker stared past the sign, searching the shadowy interior behind it for anything of value, he detected something moving deep in the back of the store. It was bipedal. And moving slowly, left to right. A zombie, that much he was sure of. Whether it was a Random or a Slog, he didn't care to find out.

After radioing a warning to the others, asking one of them to keep tabs on the thing in the pet store for him, he pocketed the radio, raised the AR level with the shops to his fore, and continued across the lot, head on a swivel and moving as fast as his aching left leg would allow.

As Riker neared *Invisible Healing - Acupuncture and Reiki*, located to the right of the hardware concern, he saw that it had been left alone, its mirrored plate-glass windows and glass front door untouched. Even during the apocalypse, he mused, the needs of our pets took precedence over personal well being. Essential oils offered none of the things a four-legged companion could provide. He knew that for a fact. While he had never been much of a dog person, that had changed the second he met Dozer. And as he thought about the gray pitbull, he wondered what kind of trouble Tara was getting the mild-mannered pooch into.

Stepping onto the cement walk in front of the reiki place, Riker slowed his gait and stole a closer look at the vehicles in front of Vern's. Sure enough, the Rubicon had been the main focus of a prolonged zombie attack. Or, more than likely, someone had driven it into a horde at a high rate of speed. The passenger side front fender was peeled back. What looked like human hair and scraps of fabric were lodged in the gap where the fender had separated from the grille. In addition to the blood and gore on the flank facing Riker, bits and pieces of skin and flesh were dried fast to the beefy front bumper; some had also become stuck in the grille's many vertical slots.

Getting a better angle on the Cherokee, Riker saw that, save for two flat tires, it was virtually untouched. Which made him doubt the attack on the Rubicon had gone down here.

Inside the EarthRoamer, Steve-O was kicked back in his seat, boots off, stockinged feet planted firmly on the dash. In his hands was the drone's remote control.

Moments ago, after starting his watch timer running, Steve-O had launched the drone and set it flying off on an easterly course. Keeping it just above treetop level, he had followed the curve of the boulevard until the drone was out of sight.

Now, forced to track the drone's progress solely via the crystal-clear image being beamed back to the screen before him, he cut the speed in half and said, "I'm turning at the next street and coming back up beside the mall."

Craning to see past the brim of Steve-O's hat, Shorty said, "Look out for traffic signals and power poles. And you should probably—"

Cutting Shorty off, Steve-O said, "Don't be a back-seat pilot, Shorty." He activated the drone's auto-hover feature, dropped his feet to the floorboard, and turned in his seat. "I can't concentrate with you yammering on. Please. Be. Quiet." He continued with the flint-hard stare until Shorty said, "Fine. Fine. I'll zip it, sit back, and watch the master do his thing."

Satisfied with the answer, Steve-O went back to his flying posture: feet on the dash, head bowed, a laser-like focus on what was taking place on the tiny screen.

Steve-O had just started the drone on the return leg of the flight when the camera picked up movement through the treetops. Trudging uphill, dead center on the gently arcing thoroughfare south by east of the mini-mall, was a large knot of dead things.

"Let's see what kind of monsters we have here." Face a mask of concentration, Steve-O flew the drone over the heads of the zombies, spun a crisp one-eighty, then stopped it fifty feet ahead of the lead zombie and engaged auto-hover.

The group was at least twenty strong, the men and boys among them wearing dark slacks and button-up shirts, the women white dresses and colorful tops. All of them bore the telltale signs of a ferocious zombie attack: purple-rimmed bite wounds to the hands and arms. Hands missing fingers and thumbs. White cartilage ringing a blood-crusted orifice where an ear used to be.

One of the men had had his throat torn wide open, the jagged mouth-like vertical wound opening and closing with each step.

Leading the group was a young undead teen. Dark, braided hair and brown eyes contrasted sharply with her elaborate white dress. A sheen of blood coated her lips, chin, and neck—it presented as crimson on her talc-white skin and reddish-black where it had sluiced over the dress's ruffles and pleats.

"Reminds me of Aunt Bea's wedding," observed Steve-O. "Only this bride is way too young to get married."

Breaking his oath of silence, Shorty said, "I think we're looking at the sad ending to that girl's quinceañera. It's a coming-of-age party Hispanic and Latino families throw for their daughters on their fifteenth birthday. Kind of like we throw a sweet sixteen party here in the States." He paused for a moment as he was ambushed with memories of his missing daughter, Megan. Finally, tone all business, he asked, "What do you think, Ace? Can you lead them away with your toy?"

Steve-O flashed a tight smile at Shorty, "It's not a toy." Regarding the screen, he said, "I shall do my best."

Vern's Hardware and Garden was locked down tight as a tourniquet, every window covered with half-inch-thick plywood, heavy-duty lag bolts securing the sheets at every corner. A liberal amount of what looked to be masonry screws were used all around the edges. The screws had been countersunk so deep into the brick façade that Riker doubted he could slip a sheet of paper under the plywood, let alone the jaws of the pneumatic spreading tool.

Whoever riot-proofed Vern's had had everything inside the hardware store at their disposal. No wonder the place was sealed up like Fort Knox.

The front door was recessed in a shallow alcove. The only chinks in the storefront's armor were a horizontal mail slot inset waist-high in the door and a half-inch-wide space that had been left between the plywood sheeting and the top of the door's brushed-aluminum frame.

Riker looked the length of the walk bordering the storefronts. Seeing he was all alone, he entered the alcove, pressed up against the door, and stood on his tiptoes.

Stretched to full extension, he was able to reach the sliver of window and peer inside the store.

Instead of seeing ghostly outlines of shelves full of product and displays beckoning from the gloom, he saw a pair of eyes staring back at him. For a moment he thought he was seeing his own eyes being reflected back at him. A half-beat later he realized the color was all wrong. While his eyes were dark brown, the eyes in the narrowed gaze staring back were a brownish-green he thought was called *hazel*.

On the back half of that heartbeat, the eyes disappeared and Riker felt something pressing hard against his crotch.

A disembodied voice said, "Freeze!" It was definitely male. Deep and raspy. Maybe a smoker. It carried a hint of a Brooklyn accent. A little like one of those mobsters in the black-and-white gangster movies Tara couldn't get enough of.

Riker said, "About all a guy can do when his family jewels are about to be blown off." He let the AR dangle from its sling, placed both empty hands in front of the mail slot, then went on, saying: "I'm just going to reach into my pocket, take out my radio, and call someone I think you're going to want to hear from."

Through the door, Riker heard the ubiquitous *crunch-crunch* sound of a shotgun slide being racked and felt a notable increase in the pressure being put on his manhood. He was sweating now. Funny how a mechanical sound no human alive liked to hear could instantly shock the primal part of the brain awake.

Eyes watering, Riker prayed that the person holding the shotgun had the sense to have his trigger finger *outside* of the trigger guard.

The male voice said, "Go ahead. But you do anything stupid, you'll be forever singing soprano."

Chapter 36

Lia spoke with Riker over the two-way radio, retrieved the requested items from the center console, then exited the Shelby.

Standing on the sidewalk beside the pickup, armed with only Olympic-caliber stamina and a sub-five-second forty-yard-dash time, Lia locked her gaze on Vern's. For some reason, Lee was still facing the boarded-over door, radio clutched in one hand, both hands held high above his head.

Why so vague over the radio? she thought as she picked her way through the ankle-high shrubs in the dirt strip bordering the lot. With nothing standing between her and the sidewalk fronting the businesses, she stole one last look at Benny in the Shelby. Seeing a thumbs-up, she stepped onto the lot and made a mad dash for Vern's.

Arriving on the sidewalk in front of Vern's a couple of seconds after leaving the safety of the Shelby, Lia ducked into the shadowy alcove and put a hand on Riker's shoulder. "What's going on?" she asked.

Remaining statue-still, Riker said, "Look down."

She moved closer and peered around Riker. Gasping, she said, "Is that a gun?"

A subtle nod, then Riker said, "I hope you know the man with his finger on the trigger."

Crouching before the door, Lia said, "Is that you, Vern? It's me, Amelia. The spider plant lady."

Instantly the shotgun barrel retreated back into the mail slot. As it did so, the hinged door slapped down over the mail slot.

As Riker felt the pressure being put on his package by the muzzle suddenly removed, every muscle in his body relaxed.

If he had been holding back a bowel movement, no doubt he would have shit his pants on the spot.

Turning to face Lia, he said, "Did you bring the stuff I asked for?"

She reached into a vest pocket and came out with the purple Crown Royal sack. It was heavy in her hand, the gold drawstring coiled around the bulging sack. As she dropped it into Riker's awaiting hand, there was a dull clank and the items inside shifted to fit the contours of his massive palm.

"And the list?"

She produced a square of folded paper from another pocket.

Riker took the list and shoved it through the mail slot. Next, he went to work loosening the sack's drawstring.

While Riker fought the tangle of string, Lia lifted the mail flap. "This guy is my friend."

The voice said, "Your friend was casing my store."

"We were hoping you were still open," she lied. "To be honest, I'm amazed you're still here. Shouldn't you be at home with your wife?"

"My love has been gone for a year now," answered the disembodied voice. "That's why I'm always working. Figure the moment I retire, I'll die a second time. But this time for real, not just on the inside."

Lia said, "You're all alone in there?"

"That's correct."

Voice softening, she stated, "It's not safe for you here."

"I know," he said. "Did you see what they did to the pet store? Took everything but the shelves. And Ms. Nguyen's salon. It's a complete loss. I don't want that to happen to my place. I want to still have a business when the country opens back up. Still have a purpose."

"I hate to break it to you, Vern. But—"

Riker put a hand on Lia's shoulder. Squeezed gently and mouthed, "Let me talk to him."

Addressing Vern through the door, she raised her voice and said, "This is Leland Riker. He goes by Lee." Looking to Riker, she added, "Lee Riker, meet my friend, Vern."

Riker said, "Pleased to meet you, Vern. I'd shake your hand, but this mitt is not going make it through the slot of yours."

Lia whispered, "Ask him where his son is. He worked here, too."

"Amelia says your son works here with you. Is he in there now?"

Even through the door, Riker and Lia heard Vern exhale. After a beat, he said, "We were watching the place in shifts. Alternating between here and my home." He paused. "That place was going to be his one day. Hell, so was this store. All of it... his. And he had to go and get bit."

Riker finally succeeded in opening the sack. Pouring some of its contents into his palm, he said, "I bet that's his Jeep."

"I told him not to drive it, what with the soft top and all," lamented Vern. "But he's hardheaded, just like his father."

Riker crouched down. "I'm sorry for your loss, Vern." A brief pause. "That list I gave you ... I have a proposition. Sounds like you're in it for the long haul. Determined to wait this thing out. Reopen when the authorities get things sorted. Am I right?" As he spoke, he could feel Lia's eyes on him.

"I remember the riots in Los Angeles," Vern said. "The Korean shop owners defending their stores against all comers. Can't blame them. It's the same with me. Hell, I'll be seventy day after Christmas. Boxing day. This store is all I have now. I'm going to need *something* to keep me busy when everything gets back to normal."

Clearly, normalcy bias has a firm grip on the man, thought Riker. Either that or the man knew something that Riker didn't.

Riker held his open hand in front of the slot. In his palm was a gold Krugerrand and two rectangular pieces of gold that, at first glance, looked a lot like cell phone SIM cards.

Vern said, "What's this?"

"*This* is an ounce and a half of pure gold. Gold was last trading north of two thousand dollars. The New York Stock Exchange was tanking so badly, people were fleeing to gold. I can imagine it doubling or tripling by the time the National Guard gets the dead rounded up. It'll probably double again when they develop a vaccine against the virus. Then when the vaccine is perfected and President Tillman starts opening everything back up, the sky's the limit. Doubt if we'll *ever* go back to fiat currency. The gold standard will return and this gold in my hand will be worth ten, maybe twelve grand. More than enough to keep your place humming along until everything gets back to normal."

Sounding hopeful, Vern said, "By the time a *vaccine* is perfected? They really have one in the works?"

Riker felt Lia's hand on his shoulder. She was squeezing hard to get his attention. As he cocked an ear toward her, she whispered, "Do not lie to him."

Hoping white lies didn't count in her book, Riker said, "I didn't hear it from a reputable source, but you'd have to imagine one is in the works. We're America. We have the CDC and AMRIID."

"I looked at your list," Vern said. "I have most of this. The dog food you'll have to find elsewhere. The chainsaw will have to be a Stihl model. It's all I carry. All I trust. As for the solar sidewalk lights. Why on God's green earth would you need three dozen of those?"

"It's for a home project," Riker said. "I'm not greedy, Vern. I'll take however many you have."

"So why would you give me what could end up being ten thousand dollars worth of gold for goods worth a third of that?"

"Supply and demand," Riker said. "We're not looters. I pay my way in life. Always have. Bottom line, Vern, is that you have what we need."

There was a long pause. Then Vern said, "My gut tells me you're on the level. Plus, Amelia seems comfortable around you. Nothing's forced."

Lia's grip on Riker's shoulder loosened.

Vern went on, "If you do something for me, Leland Riker, we have a deal. And I'm only going to take the Krugerrand off your hands. I always wanted one of those—"

Bowing his head, Riker said, "What is it?"

Vern said, "I need you to check on my son."

Lia said, "I thought Shane got bit."

"Yes, he did," Vern said. "It's what killed him. The infection was unlike anything I've ever seen. It burned him up at the end."

"Where is his body?"

Vern stuck a finger out the slot. Pointing to Riker's left, he said, "In the pet store. I put him on a four-wheeled dolly, rolled him down there, and pushed his body through the door."

After another long pause, in a funereal voice, he said, "It was a cop-out, what I did. Now I can't help but think that he probably came back as one of *them*."

Confident the shadowy form milling about in the gutted pet store's deep, dark recesses was Vern's undead son, Riker said, "I know it's a hard thing to do at a time like this, but I'm going to need you to try to describe your son for me. Tell me what he was wearing when he finally ... " He let the obvious go unsaid.

There was the sound of the door lock being thrown then the door sucked inward. Vern was standing there, hazel eyes flicking between Riker and Lia. He was wearing cotton khakis and a blue polo. A hat with the store's logo was pulled down low on his head. On his feet were well-worn black leather jungle boots. In a low, wavering voice, he said, "Shane's about six-one. He has... uh, he *had* sandy-brown hair. It was graying a little on the sides. Mustache had gone a bit gray, too. At the end he had on cargo shorts and flip flops. He wore those damn rubber things year-round. Oh"—he met Riker's gaze—"he got real cold at the end so I dressed him in his favorite sweater. It was a Christmas one." Vern chuckled. "A real natty thing with the Grinch and his sad little rein-doggy on front of it. He liked to wear it around the store because it made me laugh. He was always trying to do something to take our minds off all that was happening. There was the constant reporting on the terrorist attacks in New York and Logan airport. Then the FEMA facilities started going up downtown and at the airport. The governor's lockdown was the last straw. When they—"

Riker interrupted. "I'll do it. I'll check on Shane. What do you want me to do if, God forbid, he is one of them?"

"A vaccine only works up front," Vern said. He seemed to have regained some of the clarity he had displayed upon opening the door. The spark was back in his eyes. Shaking his head, he added, "It's too late for my boy. You do what you have to do, Leland. Destroying the brain is the only sure-fire way to put one of them things down." He pinched tears from his eyes. "I was weak. I've put down my fair share of those things before Shane ... I just couldn't bring myself to do it to my own flesh and blood."

Riker said, "I get it, Vern. I really do." A sudden flood of emotion hit him. A tremor rocked his body. Then the headache was back, bringing with it a bout of dizziness.

Vern said, "Thank you. And you be careful. While you're gone, we'll start rounding up the stuff on your list."

In response, Riker placed all three pieces of gold in Vern's palm. "Take it all," he insisted.

Before Vern could object, the radio in Riker's pocket came alive. It was Shorty. Voice sounding strained, he said, "Look alive. You've got about two dozen biters coming your way."

Chapter 37

Poking his head from the shadowy alcove, Riker fished the radio from his pocket and quickly stabbed a finger on the Talk button. Gaze locked on the distant boulevard, he whispered, "I hear you, Shorty. I don't see them from here." He rolled the volume down and opened the channel.

Shorty came back right away. "They're just down the street from the pet store. Half a block south and moving your way."

Riker said, "I just made a deal for supplies. Can you buy us some time? Maybe use the drone to distract them. Even better, see if Steve-O can use the drone to turn them around and lead them away."

Shorty came back right away. "Steve-O already tried that. He'd get their attention with the drone. Half of them would turn around and lock eyes on it, but every time he started them moving back the way they came, low-hanging tree limbs would get in the way of the drone. He tried three times. Each time he gained altitude to clear the branches, the damn things lost interest and resumed their previous heading." There was a brief pause. "Then there's the battery issue. Steve-O says the level is dropping faster in this one than the first. He thinks he's about to lose the drone, so he's bringing it home."

Exasperation showing in his tone, Riker said, "Thing's probably made in China." He let go of the Talk button and spit a couple of choice curse words. Then, over the radio, he asked, "So, Shorty, how long do we have?"

"Five minutes, max," was the answer. "If you want—"

"Forgot it," Riker shot, cutting Shorty off. "I'll deal with it." Before signing off, he relayed the crude details of his hastily hatched plan.

Shorty said, "You sure that's how you want to do it? Can't go it alone every time, Lee. You're not my guardian angel. Why you have to be a helicopter parent to everyone else is a bit baffling to me. Steve-O, your sister … sure, I can accept that. But Benny? Why don't you have him help you?"

"My mind's made up," Riker said. Before Benny, who was able to hear everything said about him on the open channel, could mount a defense, Riker rolled the volume down and pocketed the radio.

Lia said, "Let me tag along. I can watch your back while you're inside."

Riker shook his head vigorously. "You stay here and help Vern round up the stuff on the list. Feel free to add anything extra you think you might need. Just tell Vern I'll give him more gold when I get back."

She said, "If you come back."

Riker hung his head in defeat. Damned if he did, damned if he didn't. He said, "My plan is solid."

For the third time in as many minutes, Lia laid a hand on Riker's shoulder. Looking him in the eye, she said, "You be careful."

Remaining stone-faced, Riker thought, *Isn't this when the sappy music kicks in and the hero kisses the girl?* Out loud, he said, "You've seen enough killing and dying for ten lifetimes. Said so yourself a few minutes ago."

"You better go, then." She made a shooing motion just as Vern reappeared at the open door.

"Lee," Vern said, extending his hand.

Riker reciprocated. Lean and wiry, Vern was a head shorter; however, his grip was stronger than his stature would suggest. And in his palm was the gold. He said, "I'm not taking this, Lee."

No time to argue. Riker pocketed the gold. Casting a furtive glance in the direction of the pet store, he said, "I better go, the deadheads are on the march."

Vern said, "I was listening. Better go. We'll get to fulfilling your order." With that, he led Lia inside and closed and locked the door behind them.

Riker peered inside the spa as he passed it by. It was a mess in there. Bottles of hair care products, some of them leaking pearlescent goop, lay in a jumble on the floor just inside the door. The broken display case was canted to one side and partially blocking the door.

Lying on the floor between what Riker guessed were workstations where the beauticians and customers sat facing each other was a slight Asian woman. She was dead, that was for sure. She wore a wide-eyed expression. Her mouth had frozen open mid-scream—the thin lips, white with blood loss, stretched tight over a picket of mostly straight teeth.

She had ended up on her back, stuck fast to a pool of her own blood, both arms cocked in a defensive posture. The blood had dried long ago and now looked more black than red. It covered a good deal of the floor and seemed to be swallowing up all the light from outside.

The woman's white smock was torn and blood-spattered and had somehow ended up around her chin. Everything that used to reside inside her narrow chest cavity had been scooped out and was nowhere to be seen. Riker had no doubt he was looking at the work of one or more of the dead things. They were efficient eating machines.

On the woman's forehead, equidistant between almond-shaped eyes, was a tiny, bloodless hole. The lack of powder burns around the entry wound, and that there was no noticeable exit point, told him she had been put down by a single small-caliber round.

What a way to go, thought Riker. As he pushed on toward the pet store, the only solace he took from the macabre scene was that, unlike Vern's son Shane, the lady in the spa hadn't reanimated. Who was responsible for bestowing to her the ultimate gift? The gift of release? Maybe her husband? Perhaps an adult child? Whatever the case, contrary to the impression conveyed by her final death pose, she was at peace now.

Stepping between islands of broken glass dotting the walk-in front of *Wags*, Riker made his way, as silently as possible, to the sidewalk bordering the mini-mall to the east.

A couple of yards shy of the blind corner, he heard a low, mournful moan coming from the right, from somewhere deep in the bowels of the pet store. It made him think of the wind navigating the upper boughs of tall pines. As the hair on his arms stood to attention, the moan morphed to guttural grunting that was quickly drowned out by the distinct *slap, clop, slap, clop* of flip-flops striking the floor.

Turning toward the sound, Riker saw a shadowy form trundling down the aisle toward him. As it was hit by the light spilling in the big window, Riker saw the sandy-brown hair "graying a little on the sides." The mustache "gone a bit gray" was present, too. The final piece of the puzzle, the leering green face of the Grinch on the "natty Christmas sweater," confirmed to Riker that the dead six-footer staring the meat from his bones was indeed Vern's son, Shane.

As Riker waited for undead Shane to get close enough to put down with the Randall, the overpowering stench of rotting flesh reminded him that the pack of dead things was somewhere on the nearby street and heading his way.

Curiosity getting the better of him, he performed a quick turkey-peek around the corner. While letting the dead see him and then luring them away from the mini-mall *was* part of the plan, coming face-to-face with an undead teen in a wedding dress definitely *was not*.

Two things happened back to back. First, Riker recoiled and said, "The hell you get there so quick?" Then, reacting a half-beat slower, the doll-like corpse's dead eyes flicked left, its jaw dropped open, and both of its bite-ravaged hands commenced an upward sweep for Riker's face.

For a person of Riker's stature, backpedaling usually required a little bit of concentration. Doing so in a near panic and without benefit of a backward glance, he immediately learned, was *not* in his wheelhouse.

Feet inexorably tangled, all two hundred and twenty pounds dragging him backward, Riker grudgingly let go of his rifle and brought both hands up to protect his face. It was the classic defensive posture, the same the dead woman in the spa had employed, only Riker had no intention of going out like her.

Though his elbows struck the sidewalk first, it did nothing to soften the breath-robbing blow delivered to his back when his body slammed hard back to earth. Electric currents of pain rippled through both arms. As the wind rushed from his lungs, twin starbursts erupted behind his eyes and the throbbing in his head ramped up.

Though Riker knew the rest of the zombies were just around the corner—the heavy pong of death riding the air all the confirmation he needed—survival dictated that he focus solely on the danger directly in front of him.

Just as the undead girl pounced, Riker managed to get his right hand wrapped around her neck. As he increased the pressure and locked his arm to create some distance, three of his fingers plunged under a flap of skin that arced from the thing's collarbone to a spot an inch south of the bloody cavity where an ear was supposed to be. The half-moon-shaped wound looked to have been created by a single pass of a very sharp blade. It was bloodless and cold, instantly chilling his fingers all the way to the knuckles.

Fingernails painted ruby-red scythed the air in front of Riker's face. The girl was strong for her size. Which made him think he was wrestling with one of Lia's "Randoms."

As Riker struggled to get to the Randall with his off hand, the steady clack of teeth snapping dangerously close to his ear drowned out all other sound. If the rest of the herd had rounded the corner behind this one, he was blind to it and surely about to be dead meat.

Simultaneous with the big blade clearing the sheath, the zombie strained to take a bite out of Riker's shoulder. Like a rabid dog, it snarled and snapped and whipped its head back and forth. The incessant movement dislodged the nest of intricate braids wrapping its head. The ensuing explosion of fine black hair cascaded down over its face, completely blocking Riker's entire field of view.

Working blind, Riker dragged the Randall across his chest. Arm and hand now out from under the weight of the writhing form, he swept the blade up and around—a clockwise half-circle that began by his left hip and ended a couple of inches from his face. The blow was vicious and produced an awful crunch. The sound of bone losing the battle with honed steel was usurped by a wet squelch as the blade cleaved smartly through forgiving brain tissue. One second the zombie in Riker's grip was fighting like a pissed-off badger, the next it was a limp ragdoll, arms and legs yielding at once to the pull of gravity.

The rank odor of decay was overwhelming Riker as he tossed the stilled corpse aside. Breathing through the mouth, he rolled over and got up on his knees. As he rose on rubbery legs, undead Shane slammed into the waist-high window frame to his right. The impact started the entire run of window frames

vibrating and dislodged some of the remaining glass, sending it tumbling to the ground where it made a great amount of noise as it shattered into tiny slivers.

The horizontal edge of the window frame came up to the Grinch's chin and prevented undead Shane from leaving the store. Triangle-shaped glass shards protruding vertically from the frame had become buried inches deep into the zombie's gut. As the thing lunged and reached for Riker, the glass acted like oversized saw teeth, tearing into its abdomen like a hot knife through butter.

Good thinking, Vern. Whether your son reanimated or just moldered for eternity inside the empty store, probably a better place than most to deposit the body. Nobody in their right mind would venture inside, considering the shelves had been emptied of food.

Riker couldn't blame the old man for taking this route. It wasn't a cop-out. Truth be told, if Riker hadn't made a pact with Tara, he would probably struggle long and hard with the decision. For be it by blade or bullet, putting down a loved one had never once in his thirty-eight years on earth crossed his mind. Not even when his mom was dying of cancer. He'd even remanded to Tara the task of reminding the nursing staff of their mom's do not resuscitate order. So, in a way, he was just as weak as Vern.

Knowing there would be no way for him to honor his promise to Vern if he rabbited now, Riker moved toward the window. Widening his stance on the sidewalk, he reached out and grabbed a handful of the zombie's hair. Pulling the thing forward put a lot of stress on the window frame. It also finished what the jagged glass had started. There was a rush of eye-watering gas and Shane's guts spilled from underneath the Grinch sweater.

Gagging and about to throw up in his mouth, Riker stabbed the Randall into the zombie's left temple. As the living corpse ceased all movement and its eyes rolled back in its head, Riker let go of its hair, hinged over, and threw up on his Salomons. Sidestepping the spreading pool of bile and bodily fluids flowing around his feet, Riker lifted undead Shane's upper body off the window frame. A hard shove on the shoulder sent the body crashing to the floor inside the store.

Out of sight, but in no way out of mind.

Chapter 38

Riker was still mourning Vern's loss when he stepped from the low-curb and made a bee-line across the narrow end of the kidney-shaped lot. As he stepped onto the sidewalk where the north and east runs merged to become a kind of swooping arc, he was afforded a clear view up and down the nearby two-lane.

The zombie herd was farther down the road than he had expected it to be. He could see the first third of them. They were out in the open, a good twenty yards away, three abreast and trudging up the middle of the street. The rest, maybe twelve or so, were in a knot and lagging back about fifteen feet behind the main group. Though they were still partially obscured by parked cars and low-hanging branches on the trees lining both sides of the road, Riker saw that Shorty was right: They were indeed wearing their Sunday best.

Now or never, thought Riker, and he stepped off the curb. Though he already was a pretty big target, he stuck the AR in the air and waved his arms, hollering at the top of his voice, "Here I am, you stinky carnivores! Come and get me!"

All at once a whole bunch of eyes locked on him and one of the zombies in the lead element, a small dark-haired boy in a knit shirt and navy pants, broke into a head-down sprint.

Riker was reminding himself to use the knife to save ammunition, just as a second Random, a twenty-something female in low-heels and a knee-length skirt, split off from the laggards.

The self-admonition seemed ridiculous to Riker, considering he was now facing two fast movers. It became downright ludicrous when a third zombie bolted from the dwindling lead element.

Grabbing hold of the rifle with both hands, Riker risked a quick glance at the hardware store. Neither Vern nor Lia were visible at the moment. However, on the sidewalk was a growing pile of supplies. There were colorful cardboard boxes. Rubbermaid bins. A jumble of red gas cans. Various soft goods piled high to the right of the alcove mouth. And, standing out amongst it all, several humongous bags of something. Topsoil? Fertilizer?

Having used Riker's catcalls to cover the sound of his footsteps, Benny had sprinted across the lot and crouched down beside the Rubicon. He had set the gas can on the ground next to him and deployed the siphon pump next to the filler door.

Part of the plan.

As Riker looked on, Benny jammed the hose attached to the pump into the tank. The other hose he stuck into the mouth of the gas can. He immediately started cranking the siphon's side-mounted handle. In no time the can at Benny's feet began turning a darker shade of red than the others. Which told Riker gas was flowing into it. Satisfied he was seeing the least important part of his plan coming off without a hitch, he turned to face the zombie herd and trained the AR's business end on the smartly dressed undead boy.

Flicking the selector to Fire, Riker settled the crosshairs on a spot just below the kid's brow. Whispering, "I'm sorry," he pressed the trigger two times in rapid succession.

The first .308 round snapped left of the undead boy's wildly lolling head. The follow-on shot found its mark, striking an inch lower than where Riker had been aiming. Instead of punching a neat little hole between the bushy black eyebrows, the screaming hunk of lead destroyed the undead kid's tiny nose. Instantly deflected upward as it careened through the sloped ethmoid bone, the bullet broke apart, each sharp-edged fragment charting a course of its own through cranial bone and brain tissue.

The undead boy was standing straight and coming out of his shoes when Random number two filled up Riker's gunsight. Low heels clacking furiously on the blacktop, arms and legs miraculously working in concert, the thing was a few yards out and closing fast. With no time to line up a headshot, Riker aimed for center mass and snapped off a half-dozen rounds. The first pair of hits opened a fist-sized hole just under the thing's finely sculpted chin. The third entered through the mouth clean and exited the right cheek with little more than a spritz of pale dermis. Amazingly no blood, teeth, or flesh followed. Aim affected majorly by the perfect storm of adrenaline dumping his system, the banger of a headache assaulting every nerve in his head, and the AR's normal muzzle climb, Riker's next three shots went high and wide.

Vowing to put more practice in with the rifle, assuming he survived this scrape, Riker pulled a move from his gridiron days. Sidestepping left, he dipped his hips, lowered his right shoulder, then, pretending the charging corpse was wearing pads, drove his elbow up and forward, aiming for the spot the center laces should be.

The sickening crunch and crackle of breaking ribs resounded when Riker and the zombie collided. A simple twist of the hips on his part unloaded an enormous amount of pent-up energy, the move sending the female Random airborne, skirt fluttering over its face, arms and legs a blur of motion. As it crashed hard on the asphalt, the other shoe broken in two, all of its efforts immediately went into a sad attempt at standing.

Down but not out. Still, sidelining the female Random for a second gave Riker time to take aim on the final runner—a Hispanic male in its teens when it had died the first time. It was ten or so yards out and running diagonally for Riker when he put it down with a pair of shots to the face.

When Riker finally returned his attention to the female Random, it was still struggling to stand. One arm hung limply from the socket. Riker guessed it had become dislocated when the thing dropped back to earth. A length of jagged bone protruded from the other arm, causing it to buckle as soon as any weight was put on it. And adding insult to injury, the fingers on that hand were bent back at peculiar angles.

If that wasn't enough, the heel had snapped off its other shoe, further adding to the difficulty the zombie was having in rising up off the road. If this living corpse had actually been an opponent on the gridiron, Riker thought, he would most definitely be adding another morale sticker to the back of his helmet.

But this wasn't a game. This was life and death. And death was literally stalking up the road, coming for him, a wall of gnashing teeth still too numerous for him to take on alone.

231

Acting without thought of who the female zombie used to be, (there would be time to contemplate that later) Riker walked right up to it, touched the AR's muzzle to the top of its head, and pressed the trigger one time. There was no spray of bone or brain matter. No blood, either. The report was muffled as the bullet simply opened a hole in the skull and destroyed the organ running things.

Riker didn't see the zombie topple forward. He wasn't aware the escaping energy had pushed both eyes from their sockets. Nor was he privy to the brains dribbling from the entry wound. He was already staring at the zombie troop, still several yards down the road and closing.

Riker didn't need to do the arm wave thing again. No need to yell, either—every single one of them was focused solely on him.

Another part of the plan.

From somewhere behind Riker came the sound of the EarthRoamer's motor firing. The low rumble was soon joined by the reverse-gear whine of it moving away from him. When he finally stole a glance over his right shoulder, he saw three things: sixty yards down the arcing boulevard, Marge was moving right to left, with Shorty just steering the rig into a sweeping J-turn. In the middle distance, the Shelby sat all alone at the curb, unattended. Across the mini-mall parking lot, a hundred yards or so from the apex of the curving boulevard, the pile of goods in front of the hardware store had tripled in size.

What Riker didn't see, because he had turned back toward the approaching zombie herd, was Shorty driving the EarthRoamer over the curb and sidewalk to create for the big rig an entry to the lot where there was none.

The previous fight for survival, combined with the stress of being so near to a large group of flesh-eating zombies, was beginning to take a toll on Riker. He took his eyes from the plodding monsters and glanced skyward. Dark clouds were moving in from the south. Rain was about the only thing out of his control that could possibly make this any worse. As if on cue, he felt a single raindrop hit his exposed skin.

While his first, second, and third instinct was to run away from the dead things and the impending deluge as fast as his tired legs would carry him, doing so would put the others in danger. Already, some of the zombies were casting glances in the direction of the mini-mall.

"Stick to the plan," he told himself. Slowing a bit to let the zombies gain a few steps on him, he resumed the waving and hollering, putting his all into the Pied Piper routine.

***

Yelling at the top of his lungs for the better part of five minutes had left Riker a little lightheaded and his voice beginning to go hoarse on him. With barely a truck length to go to get to the Shelby, he turned away from the dead things and jogged the rest of the way.

The drone was on the hood where Steve-O said he would leave it. As promised, Benny had left the fob hanging off one of the drone's stilled props.

With the dead still a safe distance from Dolly's grille, Riker hurriedly stuffed the drone under the tonneau and slammed the tailgate shut. Only when he was in the cab and had the door closed and locks thrown did he relax a little. But it was short-lived, because as soon as he was ensconced in the relative cocoon of silence the cab provided, he became acutely aware of the fierce pounding behind his eyes and dull ache emanating from deep within his stump.

The radio in his pocket came to life. With the volume turned down low, the sound coming from the speaker was but a low hiss of white noise. He dug out the Motorola and upped the volume just in time to hear Shorty say, "I think your new friend is planning on turning your place into a Rainforest Café."

After having seen the inside of Lia's house, Riker had a good idea where the man was going with this. Thumbing the Talk key, he responded, "Let me guess. Seeds, clay pots, fertilizer, and potting soil?"

Shorty said, "Bingo. But that's not all. Your spitfire has assembled on the sidewalk here what looks like the beginnings of a major league grow operation—" he was interrupted by the Shelby's blaring horn, which stopped only long enough for Riker to tell him to get off the radio and get the stuff loaded.

"Alright, alright," Shorty flared, "I'll get my hands dirty. But tell me this: Why do you get to have all the fun?"

RIKER'S APOCALYPSE (THE PRECIPICE)

Fun, my ass, thought Riker as a pale palm slapped the window glass just inches from his left cheek.

Chapter 39

Trying hard to ignore the leering, rictus grins of the dead, Riker kept his gaze locked on the sidewalk in front of Vern's. Though the migraine he was currently experiencing was one of the worst he could remember, he continued to lay on the Shelby's horn. He winced as the screech of fingernails scraping against the outside of his door resounded inside the cab.

After enduring what seemed like a never-ending assault on his once shiny hundred-thousand-dollar ride, the others finally finished loading the last of the supplies into Shorty's EarthRoamer.

Flipping the assemblage of dead the bird, Riker fired the Shelby's engine, then placed a call to Shorty.

Talking loudly to be heard over the sonorous gong-like bangs of dead flesh striking sheet metal, Riker asked, "Almost ready to roll?"

A couple of seconds ticked by before Shorty answered. "Getting there," he said. "But I'm afraid you're going to need to come and pick these kids up."

"Not part of the plan," Riker shot. "I'll pick up Benny and Steve-O after I turn around."

"Listen," Shorty shot back, "your friends just went on one hell of a shopping spree." There was a short pause. Voice adopting a conciliatory tone, he added, "I picked up a *few* things myself. Bottom line ... Marge is filled to the brim."

Incredulous, Riker said, "The camper *and* the crew cab?"

"Affirmative," said Shorty. "I'm going to need you to take on all passengers."

Throwing the transmission into Reverse, Riker said, "On my way."

Fingernails stole more of Dolly's paint as Riker eased her from the pocket of zombies. He took the same route as

Shorty, whipping a quick J-turn, then driving up and over the curb and sidewalk, finishing the utter destruction of the shrubs the EarthRoamer had started.

Pulling the Shelby close to the EarthRoamer's rugged rear bumper, Riker powered down the curbside window.

Lia and Vern were in the shadowy alcove and engaged in an animated conversation.

On the sidewalk, Steve-O was standing with his arms crossed and watching Benny arranging items in the camper.

Shorty hadn't been lying when he said the rig was full to the brim. It was crammed floor to ceiling with everything but the kitchen sink. Seemed like half of Vern's inventory had been transferred over to the big rig. Considering many of the items were not on the list, Riker mused, maybe a kitchen sink *was* shoehorned in there.

After balancing a pair of indoor grow lights atop of a row of five- and ten-gallon gas cans, Benny tried closing the rear door. Nothing doing. It took some manipulation of the load and a great deal of pushing and shoving on the door to finally get it closed and locked.

Hate to be the person to pop that door, thought Riker. In his mind, he saw the door flying open and Shorty backpedaling away as an avalanche of stuff poured forth.

Suppressing a grin, Riker looked across the lot to his left. The dead had already made it off the boulevard, up the curb, and over the sidewalk. Two, maybe three hundred feet to go, he figured. No doubt in a minute or two they'd be here causing problems. Already he could hear their raspy vocalizations preceding them. Leaning across the center console, he called out to Vern. "You sure you want to stay here? We can take you to your house. Probably be safer there."

Vern had put on an olive Army surplus jacket. It was old and worn on the elbows and collar. Covering his wispy gray hair was a new red hat stitched with the words *Vern's Hardware*. Turning away from Lia, the proprietor said, "Vern Rossi is afraid of no man ... living or dead. I survived the battle of Ia Drang Valley. If those NVA Regulars couldn't kill me, no way these mindless things are going to."

Riker put his hands in the air. "I wasn't questioning your bravery, Vern."

Lia crossed the sidewalk. She stepped onto the Shelby's running board. Head filling the open window, she said, "His Jeep has two flat tires, Lee." She bit her lip. "I talked him into coming with us. Is that all right with you?"

Riker looked skyward. He sighed, then said, "A little late to be asking for permission."

Adding a slight tilt to her head, she said, "He's a sweet man. We could use someone with almost seven decades of life experience."

"Agreed," Riker said. After stealing a glance at the man in question, he whispered, "Vern's seventy? Damn spry for a man his age. I figured he was sixty or so."

"He's sixty-nine, Lee." Her brows lifted. "He said he was a medic over there. Worked as an EMT all through the eighties and nineties. He knows more about medicine than all of us combined."

While Riker was on the boulevard and waiting for the loading to finish, he had been filling rifle and pistol magazines. Now, as he mulled the decision, he slapped a fresh magazine in his AR and stowed the rifle by his feet.

Breaking the uneasy silence, Lia went on, saying: "I had to tell him about my dad being an airline pilot. How he went missing early on. No call. No text. Nothing. There's more to it." She shook her head.

Riker looked up and thought he saw tears.

Swallowing hard, she continued. "I mentioned how the airport brought infected people here." A short pause as she wiped her eyes. "He was still in denial about a recovery until I told him about the FEMA facility. How all the dead things escaped from it. Lee ... he already knew about the unmanned roadblocks and empty streets. He finally came around to my way of thinking when I told him what I saw with my own eyes at the county detention center."

Riker nodded slowly. "You're riding with us, Vern," was the only thing he could say. The right thing to say. No way he was going to leave another person alone to fend for himself. Especially someone who had already been so generous.

As everyone climbed aboard Dolly, the sky opened up. At first, the rain fell big and heavy, the gray impenetrable sheets pummeling the approaching dead and sounding like a squadron of tiny warplanes strafing Dolly's roof and hood. By the time they were moving again, the Shelby leading the EarthRoamer off the lot, visibility was near zero and a thin layer of condensation had collected on the insides of the windows.

***

Leaving the mini-mall behind, Lia directed Riker through an old part of Santa Fe. After following the boulevard for a few miles, and seeing only a handful of dead along the way, she had him turn to the north and traverse a mostly deserted thoroughfare hugging the city's east side.

Finally, with the northernmost part of Santa Fe drawing near, Lia had them turn back to the west. She took them on a tour through a part of the city on whose warren of streets she liked to run. The circuitous route culminated with them reaching a dirt road that shot due north for a couple of miles, to a T, where they again motored west through a couple of miles of fenced range marked as private property.

Three times they used Shorty's bolt cutters to lop padlocks and unchain gates blocking travel on the unimproved single track. A sign on the third gate had indicated they were entering federal land. The lone, well-worn horse trail that had been paralleling the road through the private tracts of land ended there.

Leaving the scrub- and cactus-flecked range behind, they continued westbound, through a fledgling development dotted with numerous homes in different phases of construction. At the eastern boundary of the new development was a street lined with freshly painted two-level homes. Gleaming white sidewalks and driveways fronted the homes. For Sale signs sprouted from lawns still somewhat green thanks to recently laid sod.

The eyes of the smiling agents on the signs seemed to follow them as the two-vehicle procession made a slow-rolling right onto an unlined side street.

"Place is deserted," observed Benny. "We should have gone through here this morning."

"All those zombies at the roadblock had me spooked," Riker admitted. "The Randoms sprinting at us from behind the dump trucks sealed the deal for me."

Benny was seated behind Riker. Matching his friend's gaze in the rearview mirror, Benny said, "'Randoms'? You mean *Bolts*, right?"

238

Riker looked the question to Lia. She repeated her observations to the others, finishing with, "So long as you remember there's no rhyme or reason as to which ones don't diminish like the others, I don't give a rat's ass if you call them Randoms or Bolts or Flo-Jos."

"They're all monsters to me," stated Steve-O. "They aren't people anymore. I shot one today. It didn't cry or scream. I think it didn't even know what it means to die."

When they left the mini-mall, Vern had claimed the center spot in the backseat. Tapping Riker's shoulder, he asked, "Was my boy one of them? Was he a monster?"

Riker heard pain in the man's voice. To keep from having to see it reflected in those hazel eyes, Riker kept his gaze locked on the road and shook his head in response.

"He was still dead?"

Again Riker shook his head. "I'm sorry, Mr. Rossi. The virus turned Shane into one of them."

Vern was a short man, maybe five-seven in shoes. Still, he had almost half a head on Steve-O. Upon hearing his worst fear put into words, Vern seemed to shrink, the back seat swallowing him up. Voice bereft of the bravado previously on display, he said, "My boy's plan was to go down there and let nature take its course. I couldn't let him do it. Nobody should ever die alone. So I sat with him in the store. We reminisced about Little League. I coached his team, you know. We talked about his mother. That led to a discussion on why he never got married. He wasn't gay, you know. Not that that's bad or anything. He … he just could not commit. I suppose that was my fault, with all the moving around. A different post every few years. Shane was always shy and quiet." Vern swallowed hard. "The store, though … Shane gave it his all when he was there. Could talk to any woman no matter how stunning she may be."

Lia said, "Your son was a nice man. Shane was always helpful."

Riker blurted, "Shane was never a *monster*, sir. I released his soul from the shell that was his body. He didn't feel any pain. I can guarantee that."

Benny was staring outside the truck, scrutinizing the darkened windows of the homes flitting by. "None of them feel pain," he said absently.

"Or feel happiness or sadness or get mad," Steve-O added. "I take back the *monster* thing, Mr. Rossi. I'm sorry. Shane was not a monster. He just got sick and stopped being himself."

Nobody responded to that. A heavy silence descended on the cab.

Without realizing it, Riker had allowed Lia to have him drive through the same residential area he had seen from the roadblock on 84 earlier in the day. If his bearings were correct, they were still somewhere south of the roadblock. Which meant he had to decide if stopping to siphon gas from some of the hundreds of cars in the northbound lanes was worth the risk. On one hand, the target-rich environment meant they would only have to stop to exit the vehicles one time. The problem with the roadblock, though, was that the presence of dead things was assured. And scattered amongst the Slogs, he knew, were untold numbers of Randoms. He'd already seen them with his own eyes. Conversely, if he were to pull over on one of these side streets, not only would they be a draw for any dead in the vicinity, the group would also be exposing themselves to anyone holed up in the surrounding homes—be they hostile or not.

He was about to take an informal survey, see who wanted to face the Bolts and who preferred to, perhaps, be shot in the back by a terrified shut-in protecting their hood, when Shorty came on over the radio. "Lee, this is Shorty. You reading me?"

Instinctively, Riker flicked his eyes to the mirror, where he saw the man behind the wheel of the massive rig. Though the EarthRoamer was following a couple truck lengths back, the big rig still blotted out the road behind them. Worried friends of the kids they'd left dead in the cul-de-sac had somehow caught up with them, Riker said, "You're coming in loud and clear." Before releasing the Talk button, he asked, "How's our six? We still alone?"

"Just us and my dust," answered Shorty.

"What's up?" Riker asked.

Lia gestured for a left turn.

"Let's find a street with a diesel rig and a couple of cars. Fill up those gas cans Vern sold me."

Sold? thought Riker as he turned west onto a block occupied by run-down homes fronted with unkempt lawns. *Turns out Vern's a true capitalist after all. Nothing wrong with that.* Glad that

Shorty was the one who broached the subject, Riker said, "Agreed. I didn't want to venture into the tangle at the roadblock. Lots of cars to choose from. But it looked like people were tailgating while they waited on the road to open. Which means there are lots of deaders roaming around."

Without allowing Riker much of a heads up, Lia stabbed a thumb to her right.

Loyally following her input, Riker hooked a hard right turn. No sooner had he begun to straighten the wheel than he found the road in front blocked with a slow-moving mass of dead things. Just as the others took notice and a babble arose in the cab, Riker stood on the brakes.

Chapter 40

Rapid-fire, Lia shouted, "Stop! Stop! Stop!"

Responding to Riker's input, the Shelby's brakes locked up, the nose dipped at once, and the load in the bed shot forward. The metallic clang of something large and metal crashing loudly against the back of the cab instantly drowned out Lia's chant, Benny's high-pitched "Oh shit!" and Vern saying: "Where in Hades did they all come from?"

When the pickup finally came to a halt on the slick pavement, all that the stunned occupants could see through the windshield were the swaying forms of several hundred walking dead.

Following a little too close, Shorty was forced to swing the EarthRoamer wide left. Though the quick reaction kept the bigger vehicle from rear-ending the Shelby, it also created another set of problems.

Faced with plowing into the front end of a tiny blue and white Smart car parked against the far curb, or trying to squeeze the EarthRoamer between the parked car and the Shelby—a tricky maneuver that would no doubt damage all three vehicles—Shorty put his trust in his rig's massive wraparound bumper.

Having just gotten the Shelby wrestled to a complete stop, an explosion of sound from behind and left stole Riker's attention from the parade of zombies, most of which were beginning to about-face in unison.

Immediately following the screech of twisting metal and crackle of shattering glass, the tiny car Riker had just passed overtook the Shelby. Only it wasn't rolling on its undersized tires. It was now airborne, the stunted rear end sweeping by Riker's window, just about eye-level to him.

A shower of broken glass accompanied the car, which was just nosing into what would be the first of three complete revolutions.

When the car came back to earth, all four tires popped near simultaneously and it went into a flat spin on the wet pavement. The crumpled vehicle continued on, careening through two dozen zombies before coming to a complete stop. The chain reaction that followed was instantaneous and unexpected.

Beginning at the terminus of the spin, where the car had come to rest atop a number of pulped human forms, the zombies began to fall away. Like a human wave circling a packed stadium, the domino effect—slow at first—quickly picked up speed, seeing nearly every one of the biters topple over.

It had all happened so fast. One second the blur of color was screaming past Riker's window, the next the EarthRoamer was stopped broadside, straddling the curb, its shadow darkening the road all around.

Before anyone in the Shelby acknowledged what had just happened, Riker craned and leaned forward to get a look at Shorty. Since the EarthRoamer sat a bit higher, the angle was all wrong. Placing the radio to his lips, Riker said, "Shorty, you there?"

No answer. But the rig was starting to roll backwards under power. A good sign.

It was all Riker could do to wait while the vehicle reversed past the Shelby. To his front, the zombies were getting back on their feet. A quick glance in his wing mirror confirmed the EarthRoamer gave more than it got. And in spades. Its front bumper wore a good deal of white and blue paint. The hook at the end of one winch cable had been pushed back into the rectangular housing. The only other damage was to the driver-side lights. The headlight was completely destroyed. After having come loose from its housing, the fog light now hung from a tangle of wires and was swinging back and forth—pendulum-like—in front of the bumper.

"You're not leaking any fluid," Riker noted. "Once you back into the intersection, stop and make sure I can get away from these things."

Shorty responded with a terse, "Copy."

The dead were now surging around the Shelby. Most began jostling against each other to get to the windows.

Riker had just started to back away from the surge, when out of the blue, Vern said, "I don't know about that Shorty guy. What's with the *Booty Hunter* hat? Message is a bit lewd, wouldn't you all say?"

Steve-O said, "I bet he got it at a truck stop."

"You think?" Benny said ahead of a soft chuckle.

"I didn't want to say anything," Lia added, "but I think that hat screams 'look at *me* ... I'm a misogynistic *redneck.*'"

Steve-O shook his head. "Shorty may be misogynistic ... but he is *not* a redneck. Tara thinks he's a nice man. She actually kinda likes him. Told me so after he stole the big truck from the new car lot."

Vern was turned in his seat and watching the EarthRoamer reversing toward the westbound thoroughfare. "Seems like Shorty went with a vehicle a little above his pay grade."

Steve-O said, "Shorty drives big trucks because his penis is small. I thought the same about Lee until—"

"*Steve-O,*" Riker barked, "let's not go there." Brows lifting, he regarded Lia, then swept his eyes across the backseat, holding each person's gaze for a beat. Finished, he said, "Can everyone just shut it down for a second? If I'm going to get us out of here in one piece, I need to be able to concentrate."

Again a brooding silence fell over the cab.

Having gained a good deal of separation from the dead, Riker cut the J-turn short and stopped on the thoroughfare, in the northbound lane, with the Shelby just off the EarthRoamer's right front fender, where he could see Shorty's face through the rig's windshield. Raising the radio to his mouth and pressing the Talk button, he said, "Please check your following distance. What we had there was the vehicular equivalent of a midget toss."

As Shorty's laughter came over the speaker, Riker saw Lia's head swivel in his direction. Finding himself on the receiving end of one hell of an icy glare, he said, "What?"

She said, "They're called *little people.*"

"Or dwarves," Vern added. "I really loved the Wizard of Oz."

Steve-O launching into a great rendition of Yip Harburg's *We're Off to See the Wizard* softened Lia's expression. Though the man sounded nothing like Judy Garland, his singing elicited a smile from Lia.

Resigned to the fact that no amount of pleading could silence the peanut gallery, Riker got them rolling north. Once both vehicles were on the move, he nodded toward the road ahead. "Get us on a nice quiet side street. Somewhere near the ramp to 84 but far enough away so those things back there won't find us." He paused to check his mirrors. "And, please, pretty please, Lia, try to let me know where to turn *before* we're right on top of it."

Finishing the last verse of the old classic, Steve-O said, "The monsters didn't get us, Lia. Stop breaking Lee's balls."

Benny chuckled. "Wow. Wingman's got your back, Lee."

Riker said, "Thanks, Steve, but I'm a grown ass man. I'll own my part in it."

Ignoring the quip, Lia said, "In one block, turn right."

Riker nodded. When the time came, to keep from running headlong into another herd, he slowed considerably and made the turn, keeping the Shelby tracking wide left and his eyes locked on the road as it was revealed to him in narrow increments.

"Napoleon is not driving up our tailpipe," noted Vern. "But he's still pretty close."

Progress, not perfection, thought Riker.

"One block and go left. I like to run through here," Lia noted. "It's a quiet little pocket of older homes. I've only seen mostly elderly folks. They usually don't drive a lot, right? Hopefully, we'll find what you're looking for."

Again, to keep from inadvertently coming up against another herd, Riker eased the Shelby around the next corner.

Lia's assessment of the block's make-up was correct. Most of the homes were single-level and had about the same size footprint as her one-bedroom back in Santa Fe proper. About a third of the homes had at least one vehicle parked in the driveway. All of the homes had their drapes pulled shut.

Only movement Riker noted along the entire block was an American flag. It hung from a standard affixed to a stucco home painted an ugly shade of brown. Though the flag was damp, a light breeze had it swaying listlessly back and forth.

Parked out front of the stucco house was an old Dodge Ram dually pickup. On the bumper was a smattering of union stickers. Rust was taking over the oxidized red paint.

Riker pegged the Dodge for a working man's rig. Which meant it was probably decently maintained and used regularly. Which in turn indicated it would likely bear fruit in the form of fuel for the EarthRoamer.

Riker said, "Those old diesel pickups usually have a pretty big tank. We'll stop here." As he slowed Dolly, he ran his window down and pointed at the decades-old rig.

Taking the cue, Shorty pulled in front of the Dodge and parked at the curb.

Riker did the same but on the opposite side of the street. He ran up his window and killed the engine. The rain had settled down to a gentle drumming on the hood and roof.

After watching Shorty emerge from his rig, gas cans and siphoning gear in hand, Riker and the others piled out and met the man beside the Dodge.

Shorty had his hat pulled down low, the Shockwave slung over one shoulder.

Riker was armed with the AR. After popping more ibuprofen pills and swallowing them dry, he regarded Shorty. "Why don't you go to work on getting diesel for your rig. My cans are all full."

Shorty said, "Better put a watch on each of our flanks." He handed the shotgun to Benny. "I could use some help here."

"Steve-O," Riker called, "you're an old hand at it. Why don't you stay with Shorty."

Flashing a crisp salute, Steve-O said, "Yes, sir," and looked to Shorty for direction.

Riker led Benny, Lia, and Vern away from the siphoning operation. Pausing on the sidewalk between the Dodge and stucco home, he said to Benny, "You take the west end." He turned, passed the AR to Lia, then sent her off to cover the intersection east of them. Pointing to the brown stucco home, he called, "Me and Vern will take the high ground on the porch. Holler if you see or hear anything."

The pair followed the short walk to a run of six stairs leading up to a four by six porch.

While Riker waited on the porch out of the rain for Vern to join him, he plucked a rolled-up newspaper off the dusty floor.

Vern reached the top of the porch a few seconds after Riker. He wasn't winded or limping and didn't seem to favor any one part of his anatomy. He was just a little bit slower. Which was totally understandable, seeing as how Riker's stride was longer than most. Seeing the unfurled newspaper in Riker's hands, Vern said, "Can I see that when you're done?"

Riker handed it over straight away. "I'll keep watch. You read the headlines aloud. Cool?"

"Governor calls for statewide quarantine. That was the right call," Vern said agreeably. "Mentions the airport shutting down because of incoming flights carrying people infected with Romeo Victor." He looked up. "Is that what this thing is called?"

Riker shook his head. "It's called Romero."

"After the movie director?"

Stunned that the man made the connection, Riker asked, "What do you know of Romero?"

"Are you kidding? *Night of the Living Dead* was a groundbreaking movie. Way ahead of its time. Took a pretty girl named Barbara to see it at the theater. She hugged on me for the entire run. I was twenty-two. She was twenty." He smiled. "Barbara was my new bride."

"Where was Shane?"

Vern drew a deep breath. Exhaling sharply, he said, "Barbara was about two months along. He was an easy baby. She didn't have any morning sickness. She went into labor at ten in the morning. I was smoking a cigar before noon."

Riker didn't respond to that. He had just jabbed a knife into Shane's head. What could he say? So he acted like he hadn't been listening and looked the length of the street, right to left. Benny was all alone near the end of the block. Nearby, on the street in front of the stucco home, Shorty and Steve-O were still filling the cans. They were mostly out of sight. Now and again Steve-O's Stetson would appear over the Dodge's bed rail. Finishing the slow pan, Riker saw Lia down by the T. She was backpedaling, real slow, toward the Shelby, the AR trained on something to her right.

Riker was fishing his radio out to see what the matter was when, simultaneously, Rose's harried voice leapt from the speaker and something slammed hard into the door at his back.

Vern started but retained his hold on the newspaper.

As Riker lifted the radio to his lips, he glanced at the door. A lone zombie, nearly as old as Vern from the looks of it, was peering at them through the rectangular window. Its bathrobe hung open, revealing a distended belly crisscrossed by blue veins. It looked like something dragged out of the grave.

The impact with the door had dislodged the horizontal blinds, leaving them attached at just one corner. As the zombie pawed at the glass, its bloated fingers making opaque slug tracks everywhere they touched, the blinds clattered against the doorjamb.

Assessing the odds of the dead thing breaching the door as slim to none, Riker answered the call. "Rose? You still there?"

"Yes, Lee. It's me, Rose," she said breathlessly. "I've been trying to get ahold of you for a couple of hours."

Entire body going rigid, Riker blurted, "Where is Tara?"

A couple of seconds passed, then Rose came back on. "She went out to work on the clearing and didn't return. I followed protocols, Lee. I called her when the first fifteen minutes had passed, and she hadn't checked in. No answer. Tried again right away, same thing. I haven't heard from her since."

"OK ... calm down. Take a breath. I'm sure it's just bad batteries. Or maybe she lost her radio. Dozer could have wandered off and Tara got lost trying to find him." He knew he was lying to himself. Damn it, Tara. Why'd you go it alone? He knew the answer before he thought it. Because he and Tara were cut from the same cloth, that's why.

Voice nearly back to normal, Rose said, "Dozer stayed here with me."

Cold ball forming in his gut, Riker turned and regarded Vern. "You better get back to the truck. Tell the others to wrap it up. We're done here."

Vern made no reply. He continued to stare at Riker—on his face, an earnest expression. Remaining tightlipped, he tucked the paper under his arm and started down the stairs.

Riker got a sense the man could tell something bad had happened. If it hadn't been apparent from Rose's tone, Riker had no doubt his own body language had conveyed the seriousness of the call.

Once Vern was out of earshot, Riker thumbed the radio's Talk button. "Start from the beginning," he said to Rose. "Leave *nothing* out."

The words tumbled rapid-fire from the speaker as Rose went over everything that had happened since Riker's last radio contact with Tara.

Riker listened, prompting for more detail only when he felt it necessary. After about three minutes of this—during which he witnessed Lia put down a Random and pair of Slogs with a sustained volley of gunfire, and the trapped zombie at his back slammed repeatedly against the door—he hurried back to the Shelby, one thing on his mind: returning to Trinity as fast as humanly possible.

Oh, what Riker wouldn't give for access to Wade Clark and his helicopter right about now.

Chapter 41

Lia's directions saw the two-vehicle convoy to the onramp to Route-84 with a minimum of turns and very little contact with the walking dead. They did, however, come across a handful of automotive pileups. They didn't let those slow them down. Where the EarthRoamer couldn't pass through cleanly, Shorty slowed it to a crawl and created a hole with its formidable bumper. After coming up against their third tangle of cars, Shorty had become so adept at nudging static vehicles out of the way that he barely had to slow down.

Every time Riker let the EarthRoamer overtake the Shelby so Shorty could put it through its paces, he couldn't help but compare the technique to a fullback opening up a seam in the opponents' defensive line for the halfback.

Ten minutes had already slipped into the past when the clear stretch of Route 84 came into view. In the far distance, Riker saw the pair of dump trucks. They were still parked perpendicular to the four-lane and blocking all access to and from Santa Fe. Adjacent to the roadblock was an entrance to 84 northbound. At the midpoint of the northbound ramp, a pair of New Mexico Army National Guard Humvees were parked grille-to-grille across the road. To their right, the dusty infield was a parking lot of abandoned vehicles. There was no going around them.

Riker cast a quick glance at the distant roadblock. "We would have had to deal with this had we come this way earlier."

"And we would have had to deal with the monsters, too," Steve-O noted.

"At the time, going around was the right decision," Riker said. "Now that we know Santa Fe is accessible the way we just came, this will have to be our go-to. Shaved a few miles off. Saved us some gas, too."

"What are we going to do *now*?" asked Benny. "Rose is all alone at Trinity."

Voice filled with confidence, Steve-O said, "Dozer will protect her."

Riker met Benny's gaze in the mirror. "Take it easy, bro. Before you start future tripping, why don't we take a closer look at the block on the ramp. I don't think it's as bad as it looks from here." He refrained from voicing his doubt that Shorty was going to be able to maneuver his EarthRoamer through the roadblock without moving at least one of the Humvees.

Hard set to his jaw, Riker drove the short distance to the ramp at half the posted limit. He braked short of the onramp and took the turn real slow, the Shelby creeping along at walking speed.

Viewed up close, it was easy to see there was more to the roadblock than Riker had previously thought. A C-shaped assemblage of cement Jersey barriers ringed the Humvees on the downhill side. The ground in front of the barriers was littered with spent brass. Unlike most of the roadblocks Riker had seen since the nationwide lockdown had begun, this one lacked the usual wheeled light standards. Additionally, there was no electronic reader board to announce what was to be expected of a citizenry just coming to learn that all future travel had been banned by the government—be it at the county, state, or federal level.

A handful of yards downslope from the roadblock, a half-dozen bullet-riddled corpses lay sprawled out across the road in positions that would have been extremely uncomfortable if they hadn't been dead. To a man, they had bled out and died where they had fallen.

The fact they were all fighting-age males, early twenties to mid-thirties, led Riker to believe these men had tried to assault the roadblock.

The long pants and assortment of winter parkas told him they had tried to use the cover of night to their advantage. That they had paid dearly for the transgression told him the guardsmen manning the block had been wearing night-vision goggles—one of the items on his list yet to be found.

As Riker slowed the Shelby and pulled off to the side of the ramp, the murder of crows that had been feeding on the corpses took flight. They circled overhead for a few seconds, cawing and swooping on the roadblock, then beat wings toward the next free meal.

Watching the angry birds retreat to the north, Riker said, "Looks like a bunch of locals tried to take back their highway."

"Sad it has come to this so quickly," Vern said. "Doesn't surprise me though. Before you kids came along, me and Shane had to run off more folks like these than I care to count."

Lia said, "They must have been desperate. I can't imagine being in their shoes."

Benny said, "You going around, Lee?" He paused for a beat. Then, voice a near whisper, he added, "Rose is all alone up there."

And Tara's at Disneyland, thought Riker. Out loud, he said, "Think Shorty can navigate around this?"

"Not much room," proffered Lia. "And those barriers will probably need to be winched out of the way."

The hillside on the left was steep, but Riker figured the Shelby could tackle it. It took all of his will power to not drive around the block, power up the embankment, and leave Shorty to fend for himself. Instead, knowing that the time and daylight burned trying to talk the man to Trinity over the radio could be better used searching for Tara, he hailed Shorty and asked the man if he remembered Buccaneer Park in Mississippi.

Shorty came on right away. "Almost died twice." He paused. "And it's Miss Abigail's final resting place. I'll never forget it."

"Same routine, then," Riker said. "I'll use my winch to move the two barriers on the right. You hook up to the Humvee behind them and pull as soon as I'm out of the way. We should be moving again in five or so."

"Copy that."

There was no way to thread the vehicles through the bodies, and Riker couldn't justify taking the time to move them. So he tried his best to avoid running over them as he nosed the Shelby perpendicular to the pair of barriers. Each time the big tires rolled over a fleshy obstacle, he said, "Forgive me." Three times he uttered the phrase before the pickup was in place.

After spooling out some cable, Riker jumped from the truck and ran the hook to the barriers. With Benny standing guard, Riker wrapped the cable around both barriers, threading it through embedded eyehooks. *Two birds, one stone.*

Back in the truck, Riker put the seven hundred horses under the hood to work. At first, until heat and friction dried the pavement, there was a little slipping and sliding. Once all four tires found purchase, the pickup lurched backward. The noise of two and a half tons of cement being dragged down the ramp was drowned out by the revving engine. The vibration from all that weight in transit, however, resonated through the pickup's frame and floorboards and manifested as a vibration felt deep in everyone's chest.

As the barriers rode over the pronounced drop-off where the shoulder abutted the infield, they toppled over and quickly ground to a halt in the damp dirt.

Riker set the brake, hopped from the pickup, and rushed over to help Benny unhook the barriers and get the cable spooled back up. Reversing the process, they ran out cables from the EarthRoamer's dual winches and hooked them up to the Humvee's frame-mounted tie-down points.

The EarthRoamer had a hard time getting the Humvee's front tires to break free. Shorty was forced to reposition Marge on the ramp a couple of times to get the angle right. All of the jockeying back and forth was taking a toll on the corpses of the would-be marauders.

Once the squat Humvee's desert-tan snout was facing down ramp, towing it from behind the remaining Jersey barriers was an easy affair.

Ten minutes lost, thought Riker as he got them rolling through the breach and past the lone Humvee still standing sentinel. Just as the Shelby crested the ramp, Riker saw the crows in his wing mirror. Still in flight, they had coalesced into a glossy black cloud. As he continued to watch, the birds winged around in front of the EarthRoamer, flared in unison, and dropped en masse on the newly ravaged corpses.

After thirty minutes of not knowing what had become of Tara, the non-stop headache assaulting Riker was joined by a feeling of despair that no amount of glass-half-full thinking would make go away.

***

Fifteen minutes later, the Shelby was nosed up to the gate to Trinity House and Riker was tapping out the access code on the keypad.

Rose awaited them on the circular parking pad. Clutched in her hands was a tightly wound dish towel. Sitting on his haunches next to her, stout shadow falling across the bloodstain that—short of a good pressure washing—was going nowhere, Dozer watched with canine indifference as the vehicles rolled toward him.

Riker didn't take time for introductions. That would come later. Right now his first priority was seeing the basement safe room Rose had described. A close second was getting eyes on the map and blueprints to the so-called Lazarus bunker.

As the passengers opened doors, Riker asked Benny to hang back a second.

Already halfway out of the truck, Benny grabbed Riker's headrest to arrest himself. "What's up?" he asked, hanging over the seatback.

Near the front of the Shelby, Steve-O was doing his best to comfort Rose, who was on her tiptoes and craning to find Benny. Lia was standing off to the side. Her body language suggested she was unsure of what she should do. Vern, on the other hand, had closed the door behind him, gone straight to Dozer, and was now busy scratching the pooch behind his cropped ears.

Riker met Rose's inquisitive gaze, held up one finger and mouthed, "Give us a second." She nodded, so he turned to face Benny. "I don't want you to make a big deal of her being alone. If you do, it'll just feed her anxiety."

Benny looked a question at Riker.

"There may again come a day when she has to hold down the fort all by herself."

"Not if I have anything to say about it."

Riker shook his head. "We're only as strong as our weakest link, Ben. Feelings aren't facts. We're going to need to build up her confidence, not cosign her fears."

Incredulous, Benny said, "Tara is missing, Lee. She isn't answering her radios. Is that lost on you?"

Unbuckling his seatbelt, Riker said, "It's not lost on me. It's all I've been thinking about since Rose got ahold of us. I'm torn up inside over this, Ben." He bowed his head. "In my mind's eye, I keep seeing her in the clearing." He paused for a beat. Regarding Benny, he continued: "And in that vision, I see a group of biters feeding on her. Just fucking ripping and tearing at her guts."

Struggling to put a positive spin on the situation, Benny said, "You and I know how Tara likes to take the bull by the horns. I'm sure she's investigating the Lazarus place. Maybe she got locked inside and is just waiting on us to rescue her. I doubt those crappy radios work inside a bunker. If that's what this Lazarus thing really is."

Riker said nothing. He was gripping the steering wheel so hard his knuckles had gone white.

Benny said, "Remember when we were coming back from a night out in Fort Wayne?"

Riker nodded. "The night you kept hitting on my little sister? How could I forget, you horny bastard." He chuckled at that. "She wasn't having it, bro."

Smiling, Benny said, "We were still kind of buzzed and stopped at that McDonalds for coffee."

Eyes lighting up, Riker said, "And Tara got herself locked in the bathroom. We thought she was driving the big porcelain bus. But she wasn't puking at all."

"And her phone was in that ratty Monte Carlo you used to drive." Smile fading, Benny said, "She's going to be OK, Lee. Just you watch. She's locked in the bathroom in this Lazarus place."

Pushing from his mind what Lazarus really meant to him, Riker elbowed open his door. "Let's check out this *bunker* Rose stumbled upon."

Chapter 42

The stairs leading down into the bunker were steeper than Riker imagined them to be. Each step down elicited a flash of pain from his overworked stump. When he set foot on the gray cement floor, he paused to survey his surroundings.

Rose's initial description of the Trinity House bunker had been nondescript and conjured up images of his parents' basement rumpus room. What he found himself staring at was in reality closer to NORAD's Cheyenne Mountain Complex than what he had been expecting to find. It was like night and day. There was so much detail Rose had left out: the multiple clocks on the wall. The bank of computers. He couldn't believe she had left out the HAM radios crowding the workbench. Though a bit old technology-wise, they would be a game-changer if they actually worked and were connected to an external antenna. The setup made the little Motorola handheld radios look like kiddie toys.

"Wow!" was the first thing that came to Riker's mind. He moved away from the base of the steps so Benny and Rose could join him.

Benny's tongue wasn't tied. He said, "It's like the bridge of the Voyager."

Riker looked a question at his friend.

"The spaceship from Star Trek Voyager."

"I only watched the Shatner reruns. If you would have said Starship Enterprise, I'd have understood." As he paced the room, he couldn't help but think there had to be a hidden egress tunnel somewhere. A lot of house sitting above that steep ass stairway for there not to be a second way out. Filing the thought away for future exploration, he regarded Rose. "Where's the map you mentioned?"

Stabbing a thumb at the ceiling, she said, "Upstairs. I lugged the stack of blueprints up as well." She pushed her glasses back to their proper perch on her nose. "Shouldn't we be looking for Tara?"

Riker nodded. Not looking forward to scaling the steps, he said, "Let's go," and shooed the couple ahead of him.

Unfolded, the map took up half of the dining room table. Riker planted his palms on either side of the map and gave it a quick once-over.

Rose edged in and pointed to the clearing. From there she traced her finger along the path running east away from the clearing Tara had been working on. "Tara said she's been up this path, just not all the way to where this Lazarus thing is supposed to be." Relocating her finger to a point north of Trinity House, she pointed out the dashed line denoting a road that cut a shallow east-west arc across the top of the map. If everything was to scale, the road wouldn't be far from the outer wall.

"This really caught Tara's attention," Rose said. "The key indicates it's a fire lane. Tara was amazed she hadn't already spotted it during her walks to and from the clearing."

"This map is old," Riker stated. "I'd guess if there is a road there, it's probably unrecognizable by now. Likely to find only a couple of dirt tire tracks overtaken by underbrush and cactus."

"Only way to find out is to take a look. First thing, though, is to go to the clearing and make sure she's just not so absorbed in her work that she's forgotten about the radio check-ins."

Benny said, "That's not like her."

Steve-O was throwing the ball for Dozer. Riker called, "Coming with?"

Adjusting his Stetson, Steve-O said, "If the pretty lady is lost, I want to help find her."

"Get a coat," Riker instructed. "Probably want to grab some water. Since there's only about ninety minutes of sun left, be smart to grab a couple of headlamps, too. And maybe change out of those fancy boots. Wouldn't want to scratch them up on day one."

Steve-O said, "My dad used to say even fancy boots were meant for wearing." The heels clicked on the wood floor as he strode off to fill a couple of water bottles.

Regarding Lia and Vern, who had been standing on the periphery, Riker said, "Who's coming? It's about a mile and a half round trip. If you don't want to, you're welcome to stay behind and keep Rose and Dozer company."

Rose looked to Riker. "Tara's my friend. I want to help look for her."

Benny beat Riker to the punch. "You should stay back and monitor the radios. Besides, Lee's friend, Shorty, found us. He's out getting stuff ready. You'll meet him later."

This spurred Rose to ask: "Did you find Crystal?" Her tone was hopeful.

Benny nodded. "She was at the county lockup…" He paused. The look on his face conveyed what he had left out.

Rose exhaled sharply. "She's one of those things, isn't she?"

Benny told her about Riker and Lia rescuing Warden Littlewolf and her men. He left out Luther Carr's gruesome death. He also kept quiet about the cul-de-sac gunfight.

Riker said, "Littlewolf confirmed that Crystal did not survive the outbreak inside. I don't think a single prisoner got out alive."

Crestfallen, Rose took a seat on a stool. Regarding Riker, she said, "Thanks for checking for me." She hefted the Motorola off the counter. "I'll stay and watch the cameras. Be sure to keep in radio range."

Riker said, "Vern sold us some new long-range jobs. Shorty's putting batteries in them."

She said, "Sold?"

Benny said, "Long story."

After committing the map to memory, Riker scooped up his AR and headed for the door.

Shorty was waiting beside the EarthRoamer. He passed a radio to Riker and kept one for himself. "They're all set to Channel 10-1." He handed a third radio to Steve-O. "Take that to Rose. Tell her it's good to go." Steve-O accepted the radio, flashed a salute, and hustled off.

Shorty had an assortment of weapons and gear laid out on the motor court pavers. Looking to Lia and Benny, he said, "Pick your poison."

Benny said, "I'm good with the Glock," but he still took a headlamp and snugged it on.

Lia had already retrieved the plastic rifle case from the Shelby and had taken her scoped bolt-action rifle from the protective foam-padding. It was futuristic looking; the milled aluminum stock outfitted with a multi-adjustable cheek-weld and padded stock extension. She selected the appropriate ammunition for her rifle and went to work loading the tiny .22 caliber rounds into the pair of magazines she'd taken from the case.

Eyeing the rifle, Shorty said, "Anschutz, eh? That thing probably cost you more than that Smart car I destroyed back there. You rich?"

She shook her head. "My dad bought it for me. He's ... *was* an airline pilot."

He asked, "You need a pistol?"

"I'm good for now. It's not like we're going to war, right?"

Shorty raised a brow. "Better to be prepared and not need it." He chose a .22 caliber semiautomatic pistol that had been among the spoils he found inside the EarthRoamer. "Takes the same ammo as your tack driver. Ten-round magazine, too."

Lia took the pistol without protest.

Riker had been watching the exchange. While he didn't think his opinion of her could go any higher, the way she went with the flow and accepted the offering bumped it up a couple of notches.

"Take what you need," Shorty said to Riker. "I'm about to close up shop."

Though the handcrafted knife on Riker's hip had a long, sharp blade, he selected a machete and attached it to his belt opposite the Randall.

"We going to be doing a little bushwhacking?" Shorty asked.

Riker mentioned the Lazarus place and fire lane leading up to it. "If the bunker is actually there, I have a feeling it has been a long time since anybody's used the road."

Shorty picked out a machete with a safety-orange handle. It was nicely balanced. He shoved it into a side pocket of his backpack and shrugged the pack on.

"Blades are real sharp," Vern called. He was standing by the entry and watching the goings-on. "Ran all of them over a whetstone myself. It's the little things that keep my customers from going to the big box stores."

Kept, thought Riker. *Past tense. There are no more customers. Or big box stores for that matter.*

Shorty called, "Steve-O! We're on the move."

A beat later, Steve-O emerged from the side door to the garage. He was still wearing the red boots. He'd swapped the windbreaker for a western-style jacket complete with suede fringe. In his hands was the colorful NERF gun. Orange-tipped darts could be seen in the clear plastic magazine. And though the white Stetson was pulled down low, the brim couldn't hide the wide smile on the man's cherubic face.

"Got fresh batteries," he called. "Let's do this."

Turning to Riker, Shorty asked, "Think he's ready for a big boy piece?"

Riker shook his head. "Not yet."

"When?"

"Soon," Riker said as he strode off toward the back of the house.

While they made their way counterclockwise around Trinity House, Shorty provided a running commentary. "You choose the place?"

"All Tara," Riker responded. "It came furnished, too."

"Came with more than home furnishings," Shorty noted. "And for so big a place, it sure blends in with the countryside."

Benny said, "Can't even see the roof from the road. Wouldn't know it was here unless you've been here before."

Riker stopped in front of the recessed door. He had in one hand a keyring full of keys to the house. Selecting the keys for the locks, he made a quick call to Rose. "What do you see on the monitors?"

"All clear except for the front."

"What's going on up there?"

"Looks like you picked up some zombies on the way back. A small pack of them way down at the end of the feeder road."

Riker said, "Keep an eye on them. Let us know if you see anything out of the ordinary."

Sad days, he thought, *when a group of dead humans trooping around* is *the ordinary.*

Rose came back and warned Riker of the corpses he was about to find on the opposite side of the gate.

"I can already smell them," he responded. "You're in charge until we get back." He pocketed the radio, then unlocked the door.

Rose hadn't been kidding when she said, "Tara made a mess of a few by the back gate." They were sprawled where they'd fallen, each headshot skull encompassed by halos of clumped brain tissue and congealed blood.

Shorty said, "Wouldn't want to tangle with the person who did this."

"It was Tara," Steve-O noted. "She's gotten real good with her pistol."

Riker stepped aside so the others could file through the open door. Gesturing to Shorty's Booty Hunter hat, he said, "Tara sees that on your head, I can almost guarantee there's no way to avoid tangling with her."

Lia said, "I think you're right about me liking your sister, Lee."

While Riker locked the door, Shorty removed the hat and looked at the image. "I forgot all about this," he lied and tossed it into the nearby underbrush.

Riker assigned marching order, with Steve-O, Lia, and Shorty in the middle. Benny was to lag behind for a few seconds, then set off after the rest, his job: stopping every now and again to listen for anyone or anything that may be tailing them.

Once the group had started up the path toward the landing pad, Benny spent the time retrieving the hat. Before he fell in behind the others, he snugged the gas station gem onto the head of the bald corpse. He figured it would be the perfect icebreaker once they found Tara safe and sound and all returned to Trinity House together.

Chapter 43

"We're here," Riker said as he emerged into the clearing. Presently it was entirely in shadow, the westering sun having dipped below the treetops hours ago. The chill in the air made him shiver as his gaze toured the open space. His heart sank and the cold finger of dread was back and working its way up his spine when he saw the axe and bow saw sitting all alone in the center of the clearing. He also noted the head-high pile of brush on the periphery. What he didn't see was three or four hours of forward progress on the job at hand. While the ground Tara had been working on earlier was now mostly cleared of brush—maybe a two-hour job for one person—the perimeter still needed much attention.

"Spread out and search the ground for any clues. Maybe a radio or the keys to the gate." That Tara had taken two radios with her and still hadn't checked in with either had been nagging him since he learned she had stopped checking in.

Lose one radio? Maybe. Both? Not a chance in hell. Which was why the dreaded thought of "foul play" being the explanation for her disappearance was becoming more of a reality to him with each passing second.

While the others walked the clearing, heads down, flashlight beams sweeping the ground, Riker made his way east, to the far side of the clearing, where a second trail snaked off into the gloom.

Lia had followed close behind. When they got there, she illuminated the narrow path that, at first blush, appeared to be no more than a game trail. Pointing to a spot where the hard-packed soil was a little darker than the rest, she said, "Those scuff marks in the dirt, were they here before?"

"I don't know about those," Riker responded, "but these bushes look like they've been pushed apart." He grabbed ahold of a gnarled branch jutting out across the path. It was waist-high to Lia and had been bent back to the point that it had snapped under pressure. "Someone's been through here," he noted. "Could have been one of the zombies. I highly doubt it, though." He paused and looked about the clearing. "I'd bet the house Tara went exploring. The Lazarus place was probably calling to her—"

"Like the Siren's song," Lia finished.

"I don't know about all that," he conceded. "It certainly has *my* attention, though."

"So you think she found the place, went inside, and she's *still* exploring it?"

"I don't know what to think." He called the others over. Once they had assembled and were standing around him in a loose semicircle, he went on, saying: "Same thing as before. I'll take the lead. Benny, you get the rear." Half expecting a smartass comment due to his poor choice of words, Riker looked to Shorty. The man was standing ramrod straight, eyes roaming the forest, shotgun at a high-ready. On his face was a look equal parts worry and exhaustion. Throw in a pounding headache, and that was exactly how Riker felt.

NERF rifle at port-arms, Steve-O said, "Where is Tara? I'm real worried about her."

Lia bent down and whispered something in Steve-O's ear. He looked to her and a half-smile creased his face. Whatever she had said, Riker thought, it had lifted his spirits. Making a mental note to himself to remember to ask her about it later, he dragged the machete from its sheath and started cutting them a path through the foliage.

***

Ten minutes after leaving the clearing, Riker was standing on level ground and staring at the rounded crest of the hillock he had previously only seen from a distance. Viewed from the twisting access road leading to Trinity House, the nub of earth protruding over the surrounding trees was not at all impressive. Up close, however, it was enormous. He could easily imagine a geologist and architect and engineer all collaborating on ways to carve from the peak a hole large enough to accommodate the massive multi-level subterranean Lazarus complex depicted on the blueprints.

"So where's the vault door?" Shorty joked. He had loosened up somewhat during the short hike, becoming quite chatty with Lia and Benny.

Riker ignored the quip. Envisioning the map in his head, he turned to the north, putting the hilltop off his right shoulder. "First things first," he said to no one in particular. "Let's spread out and look for the road. We find one, chances are the Lazarus bunker is real and it'll lead us to it."

Keeping a few yards separation between them, they all walked north, toward a nearby picket of mature trees.

"Got it," Steve-O called and then started humming *On the Road Again*—his favorite Willie tune.

Ducking around a wide tree trunk, Riker said, "On the road again is right, Steve-O. And it's more than I expected to find." The brush-choked single-lane dirt track he had imagined was actually wide enough to accommodate the Shelby. Thanks to the overarching branches, there was zero chance of the EarthRoamer making it up here without a lot of advance pruning.

Lia said, "I think we should follow it."

Benny got Riker's attention. "Try the radio again. Even if she is inside, maybe we're close enough now that our signal gets to her."

Doubtful, thought Riker. A bunker is supposed to keep things out. Things like gamma rays, nuclear fallout, a nasty virus as well as the desperate people hell-bent on escaping all of the above. No way radio frequencies were going to leach in or out. But, given the elevation gain, if Tara was *outside* and within a ten-to-sixteen-mile radius from their current position, with the new radio's extended range, he might be able to push a signal out to her.

Checking the channel and sub-channel, Riker pressed the Talk button. "Tara? It's Lee. Can you hear me?"

Everyone had frozen in place and turned their attention to the radio in Riker's hand.

A minute passed.

Nothing.

He tried again.

Silence on the other end.

Pocketing the radio, Riker said, "That settles it: We walk the road."

Benny moved close to Riker. "East or west?"

"East is uphill. If that doesn't pan out, we follow the road back down to Trinity."

"Maybe she got bit by a coral snake," proffered Steve-O. "Did you know that they are the second most deadly snake in the world?"

Riker said, "Negative, Ghost Rider."

Benny shuddered. "I hate snakes almost as much as I hate spiders."

Shorty said, "Who knew we had Steve Irwin in our midst. The man in the white Stetson makes a valid point."

Steve-O smiled at the compliment.

Lia said, "Coral snakes are native to *southwest* New Mexico. Rarely do you find one here. Rattlesnakes are a dime a dozen, though. I have to be careful when I'm out desert running. Then there's wild boar and javelina to worry about. Their tusks are razor-sharp and can gut a man. I've seen both in the wild."

"A rattlesnake bite isn't going to put you down right away," Benny said. "Tara would have time to get back. Wouldn't she?"

Riker heard the doubt in his friend's voice. Having had enough, he said, "We're talking about my sister. Not some anonymous hiker from New York who's gotten lost on a vacation walkabout." He went silent, raised his AR, and marched off to the east. As he followed his own lengthening shadow, with each step he took it was becoming more and more difficult for him to believe that a good outcome was on the horizon.

***

They emerged from the tree line ten minutes later, at a spot where the road widened and started a shallow climb around back of the hilltop. A quarter mile or so from the flat spot on the hilltop's west side, the road leveled out and made an abrupt ninety-degree turn to the right.

The road was flat and smooth and ran laser straight for sixty feet or so before dead-ending at a near-vertical section of hillside covered by some kind of creeping vines, their large woody roots showing through in places.

Lia said, "Trumpet vines. They flower in spring and summer. Pretty colors, too. Damn hard to keep in check, though."

"I can tell," Riker said. "Perfect choice of plant to cover a secret entrance." Though it wasn't showing in his demeanor, his mind was running a mile a minute. He wanted to rush to the end of the road and start ripping away the dying vines. Two things held him in check. First, he didn't want to do so just to find dirt underneath there. It would crush him. Secondly, he wanted to call Rose and give her a quick rundown before they went any further.

As Riker checked in with Rose, he walked his gaze along the short length of road running away from him. It looked undisturbed.

Finished with the call, Riker walked forward and rejoined the others at the wall.

Steve-O was already up to his elbows in vines.

"Watch for snakes," Lia called.

Running a hand through his lengthening salt and pepper hair, Shorty said, "Knock yourself out. I'll supervise. Have to admit, though. If you were going to build yourself a nuclear bunker, sure makes sense to have your blast doors facing away from the place most likely to take a direct hit from a nuke."

Letting a handful of vines fall back over the wall, Lia said, "What threat is Santa Fe to the old Soviet Union? They going to corner the world's turquoise supply?"

Riker fixed her with an icy glare.

She raised her hands. "Sorry. I know this is no time to be joking." She pointed away from the hillside, north by west, where the sun was playing off the bottoms of distant clouds. "Los Alamos would be targeted before Santa Fe or Albuquerque."

Shorty said, "And how'd you reach that conclusion?"

"My dad was Air Force. He flew Buffs at first. Then he moved from B-52s to the new B-1 and, finally, toward the end of his career, he drove B-2s out of Whiteman in Missouri."

Riker asked, "What does that have to do with a nuke hitting here?"

"Dad was active during much of the Cold War. Always talked about the end of it all. How it came to a screeching halt. About the Berlin wall coming down being a big deal. Their operational tempo slowed considerably up until Volkov and his oligarch friends took power in Russia. Towards the end of Dad's

267

career, before he started flying airliners for Alaskan, he started writing a book about his being a part of the nuclear triad."

Explains why he named his daughter Amelia, thought Riker. *Namesake is only one of the most influential women in aviation history. One of the bravest, too.* He crunched the numbers in his head and decided that if her father was still active duty during the end of the Cold War, then Lia was likely in her late twenties or early thirties. She sure didn't look it. And wouldn't that make her a little too old to be an Olympian? Since he knew nothing about the biathlon, he refocused his attention on the task at hand.

As Riker grabbed another handful of vines and began pulling them away from the hillside, he said, "So why Los Alamos?"

"Los Alamos National Laboratory is still doing research in nuclear energy, nanotech, and other cutting-edge technology. Read about it in the *New Mexican.* They theorized it's one of hundreds of sites Russia would hit. China probably has a bomb targeted here, too."

Shorty said, "So we have a Steve Irwin, and now we've got Bill Nye the Science Guy. What's next?" He looked to Benny. "Go ahead. Spout some facts. I'll give you a nickname, too."

"No need," Riker said. "I just found something. A smooth surface. It's probably a wall." He looked to his immediate left. "Shorty, Steve-O … give me a hand."

Steve-O was still singing a Johnny Cash song as he hustled over. Something about a man coming around and taking names.

Shorty, on the other hand, paused for a beat. He smiled and said, "And now we have an archeologist in our midst. Be right there, *Indiana.*"

Chapter 44

Even as Shorty was asking, "Whatcha got, Indy?" Steve-O and Riker were busy ripping away a long swath of the invasive flora.

Hearing this, Steve-O stopped what he was doing, turned to face Shorty, and said, "We found a garage door."

Riker said nothing. He was tearing furiously, hand over hand, and throwing the shredded leaves and broken lengths of vine over his shoulder.

Meanwhile, Lia had stalked off to the far edge of the road and was busy pulling a section of vines away from the wall. The vines were in shadow and looked much greener than the rest.

"These are fake," she called. "Some kind of plastic. Like the decorations you put in a fish tank." She grunted and pushed the vines aside. "There's something behind here."

All heads turned in Lia's direction.

She said, "I think I just found a Judas door."

Shorty said, "Is it inset into a roll-up deal? Or a vault door?"

"The former," Lia said. "It's sturdy, though. Probably thick steel or some kind of exotic metal. I'm no expert, but it sure doesn't look like it's bombproof."

"Neither is this," Riker said. "They weren't on the blueprints. Makes me think the vault door is beyond this. Which I suspect is hiding a motor pool of sorts."

Lia bellied up to the door. She ran her hand around the barely perceptible seam. It came away covered with dust and spider webs and husks of dead bugs. "This door hasn't been opened in a long while."

Everyone formed up around the woman.

Riker said, "Don't move," and knelt by Lia's feet. He gasped as he did so. After wiping sweat beads from his forehead, he inspected the ground around Lia's trail runners. "Show me your sole," he demanded.

Looking to Steve-O for affirmation, Shorty said, "I'll take things Satan says for five hundred, Alex."

Steve-O said, "Jeopardy?"

"Bingo," Benny replied. "Shorty, it would seem, is full of jokes today."

"Better than being a sourpuss all the time," Shorty sneered. Softening his tone, he added, "I'm high on life, Benji. Might want to try lightening up."

Riker ignored the quip and the responses to it. He got it. People had their own ways of dealing with this new normal. And Shorty's coping mechanism was humor. Albeit poorly timed and usually inappropriate. Riker, on the other hand, chose to just tackle life one day at a time. At night, before closing his eyes, he thanked whoever was up there for seeing him through the day unscathed. Upon waking, before knocking out his mandatory pushups, he asked said entity for a repeat. Nothing less, nothing more. If *more* happened, and it was all good, he considered it icing on the cake. The only question he occasionally asked of this *whoever* was why he and those around him had been chosen to live while millions had died and come back as zombies. The answer never came.

Lia felt Riker release his hold on her ankle. "What are you doing?" she asked.

Riker said, "Comparing the pattern on your Nikes to the prints on the ground. They're all you. Tara never made it here." He rose. "We need to go back, but not the way we came."

Shorty said, "We're not going to explore Lazarus?"

Riker was already on the move, AR unslung, its deadly end leading the way. Over his shoulder, he called, "*After* we find Tara. Come on, damn it. We're burning daylight."

***

Riker saw the mountain bike before anyone else. It was on its side in the middle of the road with only its wheels and handlebars visible. Most of the bike's frame and its seat and pedals were obscured by the strip of tall grass splitting the road in two.

270

To his left was the beginning of an unimproved trail. No doubt it would spit them out at Trinity House. The seam in the bushes looked nearly identical to how they initially found the one across from Trinity's rear wall. If someone had come through here today, they'd taken great care to conceal their passage and had likely been scratched to hell upon emerging on the other side.

To Riker's right the road was crowded in on by mature trees and some kind of low scrub that liked to grab at clothing and was quick to cut any exposed skin its inch-long spikes came into contact with.

Thinking he might have inadvertently led them all into a trap, Riker made a fist and raised it high for all to see.

Shorty read the signal first. He stopped at once, restrained Steve-O with one arm, then trained his shotgun on the forest to his immediate right.

Lia and Benny had been talking to one another and nearly ran into Steve-O.

The transgression drew a steely glare from Shorty, who had taken a knee and was in the process of having Steve-O do the same.

After a few long seconds spent looking and listening for anything out of the ordinary, Riker decided it was safe for him to go ahead and take a closer look at the bike. As he rose, he showed Shorty his palm and mouthed, "Wait here."

Riker crept forward until he was standing over the black high-dollar mountain bike. It was only when he saw the bike in its entirety that he realized he'd seen it before, and he knew unequivocally who was behind Tara's disappearance.

After inspecting the ground all around the bike, he fished his multi-tool from a pocket, flipped out its short blade, and gently probed the grass under the frame tubes. When he failed to detect any wires connected to the bike, or metal objects hidden in the grass underneath it, he took a deep breath and stood the bike up. Balancing the bike on its knobby tires, he noticed something taped to the downtube. Closer inspection revealed a plastic sandwich bag. It contained a folded square of paper. A note.

Benny said, "What is it?"

Riker held the baggie up. "Demands, no doubt."

Lia asked, "Is the bike Tara's?"

271

Riker shook his head.

"I've seen it somewhere before," Shorty said. He paused for a beat, watching Riker open the bag. Finally, he went on, saying: "The *nephew* was riding it when he first came to my dock to ask about a ferry ride across state lines." He shook his head wildly side-to-side. "Shorty, Shorty, Shorty. Look what you fucking did, you greedy bastard."

Riker had unfolded the sheet of paper and was reading the message scribbled on it. "It was my idea," he shot, eyes still flicking over the words. "I take sole responsibility. It was a shitty move to undercut those people. But in that moment, I only cared about getting Tara and Steve-O off that dock. Staying out in front of the rolling lockdown was more important than anything. Making enemies was a risk I was willing to take. Getting stuck behind the iron curtain they were throwing up would have been a death sentence."

While Riker was talking, the others had crowded around him.

Steve-O put a hand on Riker's shoulder. "It's all right, Lee. Your heart was in the right place."

In a low voice, Benny asked, "What do they want?"

Riker met his friend's gaze. "Me. They want me to ride the bike downhill. I'm supposed to come alone."

Lia broke an uncomfortable silence. "Or what?"

Pinching away a tear, Riker said, "Think the worst and multiply it by a thousand. I'm not going to read it again. Makes my stomach turn. Especially since my sister is no stranger to her own body being violated."

Lia crossed her arms and looked away.

Thinking of Rose in the house, all alone with Vern, Benny took his radio from a pocket. "I'm doing a check-in."

Riker said, "Ask Rose what she sees on the monitor." He checked his watch. "It's going to be dark in less than an hour. Full dark in two or three." He handed the AR to Lia then loosened his belt and removed the Randall and holster containing the Sig Legion.

Finished checking in with Rose, Benny said, "The biters have made it to the gate and are hanging around. There's only three. Other than that, she's seen nothing else to cause alarm."

Riker nodded toward the overgrown trail leading to the rear of Trinity House. "You're going to make a lot of noise breaking through the thicket. Which means you'll be in the same boat as Tara and will have to deal with the zombies when you reach the gate." He handed over the Sig and knife, then dug out the keys to the perimeter wall door. "Have Steve-O tackle the locks. While he works to get the locks thrown, the rest of you need to have your guns out and your heads on a swivel."

Having composed herself, Lia said, "You're going in completely unarmed?"

"One of their rules," Riker said soberly.

Lia made a face. "Their? Plural? There's two of them?"

Benny said, "Weren't there three at the docks?"

Riker nodded. "There may be more by now." In his mind's eye, he saw the pickup with the caveman decal. Then a memory was triggered. "I should have known they'd be a problem. Now I remember seeing New Mexico plates on their truck."

Benny said, "How in the hell did they find you?"

"Looks like I'm about to find out."

Lia said, "You can't go like a lamb to slaughter. Maybe some of us can tail you from a distance. Or Steve-O can shadow you with the drone."

Riker shook his head. "I have no choice. Tobias wants his pound of flesh. It's either coming from me or Tara. My decision led up to this." He pinched the back of his neck. Rubbed it vigorously. The headache, plus all the accompanying stabs of pain brought on by high stress, was back.

Riker had Lia watch the road as he pulled Benny aside. Out of earshot of the others, he said, "The property and house belongs to you and Steve-O if, God forbid, me and Tara don't make it back."

Benny tried to protest.

Silencing the man with a raised hand, Riker went on, saying: "Shorty may be a bit coarse, but he has integrity. He does what he says he is going to do. Work with him. Try to get along."

"What about the helicopter pilot?"

"Wade's solid. Take him at his word." Riker pointed toward the clearing. "You need to get those solar path-lights strung up in the trees around the clearing. Get them as high as you can. All of them. I'm pretty sure they will have taken on enough of a charge before sundown to power them through the night."

"You want them mounted to the bigger trees on the periphery?"

Riker nodded. "If you can, put on some headlamps and take the chainsaw to the ones I marked."

"We're talking about *tonight?*"

"They need to be up as soon as possible," Riker stressed. Then, tone all business, he said, "Treat Steve-O like an equal. Like a grown ass man. Give him a gun. I think he's ready."

Riker singled out Shorty. "You and Benny need to work together while I'm gone. If I don't return—"

Shorty shushed Riker and gestured for the note. Note in hand, Shorty said, "You're coming back, Lee." Shorty's eyes flicked rapidly back and forth, and his lips moved as he read the note. "They want you to take a radio. Good! Gives me an idea." He shared his thoughts, then reached into his back pocket and took out his wallet. From the wallet, he retrieved a manila envelope and gave it to Riker. It was no bigger than a pack of gum and contained something rigid. "Instructions are inside," Shorty said. "I always carry one of these. Started doing it back in my smuggling days."

Riker said, "I'm supposed to bring the radio and nothing else."

"So you hide it."

"Where?"

Steve-O had been looking on. He said, "In your bionic leg, Lee."

"Good thinking," Riker said. *They'll search it first thing* was what he really thought.

"In your Salomon," Benny suggested. "Slip it under the insole?"

Shorty said, "There's always the prison pocket."

Riker's head took on a slight tilt. "Prison pocket?"

"Keister it," Shorty said, keeping a straight face. "Conceal it in your anus."

Obviously listening in, Lia said, "That's gross."

Raising his arms in mock surrender, Riker said, "I'll figure something. Just not *that.*" He dragged Steve-O over and hugged the man. Before letting go, he whispered something that made Steve-O smile. Riker did the same to Benny, patting his back as they parted. With that out of the way, he threw a leg over the bike and, without another word or glance over his shoulder, pushed off and put his feet on the pedals.

Chapter 45

To get used to the bike, Riker took it easy at first, going heavy on the brakes and allowing gravity to pull him downhill. After a hundred yards or so, he pedaled furiously for a short while. While his knees came close to hitting the handlebars with each revolution of the cranks, the bike's front and rear suspension allowed him to remain seated, which in turn relieved pressure where the prosthesis came into contact with skin and scar tissue. A full day's worth of activity, most of it rather strenuous, had led to him feeling his heartbeat on the tip of his stump and phantom pins and needles where his lower leg used to be.

After coasting for a couple of minutes, Riker braked and dismounted. Figuring his average speed to have been somewhere between ten and fifteen miles per hour, and that he'd been on the bike for three, maybe four minutes, he ran a couple of quick calculations in his head to determine how far he'd traveled.

The first, using the lower estimate of each variable, put him roughly half a mile from where he'd started. Plugging in the second set of numbers suggested he was a mile removed from Trinity House. Either way he sliced it, assuming the narrow road spit him out near the highway, he had a couple of miles to go, and little daylight left.

Working quickly, Riker stripped off the prosthesis, then yanked the silk-like stocking off the stump. Designed to reduce chafing, the stocking had slipped down on one side and was dotted with blood. Where the scar tissue on the inside of his left knee had been in prolonged and direct contact with the carbon fiber of the prosthesis, an inch-long fissure had opened up. It had become inflamed, the edges purple and red and oozing blood.

He took the envelope from his pocket, extracted the contents, and unfolded the slip of paper. The directions covered both sides of the paper. He put his leg up on the bike, propped himself up on one elbow, and read them beginning to end. He had to squint to get through it. Finished, he crumpled the instructions and envelope and chucked the wadded-up paper ball into the underbrush.

The air hitting the stump felt good. Aside from his mandatory twenty-two pushups, taking the prosthesis off was the best part of any given day. Unfortunately, given his sister's predicament, he wouldn't allow himself to enjoy the downtime.

It was a task he'd been dreading since the words *prison pocket* crossed Shorty's lips.

He took out the multi-tool, unfolded the two halves, and deployed the blade. As he steeled himself to what he was about to do, he tried to remember if the tool had come into contact with infected saliva or blood. He couldn't remember. Days and actions all seemed to blend together since the dead began to walk. Didn't matter now. There was no way to sterilize the blade.

So he bit down hard on his shirt collar, took a deep breath, and worked the sharp edge of the three-inch blade into the fissure. A bit of sawing was required to loosen the worm-like length of scar tissue from the healthy flesh underneath.

The mantra *Don't scream* was marching through Riker's head as he inserted the tool into the wound. When he was finished, the initial wound was twice the size, his face had broken a sheen of sweat, and endorphins were flooding his brain.

Rambo had made it look so easy in *First Blood*. In reality, from start to finish, it was all Riker could do to keep from passing out. Silver lining: He hadn't screamed. He had, however, bit down on his lower lip hard enough to split it. Yet another source of pain to add to the others currently fogging his brain.

Once Riker had caught his breath, he pocketed the multi-tool and donned the sleeve and prosthesis, wincing in pain as he snugged the latter tight to the stump. As he rose, he could feel the strip of metal being driven deeper into the fresh wound. Every movement thereafter—from throwing his leg over the bike, to planting the Salomon-clad bionic on the pedal and applying pressure—was a stark reminder of what he was willing to go through to spare Tara's life.

Remembering he was ordered to come with the radio and nothing else, he retrieved the multi-tool from his pocket and tossed it into the woods.

For the first time since reuniting with Tara in Middletown, he was completely unarmed.

As he got to pedaling the bike, he became aware that for once in his life, though he didn't have a plan, he was fully committed to playing whatever cards Fate was about to deal him.

Strangely, he was at peace with it.

***

Riker had only covered a few hundred feet from where he stopped last when he noticed the strip of grass suddenly go from standing at attention to looking somewhat beaten down in places.

It appeared that someone had driven a vehicle to this point, parked it, and trekked uphill to Trinity House. The presence of tire tracks, the tread an aggressive off-road pattern, supported the theory. That there had been no obvious signs of a struggle near where Riker found the mountain bike had led him to believe his sister was somehow incapacitated or overpowered and then carried away. Taking Tara's slight stature into consideration, and that the grade was working in the kidnappers' favor, lugging a little over a hundred pounds of dead weight in a fireman's carry for a mile or so was doable. Even for a wiry teenager and someone Tobias Harlan's age.

***

Roughly three miles from where Riker had picked up the tire tracks, the trees began to thin. Under the bike's tires, the dirt road was nearly flat. Dead ahead, a picket of tall trees was silhouetted by the faint glow of the sun's last stand.

In the middle distance, a paved road ran left to right. The closer Riker got to it, the more evidence he saw of recent activity. Numerous tire tracks, older and obviously preceding the ones he was following, could be seen arcing across the grassy strip. Suggestive of a heavy vehicle having loitered here for some time, the underbrush crowding the left side of the dirt road was crushed down. Branches on some of the bushes had been snapped. A long ten-foot stretch of the spiny bushes bordering the dirt track had been completely uprooted. To Riker, it looked as if the damage may have been caused by the spinning tires of a vehicle making a frantic U-turn.

Food wrappers and beer cans littered the recently disturbed ground.

Riker didn't stop to investigate. Wasn't in the orders. Instead, seeing that the road he was on was close to spilling onto the paved two-lane, he coasted to the T and came a complete stop.

To Riker's left, the road curved twice then disappeared into the low hills skirting Trinity House to the west. Santa Fe was in that general direction, too. Everyone he had asked for an opinion had agreed the captors would not be holed up in the city, or anywhere close.

Off of Riker's right shoulder, about fifty feet from the T, a pair of zombies were rising up from the road. When they turned to face him, he saw the fresh blood dripping from their open maws. Their knees were also stained red. Behind the zombies, stretched out across the far lane, was a partially clothed corpse. The feet were clad in brown leather hiking boots. They were small and needed resoling. Though Riker didn't know whether he was looking at a woman's corpse or that of a small man, he did know it was a recent kill, and that his presence had just interrupted a feeding session. Off to one side was a Kelty backpack. On the shoulder, still rolled up tight, was a red sleeping bag.

The pair of zombies now staring him down were both males. The advanced stage of decay suggested they were a couple of Romero's first victims. *Early Turns*, or *ETs* for short, was what Benny had taken to calling especially road-worn specimens such as these.

The older of the two, probably a proud grandpa prior to dying the first time, wore a tattered Grateful Dead shirt and khaki walking shorts. No shoes on its feet. Everywhere they touched the road, a yellowish-green slick was left behind.

Oh the irony, thought Riker. *Keep on Truckin'. Not like he has any choice in the matter.*

The other was dressed like a clown: white coveralls decorated with red and yellow polka dots, ruffles on the sleeves and cuffs. On its feet were ridiculously oversized black shoes. They were polished to a high sheen.

A sign hung from a length of twine strung around the clown zombie's neck. With each step the twenty-something thing took toward Riker, the sign jerked and bounced wildly. If not for the hunger evident in its shark-like eyes, Riker would have found humor in the get-up and how the toes of the clown shoes vibrated when they struck the asphalt.

The sign bore a message. Even from a few yards away, Riker needed to squint to read it.

Eyes are on you, Lee Riker
Radio to Channel 12-12
Continue riding north

The zombie wearing the sign had only taken a few more steps when all forward motion was arrested by the thin rope encircling its waist. Following the taut length of rope with his eyes, Riker learned that the other end disappeared underneath the partially consumed corpse.

"Stick around," Riker said as he pulled the radio from his pocket. It was still powered on and tuned to 10-1. He broke squelch one time, real quick. As if it had been inadvertent. Or an accident, maybe due to the size of his hands. *North* was how it was supposed to be interpreted by the people who mattered. A capital offense to Tobias if he saw it for what it was.

Bringing the radio to where he could see the LCD display, he complied with the first order on the sign.

Praying he wasn't outside of radio range of Trinity and that his covert message wasn't just lost in the ether, he mounted the bike and got underway.

As Riker steered the bike wide right to avoid the zombie in the Grateful Dead shirt, he thought, *What a long strange trip, indeed.*

Riker had barely made it a hundred feet north of the zombies when from his blind side a long burst of automatic fire broke the still. *Full auto.* He'd heard some soldiers in-country call a full magazine dump *rock and roll.* The range officer discouraged it. Even going so far as to make the point that accuracy suffered greatly due to the inevitable muzzle rise.

It dawned on Riker that he hadn't heard that kind of a prolonged fusillade since Iraq.

As a result, he ducked instinctively and turned his head toward the sound. In the next beat, he felt something heavy strike him in the back. Squarely between the shoulder blades. A big target. Difficult to miss. Even on full auto.

Riker's first thought was that the fatal shot had come from the same direction as the second-and-a-half-long burst of fire. As he pitched forward off the bike, arms and legs instantly useless and leaden, he cursed himself for failing Tara.

He hit the ground headfirst. Then, with a tenuous hold on consciousness, he went limp and his feet traded places with his head. The short journey across the road's cool surface ended with him lying in the fetal position on the two-lane's right-side shoulder, the bike on top of him, and unable to form a coherent thought or cry out for help.

The last thing Riker remembered before everything faded to black was the appearance of two pairs of combat boots and then somebody probing his neck for a pulse.

Chapter 46

Riker came to flat on his back, completely naked and wearing a blindfold made from material so thick it blocked out any and all light. When he tried to sit up, he immediately learned it wasn't happening thanks to the cuffs biting into his wrists and right ankle. And to add insult to injury, the cuffs keeping him in a permanent spread-eagle position were anchored so close to the table that he could only lift his hands a few inches off its cool surface. His good leg was trapped in the same manner. Strangely, whoever had strapped him down had ignored his left leg.

Still, if he was ambushed by an itch, there was no way in hell it was getting scratched.

The air was cool and smelled like the ocean and freshly disturbed soil. He had a strong feeling he was inside. Probably in a basement. Which begged the question: Why the briny odor?

Riker had never felt so vulnerable in his life.

Silver lining to the nightmare he had just awakened to—he hadn't been shot. Where he thought the round had struck his back, there was just a burning sensation. And constant pressure. Like there was some swelling involved. Save for the initial punch, the aftereffects were more akin to a wasp's sting than a gunshot wound. Lord knows over the last week or so he'd heard all about being shot. From the searing pain to the itch he couldn't scratch, Benny had made sure to share all the little details with anyone at Trinity House who would listen.

As Riker lay there trying to make sense of what had happened—why the gunfire and no gunshot wound?—he realized he was very thirsty, that his mouth and lips had gone dry as the Sahara. Though his tongue was semi-numb, he could still feel something pressing against it. When he probed the item, he discovered it was round and smooth and was keeping his jaw locked wide open. Which in turn was putting great stress on all of the associated joints and muscles. When he tried to call out, his words were reduced to unintelligible grunts.

Think, think, think.

The only thing he remembered following the sting to his back was the ground rushing toward his head. He remembered absolutely nothing between his head hitting the road and coming to in his present condition.

It suddenly dawned on him that the hit to the back had most likely been a dart shot from an air gun. The time loss and foggy brain were probably due to the combination of the tranquilizer used in the dart and yet more brain damage caused by the ensuing impact. He was no stranger to concussions. Still, thanks to the latent effects of the sedative, he couldn't tell if his headache was a remnant of prior damage, new trauma, or side effects of whatever drug had been administered by the dart.

Didn't matter, he reminded himself. For if he kept worrying about the past, no way he was going to survive the day—or night—whichever it may presently be.

One at a time, he tested the anchor points, straining with all his might. No give whatsoever. All he got for his efforts was the knowledge that the drugs were still sapping his strength. Best to conserve what little he had. So instead of worrying about things he couldn't change, he began to plan his escape.

***

Riker had no way of judging the passage of time. He didn't know if he'd been awake for ten minutes or an hour and was chewing on whether or not he was going to speak to his captor when he heard the *snik* of a lock being thrown. Next, the squeal of hinges in dire need of lubrication sounded somewhere above and behind his head. Somewhere in the distance, an engine was purring softly.

Generator?

Hollow footfalls came next. As Riker lay still, playing dead, they grew louder and drew nearer. When the footfalls ceased, a light scuffing noise commenced. The new sounds lasted a couple of seconds and ended with Riker sensing that someone was danger close to him. In his personal bubble. The sensation of air being displaced near his head made him think that the *someone* was standing over him. Probably examining him as if he were a specimen in a petri dish.

The sound of a person breathing confirmed Riker's hunch. It was coming from his left. A couple of feet above his head. It was also a bit ragged. Was he or she a smoker? Could descending the stairs be to blame?

Control what you can. It was advice given to him by an anger management counselor. The same counselor who had told him humor was a good way to combat a flare-up. To nip it in the bud. An off-ramp from the next level: violence.

Humor had no place here. So Riker resorted to the former advice. He had counted the hollow-sounding footfalls: *twelve.* The shuffling sounds afterward had accounted for probably half as many.

He added this new information to what little he had already compiled and went over it in his head. He was pretty certain he had ended up in someone's basement dungeon. He was naked and completely immobilized. Which meant that the twelve stairs to freedom just a few feet from the crown of his head might as well be a mile away.

For now.

Resigned to the fact he was going nowhere if he couldn't get free of his bonds, he thought through his options. He came up with only one: reason with his captors. Build a rapport with them and hope something good came of it.

A tall order, indeed.

The raspy breathing ceased for a few seconds, then the person spoke. "Just you and me, Lee Riker." The male voice was even and measured. "I've missed having my very own captive audience of one. I bet you're a good listener. Am I right?" He paused for a few seconds. "I sure hope so. Because you need to hear a few things before I let you say your piece. And your story better be good. If it is, if I believe you had no choice but to do what you did, I'll grant you a quick death. But if your story is unconvincing, I'm prepared to go the long haul. It's not my first rodeo, Lee. While this little space of mine doesn't have all the accoutrements of the black sites I'm used to, it'll do. I have spent a lot of time and put some effort into getting this place ready for this glorious day."

As soon as the man had said "Just you and me," Riker knew his captor was the man he'd duped into letting him reposition the vehicles on Shorty's ferry, *Miss Abigail.* The same man he had ultimately left stranded on shore during the first frantic seconds of a zombie attack. In his mind's eye, Riker saw Tobias Harlan's jaw drop as the man realized that not only had he just lost his spot on the ferry, but that he also had to deal with the Bolts streaking down the dock toward him. As acceptance washed over the older man's narrow face, the nephew, Jessie, was bringing a rifle to bear on the departing ferry.

Riker had been waiting for the storm of bullets when he heard Tobias order the nephew to check his fire and engage the Bolts.

As the ferry finished its slow turn and reversed course, motoring away into the inky black, the last impression Riker had of the unfolding scene was Tobias and the kid breaking contact and sprinting for their pickup. That snapshot in time, of the pair heading for safety, had helped Riker deal with the awful feelings associated with the decision he was going to have to live with until he drew his final breath, which, given his present situation, and Tobias's demeanor, was rapidly approaching.

It suddenly dawned on Riker, after having just revisited his unconscionable misdeed, that Tobias was no over-the-hill new-age hippy as his dress and demeanor had suggested. Everything Tobias had done on the dock that night had been tactically sound. There was no hint of panic. He had prioritized the threat, saving retribution for later. And *later* had arrived.

Where's the wife now? Riker wondered. *The nephew? Is it really just you and me alone in your dungeon?*

The answers to Riker's unasked questions came in an oration that was more flood-of-thought than a one-sided conversation.

Tobias began by saying, "I bet you want to know how we found you?"

Riker wanted to nod but stifled the urge. *Pretend you're on the couch, Toby. Go ahead, you can tell me everything.*

"That Shelby of yours is a rare model. Dealer plates were New Jersey. The Jersey Motor Vehicle Commission only tagged three in the last year. One blue Shelby Baja in the last month. Your name was on the temporary tag. Not too many Lelands on the books. Bank records led to some escrow records. From those came the address to your place on the hill." He paused. Riker felt eyes on him.

Satisfaction evident in his tone, Tobias added, "It pays to have friends in high places. It's a shame your sister got dragged into this. Under the influence of my very own drug cocktail, she told me that you kept her and the retard in the dark prior to your dishonorable deed. If you hadn't have done that, I would feel a bit better at having used her as bait."

We, thought Riker. *Where's this other person?*

"Why the vendetta if I'm still above ground? Because, Lee Riker"—Tobias's voice suddenly rose a couple of octaves— "my wife died as a result of us getting trapped in the surge to escape the marina. Some teens tried to carjack her at gunpoint. Me and the boy arrived back at the truck just as the punks were breaking her window. They all died as a result of their poor judgment. Two got the Mozambique treatment courtesy of Tobias Harlan. Two to the chest, one to the head. A runner got the kid who had broken out our window. It took a chunk of the kid's ear, then went for Maria's arm." He paused again. Then, in a funereal voice, he said, "She lasted six hours. I thought the turn would be peaceful. I was so wrong. I could see her fighting it. She lost the battle." He exhaled sharply, then grunted. "You got two birds with one stone. Watching her changed the kid. He's taken to chopping off their arms. Making pets of them, then blowing the hell out of them after a short while. His behavior is becoming riskier by the day. I'm afraid he has a bit of a death wish. Only thing I can think of to explain his recent actions."

Explains the clown zombie with the sign around its neck, Riker thought. *You'd have to get danger close to dress it up, let alone hang a sign on the thing.* A noise he immediately attributed to water sloshing in a large vessel grabbed his attention. Though he had been hanging on Tobias's every word, he had remained still throughout. Did his best to keep his respiration even. To stay calm in the face of danger and, as he feared he was about to find out, in the presence of crazy.

Calm lasted about five seconds. All the way up until the point when a wet cloth was put over his nose and the first drops of cold saltwater hit his face. By the time the third second had ticked into the past, he thought for certain he was drowning. After five drawn-out seconds, each seeming to last longer than the previous, he was thrashing his head side-to-side and arching his body as far off the table as possible.

Riker's stump took a beating from hammering repeatedly against the hard surface. In a way, he thought, it would have been better to have been put into four-point restraints, not just the three.

He had no idea how long the waterboarding session had gone on. Once, just before he passed out, Tobias had said, "Impressive, Lee. You're going … be … tough nut … crack." Due to the continuous splashing noises from the slow torrent hitting the wet cloth, Riker missed hearing some of the words. But he got the gist—he was persevering, and Tobias Harlan wasn't happy about it.

Crazy arrived the moment Riker came to. He was still strapped to the table, the surface of which was now tilted ninety degrees to the right. Water ran across his face, left to right, ear to ear, then fell to the floor, pattering softly somewhere below his right cheek.

Did the table convert into a rotisserie? As he thought it, he imagined the thing in his mouth was a shiny red apple and he the hog on the spit. Not too far from the truth, he would soon learn.

Tobias was hollering crazily at the top of his voice as he waved smelling salts under Riker's flaring nostrils. Compared to having a steady stream of saltwater forced into his nose and mouth, this was nothing. So he went back to the comatose act.

"Don't die on me, motherfucker," Tobias bellowed. Riker felt the sting of a hard slap to his left cheek. Then, voice strangely calm, Tobias went on, saying: "You can't die on me. I won't allow it. I'm not done with you yet. You left us on the precipice back at Shorty's dock. Stole safety right out from under our noses."

Just as an intense spasm corded the muscles in Riker's neck, the table was spinning counterclockwise. As Riker was returned to his original face-up position, he heaved and warm salty water purged from his lungs and sluiced around the thing in his mouth.

The respite Riker was hoping for didn't arrive. Before he could draw a breath, the cloth was back and so was the water. Riker didn't count the seconds this time. No reason to. Nothing he brought to mind to distract him from what was happening could rise above the fight and flight impulses emanating from the reptilian part of his brain.

It went on and on like this for an indeterminate amount of time.

Finally, after coming to for the seventh or eighth time, this time on his back, with a searing pain in his chest and every nerve ending burning like tiny suns gone supernova, the blindfold was ripped from his face.

As Riker clenched his eyelids to ward off the light bombarding his retinas, he felt someone manipulating the straps holding the gag in place. When the gag came out, so did Riker's one burning question: "Where the *fuck* is my sister?"

Chapter 47

The answer to Riker's question was delivered with a closed fist. He was still seeing the stars and tracers brought about by the tightness of the blindfold when the unexpected blow snapped his head to one side.

"You'll learn Tara's fate when your suffering matches mine," Tobias growled. "Until then, you don't talk unless I order you to talk. And when that order comes ... seeing as how I just saved your life with a shot of adrenaline—the first *fucking* thing I want to hear from that rotten mouth of yours is a sincere 'thank you.'" He paused and raked a hand through his lengthening hair. "I've only had one man die on me and stay dead. Wasn't going to let you off that easy." The ragged breathing was back. The man was enraged, Riker thought. He'd been there more times than he could count. It had all started on Route Irish. He blamed himself for not seeing the IED. Even more so than the animals who had planted it.

Another blow landed on Riker's cheek. It was delivered openhanded and with much more force than the last.

"Look at me when I talk to you, Lee Riker. At least afford me that respect."

Riker opened his eyes, then quickly closed them against the glare from the lone trouble light strung overhead. Though the bulb was an LED item and threw a uniform bluish-white light, Tobias still presented as a misshapen silhouette against a cluttered background.

"How's it feel to die and come back? I've had jihadis tell me they saw their seventy-two virgins." He let loose a wicked laugh. "What did *you* see?"

Riker said nothing. He hadn't been ordered to speak. As his eyesight slowly returned to normal, he walked his gaze about the room.

The torture table was installed in an unfinished basement which he could only see about two-thirds of. The exposed floor joists directly above the table were dust-covered and home to cobwebs and shiny husks of dead bugs.

The room beyond Riker's feet was piled high with plastic bins. The contents of each bin were indicated by words written on lengths of white tape: **X-MAS ORNAMENTS**; **HALLOWEEN DECORATIONS**; **OLD WINTER CLOTHES**; **PHOTOS AND DOCUMENTS**.

The wall behind a nearby workbench to Riker's left contained vintage hand tools: files, wrenches, pliers, handsaws, a hammer. His stomach turned when he saw that the work surface was crowded with brand new power tools in all the colors of the rainbow.

On the floor beside the workbench was a pair of welding tanks. Hoses attached to metal welding guns were coiled atop the larger of the two tanks.

On a shelf underneath the workbench was a boxy device used to jump-start dead batteries. No doubt that would come into play sooner or later.

Above the workbench was a tiny rectangular window. It was dark outside. Clearly, the window was way too small for Riker to fit through. He even doubted Tobias could squeeze through if he greased his hips and tried really hard.

An extension cord snaked up the wall and to the outside via a hole punched through one of the windowpanes.

Tobias walked over to the bench. As he started pawing over the assortment of power tools, Riker saw that he was dressed in a camouflage fleece zip-up and desert-tan tactical pants, the cuffs of which were tucked into worn combat boots. He also noted that there wasn't a single piece of silver and turquoise jewelry to be seen on the man, not even a wedding band—a sharp one-eighty since Riker had first met him on the highway near Shorty's place.

On the wiry man's right hip, riding high in a saddle-brown leather holster, was a Colt M1911 pistol. On the other hip, snugged side-by-side in a leather mag pouch, was a pair of slim, single-stack magazines.

Tobias turned to face the torture table. To Riker, he looked younger, more spry than he had at Shorty's. In one hand Tobias held a safety-orange cordless drill. Riker noticed his eyes were no longer those of a stoned new-age hippie on holiday. There was a fire in them now. A whole lot of crazy, too. Like a needle on a polygraph machine, those slate-gray orbs were in a constant state of motion.

Riker figured his assessment of the older man fit, for even as he had been spilling the hows and whys, the captor was no doubt gauging reactions to the information. Judging him by his body language and changes in respiration. Trying to mine fact from bullshit, the latter of which Riker hadn't been shoveling.

Riker had a hunch at this point the interrogation would shift to the verbal variety for a short while. Tobias plugging the drill into the trouble light told him otherwise. As he closed his eyes, every muscle in his body clenched and his heart raced wildly in anticipation of the drill's telltale whine and eventual bite of its bit, the beautiful squeal of unoiled hinges bought him some precious time.

Chapter 48

"Uncle Tobias, you there?"

Tobias Harlan looked toward the stairs. He said, "Did you complete everything on the list?"

Riker heard heavy footfalls coming down the steps. He was on six when a voice he recognized as belonging to the nephew called down. "Mostly."

Tobias shook his head and put the drill back on the workbench. "Mostly? I didn't send you off to build a rocket."

Jessie said, "I dumped the body"—hearing this, Riker whipped his head around and strained to see up the stairwell. It was gloomy, so a pair of muddy boots was all he saw—"but couldn't find a roamer. They're always around when you don't want them to be. But when you—"

Meeting Riker's wide-eyed gaze, Tobias said, "And here I thought you found a fresh one and was just playing dress-up."

Jessie made it to the bottom of the stairs and took up station opposite his uncle. "I didn't see any. I should have checked that box yesterday. Snatched a slow mover from that herd going north." Indicating the water pooled on the cement floor, he said, "How'd he take the water torture?"

"He's too tough for his own good. Blacked out several times. Only died on me once." Tobias flashed Riker a wan smile. "Ten minutes with the Dewalt and I'll have him begging for me to end it."

"Just like Aunt Maria."

Tobias chuckled. "Not exactly," he said. "That'll come after."

Riker had been following the conversation, eyes flicking between the uncle and nephew when they spoke. Like the uncle, the nephew had undergone somewhat of a transformation since Riker had seen him last. But this one-eighty was nothing like the uncle's. Jessie no longer looked healthy. He'd initially come off as lean and wiry. Athletic, actually. Now he was stick-thin, cheeks hollow, dark bags below the eyes. His clothing was appropriate for the weather, but it was dirty and carried on it a faint odor of death. Greasy and unkempt, his dark brown hair was plastered to his head.

Clearly, the apocalypse was taking a toll on the teen. Unlike the uncle who was squared away, Jessie was riding the express elevator into the abyss.

Averting his gaze, Jessie said, "I went a few miles east. I can go back out and head north if you want. With all the roamers we saw yesterday, there's got—"

The uncle cut him off. "I know where one is. You remember the farmhouse with the rusting trucks in the yard? South of here … set way back from the highway?"

The nephew shook his head. "Not really. They all look the same in the country." He made a face. "Is it a runner or a walker? If it's a runner, you better let me handle it." He paced to the end of the table and locked eyes with Riker. "How's it feel to be stranded knowing the roamers are on the way?"

Riker would have shrugged if possible. Instead, he winked and smiled.

"He *didn't* know," Tobias growled. "Now he does." He lit a cigarette, then took a long drag. Blowing the smoke out through his nose, he regarded the nephew. "It's a *walker*."

Trying hard to recover from the slip of the tongue, Jessie looked at Riker. "That was just a figure of speech. There's no herd on the way." Looking back to his uncle, he said, "Draw me a map. I'll go out and fetch the thing."

Shrugging on a tan Arc'teryx shell, Tobias said, "You had your chance. Stay here and watch him. Don't get too close. Keep your radio on. And for fuck sake, leave his damn stump alone."

***

There was a long uncomfortable silence between Riker and the nephew. It began with the uncle's admonition and wasn't broken until the engine noise from the retreating vehicle had faded to nothing. During that time, five minutes, Riker guessed, he'd heard twelve ascending footfalls and the squeal of the unoiled hinges as the door to the stairwell opened and closed.

Next came the telltale *snik* as the uncle threw the lock to the stairwell door.

Dust motes rained from the floorboards overhead as the clomp of combat boots sounded from one end of the house to the other. The footfalls had stopped somewhere above the plastic bins, beyond Riker's feet, where the distinct noise of another door opening and closing drifted down from above.

The engine that had fired up was a big V8, likely the same one powering the gunmetal gray pickup with the caveman camper. Finally, with the nephew still staring at him, Riker saw the dual cones of the pickup's headlights sweep the basement window.

The basement was illuminated briefly by the weak yellow spill, then went all gloomy again as the vehicle motored off, the engine noise moving from left to right.

Assuming the uncle had driven south, Riker figured that if he got out of here, he was going to strike off in the same direction, and never look back.

No sooner had the engine noise dissipated than the nephew asked Riker how he lost his leg.

After spending a beat deciding whether he should bullshit his way through an answer that might curry favor, or if the truth was the way to go, Riker decided on the latter. Too many moving parts with the former. Too easy to get tripped up. Given the drastic change in the kid's appearance and demeanor since Riker had seen him last, no telling what he would do if he detected the deception.

"You want the long version or the Cliff's Notes version?"

The nephew pulled a five-gallon bucket over to the head of the table, flipped it over, and sat down hard.

"Give me the full story. All the gory details."

"I was deployed to Iraq right out of basic. Motor Transport Operator. Eighty-eight, Mike is the MOS. Eventually, I was trained in-country and tasked with driving personnel around in an up-armored Humvee. Sometimes it was an armored Land Cruiser or Suburban. I got hit one day going down Route Irish. Had a high-level diplomat in back of my Land Cruiser."

"IED?"

Riker lifted his head off the table and nodded as best he could. "Shaped penetrator. One of those things the insurgents were getting from the Iranian Quds Force. Cut right through the lower door sill. Took my leg right with it. The diplomat's security detail bought it too. A couple of seasoned operators."

Jessie perked up. "SEALs?"

"I honestly don't know their military backgrounds. The way they were dressed led me to believe they were CIA. Special Activities Division, I assume. Nobody told me. Need to know and all that. Still don't know to this day."

"That how you got the burns on your head?"

"A lifetime of headaches, too."

Riker's stomach rumbled.

The kid said, "Why'd you do it?"

"I was scared." Riker paused. Speaking forcefully, he said, "Tara and Steve-O had nothing to do with it."

"I know."

"What did you do with Tara?"

Eyes downcast, the kid said, "I killed her. Uncle told me to do it. He's all I got now that Maria is gone. She kept him even-keeled. Now that she's not here ..." He glared at Riker.

Riker met the glare with a thoughtful look. In reality, he was burning inside. The rage coursing his veins might as well been molten lava. He sighed and said, "I'm so sorry it went down like it did. If I could take it back I would."

"My family was on vacation. Hawaii. I burn easy. Why I hate the islands. That's why I was on the road trip with my aunt and uncle."

Riker's stomach protested again. It gave him an idea. Remaining calm, he said, "Where did you dump the body?"

"Where she would be found by your people."

Riker thought, *He knows Steve-O isn't alone at Trinity House.* The scrap of info led him to believe the pair had been surveilling the house for some time. What bugged him, though, was that the kid was still looking away, or at the floor, anywhere but making direct eye contact.

The kid said, "I left your fake leg with her body. Uncle said it would send a message."

This time eye contact was achieved. Wondering what had changed, Riker asked, "What's the message?"

"You and yours fucked up big time."

"Tell me something I don't already know." Riker sighed, even as his stomach roiled. The gurgling was so loud that the kid rose and moved the makeshift stool aside. Riker said, "I think it's the sedative your uncle used."

"Do *not* shit yourself," the nephew said. "I'm the one who's going to be cleaning the table before we break it down and leave."

Nodding to a blaze-orange bucket with a home improvement store's logo on one side, Riker said, "Let me go in the bucket. You can uncuff my weak arm and my right leg. I'll hang my ass over the bucket and do my business."

"There's nothing weak about either of your arms. You watch Game of Thrones?"

Riker just stared at the ceiling.

"A couple more inches and a few more pounds and you'd give the Mountain a run for his money. As it is, you're every bit as big as the Hound."

"That's all Greek to me," Riker said. "Listen, I won't try any bullshit. I have *one* fucking leg." He thought of his recently deceased mother. Pictured her gaunt face. How her body had looked, ravaged by cancer, so frail on that deathbed. The tears that came were real. "Just let me have a little shred of dignity. Call it the last request of the condemned man."

The kid stared at Riker for a long while. Finally, he said, "Stare at the wall. *Do not* look at me."

One moment Riker had been staring at the earthen wall, the next he was all clenched up, the sting of a thousand hornets ripping across his exposed skin. Why he hadn't gone and shit himself during the two seconds of living hell was a mystery. Perhaps his sphincter had closed up like a Chick-fil-A on Sunday. Lord knows every other muscle had gone tight as a cable holding up the Golden Gate bridge.

When the clicking noise behind Riker's left ear finally ceased, the assault on his body was still in full swing. As his muscles twitched and drool spilled from one side of his mouth, he realized Jessie had hit him with a stun gun.

Taking advantage of Riker's incapacitated state, the nephew quickly removed the left wrist and right leg cuffs. With the right wrist cuff still attached to the table, he shoved Riker's quivering body toward the table's opposite edge. Staying clear of Riker's freed left hand, Jessie ratcheted the cuff on Riker's good leg to the table's sturdy base.

Feeling was just beginning to return to Riker's extremities when the nephew lifted his shirt to show off the pistol stuffed in his waistband. "You try anything," he said matter-of-factly, "I'll shoot you in your good knee."

Raising the freed hand in mock surrender, Riker said, "Promise. Scout's honor." He sat on the bucket. It was awkward, his balance compromised greatly due to the fact his right arm was stretched diagonally across the table and his right leg was splayed out to his side. He grunted and pushed hard. The result was the loudest and wettest sounding fart he'd ever let loose. That his bare butt was hanging out and the kid was watching made it all the more disgusting.

Even to Riker, the smell was noxious. Stomach-turning, really.

Another byproduct of the tranquilizer?

Riker continued to groan and grunt and fart, the empty bucket acting as an amplifier for the latter. After enduring a couple minutes of this, the kid made a move for the stairs. "You have exactly two minutes to finish your business."

Riker said, "Before you go … can you give me something to wipe with?" His forehead was dotted with sweat.

Incredulous, the nephew said, "Don't go thinking I'm gonna go upstairs and fetch some asswipe for you. I'm not stupid. No way I'm leaving you all alone down here." He covered his nose with his shirt. "I'll be on the stairs, though … as fucking far as I can get from that invisible cloud your asshole is spewing."

"How about you let me use one of those shop rags on the workbench?"

The nephew shook his head. "Use that stump cover of yours. Won't be needing it anyways." He turned and stomped up the stairs.

Riker counted eight footfalls. *Two-thirds of the way up.* When the footfalls ceased, he assumed the kid had turned and sat down on a step. Question was: How much of the torture table was visible from the kid's new vantage?

After a quick glance at the stairwell, during which Riker saw only the nephew's boots and about a foot of his pants legs, he ripped the cover off his stump and worked two fingers under the inflamed worm of scar tissue. As he did, he kept his eyes glued on the nephew and continued the grunting and groaning.

Blood warm and sticky on his fingers, Riker had a hard time grasping the tool. Once he finally had it trapped between his thumb and pointer finger, he stood and reached across the table. With his entire weight supported on the one wobbly right leg, and the stump stretched horizontal to the floor and providing a modicum of counterbalance, he worked the metal shim into the only opening the directions indicated it would work in. While one would think handcuffs needed to be defeated by picking the locking mechanism through the keyhole, that was not the case. As Riker probed the opening, he made a mental note to ask Shorty if he had ever had to use the tool. Knowing Shorty, if he had, the story was going to be a whopper. First things first, though: Riker had to make it home.

"You almost done?"

Riker moaned and worked the shim in the housing that accepted the claw part of the cuffs. Pausing the faux noises, he said, "It's those fucking MREs we've been eating."

The nephew said, "The freeze-dried shit my uncle stocked up on does the same to me."

Bullshit, thought Riker. *It's the opioids clogging you up.* He'd seen a few people hooked on the things. One of the side effects was a slow-moving digestive tract.

"Thirty seconds," said the kid. "Pinch the loaf and wipe. I'm done sitting here in the dark."

Riker worked the tool an inch or so into the thin slot between the notches on the claw and the body of the cuff. When he felt tension, but *before* he heard a click, he rolled his wrist back and forth. The subtle movement caused the claw to retract from the housing. There was no sound save for the rattle of the chain securing the cuff to the table. He set the open cuff down slowly on the table, then quickly swapped the tool to his dominant hand.

Removing the first cuff left-handed had burned nearly a minute. Now that he'd done it once, popping the cuff on his right leg with his dominant hand took but a few seconds. As he reached across the table and grasped the open cuff in his right hand, he called out, "All done."

The kid rose and clomped down the stairs. Riker's count was at five when the kid said, "No funny business." Riker was looking at the ground on the far side of the table, watching and waiting for the kid's shadow spill, when the scuffing sounds told him the kid was approaching from behind.

Armed with this knowledge, Riker turned his head a few degrees to the right. Peering over his shoulder, he spotted the nephew out of the corner of his eye. Jessie was still a couple of yards distant, stun gun in hand, and approaching the head of the table with extreme caution.

He said, "You move, I shoot you in the spine."

Yeah, right, Riker thought as he released his hold on the handcuff, balled the hand into a fist, and started his right arm rocketing around on a flat plane whose terminus he intended to be upside the kid's right temple. Instead, due to a combination of poor lighting and a narrow viewing angle, Riker's backhand caught the kid on the right side of the neck. While not incapacitating, the force of the blow was sufficient to send the kid sprawling in one direction and the stun gun tumbling from his hand. Knowing the kid still had the pistol tucked in his waistband, Riker dove across the table after him.

Chapter 49

The blow to the kid's neck must have been more effective than Riker first thought because the gurgling noises he was making were in no way normal.

Before Riker's outstretched body had completely cleared the corner of the table, he had gotten ahold of the kid's shirt with one hand and a fistful of hair with the other. As Riker's upper body slithered from the table and rocketed toward the cement floor, the kid was dragged down with him.

As Riker twisted his torso mid-fall, he witnessed the kid's chin clip the workbench. Then, like he'd received a Sugar Ray uppercut, the kid's head snapped back and his upper body bent backward. Eyes rolling back in his head, arms and legs suddenly limp, the kid made no attempt to stave off the imminent head-first collision with the floor.

Riker came down hard on the wet concrete, his entire left side absorbing the impact. Pent-up momentum sent him on a collision course with the welding gear. He hit the steel gas cylinders headfirst, the impact causing them to clink together and wobble back and forth. With the coiled hoses and welding gun preceding it, the larger of the two tanks came down hard across Riker's stump.

As Riker pushed the tank off his stump, the other scythed the air near his left ear, clanged against the cement floor, and rolled away toward the base of the stairs.

The pain at the end of the stump was intense. Riker feared the tank steamrolling along the nub may have completely torn away the scar tissue.

There would be time to lick wounds later. He quickly transitioned to his hands and knees, crawled over the unspooled hoses, and ripped the pistol from Jessie's waistband.

A quick glance at the kid's face told Riker he was beginning to recover. A flurry of punches to the head—*ground and pound* to the UFC announcers—rectified the situation. Not wanting to kill the kid—at least not yet—he had pulled most of the punches.

Seeing the kid's eyes taking another tour of the inside of his skull, Riker grabbed hold of the workbench and pulled himself off the floor.

The pistol was a semiautomatic made by Taurus. There was one nine-millimeter round in the pipe and fifteen in the magazine. He placed the pistol on the workbench, then plucked the five-gallon bucket off the floor and placed it upside down next to the table. Using the bottom of the bucket as a platform to steady his stump on, he leaned over, grabbed twin handfuls of the kid's clothing, then hauled him onto the table.

Though the kid's hundred and fifty some-odd pounds were in the form of dead weight, and his arms and legs flopped about like overcooked spaghetti, for Riker, the job of moving him from the floor to the table was child's play. He straightened the unmoving body on the table so that it was oriented exactly as he had been: face up, head towards the stairs, feet aimed at the wall of plastic storage bins. He ratcheted the cuffs to the kid's wrists and right ankle. Without a fourth pair of handcuffs in sight, to keep the kid's left leg immobilized, Riker lifted the smaller of the two welding tanks from the floor and laid it across the table, positioning it so that its entire weight pressed down on both of the kid's ankles. Lastly, he wound the attached hose around the kid's left shin, snaked it around the table leg, then secured it with a double knot.

The kid was wearing a headlamp on his head and Riker's watch on his right wrist. Riker donned the headlamp and switched it on. He relieved the kid of the watch and strapped it onto his left wrist. Noting the current time—not quite 10 p.m.—he calculated that he'd been gone from Trinity House for nearly five hours.

He rifled through the kid's pockets, finding a folding knife, spare loaded magazine for the pistol, plastic baggie half full of round green pills, a small key that fit the handcuffs, and a two-way radio, its LCD screen glowing a soft shade of orange. He put the items on the workbench next to the pistol and power tools.

Resisting the urge to go and look for his own clothing, Riker scooped some of the activated ammonia ampules off the floor and used them to bring the kid back to the present.

It took a couple of seconds for the harsh chemical to take effect. Finally, the kid turned his head away from the ampule and opened his eyes. Up close, illuminated by the headlamp's blue-white beam, the kid looked like one of the dead. His face was pale and gaunt, the eyes vacant and crisscrossed by tiny red capillaries.

Matching the kid's gaze, Riker said, "How did you do it?"

"Do what?"

Amazed the kid could talk, considering the blow to his larynx, Riker said through gritted teeth, "Kill my sister. How'd you do it?"

Eyes widening, head rocking side to side, the kid said, "My uncle ordered me to. But when it came time, even though she was drugged, I couldn't do it."

Riker stared murder at the nephew.

"I swear I didn't do it. I was lying to my uncle when I told him I had." He took a deep breath, then looked away. "She was still out cold, so I zipped her up in a sleeping bag, tossed one of her radios in the bag with her, and left her lying there on the side of the road."

Riker had snatched the drill from where the uncle had placed it. Plugging it into the outlet on the trouble light, he growled, "What road?"

"Right where we ambushed you."

Not believing a word the kid had said, Riker asked, "The clown zombie wearing the sign—your doing?"

The kid nodded. "Dressing them up passes the time. I'm so bored out here. All my friends are gone. I got nothing to do—"

Interrupting, Riker said, "Nothing to do but take Oxy and play king in your apocalyptic fantasy world."

The kid remained tightlipped.

"The young lady you tethered the zombies to? What did you have to do with her *condition*?"

"When we found her the geeks were already feeding."

Riker said nothing. In his mind's eye, Tara was being defiled. He heard her pained screams, her begging breathlessly for a quick death.

"If you didn't kill my sister," Riker said, lowering the drill bit close to the kid's eye, "leaving her alone out there was just prolonging her death. You know what happens when a person gets bit." He pulsed the drill. Once the shrill whine subsided, he asked, "Where are we?"

The kid hesitated, so Riker moved the drill lower on his body, pressed the bit hard against his manhood, and repeated the question.

"We're in an abandoned farmhouse way off the beaten path. The main road is a few miles west of here."

"Where is Santa Fe in relation?"

The kid thought about it for a second. Finally, he said, "About twenty … maybe twenty-five miles south of where the road Ts with the main road." *Which means Trinity House is halfway between the two*, Riker thought. Setting the drill aside, he asked, "What'd you do with my clothes and shoes?"

"Uncle cut your clothes off and left them on the road with your shoe. Since he had a tracker on the bike, he thought you might have a tracker on you, too. Better safe than sorry is his motto. At least it has been since you fucked us over at Shorty's."

"Better you than us," Riker said. He glanced at the radio on the workbench. "What's your check-in protocol?"

"Uncle is pretty strict about it—"

The kid was interrupted by the soft warble coming from the radio.

Riker rested the drill bit in the corner of the kid's left eye. Keeping pressure on the drill, he reached back and grabbed the radio. "Answer it like you normally would." He held the radio in front of the kid's mouth. "You warn your uncle, I will take the eye. Are we clear?"

The kid nodded. Riker thumbed the Talk button and mouthed, "Act normal."

"Hey, Uncle Tobias," said the kid, his voice a little hoarse. "Did you find your walker?"

Simultaneous to Riker releasing the Talk button, he backed off on the drill.

"Right where I thought the abomination would be," Tobias answered. "Still wandering the equestrian center with all

303

the dead horses in the pasture. Turns out the carcasses are all in varying stages of decay. Figure the thing had been stalking them since all this started. Likely ate its way through all of them over time. Probably one kill every couple of days or so. I found huge piles of dead meat here and there in the pasture. I think you were right. These damn things don't digest the meat they eat. It just builds and builds and eventually their internals rupture and the meat falls out of their ass." The radio went quiet. Riker guessed the man was shaking his head in disbelief. When the uncle finally came back, he said, "How's our *friend?*"

Riker mouthed, "Passed out cold," then thumbed the Talk button.

The kid repeated verbatim what Riker had said.

"Good," said the uncle. "Let Goldilocks sleep. Hey ... I forgot to feed the generator before I left. Remind me to top it off when I get back. Wouldn't want to lose power while I'm in the middle of *working* on the doomed man."

Riker nodded and depressed the Talk button.

"I'll try to remember," said the kid, his voice wavering a bit. Whether it was from stress or the blow to the neck, Riker didn't know.

"It's a simple task." After a short pause, Tobias asked, "How many pills did you take?"

Riker mouthed, "None," then reopened the channel.

"None yet," said the kid.

"Better take one right now!" Tobias shot back. "That's an order. Can't risk you going into withdrawals on me. And take some Ex-Lax. Get things moving down there. I'll be back in fifteen."

Riker thumbed the Talk button. The kid said, "Copy that."

Tossing the radio onto the workbench, Riker said, "He's *encouraging* you to take drugs?"

The kid nodded. "Said he's titrating me off of them. Whatever the fuck that means."

"Why'd he leave you so many?"

"He's testing me. Keeping me honest."

Riker left the kid alone and went and pawed through the bin marked **OLD WINTER CLOTHES**. Inside he found a long-sleeved flannel shirt that he shrugged on and was able to get buttoned most of the way up. Since the cuffs fell mid-forearm on him, he rolled them up to his elbows. The jeans in the bin were all too small. Picking the largest pair of the lot, he pulled them on and ran the zipper up as far as it would go. The pants remained open at the waist, but the zipper held. Using the kid's folding knife, Riker cut the left pant leg off just below his stump. He ran a couple of lengths of silver duct tape around the end to keep the excess denim from flapping around.

The other pant leg fell to mid-shin on his right leg. All in all, the ensemble was tight and a little restrictive in all the wrong places.

Hell, he thought, *better than the alternative.*

Unfortunately, there were no shoes mixed in with the clothes.

Taking the bag of pills from the workbench, Riker said, "I'm going to kill your uncle when he gets back. No two ways about it. You … I'm going to let you choose your own fate. Do it yourself"—he shook the pills in the bag—"or"—he picked up the drill—"I can do it for you."

The kid closed his eyes. When he reopened them, the look he gave Riker was one of resignation. Like he knew this train was long due coming into the station. Flicking his eyes to the baggie, he opened his mouth wide, like a baby bird.

Riker obliged the kid, feeding him a handful of pills, then letting him drink water from a half-full bottle he found on the workbench. Without another word, Riker scooped the items from the workbench. The radio, spare mags, and knife went into his pockets. With no waistband to stuff the pistol into, he tucked it away in a back pocket.

A quick search of the basement turned up no crutches or even a cane. However, there was a deflated raft and pair of plastic oars for it. Though the oar didn't reach up to his armpit, it was load-bearing and would do in a pinch.

Riker scaled the stairs. At the top, before opening the door, he said, "Sweet dreams, Jess."

Chapter 50

The house Riker had been brought to against his will was a two-story affair. It was well lived in. Judging by the figurines, vases, and crocheted doilies placed underneath anything sitting on the vintage wood furniture, the people who had called the place home were vintage as well.

Riker decided against going upstairs. No time for that.

After a quick tour of the living room, formal dining area, bathroom, and lone main-floor bedroom, he circled back to where he'd started.

Coming off the stairs to the basement, the galley-style kitchen was clean as could be. Adjacent to the closed basement door was a second door that led to a mudroom featuring multi-paned windows that looked out onto the back and side yard. Another door to the right was inset with a square pane of glass and led out to a driveway. The driveway began at some point out of sight to the right and ended at a small garage a short distance from the back door.

Glare from the liberated headlamp reflected off the window glass as Riker searched the tiny mudroom for anything of use—shoes, at the top of the list.

An old double-barrel side-by-side shotgun was propped up behind the door. Cracking the barrel, Riker saw that it was loaded with a pair of 12-gauge shells. Examining the shells under light told him that one was buckshot, the other a slug.

Grandpa and Grandma were ready for varmints *and* zombies.

On the floor by the door to outside were two pairs of rubber galoshes. One pair was bright yellow, the other basic black. The larger pair happened to be the yellow pair, the rubber new and pliable. Riker crammed his size-twelve right foot into the size-ten boot.

The fit was tight but better than nothing.

Riker took the shotgun, opened the door, then maneuvered the short stack of stairs, the makeshift crutch flexing greatly under his weight.

To his left, where the cement driveway ended, he heard the generator purring away inside the garage. To his right, the driveway curled off into the dark. It was paralleled by a waist-high picket fence that Riker guessed followed the driveway all the way to the distant road.

As Riker was looking around for somewhere to lay low and wait for Tobias's imminent return, something he heard the uncle say to the nephew over the radio sparked an idea.

After a final look down the driveway, mainly to gauge distances and angles, Riker hauled the garage door open. Inside the garage was mainly stuff used for lawn care and gardening. Bags of fertilizer were piled in front of a side door. Cobwebs covered the window looking out on the backyard. An old motorcycle leaned against the far wall next to a workbench.

Perfect.

Riker pulled the door closed, sealing himself in with the noisy generator. Not wanting to succumb to carbon monoxide poisoning, he went to the back window and, using the shotgun barrel, broke out most of the glass.

The generator was on the floor by the wall opposite the house.

Putting the garage wall at his back, Riker took up station behind the generator. To his left was the rollup garage door. Four square windows ran horizontally across the top of the rollup. They were each about the size of a basketball and nearly opaque thanks to accumulated grime and industrious spiders.

Riker pressed his back to the wall, then shifted all of his weight onto his good leg. As comfortable as he was going to get considering the circumstances, he scraped a quarter-sized portal from the grime on the window nearest him, then parked his gaze on the gloomy stretch of driveway.

***

Riker had been waiting and watching for ten minutes when the weak yellow spill of the pickup's headlights swept the end of the driveway. The lights dipped and rose as the vehicle chugged toward the garage. No sooner had a dark-colored pickup ground to a halt on the gravel drive roughly two truck lengths from the back door than the lights snapped off and it began the first leg of a three-point turn that would ultimately leave the rear of the camper facing the garage.

Riker could hear little from outside over the rattle of the generator. When a pair of lights mounted on the top corners of the camper flicked on and bathed the entire cement pad in stark white light, he had to raise a hand to shield against the glare.

As Riker sank further back into the shadows, he saw Tobias round the corner of the pickup and stop abruptly at the far edge of the light spill.

Once Riker's eyes finally adjusted to the sudden change, he was able to make out the caveman sticker on the back of the camper. On a bike rack under the sticker was the bike he had ridden from Trinity House. It was sharing space with two other high-dollar mountain bikes. *His and hers.* And, totally out of place, lashed horizontal to the cargo platform jutting out from the rear bumper, was a writhing human form. It was hooded and naked, shriveled male anatomy on full display.

The walker from the equestrian center. The last piece of the puzzle that would make Tobias Harlan's revenge complete. Not going to happen, Riker thought as he bent down and shut off the generator.

Looks like Jessie didn't follow through for you. What are you going to do now?

Tobias was in the middle of rolling the zombie off the platform when the generator sputtered one last time and the light behind the basement window winked out. What Tobias did next was not quite what Riker had anticipated. One second he was helping the hooded zombie to its feet, the next he was going to ground behind the pickup's right rear tire.

Fuck, fuck, fuck, thought Riker. Whispering to himself, he said, "It's just out of gas, Tobias. Come and take a look. You know you shouldn't put your trust in an addict you're feeding pills to."

The uncle's voice emanated softly from the radio in Riker's pocket. Though he was whispering, it was clear by the tone that he was not happy with the nephew's performance.

After a minute or two of radio silence, Riker watched Tobias commando crawl from cover. When the man reached the darkened basement window, gun in hand, a flashlight in his other hand flicked on. Craning to see into the basement, Tobias aimed the narrow beam into the void.

Cat's out of the bag now. Being mindful to stay away from the bars of light coming through the rollup door's windows, Riker snatched up the oar and retreated further into the garage.

As he reached the left rear corner and was making himself as small as possible on the floor, three tremendous booms rattled stubborn shards of glass from the window he'd broken earlier. He heard the rounds crackle the air nearby. Still possessing an enormous amount of kinetic energy, the screaming hunks of lead slapped the rear wall above Riker's head, knocking hand tools from a pegboard mounted there.

Three nickel-sized bullet holes appeared in the rollup door to Riker's fore. They were an inch or two apart and would have rendered him a eunuch had he still been standing near the generator.

Dust motes danced in the light lancing through the jagged holes.

Riker immediately went from a seated position to lying flat on his back. Head toward the rear wall, he spread his legs, trained the shotgun dead center on the garage door, and drew back both hammers.

Four more deafening booms broke the still.

Four new holes appeared magically in the door where Riker was aiming the shotgun. The rounds crackled the air maybe a yard to Riker's right and punched identically spaced holes through the wall beneath the rear window.

Patience of Job, Riker thought. *Let Tobias make the mistakes.*

Shifting his gaze to the back wall, Riker saw a pair of shadows. One of the dark blobs was moving erratically back and forth. *The zombie blindly roaming the drive.*

The other shadow was static, darkening the wall just to the left of the broken window. Riker imagined Tobias adopting a Weaver stance near the stairs to the mudroom, the big .45 about to belch more lead into the garage.

Riker's hunch was correct on the latter count. Three more booms preceded three new holes appearing in the rollup door's thin aluminum skin. Only these holes weren't waist-high. They were low to the ground. Though the rounds didn't find flesh, dozens of razor-sharp shards of cement displaced by one hundred and eighty grains of hurtling lead did. Riker gasped and nearly dropped the shotgun as a tsunami of white-hot pain rippled up his entire right side.

The light coming in through the new holes confirmed to Riker that his adversary had indeed fired the last barrage from somewhere near the short stack of stairs. The downward angle the light bars took from door to floor suggested Tobias had been trying to skip the rounds off the cement.

Feeling hot blood seeping from multiple unseen wounds, Riker risked a second glance at the rear wall. The roving shadow was still there. The static shadow was not.

Hoping to stay one step ahead of Tobias, Riker spun a one-eighty on his back and, summoning all the strength in his weakened right leg, pushed himself away from the rear wall. Lying on his back, a few feet from the wall, dual barrels trained on the window, he swallowed the pain and listened hard.

***

As the minutes slipped into the past, the only thing Riker saw moving was the shadow on the wall. Matching the movement was a scuffing sound Riker figured to be coming from the zombie's bare feet as it wandered the cement parking pad.

Come on, he thought. *You hit me. You heard me cry out. Maybe I'm bleeding out. If I do, there goes your chance to make me pay. Show yourself, fucker.*

No sooner had he thought it than a silhouette—just a shade lighter than the inky black of night—edged out from the left side of the window.

Patience, Riker chided himself. *He thinks you're dead. Act like it.*

Following his own orders, Riker held his body stock still. He even held his breath. Only giveaway that he wasn't dead was the shotgun balanced atop his left thigh. With his knee bent and stump planted on the floor, the shotgun's deadly end was aimed upward, at a spot on the bare wood between a pair of vertical two-by-four studs and equidistant to the floor and window.

The silhouette's head inched further into the void, then the Colt .45 broke the plane.

Simultaneous to Riker pressing both triggers, flame and a single booming report erupted from Tobias's pistol.

Momentarily deafened by the simultaneous booms, Riker saw a manhole-sized gulf appear between the studs, exactly where he'd been aiming the shotgun. Whether the one-ounce lead slug had passed through the wall first, or the double-ought buckshot provided an opening ahead of it, Riker had no way of knowing.

What he did know, however, was that Tobias Harlan bore the brunt of both loads. Judging by the guttural grunting filtering in from outside, barring a miracle, the man would not be getting up.

In the millisecond after Riker had processed all the information flooding his brain, he realized the single round fired by his adversary had found flesh. The entry wound was three inches north of the end of his stump and pulsing blood at a terrifying rate. If there was an exit wound, he couldn't see it.

Tourniquet!

First thing though, Riker needed to be sure Tobias wasn't getting up. So he rolled over and went up on all fours. The pain was excruciating, causing him to gulp air just to stave away the stars dancing before his eyes. After a moment, he slowly stood upright.

Riker wrenched the motorcycle's side-view mirror off. In a move both dangerous in nature and similar to the one that had gotten Tobias shot, he raised it slowly, like a periscope, into the ragged hole.

A morbid scene was reflected back at Riker: The uncle was sprawled out flat on his back, arms outstretched, black pistol a yard from his flexing fingers. A growing field of crimson dominated the front of the tan Arc'teryx shell. Evidence as to where the slug had struck the man was the gaping, bloody hole where the outdoor company's prehistoric bird logo should have been.

Beaded sweat ran down Riker's forehead as he ripped both sleeves from his shirt. He quickly tied the cuff ends together, wrapped the makeshift tourniquet around his leg a few inches above the entry wound, and tied the loose ends together. Finding a wooden tomato plant stake mixed in with the gardening supplies, he broke it down to a manageable size and slipped it into the knot. Turning the piece of wood tightened the tourniquet substantially, which in turn stopped the bleeding.

Over Riker's own labored breathing rose the sounds of a dying man. After a few seconds of listening to the thrashing and moans, during which Riker had decided to just wait for Tobias to bleed out, he used the mirror to make sure what he was hearing jived with the image in his head.

In just a handful of seconds, Tobias had spun himself around a few degrees, not toward the gun, but away from it. On his face was an expression equal parts horror and pain. He raised his left arm a few inches off the ground. In the next beat, the zombie entered the picture and fell to its knees at the dying man's side. That it was still hooded was no deterrent. Its own raspy growling rising over the uncle's low moans, the creature dove onto his bloody chest, strong blunt fingers ripping and tearing at flesh and organs alike.

While Riker didn't really believe in the Butterfly Effect—the phenomenon whereby a minute localized change in a complex system can have large effects elsewhere—if he could replay the night at Shorty's and take back the wrong, no matter the outcome, he probably would.

Snapping back to the here and now, Riker grabbed ahold of the wooden window ledge and pulled himself up.

Though Tobias's eyes were darting back and forth in his skull, it was clear his life was fading away. His earlier feeble attempt to ward off the zombie had proven to be his last stand. Now, arms at his side, all the fight was in the past.

Riker took the pistol from his back pocket, press checked to make sure a round was chambered, then shot Tobias Harlan dead.

"Sorry it had to come to this," Riker whispered.

The zombie stopped feeding the second Tobias went limp. Still chewing on a length of ropy intestine, it rose and staggered to the window.

Riker collected the oar and took a step back from the window. Taking a screwdriver from the pegboard, he waited until the zombie showed its face in the empty window frame, then buried the tool up to the handle in the thing's right eye.

Feeling a little woozy, from blood loss, he guessed, Riker made his way to the rollup door. Prior to hauling it up, he peered through one of the holes.

The camper's rear lights were still ablaze.

Clear. No new zombies.

Lifting the garage door took a lot out of Riker. Wiping sweat from his brow, he glanced over his shoulder. The lights atop the camper shell shone off the pool of blood where he had been lying. It was larger than he had imagined as he lay in its warm stickiness. The trail that he'd left from the rear window to where he now stood was startling to look at.

Tightening the tourniquet, Riker set off to check one last box.

Kneeling before the basement window, he flicked on the headlamp and used its weak beam to probe the gloom. Though the light didn't penetrate very far into the tomb-like darkness, it did wash over the still form on the table. Shifting the beam a few degrees to the right revealed the nephew's upper body and vomit-covered face: eyes wide, mouth agape. It looked to Riker like the kid had fought the Grim Reaper to his last breath. A last gasp that ultimately had led to the kid drowning in his own puke.

Riker hoped that was how Tara had gone out. Swinging and kicking, struggling to take her own pound of flesh from the kid who'd just been delivered a fate spawned by a Butterfly Effect of his own making.

Chapter 51

Fifteen miles southwest of the charnel house where Lee Riker was waging a battle to remain conscious, skeletal muscles in his sister's prone body were twitching wildly. Internally, major organs were also tremoring and in the process of entering a phase in which there would be no return.

While Tara's eyes moved rapidly behind clenched lids, deep inside her brain the hypothalamus was working overtime to slow the changes occurring within her body. Concurrent with all of this, in the rear of her brain, neurons were firing, the activity elevating in frequency and instrumental in activating her fight or flight reflex.

Awakened by the chattering of her own teeth, she was instantly aware that something was moving about in the dark real close to her.

As she listened hard, trying to determine the source of the shuffling sounds, her mind was quickly processing other stimuli. Though she had no idea *where* she was, the cool, silk-like fabric brushing her hands and forearms gave her the sense she had been placed inside of something.

A coffin!?

That didn't make sense. At every open casket viewing she had ever attended, the deceased loved one was swaddled in overstuffed fabric. So much so that the corpse appeared to be floating within the casket's tight confines.

That wasn't the case here. Through the thinly padded fabric, something cold and hard was pressing against her back. As she sat up, the material cascaded from her upper body. The instant bite of cold desert air made her nipples stand at attention. She ran a hand down her body, from her neck to her knees, and learned she was completely naked. Last time this had happened to her she had been drugged in a nightclub back home. That time

314

she had been raped by a stranger. She had known right away upon waking that she'd been defiled. Oddly, this time, though the dry mouth and banging headache convinced her the drug the kid had used was similar to whatever the rapist had slipped into her drink that night long ago, she was confident this time it had ended there. That he hadn't taken advantage of her. That she was alive was a miracle. Last thing she remembered before the kid had clamped his hand over her mouth was the order that she was to be killed and dumped near "that asshole's house." The uncle had also told the kid to "take the leg and leave it where it will be found."

Tara's stomach clenched.

They have Lee.

A little bit of feeling around in the dark told her she had been left inside of a partially zipped sleeping bag with no kind of a cold-weather rating. Seeing her breath cloud before her face, Tara guessed the temperature had dipped into the low fifties. Add in the chill from the steady breeze hitting her in the face, the temperature on her skin was likely closer to forty degrees.

The cheapo bag was atop the left lane and aligned with a dirt and gravel shoulder. A few feet beyond the shoulder was a metal guardrail. Beyond the guardrail was an impenetrable wall of waist-high scrub brush.

On the ground beside the bag, its outline in the dark instantly recognizable, was her brother's carbon-fiber-wrapped prosthesis.

Rising and stepping out of the bag, Tara turned a half-circle and saw the source of the noises: a walking corpse. It was staggering her way and presented as a faint outline against the dark backdrop of night. Thankfully, she thought, it was a Slog—one of the slow movers.

The cold was affecting it badly, too, slowing it to about half speed. The scuffing noise she had heard was the creature dragging its feet. Each labored step that brought it closer to where she stood ground a little more tread off the already road-worn Converse sneakers.

Tara was shivering uncontrollably. Keeping one eye on the zombie, she snatched up the bag, unzipped it all the way open, and turned it upside down.

Something with considerable heft came tumbling out of the bag. It struck the top of her foot, bringing forth a yelp of pain. Crouching down, she discovered two items on the road. One was her teal two-way radio. The other was a Petzl headlamp. She was also reminded of how she'd come to be incapacitated: two closely-spaced welts on her ribcage that radiated intense pain with her every move.

Wincing in pain, she rose from the crouch. Praying the kid hadn't played a cruel hoax on her by not including batteries, she flicked the headlamp's switch. At once her legs from the knees on down were awash in a cone of blue-white light.

"Hell yes," she blurted. Too cold to fist pump, she instead did a little dance in place. "Let's check the radio for juice."

Depressing the power button brought the LCD screen to life.

Though the wound on her side had a heartbeat of its own, Tara snugged the sleeping bag tighter around her shoulders and turned a quick three-sixty. "Yes! Thank you, Lord."

A wavering moan escaped the approaching zombie's pistoning maw.

"Shut your pie hole, rottie face. I'm about to place an important call."

Tara selected the channel Rose had last been monitoring from Trinity House. Hoping she was within range of the base station, or any friendly listening on a radio, she said a silent prayer and depressed the Talk button. "Anybody there? This is Tara. I'm freezing my tits off. Rose? Benny? Steve-O?" She cleared the channel and prayed for a reply.

The zombie had drawn to within two dozen feet when the unexpected warble and follow-on burst of squelch erupted from the radio's tiny speaker. Tara had been holding her breath and watching the moaner trudging ever closer and, startled by the noise, nearly jumped out of her skin. A male voice followed the static. "We hear you, Tara. Where are you?" It was Benny.

"I don't know where in the hell I am," she responded. The tears were flowing before she had even released the Talk button.

"Are you able to walk the road and find a mile marker or any other kind of signage?"

"My legs aren't the problem, Benny." Throwing a hard shiver, she added, "I'm naked and fucking freezing." She donned the headlamp. "Give me a second. I have something I need to do."

Arms outstretched, its gait still achingly slow, the zombie was now so close that, though it was downwind, the stink radiating from it was enough to gag a maggot. Salivary glands kicking into overdrive—a surefire sign she was close to puking—Tara backed away from the zombie. Picked up by the lamp beam, some thirty feet up the road from where Tara had come to, was a trio of corpses. On the far shoulder, beyond the last of the unmoving bodies, was an orange backpack.

Still shivering uncontrollably, Tara made her way to the first pair of corpses. Both were males and had turned some time ago. Inexplicably, one was wearing a clown costume, goofy shoes and all. The other wore a Grateful Dead shirt and walking shorts. Both were in advanced stages of decay and bullet-riddled from crotch to sternum. Each had been granted second death by a single round fired from close range into the temple. The contents of the clown zombie's stomach had spilled out onto the road. The beam of light played off its last bloody meal.

Whoever did this to the roamers was a very angry individual. The shooter had also wasted about twenty-five too many rounds putting these two down.

The third corpse was that of a thirty-something woman. She lay in a pool of her own blood. It contrasted sharply with her pale white skin.

Tara quickly concluded that the flesh missing from the dead woman's neck and arms and the human detritus on the road not ten feet away was one and the same.

The real mystery here was who had put her out of her misery with a single gunshot between the eyes.

Letting the dark reclaim the corpses, Tara moved the cone of light to the backpack. She picked it off the road and rifled through the side pockets. Nothing of use. Next, she went through the main compartment, finding a small one-man backpacking tent as well as a portable stove, lantern, and a hand-pump water filter.

Tara ripped open the tent sack and dumped the contents out on the road. In addition to the nylon tent, there was a tangle of tethered poles and a number of aluminum tent stakes.

Ignoring the fabric and tent poles, Tara selected one of the stakes. It was six inches long and pointed on one end.

Brandishing the tent stake in her right hand like a makeshift dagger, Tara turned to face the zombie. She waited until it was within five feet of her then let the sleeping bag fall around her ankles. Under any other circumstances, the action might have been seen as some kind of invitation. She was hoping to get the zombie to key in on the sudden movement, not her naked body.

Nothing doing. The monster kept on stepping, all the while staring the meat from her bones.

"You hungry?" she said, thrusting the tent stake out in front of her. "Feast on this."

It took every ounce of will power Tara possessed to remain rooted in place as the monster's gnarled fingers drew dangerously close to her face. Once the thing was fully committed to the clumsy lunge, Tara ducked under its outstretched arms. Now on its right flank, she jabbed the stake at its right eye. It was a short stabbing stroke. There was a grating noise as the stake caromed off bone and dug harmlessly into rotten flesh.

"Fuck, fuck, fuck," she wailed. Knowing that the headlamp was as much a beacon to the zombie as her naked body, she switched it off. Hustling back to the sleeping bag, she snatched it up off the road and found two of its corners by feel.

Hoisting the bag in the air, she positioned it between herself and the monster—much like a toreador would his cape to the bull—and called out in the dark to get its attention.

"Over here, dummy."

She heard sneaker rubber scuff the road as the thing turned to face her.

"Here I am." She shook the bag, hoping the sound would be as much attraction as her voice. "Come to Mama."

That did it. Head angled forward, the zombie plodded straight for her. At the last moment, she flung the bag into the air above its head. The bag billowed open then began to collapse in on itself, falling exactly where she needed it to. Head and shoulders fully shrouded, the zombie stopped in place, blindly reaching for the meat it knew was there somewhere.

Sidestepping the reaching arms, Tara swept its legs and pounced atop the prostrate form. Pinning one arm with her right knee, she stabbed it about the head and neck until it ceased moving underneath her.

When Tara paused to catch her breath, she realized the arm flailing against her bare skin had left a road map's worth of scratches all up and down her left side. Though she couldn't see them, she felt rivulets of blood already tracking down her ribcage.

After removing the embedded stake, she flicked on the headlamp, collected the stinking sleeping bag, and went back to retrieve the radio and Lee's bionic.

Wrapping the soiled bag around her shoulders, she looked to the night sky. To the left of where the dirt road met the paved road, light from the slow rising moon was glinting off the bottom of high clouds. The ambient light also revealed the faint outline of a low peak rising up behind the dirt road. In the middle distance, the jagged crowns on a phalanx of firs were just gaining definition. Though the vantage was different, it was all familiar to her.

She thumbed the Talk button. "I don't need to walk the road, Benny. I'm confident I'm super close to where the fire lane on the map meets the main road."

"Wait there, then," Benny ordered. "We're coming to you."

Breaking back into the open channel, Tara said, "Bring me some clothes. My Salomons. And a gun. Never thought I'd feel so naked without one."

"You bet," replied Benny. After filling her in on the new arrivals to Trinity House, he asked, "Need anything else?"

Tara's stomach rumbled. "Bring water and something for me to eat. An MRE. Sardines. Vienna sausages. At this point, I'd scarf down just about anything."

Chapter 52

Twenty-five miles south of the T in the road where Tara had been dumped, former Army aviator, Wade "Griswold" Clark, was piloting an Ohio Army National Guard UH-72A Lakota over a mostly dark section of Santa Fe proper.

Based on the civilian Airbus EC-145, the Lakota was similar in size and maneuverability to the helicopters the forty-eight-year-old son of a Texas oil baron had flown for the Manhattan, New-York-based charter outfit where he had most recently worked. This particular helicopter had been specially modified for a multi-mission role that included search and rescue and VIP recovery.

While not as cushy as the rides the elites Clark had been rescuing were accustomed to, not one of his customers had balked at boarding her. Being surrounded by ravenous dead was indeed a great socioeconomic equalizer.

Positioned lengthwise on the right side and accessible via the clamshell doors at the rear of the helicopter was a single stretcher.

On the left side, loomed over by a sliding door fitted with a large rectangular window, were three adjoined forward-facing seats. Across the aisle and separated by the cockpit pass through was a pair of rear-facing seats.

In the left seat up front, helmeted head tracking something off to the helo's right, Sarah "Country" Rhoads gestured with a gloved hand to where she was looking. "Santa Fe Regional must have been a major shit show at the end." Employed by the same charter outfit as Clark at the onset of the Romero virus, forty-two-year-old Rhoads had been lured away by Clark to do contracting work for the DoD. Having flown alongside Clark in the sandbox during the early days of the war in Afghanistan, back when the rubble pile that had been the Twin

Towers was still smoking and the full-scale invasion of Iraq had yet to happen, the promise of triple the pay and adrenaline-pumping missions was impossible for Rhoads to resist. It was the third time over the last five years that Rhoads had followed her former commander on to bigger and better things. First, it had been flying geologists in and out of Alaska. Checked some bucket list items during that two-year contract. Considering how fast Manhattan had fallen, with the bridges and tunnels being blown in order to contain the undead, she considered her abrupt departure from her former employer the best decision she had ever made.

Now, having just come from Army Aviation Facility 1 in Columbus, Ohio, where a frantic return to base call saw them do just that, only to find the facility in much worse shape than Santa Fe Regional, they were both suddenly out of a job.

"You have the bird," Clark drawled. "Let's make a quick orbit over Santa Fe Regional. See if we can get anything moving on the FLIR."

"Copy that," Rhoads replied, "I have the bird."

Theoretically, the "bird" belonged to the United States Government. At the moment, barring further instruction from either the DoD or Department of Homeland Security, the "bird" was in their collective care.

Whereas the Airbus AS365 Dauphin they flew in their previous lives could be called the Cadillac Escalade of helicopters, the Lakota was more Ford F-150. Utilitarian and reliable, the Lakota—most often utilized as a medevac asset— was rumored to replace the venerable Kiowa Warrior.

While not as fast or comfortable as the Dauphin, the unarmed Lakota was far superior where communications, navigation, and sensor capabilities were concerned.

Hands flashing over the glass cockpit's touchscreen while the helo banked to the left, Clark brought the Advanced Targeting Forward Looking-Infrared pod (FLIR for short) online and spun it around in its nose-mounted gimbal.

As Rhoads started the wide clockwise orbit, the bird slightly nose down and listing a few degrees to the right, Clark kept the FLIR pod trained on the ground a thousand feet below. The moving black-and-white imagery picked up by the high-tech optics suite and beamed onto the cockpit display revealed only the static hulks of passenger jets and a pair of helicopters.

Scattered among the aircraft, most of them boxy and low-to-the-ground, were a myriad of wheeled vehicles used to transport baggage, in-flight meals, and move the airplanes about the tarmac.

Their cadaverous bodies presenting like gray ghosts against the dark, cold background, no less than a hundred dead things patrolled the tarmac, runways, and grassy infields where the sprawling quarantine facility had been thrown up.

"The dead own this one, too," Clark stated soberly. "Next stop ... Trinity House."

Being one of the more junior, but not necessarily less experienced aviators at her previous job, Rhoads instinctively offered the controls back to Clark.

Though Clark had transitioned out of Army aviation ahead of Rhoads, and had done so at a higher rank, in his eyes they were equals. "Keep her," he said. "Take us to the waypoint. If the work on the LZ is not finished, I'll scan the ground for an alternate."

"Copy that," Rhoads said as she fed the twin turbines more juice and broke from the racetrack orbit. As she upped the Lakota's airspeed to a tick under eighty knots, the ground below—as seen through her four-tube night vision goggles—resembled a turbid green river as scrub, cactus, and the occasional building flashed by. Off to the right, on the periphery of her field of vision, was a cluster of buildings that caught her attention. "What's over there?" she asked, pointing in the general direction.

Panning and zooming the camera, Clark said, "Looks like a prison. Fencing topped with concertina. Lots of zekes in the yard and parking lots. Yeah ... gotta be a correctional facility."

"Sucks to be them," Rhoads stated.

"Definitely, with Romero still burning across the country," replied Clark. "Doesn't look like anyone could have made it out of there alive."

Rhoads said, "Would you stick your neck out to save a bunch of felons?"

"Point taken."

Bringing the Lakota up to one thousand feet AGL, Rhoads said, "Fifteen mikes out. Any way you can give them a heads up that we're en route?"

"Negative," Clark said. "They're aware I'm coming today. But that's it. Haven't been in contact with Lee since cell service went tits up."

Rhoads was one of the "boys" in and out of the cockpit. Clark had never seen her blush. Doubted anything he could say would ever bring color to her cheeks.

Rhoads said, "That's a helluva wide-open window, Grizz. What are you, the cable guy?"

Clark chuckled. Both at being called Grizz—the abbreviated version of Griswold–and his memory of that old comedy flick.

Rhoads said, "Five minutes out," and started grabbing more altitude. Viewed through the NVGs, the peak rising over the general area her waypoint was taking them looked like the top of a poorly executed serving of soft-serve ice cream. The top was rounded, with a sharper, secondary peak sprouting, like a conjoined twin, from the peak's eastern flank. To the left of the peak, southwest of the tree line, was a rambling structure. Equidistant to the two points, glowing like an angel's halo, was the landing zone.

"One o'clock," Clark said. "Lee came through."

Rhoads said, "What's it lit up with? Tiki torches?"

"Can't be sure, "Clark replied. "But whatever they're using, it works for me."

"Looks like a burning ring of fire."

As the helo drew nearer, two things became evident. First was the pair of headlights moving down the hillside's southern flank. They belonged to a large pickup truck wheeling downhill toward the road west of the peak. It was speeding, taking the curves like the police were hot on its tail.

Second was the change in the "ring of fire." As the helo came in from the south and banked to the east, the circle of lights morphed into an upside-down teardrop.

Rhoads asked, "Think the cone's going to be in the clear?"

Clark nodded. "Affirmative. I was expecting to arrive here in the Dauphin. So I tasked them with expanding the LZ. Worked in a ten-foot buffer for us, too. From the looks of it, they went above and beyond to make extra room for the tail rotor."

Flaring the Lakota, Rhoads said, "I have movement."

Clark rotated the FLIR pod, bracketing the forms on the active matrix LCD. Zooming in, the two people—or at least the parts of them not covered by clothing—glowed white-hot against the ragged tree line behind them.

Rhoads bled airspeed and altitude as she brought the Lakota in from the west. With the skids maybe a hundred feet above the ground, high-intensity landing lights bathing Trinity House in a huge passing blue-white cone, she threaded the Lakota expertly through a pair of tall trees. Having "split the uprights," she dropped them down into the elongated end of the LZ, flared hard, then settled the bird atop the uneven patch of recently cleared ground.

Clark bumped fists with Rhoads. "Like you wrote the book on tight LZ landings." He looked off to his right. "Who do we have here?"

Two forms glowed green in their NVGs.

Rhoads said, "One woman, one man."

Clark said, "Those aren't the Rikers. The guy fits the description of their friend, Benny."

Rhoads asked, "What do you want to do?"

"Keep her hot." Clark grabbed a suppressed H&K MP-5 submachine gun from the floor behind his seat. "I'm going out to *communicate.*"

Chapter 53

The helicopter that had just carved a right-to-left path across the night sky could still be heard off of Tara's left shoulder when a second engine noise rose over the rapidly diminishing din. Slinking off into nearby bushes, she crouched down and drew the sleeping bag tight, leaving only her face exposed. Trying to be one with the foliage pressing all around her, she remained still. Wisps of her own breath curled around her face as she kept her gaze locked on the distant spot in the road where she guessed the vehicle would soon emerge.

She saw the faint glow of headlights wash treetops way off in the distance. As the whine of the helicopter turbines faded to nothing, she recognized the noise of the approaching vehicle for what it was. The powerful roar of the big engine. The low throaty exhaust growl.

Definitely Dolly! No doubt. But who's driving?

The headlights swept the near corner. Growing larger by the second, the twin suns came down the road, straight for her, bouncing and jinking with the road's rise and fall, slowing only when the vehicle reached the T in the road.

Tara signaled the vehicle with two quick strobes from her headlamp. She rose and stepped over the guardrail. Picking her brother's prosthesis off the shoulder, she leaned against the guardrail, waiting as the pickup slow-rolled up to her.

The *"we"* in *"we are coming to you"* ended up being Shorty. He looked like a kid behind the wheel of the big pickup. Though Tara had talked to him earlier, she didn't expect him to be the one coming to get her. Still, the little man was a sight for sore eyes. Even after all that had happened today, Tara was anxious to ask him how the rest of the United States—hell, the rest of the world for that matter—was faring in the age of Romero. But that could all wait. Finding her brother was the utmost priority.

Suddenly aware that she was naked as a newborn underneath the sleeping bag, Tara dropped the prosthesis and turned away from the pickup. Making a *gimme* motion with one hand, she called, "Throw me my clothes and shoes."

Killing the Shelby's lights, Shorty said, "I'll deliver them to you. I promise I won't look." He opened the door and climbed to the road, clothes and shoes wrapped in one big bundle. He walked backward, eyes averted, about ten paces in all.

Tara said, "That's close enough, Shorty. Put 'em down."

Bending at the waist, he arranged the clothes and shoes in a neat pile, then put a belt and the holstered Sig Legion atop it all. Lastly, he laid down the winter coat Benny had thrown in as an afterthought. Keeping his gaze trained skyward, he retraced his steps to the idling truck.

"Stand behind the door while I dress." Tara pawed through the clothes until she found her undergarments. She stepped quickly into her panties, then nearly jumped into her jeans.

Eschewing the bra for a tee shirt and fleece sweater, she slipped her arms into the coat and zipped it to her neck.

The shivers continued wracking her body as she stuffed her bare feet into the Salomon hikers.

"Why not bring me a Glock?"

"Benny said he didn't want you to think he was patronizing you. I think Benny is afraid of Lee's hand cannon."

The Sig *was* big in Tara's hand. Almost too big. Still, she went through the motions, dumping the mag and press checking the slide. Good to go. She threw the safety on and slipped the pistol into her waistband—the belt and holster would have to wait.

The next thing out of Tara's mouth was not a greeting. And like her tremoring body, the tone of the question lacked even a semblance of warmth.

"Where'd you come from?"

Always the smartass, Shorty said, "Trinity House."

"No shit, Sherlock."

"After talking to you earlier, I turned around and drove back into Santa Fe. Ran into Lee at the county lockup." He breathed in deeply, then exhaled. "There's more to it. I'll tell you all about it later. It's a long story."

Tara nodded.

"Get in and warm up. I've got the heater running." Shorty craned around the open door. "What about your bra? Just going to leave it there on the road?"

"I'm done with those fucking things."

Shorty made no comment. He clambered aboard and shut his door.

Once Tara was inside the warm cab, he said, "What's with the aerated biters?"

"I killed one. The others were here already. Shot up by the nephew, I presume."

"Fucking clowns." Shorty threw a shiver. "Living or dead ... I hate the things."

"You and me both. They ruined the circus for me."

"We all float down here." He passed a water and sack full of power bars to Tara. "That writer dude has a sick and twisted mind."

Tara made no immediate reply. She was two bars down and had guzzled all the water when she said, "Much better than sardines or Vienna sausages. Thank you." She tore open another cereal bar and gestured with it toward the distant hillock. "We going to go?"

Shorty started the truck on the first leg of a three-point-turn. "How's Lee?"

"No idea," she said, truthfully. "I don't even know if he's alive. I can't even get a sense of it either way." He grunted in response. Nothing he could think of to say seemed appropriate.

No sooner had Shorty gotten the Shelby pointed south than both of the two-way radios in the cab came to life. "Did you find Tara?" sprang from both speakers. It was Benny. He sounded a bit winded.

"You take the call," Shorty said. "I insist."

Chewing and swallowing the last of the cereal bar, Tara put the radio to her mouth and pressed the Talk button.

***

Five minutes had passed since Tara had gone over everything she knew about her captors—which was little. Before she had signed off, decisions had been made, one of them not so popular.

No way in hell was she going to stay behind with Rose to watch Trinity House while her brother was in trouble. The military never left one of their own behind, and neither did the Rikers.

A sure tell that the people coming along on the search had finished collecting their gear and gunning up was the turbine noise echoing down from the hilltop. In a few short seconds, it had risen from a soft whine barely audible over the night sounds to a banshee-like howl that could be heard inside the parked Shelby.

As they waited to be picked up, Shorty spent the time topping magazines and giving his compact Glock 19 a looking over. He had already backed the Shelby off the highway and parked it on the fire lane. To make it easier for the helicopter to locate them, he kept his foot on the brake pedal, tapping it every once in a while to add a strobe effect to the bright red lights.

Tara was on full alert through all of this, eyes constantly touring the mirrors. As she kept probing the dark all around for any sign of zombies or breathers, she marveled at how far sound traveled now the once-bustling world had been stripped of all extraneous background noise. The night sky had benefited, too. Without the halide lights ablaze along the highways and byways and the neon-like glow hovering over nearby Santa Fe, every cloudless night seemed to her like a visit to a planetarium. The Milky Way was a tapestry of four hundred billion stars that stretched from one end of the night sky to the other. Constellations were easily discernable. Seeing satellites carve laser-straight tracks across the inky black gave her hope society would one day crawl from the foxhole the tiny virus had them all cowering in.

Seeing the helicopter's lights growing larger and tracking straight for the Shelby's tailgate, Shorty turned to Tara. "They see us."

Tara said nothing.

"You know," Shorty said, "I'm more to blame than Lee for the situation he is in. The shit you endured, too." He shook his head. "For that, I am truly sorry."

"Oh, hell no," Tara shot. Her head bobbed with every word. "Lee is a grown ass man. He could have just as easily let those folks on the ferry and allowed the cards to fall however God intended them to. But, no, he had to overthink things. He's good at that." She went quiet for a beat. With the noise of the approaching helicopter threatening to drown her out, she went on, saying: "However ... knowing what I know now, can't say that I'd have either of you change what you did. Those folks weren't straight out of Mayberry. More like straight out of Woodbury."

As the helicopter skimmed over the pickup, its bright spot flicked on, bathing the T in the road and a good deal of the surrounding area in bright unnatural light.

Shorty had collected his mags and was holstering the Glock as the helicopter flared hard and landed parallel to the two-lane's dashed yellow line. Killing the rig's lights, he said, "So where's this Woodbury?"

"Fictional television town. It's not important." She zipped her coat up to her chin and stepped into the chill night air.

Turning her face away from the leaves and sand kicked up by the helicopter's whirring rotors, she tucked the radio in a pocket. She cinched the belt around her waist and secured Lee's holster. Moving the Sig from her waistband to the holster, she stalked toward the tan behemoth filling up the road.

Riker was fighting to remain conscious as he drove away from the farmhouse. Taking a right at the T had seemed logical at the time. Now, coming to a second T, where the unimproved road he was on met a two-lane highway, he had a decision to make.

Awash in the weak yellow spill of the idling pickup's headlights, the confluence of gravel single track and smooth lined blacktop bore a strong resemblance to the junction near Trinity House.

Confused as to which direction he was really facing, he tried the radio again. *Nothing.*

You have a fifty-fifty chance of getting it right, Lee.

Though the headache was getting worse with each passing second, and his vision was foggy around the edges, he had a strong feeling he was facing east. Which meant a right turn would have him heading south.

Right it is.

He fed the engine fuel and cranked the wheel hand-over-hand until the pickup was straightened out on the two-lane and moving forward at a strong clip, the tires straddling the dotted line, headlights woefully inadequate against the thick dark.

Mesmerized by the gnarled fence posts flicking by on the edge of his vision, Riker lost all track of time and distance. As he steered the ungainly rig through the high desert landscape, the road undulating and twisting back on itself as it dove in and out of arroyos, he maintained a white-knuckled grip on the wheel. It was about the only thing he had control of when the pickup came up over a rise and the headlights painted the horde of dead things spanning the road.

Packed shoulder to shoulder from guardrail to guardrail, the leering mob of rotting walking corpses was a scene yanked straight from his worst nightmares.

THUD!

CRACK!

BANG!

The morbid sounds of bodies caroming off the truck and flesh and bone losing out to the vehicle's tonnage told Riker none of this was a construct of his subconscious mind.

It all happened so quickly. The stomach-churning noises seemed to go on forever. In reality, they lasted only until the pickup had ridden over enough bodies that it became high-centered and could go no further—a few seconds at most.

Still under power, the rear wheels continued to spin. Cutting the engine, Riker let his hand drift to the tourniquet. It had come loose. The borrowed pants. The ratty seat cover on the bench seat. The carpet underfoot. It was all blood-soaked.

Had the stench of the dead not been so overpowering, he would have noticed the metallic stink of his own spilt blood.

Riker took inventory of his situation. He had the kid's Taurus and fifteen rounds for it. In the glovebox was his sister's Glock and one spare extended magazine—another thirty-five rounds.

He flicked on the rear auxiliary lights and scanned the mirrors all around. The zombies that had been out ahead of the throng had circled back and were now crowding around the pickup's front end. More were pressing in on both flanks.

Fifty rounds to clear more than a hundred zombies. Not going to happen. At this point, he thought, maybe he would only be using one.

A pale face entered Riker's peripheral and slammed hard into his window. A semi-opaque sheen of fluids accumulated as the forty-something male continued to head-butt the glass. By the third impact its front teeth were broken, the remaining shards quickly rendering its lips to ribbons of rotting flesh.

A multitude of ashen hands slapped the hood and windshield.

Trapped inside the cab, the throaty moans, resonant bangs, and ringing screech of nails scraping the pickup's exterior was torture to listen to.

Riker wasn't subject to the cacophony for long. For a minute after getting himself into this predicament, darkness crowded out the light, his chin hit his chest, and, releasing the tension he'd been applying to the tourniquet, his fingers went slack.

Chapter 54

Tara had her hand raised against the glare of the bright
landing lights as she approached the helicopter. She couldn't
make out any details behind the windows, so she had no idea
who was aboard. Seconds after the helicopter had flared and
kissed the road under the steady hand of the pilot, a door on the
left side opened and a figure emerged. The figure closed the
door, hustled around the noisy craft's rounded snout, and ran to
meet Tara and Shorty. Given the helmet and olive-green flight
suit, Tara wasn't surprised she didn't recognize the person.

As the figure closed the distance, Tara saw that the flight
suit was filled out in certain places a man's physique didn't reach.
She saw the nametape on one rounded breast: *Rhoads*. Though
the person wore a flight helmet that covered most of the face,
the smooth features and ready smile was all woman.

The woman's eyes were narrowed against the flying
debris. Affixed to the helmet up front was a pair of four-tube
night vision goggles. Tara knew what they were only because Lee
had expressed interest in getting a pair or two of them.

The word *Country* was painted on the side of the helmet
facing Tara.

She thought, *Country Rhoads ... cute call sign.*

"Sarah," said the woman, extending a gloved hand and
shouting to be heard over the thrashing rotors. "This way.
Follow me."

Rhoads led the pair to a door on the helicopter's right
side, hauled it open, and ushered them both inside.

Rhoads helped them to seats and set them up with
headsets. From her front-facing seat on the left side of the cabin,
Tara had a clear view of the pilot and a partial view of Rhoads.
Aglow in the landing light spill and visible from the massive

window to her left was the road and shoulder and the twenty-foot run of barbed wire fence bordering the road.

A bulb inside the roomy cabin cast three seated figures in its dim red light. Tara immediately recognized Steve-O. He was sitting opposite her, back to the bulkhead, and grinning like a fool.

The other two were the pair Benny had mentioned over the two-way radio. Lia was the "twenty-something-white girl," her lithe body draped in expensive-looking cold-weather running attire. Contradicting the tight-fitting ensemble were the muddy Nike trail runners on her feet. Propped against the seat next to the young woman was an exotic-looking rifle. Tara didn't know anything about her save for her first name, general age, and that Lee had seen something special in her. Benny had said as much.

If the chick knew her way around a firearm, Tara decided, then she definitely belonged on Team Riker.

Sensing the scrutiny being directed her way, the younger woman nodded and flashed Tara a warm smile.

The other person was lean and sinewy and in Benny's words, "pushing seventy." He had said his full name and reached a hand out to Tara when introduced. For a man more than twice her age, Vern Rossi had a helluva firm grip. Even in the red glow, she could tell the man's clean-shaven face was tanned. Smile lines bracketed deep-set hazel eyes. Noting the squared-off jaw and picket of straight teeth, Tara thought to herself: *No way this dude is pushing seventy.*

Gotta hand it to, Lee, she mused. Always did have a penchant for bringing home strays. But five in one day? Better call Guinness because this was a new record.

The pilot in the right seat craned around and met Tara's gaze. It was Clark, the charter pilot who'd whisked her, Steve-O, and Lee to upstate New York in a helicopter much nicer than this. Lee had heard from him earlier in the week but only half expected him to show.

At least all the hard work spent widening the clearing had not been in vain, Tara thought as she nodded and flashed a thumbs-up. A beat later Clark's voice sounded in her headset. "We meet again. I only wish it were under better circumstances."

"Me too," replied Tara.

"Where do you think they took your brother?"

Tara looked to Shorty, who was next to her and listening to the conversation over his headset. He gestured toward the cockpit, saying: "Lee broke squelch one last time before he went radio silent. We had agreed one click for right. Two for left. I'm confident he hung a right here at the T."

Tara said, "I wish I could help. But I got nothing but snippets of things I overheard. They were pretty careful with what was said around me."

As soon as Rhoads was buckled into the left seat and had her NVGs parked in front of her face, the turbines roared and the helicopter launched into the night sky.

Still smiling, Steve-O said, "I'm glad you're OK, Tara." He paused. The smile faded. He asked, "Is Lee going to be OK?"

"He's in my prayers," she said. "Best put him in yours."

Dipping the bird's nose, Clark said, "Can you tell me what we're looking for? Maybe a description of the vehicle associated with the people who took your brother?"

Tara looked to Shorty. He said, "Gray older model pickup. Chevy, I think. It had a camper shell with a bike rack on back—"

Interrupting, Tara said, "The camper shell is tall and dirty white... almost yellow. And there's a big ass decal of a cartoonish caveman holding a club. It's on back beside the door."

Vern broke into the conversation, adding: "Tara was taken captive five hours ago. Considering all of the back and forth trips it took to abduct her and Lee, plus the roundtrip to bring her back to where they dumped her, the place they're staging from has got to be fairly close."

Shorty said, "Vern's got a point. With all the roadblocks and biters south of the Rikers' place, I have a hard time believing the dirtbags would establish a base anywhere near Santa Fe."

Tara leaned forward. Making eye contact with Shorty, she said, "The older man wanted Lee's leg left alongside my dead body. I'm willing to bet every ounce of gold we have that he plans on dumping Lee back here when he's done with him."

Lia said, "Which means they're probably still somewhere close."

Shorty said, "The kid showed you mercy on his own accord?"

Tara said, "I'm alive and kicking. I said maybe five words the whole time. So it was nothing I did. That's for sure. After I got hit with the shocky thing … stun gun or whatever, they gave me something similar to a date rape drug." She shook her head. "I was completely out of it right away. The couple of lucid moments I did have, I was talking gibberish. Don't recall any other details other than what I mentioned already. I think I was dosed again right before I was dumped on the road where I woke up."

As the helicopter leveled off a couple hundred feet above the road, Clark came on over the shared comms. "I'm thinking we follow the road out ten or fifteen miles. Along the way, we'll make note of all the roads branching out left and right. We double back either east or west, we can decide which direction when we get to our turnaround point. I'll have our return leg take us over ground on the side of the road with the most feeder roads branching into it. I'll fly a grid pattern until we see something or rule out that particular side as viable."

"That would be a good strategy," Lia said. "If all of us had a pair of those night-vision goggles."

Clark said, "Just keep on the lookout for light on the ground below. You'd be surprised how easily your eye picks it up. See something, say something."

Keeping her eyes glued to the spotlight-lit road scrolling by down below her window, Tara said, "Do you have a plan? Any idea what we're going to do when we find them?"

Clark said, "I'll keep the bird tracking the same course and maintain a steady speed until we're well past the sighting."

Vern said, "Smart. Then turn back and recon from a standoff position."

"Exactly," Clark said, "Country can put the FLIR on them. We pick up some hotspots, human forms, heat from an engine block … we put down at a safe distance and approach the place on foot."

"I'm going, too," Steve-O said. "Lee needs all the help he can get."

Tara said, "I wouldn't dream of asking you to stay behind, Steve-O." With seven bodies in the helicopter, it was beginning to get warm. She unbuckled only long enough to shrug off her parka. Regarding Steve-O, she went on, "You saved our butts more than once since we met in Indiana. You're part of Team Riker and have the ink to prove it."

Shorty said, "Did I bring the wrong coat?"

Tara shook her head. "I'm sweating like a whore in church. Might be the drugs wearing off. Plus, if I need to move about in the dark without making noise, ain't going to happen in that stiff ass thing."

Clark said, "Five miles in. Ten to go." He was keeping the helicopter at a height where the spotlight illuminated both sides of the road, plus about ten or so feet beyond the guardrails paralleling the road. Even clipping along at sixty miles per hour, a break in the white steel barrier would not go unnoticed.

Sadly, Tara hadn't seen a single road branching off of her side. Looking to Lia, she asked, "You see anything yet?"

Wearing a pained look, Lia said, "One dirt track. It was overgrown as hell, though. Didn't look recently traveled."

Vern was strapped in next to Shorty. He leaned over and craned to see out the window being crowded by Lia. "I used to ride dirt bikes out here. If my memory serves, there are a couple of improved roads on your side. One shoots off to a campground. It's about a mile in. There's also an old mining operation a couple of miles past that. Me and my boy used to go shoot there."

Shorty said, "The second road? Where does it go?"

"A few private residences. The Gymptegards' place is closest to the highway. It's about a mile or two back. An old two-story. Someone's homestead way back. The rest are mobile homes. You know, those single-wide aluminum-skinned jobs."

As Clark said, "Ten miles," Lia saw the first improved road. It was a two-lane that shot straight for a few yards, then snaked off to the left, disappearing into the dark void. Getting Tara's attention, Lia said, "Just saw a paved road. Looked promising."

Tara nodded but didn't make eye contact. Good thing, too, because on her side she noticed another road branching off the main highway. It was narrow and paved, with a mailbox on a post planted in the dirt just off the narrow shoulder.

She made a mental note in case Rhoads had somehow missed it.

Sure enough, Vern's memory had served him well. The road to the Gymptegards' homestead became visible outside

Lia's window at the exact moment Clark came over the comms to inform everyone they had just reached the fifteen-mile mark.

Lia said, "There's another good prospect on my side."

Vern tapped his head. "I still got it up here."

Tara said nothing. She was focused on the landscape outside her window, disappointed they'd seen so few roads to follow. In fact, she was about to insist they stretch the northern leg of the search another five miles when the Lakota slowed substantially and started a gentle turn to the right. As the craft came perpendicular with the road below, she saw, far off in the distance, a halo-like bubble of white light. It was near to the ground and wasn't flickering like a campfire might.

She blurted, "I see something," and started stabbing a finger at her window.

Chapter 55

"That's the truck," Tara said. "No doubt about it."

Country had already trained the FLIR camera on the pickup and determined the only hotspots other than the lights ablaze on the rear of the camper was the engine block and a lone person slumped behind the steering wheel. The one sure thing they could make out about the latter without moving in and hitting the pickup with the spotlight was that it wasn't a corpse they were looking at on the cockpit display.

The walking corpses showed up on the screen as ghostly gray forms. They stood three deep around the front and sides of the pickup. Fifteen or so had become trapped underneath the pickup, their arms and legs still moving. A handful of them milled about in the light spilling behind the shell, the majority of them congregating near the narrow rear door.

Maybe, Tara thought, they were holding out hope something worth eating would eventually emerge from within the camper. The notion was informed because she had repeatedly witnessed the dead doing things the living used to do. Everyday activities: hanging around a bus stop for a bus that was never coming. Loitering in front of a convenience store long since plundered of anything of use. Sitting on a park bench for no apparent reason. After all, the dead didn't tire. They didn't sleep. Why would they need to rest?

The thought that they somehow acted on tiny snippets of memory scared the hell out of her.

The possibility that her brother may be the person in the surrounded vehicle and could very well be injured or dying brought on a rage she didn't know was inside her.

Spittle flying, Tara said, "What the fuck are we waiting for? This thing has guns, right? Shouldn't you be thinning the herd with them?"

Rhoads said, "We're unarmed."

"You gotta be kidding me. This is an Army helicopter, right?"

Nodding, Clark said, "I'm sorry, Tara, but her main role is evacuating wounded from the battlefield."

Tara looked about the cabin. One at a time, she briefly locked eyes with everyone around her. Finished, she said, "Then we better get our asses down there and see if that's Lee."

Leaning in, the safety harness taut against her shoulder, Lia said, "I have an idea," and proceeded to go over it, step by step.

Lia's plan was simple, but dangerous—especially for her.

Tara locked eyes with Lia once the younger woman had finished talking. "You don't have to do that," she said. "You don't owe Lee anything. Besides, we have enough ammunition to put all of those things down."

As the helicopter came out of the hard-banking counterclockwise turn that took it wide right of the static pickup, Lia said, "How long is that going to take? Five minutes? Ten?"

Now a half-mile north of where Clark had initiated the maneuver, he brought the Lakota parallel to the two-lane and began a steady descent from a hundred feet.

Flicking on her headlamp, Lia said, "Lee might not have five minutes. Nothing you say is going to change my mind." What she didn't say was that she still owed Lee for saving her ass in Santa Fe.

Shorty had fished some chemical light sticks from a pouch under his seat. He tore the packaging and handed them to Lia.

Hands in the air, Steve-O said, "What if there are a whole bunch of Bolts down there?"

"I'll be OK," Lia promised. "I've outrun plenty in my day. Besides, Randoms aren't very bright." She stuffed a spare mag for her rifle into the waist of her spandex leggings. "You do your part, I'll do mine." She took her headset off and set it aside. Cracking the pair of red chemical lights, she shook them hard to activate them.

The landing was smooth, the Lakota's skids settling on the blacktop with a soft scraping noise. It was nearly perpendicular to the road, the entire left side bathed yellow by the distant pickup's headlights.

Working together, Steve-O and Vern hauled the right-side sliding door back in its tracks.

Without a word, rifle slung on one shoulder, light sticks clutched close, Lia hopped onto the road.

As Steve-O and Vern worked to get the door closed, Tara watched Lia move around the front of the helicopter and wave the light sticks back and forth in front of her. Peering out her window, she saw that every zombie was now looking in the Lakota's direction: a hundred set of eyes, white against the dark, the meat in the pickup already forgotten about.

About the same time Vern was throwing the latch on the closed side door, and the Lakota was going light on her skids, a number of Bolts broke away from the throng of dead things. Heads down, arms and legs pumping, they came running down the centerline, the noisy helicopter seemingly their sole concern.

As the road dropped away outside Tara's window, in unison, the dead things altered their course, putting Lia with her glowing red batons directly in their path.

With the trees and road rapidly growing smaller, Clark yanked the Lakota around counterclockwise and aimed the nose for the field opposite the road. As the craft gained more altitude and its nose dipped, Tara watched Lia break into a full sprint, six or seven Bolts hot on her trail. She cut a diagonal path across the road, leaped the ditch with all the grace of a gazelle, then came up against the barb wire fence rising over the ditch.

By the time the Lakota was on the east side of the road and nosing around to the south, its ultimate destination their original starting point, Tara had lost sight of both Lia and her pursuers.

For Lia, scaling the barb wire fence was a lot harder than she'd expected. The moment she had put her foot on the lower strand and went to push off, the wire she thought would support her weight sagged like the roof on a hundred-year-old barn. While that was happening, she had both hands wrapped around the upper strand and was in the process of bringing her other leg up and around.

When the lower wire suddenly dropped six inches, so did her left leg. Similar to the jolt one would receive from stepping off an unexpected curb, the sudden change in footing shifted her entire body weight forward, causing the rifle to ride up her back and hit her behind the ear. As a result of the stinging blow, her fingers snapped open reflexively.

Momentarily stunned, up became down.

Unfortunately for Lia, she came down hard on the upper wire. Fortunately for Lia, the rifle strap absorbed the majority of the damage the rusty barbs would have wreaked on her upper body.

Before she could get a hand out to brace her fall, she was face up and on her way to an unavoidable introduction to New Mexico hardpan.

When the Lakota came out of the wide turn, Tara got a little lightheaded. Must be the drugs still in her system was her initial thought.

The only person in the cabin not affected negatively by the aggressive maneuver was Steve-O. A wide grin had formed on his face and he had pumped his fist the entire way.

Tara had seen Vern getting thrown around a bit. Maybe he wasn't as spry as she had at first thought.

Shorty was actively searching for an air sickness bag and failing miserably. In the end, just as the helicopter flared hard and everyone aboard was being subjected to several positive Gs, the man who was at home on the sea finally succumbed.

The stream of vomit came fast and furious. To say Linda Blair would be proud wasn't much of a stretch. Hot and sticky, it coated the floor as well as his fancy red cowboy boots.

The helo kissed the road and Vern and Steve-O unbuckled and did their thing with the right-side door.

As the door hit the stops, kerosene-tinged air rushed in and mixed with the acidic stench of Shorty's handiwork.

Rhoads was first out of the bird. MP-5 in hand, she closed her door and took up station near the tail assembly—her job: watch their six and ensure nothing, living or undead, walked into the whirring tail rotors. For if anything came into contact with the Nomex and carbon fiber item, everyone, her included, would be facing a long walk to Trinity House—or worse—having to fight off a hundred hungry zombies.

Everyone else had a pre-assigned role. Tara's was to get to the pickup and see if the form they all saw on the helicopter's display was indeed her brother.

Spittle and chunks of half-digested food dripping down his jacket front, Shorty followed the other two men out the open door. Glock in hand, he motioned for Steve-O to go to the right. With Vern keeping pace, Shorty put his head down and sprinted the thirty yards to the high-centered pickup.

Last through the door and on the verge of emptying her own stomach, Tara followed after the others. When she arrived at the pickup's driver-side door, Steve-O and Shorty were already out in front of the rig and putting down straggler zombies. In the distance, momentarily blotting out the light from her headlamp, Lia's rifle barked and spit fire.

The number of corpses crushed underneath the pickup was staggering. A dozen, maybe two, had been compressed waist-high to her. Lit up by the landing lights, ghostly faces peered out of the thicket of twitching arms and legs. Eyes staring out from the gloom tracked Tara's every move as she planted a hiker on a zombie's twisted back, took ahold of the wide side mirror, and pulled herself over the deadly tangle.

Slender fingers on a gnarled hand drummed a beat on the toe of Tara's Salomon when she planted a foot on the running board.

The zombies had smeared the driver-side window with their bodily fluids, so Tara craned around the A-pillar and looked through the windshield.

"Lee," she hollered and banged on the glass. "Wake up." He was ashen-faced and looked small slumped behind the steering wheel.

On the verge of tears, she tried the door handle.
Locked.

"Damn it all to hell." She tugged the Legion from the holster and smashed it into the window. The glass held, but she could have sworn her brother had reacted to the noise.

The second blow with the big pistol did the trick. As glass showered Lee's slack face, he flinched, and his eyes snapped open.

"Tara," he said. "Am I in Heaven?" His voice was weak and hoarse.

"Shhhh," she called. "Don't talk. We're going to get you home."

"Are Mom and Dad here?"

"No, they aren't." She reached in and unlocked the door. "Because you're alive, dumbass."

Barely.

When Tara opened the door, she was immediately overwhelmed by the odor of freshly spilt blood. It left a coppery taste in her mouth and started her gag reflex going again. Seeing the tourniquet tied loosely around her brother's left thigh, she reached down and rectified the situation, tightening it a couple of turns, then tucking the length of wood under the cord. Why Lee hadn't done this himself was beyond her.

A quick glance out the passenger window told her there was a whole lot going on along the desolate stretch of highway. On the fenced-in field, a quarter mile or so north of the pickup, Lia was being pursued by the last of the Bolts. Two of the fast movers were down outside the fence, their bodies sprawled out on the shoulder. Another was slumped face down over the sagging run of fence. Two more Bolts were prostrate and unmoving on the ground just inside the fence.

In the middle distance, Shorty had just shot a Slog point-blank in the face. As the creature collapsed to the ground, Tara's attention was drawn to the opposite side of the road, where Steve-O stood, arm extended, a small black pistol in his hand. Before Tara could process what she was seeing, orange flame licked from the barrel.

The report was nothing compared to the staccato cracks produced by Shorty's Glock. In fact, the little Sig Mosquito was quieter than Lia's rifle. Which seemed strange because the report from Lee's high-dollar long gun was loud enough to loosen a person's fillings.

Vern was now a few yards in front of the pickup, near the ditch on the right, down on one knee. With Clark's suppressed MP-5 tucked tight to his shoulder, body rocking subtly with each round delivered toward the returning zombie horde, the slight man seemed as if he had been born with a rifle in hand.

Tara waited for a break in the gunfire, then bellowed, "Vern ... I need you to get the stretcher from the helicopter."

Squeezing off a few more rounds, Vern rose and set off for the Lakota.

With one hand working to loosen her brother's seatbelt, Tara called for Shorty and Steve-O to come and help her get Lee out of the cab.

Steve-O arrived first. He was pale in the face, the pistol out of sight, presumably in a coat pocket. With that major concern out of the way, Tara said, "I'm going to join you on the ground. Reach up and help brace Lee's body. And watch your step. These things under the truck are grabby mofos."

Without warning, Steve-O drew his pistol, stooped over, and shot dead the two zombies posing the problem. As he dumped the pistol in a pocket, barrel still smoking, he launched into a rather good rendition of Marty Robbins's *Big Iron*.

"Damn it, Steve-O," said Tara. "Warn me next time you take that *big iron* off your hip."

Steve-O stopped singing long enough to say, "It's a small iron, Tara. And it's in my pocket."

"Help me here." She had Riker on his back and had ahold of his left arm, bracing his two hundred and twenty pounds with all her might. "Grab his arm and pull when I say to."

Arriving at the same time Vern was back from the helicopter and arranging the litter and first aid box on the road, Shorty said, "Move aside, Steve-O. We need you to be ready to grab his legs so we can get him on the stretcher without dumping him onto the deadheads." He took Riker's muscled right arm and slowly backed away from the open door. "He's one big dude."

One look at Riker's face in the light from the chopper gave Shorty a bad feeling. Of the small handful of people he had watched die in front of him, all of them looked like his new friend.

Vern snaked an arm in as the others were placing Riker on the stretcher. Pressing his fingers to Riker's neck, he said, "Pulse is faint." He paused and looked at the others. "I've seen plenty of men reach this stage. He's lost a *lot* of blood." He paused and pressed his thumbs to his temples. "I'm afraid he's dying."

Staring hard at the older man, Tara hissed, "How do we *avoid* this fucked-up situation?"

On the verge of tears, Steve-O said, "He's my first best friend." Wiping the tears, he shot Vern a worried look. "You have to save him."

Vern stared at Steve-O, thinking. In a flurry of motion, he popped open the first aid kit and tore into the medical supplies.

A pair of gunshots rang from the other side of the pickup. Then, at their back, came a series of soft pops that could only be attributed to Rhoad's suppressed submachine gun.

Seeing that the dismounted pilot had handled sufficiently the small group of zombies that had drawn close to the Lakota's rear rotor assembly, Vern shifted his attention back to Tara. "What's his blood type? Do you know?"

Tara looked skyward, thinking. "I don't know. O something. I remember one time Mom saying me and Lee were compatible."

"He can have my blood," offered Steve-O.

Shorty said, "I'm A positive. Don't know how it all works, though."

The moment Tara had said *"O something,"* Vern had started rigging a length of tube with a wicked-looking needle. On the other end of the tube, he hooked up an empty liter blood bag.

About the time Shorty was finished offering up his own blood type, Vern had already rubbed an alcohol swab on Tara's arm and was piercing the sterilized skin with the needle. He waited for the yard-long catheter to go completely red with blood, then gave the bag to Tara. "Hold this. Tell me when it's half full."

Vern grabbed hold of one end of the litter. Looking at Shorty, he said, "On three we lift," and counted up from one.

It was an uncoordinated slog getting the litter to the Lakota without dropping Riker off the thing.

Once the litter was in back of the Lakota and Tara had crawled into the cabin and grabbed the forward-facing seat closest to her brother, Rhoads closed and latched the rear clamshell doors.

Vern hopped in and took the rear-facing seat by the left side window.

Shorty helped Steve-O take the center seat next to Tara, assisted him with the complicated safety harness, then passed headsets all around.

To make it easier to recover Lia from the sloped field, Shorty buckled in next to Steve-O, leaving the seat by the right-side sliding door open for the young speed demon.

Clark stole a quick peek into the cabin. Seeing that everybody was accounted for and had properly secured their weapons, he spooled up the twin turbines and coaxed the Lakota into the night sky. Turning toward the rising moon, he dipped the nose and followed the road, keeping only thirty feet between the skids and fast-moving ribbon of gray.

Tara was watching her own blood seep into the bag when the helicopter banked hard to the right, quickly shedding the meager altitude it had gained, and came to an abrupt halt in the air a handful of yards east of the road. As the spotlight flicked on and the field was bathed in its bright white spill, Tara saw Lia. Strangely, the woman was sitting down on a patch of ochre-colored ground, one hand in front of her face to ward off flying dirt and debris, the other clamped around her right ankle.

A pair of twice-dead zombies were on the ground nearby. The rifle and a small pistol lay in the dirt next to Lia. Even as the Lakota settled softly back to earth, she made no effort to stand. She was doing the opposite of what someone needing a ride would do: She let go of her ankle and waved them off.

Seeing the blood on Lia's palm and knowing exactly what it meant, Tara shook her head, saying to herself: "Poor girl is as good as dead."

Shorty had already unbuckled and was helping Vern open the right-side door.

View momentarily blocked, Tara said, "I wouldn't do it. She's gone and gotten herself bit."

Shorty looked over his shoulder. "How do you know?"

"Look at her hand." Tara stabbed a finger at her own palm. "I saw the blood. She'd been holding her ankle with the same hand."

Clark had been hanging on every word. Regarding Shorty and Tara, he said, "We don't leave the living behind." He looked at Rhoads, then made a chopping motion with one hand.

Without a word, Rhoads unplugged her helmet, slipped out of her harness, and elbowed her door open.

Tara watched the female pilot step to the ground, then, inexplicably, turn back around and take a long, slender item from the space beside her seat. When she turned back to face Lia, her face was a mask of grim determination and Tara saw the item for what it was: a big ass machete sporting a neon-green handle.

Horrified by what she feared she was about to witness, Tara pleaded with Clark to stop Rhoads. Have her come back and get a gun to do the job. At least give the young woman a chance to go out on her own terms.

Clark said nothing. No response. No eye contact. He was watching intently as Rhoads closed the distance to the seated woman.

Tara heard nothing coming out of the headset. No white noise. No soft clicks followed by rotor sounds. Nothing. All put together, she came to believe she'd been locked out of the previously open channel.

Hands trembling, she worked at releasing her safety harness.

"It can't be helped," Shorty said, placing a hand atop Tara's. "She knew the risk involved."

Hollering to be heard, Vern said, "Clark, we need to get going."

Steve-O was back to biting his knuckles. He stopped long enough to say, "What's going on?"

Tara was about to answer when she saw Rhoads kneel beside Lia. She stayed on one knee like that and seemed to be having a conversation with Lia. Finally, the younger woman nodded, laid back on the ground, and put something between her teeth.

The only person in the helicopter ready for what happened next was Clark. He bellowed, "Don't look," but continued to watch the event unfolding fifty feet away.

Tara drew in a deep breath, then watched in horror as Rhoads raised the machete high overhead. Knowing what was to come, Tara tried to exhale, but her lungs wouldn't cooperate.

Light glinted off the machete as it hovered at the apex. As the pilot commenced what could only be described as a vicious, downward chop, Tara averted her eyes. When she finally lifted her gaze, a couple of seconds had elapsed and, inexplicably, Lia was back to sitting, still alive.

Tara had a million questions, but the words wouldn't come. The dam finally broke when she saw Rhoads turn back and flash a thumbs-up.

"What the hell is going on here?" Tara asked.

No answer. Instead, in her headset, Tara heard Clark say, "Rhoads needs help. One person. The ground here slopes uphill, so duck until you clear the rotor."

Steve-O was first to unbuckle and was out of his seat while the others were still staring questions at the pilot. Before any objection could be raised, he was out the door and on the run, head down, boot heels kicking up dust, the headset wire whipping his back with each determined step.

Tara examined the bag in her hand. It was a little more than half full, the blood viscous and warm. She looked a question at Vern, who took the bag out of her hands and squeezed past Shorty, leaving him all alone at the open door.

Craning to see around the man who was busy removing the catheter from her arm, Tara witnessed Rhoads and Steve-O helping Lia to stand. Though they were at the periphery of the ring of light, it was clear Lia was balancing on one leg. Her right leg, the one whose ankle she'd been cupping, was missing from mid-shin on down.

Tara's stomach churned at the thought of the gruesome task Rhoads had just undertaken. She said, to nobody in particular, "How in the hell is that woman still conscious?"

Shorty asked, "Did she just do what I think she did?"

Answering them both, Clark said, "Rhoads shot her up with morphine. It's probably just now taking effect." He paused. "It was that or certain death. And then—" Everyone knew what happened after the bite, so he let it hang in the air.

Finished starting Riker's transfusion, Vern said, "I've witnessed a few battlefield amputations. Mostly due to mines or gunshot wounds. Never saw one by machete. And I'm guessing, judging by the way Rhoads handled it … cool as ice, all business, that it wasn't her first."

"No it wasn't," Clark said. "And I'm sure she's feeling it to her core."

The three were nearly to the Lakota when Lia's head suddenly lolled forward.

Vern handed the bag of blood to Tara, then met Steve-O and Rhoads at the door. Taking one of Lia's hands, he helped guide her to the nearest seat. As he strapped her in, his gaze wandered to the tourniquet. It was a high-tech item. Something he'd never set eyes on before. And it was doing the job of keeping the blood in check. The amputation, maybe six inches below the kneecap, was far from surgical. While it was a straight cut, the bone was splintered on the end and ragged streamers of dermis trailed off the edges.

Vern sighed. Not only was he going to be plucking lead and shards of concrete out of the big fella, but now he was looking at having to perform some cauterization and a whole lot of suturing.

Seeing Rhoads strapping in, Tara quickly shrugged off her fleece, handed it to Vern, then helped Steve-O into his safety harness. After wrapping Lia with the fleece, Vern took his seat and buckled up.

Without warning the Lakota shot skyward. Tara reached back and grabbed hold of her brother's hand. It was cold to the touch.

Steve-O leaned forward in his seat. Straining hard against the harness just to make eye contact with Vern, he asked, "Is Lia going to make it?"

Vern said, "I have no idea. She's a world-class athlete, so I'd assume—"

Interrupting, Clark said, "Doesn't mean squat. If she's within the golden five minutes, she's got a fifty-fifty chance. It all depends upon whether or not Romero got into her bloodstream. If it did, she's done for."

Rhoads passed back a pair of flex cuffs.

Knowing what was expected, Vern took the cuffs and bound the young woman's hands at the wrist.

Tapping Vern, Tara asked, "Is my brother going to make it?"

Vern said, "Thanks to you, I give him an eighty-percent chance. Know that I am praying hard for him. Lord knows I owe him."

Tara didn't have to ask why. Lee was a giving soul. She gave his hand a squeeze, knowing surely it was something of monumental importance to the old man.

RIKER'S APOCALYPSE (THE PRECIPICE)

As the helicopter banked hard to the right, putting dead in their sights the distant hill on which Trinity House sat, Tara felt Lee's mitt-sized hand firm up around hers.

Look for Book 4 of Riker's Apocalypse in 2021.

###

Thanks for reading! **Reviews** help. Please consider leaving yours at the place of purchase. Please feel free to Friend Shawn Chesser on Facebook. To receive the latest information on upcoming releases first, please join my mailing list at ShawnChesser.com. Find all of my books on my Amazon Author Page.

Also by Shawn Chesser

CUSTOMERS ALSO PURCHASED:

 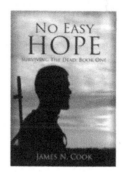

JOHN O'BRIEN
NEW WORLD
SERIES

JAMES N. COOK
SURVIVING THE DEAD
SERIES

 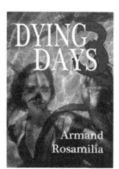 

MARK TUFO
ZOMBIE FALLOUT
SERIES

**ARMAND
ROSAMILLIA**
DYING DAYS
SERIES

HEATH STALLCUP
THE MONSTER
SQUAD

Made in the USA
Monee, IL
22 September 2020